FICTIONI
Hosack, M.
10/16 $16

By Mark Hosack

The Good Spy Dies Twice

Identity

THE GOOD SPY DIES TWICE

Book 1 of the Bullseye Series

MARK HOSACK

WIDE AWAKE BOOKS . LOS ANGELES

Please contact: mhosack@gmail.com

Cover Design: Yen Tan

hardback ISBN: 978-0-9978505-2-9
paperback ISBN: 978-0-9978505-1-2
eBook ISBN: 978-0-9978505-0-5

2016 Wide Awake Books

First edition September 2016

more at the author's website: www.markhosack.com

For Mom and Dad

Who taught me that nothing good happens after midnight...

PROLOGUE

HE HEARD IT...he finally heard it!

Well, he *thought* he'd heard it. He couldn't be sure. His head was still ringing from a massive—and quite unexpected—electrical shock.

One minute Brody had been climbing an old chain-link fence that encircled the mountain—listening intently through his headphones—the next he was flailing backward, thrown by an electrical jolt that had struck like lightning.

Only it wasn't lightning.

The shock had most definitely come from that fence.

Brody had landed flat on his back on the frozen earth, and the impact had knocked the wind out of him.

Now gasping, he sucked on the cold Russian air, his body desperate for oxygen, but his mind racing for something else.

The sound he'd heard while climbing the fence—the one that practically had vibrated the headphones right off his head—that hum...*it was real!* And it was right there on his—

Audio recorder.

Oh, shit.

Where was it? His recorder?

His headphones were still on his head, but his audio recorder had bounced out of its satchel. It had been a short fall, just ten feet or so. It couldn't have gone far, and so long as it wasn't damaged...

His heart sank into his guts.

What if it was broken? After traveling thousands of miles to Russia? After stealing away from his sleeping fiancée in the dead of the night and driving for nearly twenty-four hours, nonstop? After sneaking into an abandoned Soviet-era military installation?

It had been a difficult and expensive journey, but his news team was desperate to find this rumored "hum," and he'd been willing to do whatever it took to record it, so to have his freakin' audio recorder break after finally capturing it...

Well, wouldn't that be just his luck?

Groping around in the darkness, he finally found the small book-sized recorder, half-submerged in the snow. He examined it breathlessly. Much to his relief, the LED display was still glowing blue. *Thank God.* He plugged his headphones back in, rewound the recorder and hit Play, then listened carefully.

Brody hadn't known what to expect when he first arrived in Dagestan, near the mountain village of Gimry. The locals—a battle-weary, dubious bunch—told him that the telltale hum could only be heard for short moments at a time, if at all. So he'd started recording just as soon as he parked his rental car on the shoulder of the mountain road, probably a quarter mile from the first fence he'd hopped.

As he listened to the playback, he heard his rental car door close quietly, and then the scuff of his boots as he made his way to the first chain-link fence (the one that *hadn't* shocked the shit out of him). He listened to himself climb the first fence without incident, then drop to the other side, and then the swish of his pants and the creak of metal as he climbed the second fence.

It was then, as he was nearing the top of that second fence (the one that *had* shocked the shit out of him), that he heard the hum. It was in the background, but it was most definitely there. A distinctive sound—an undulating warble that pitched upward shortly before disappearing into the ether. And then he heard his own scream as he grabbed hold of what must have been a still-live wire on the old electric fence, the swoosh of air as he fell, and a jolting silence as the recorder hit the earth and bounced from its carrying case, which is when it must have stopped recording.

He rewound the recorder and listened again. Just to be sure.

Yup. There it was.

The hum.

He *had* it.

Looking at the mountain, and at the second fence—a fence still alive with electricity—Brody realized that there was no need to go any farther. He had what he'd come for. Now he needed to start the long drive back to Moscow, to give the audio to his boss, Jake Boxer, so that he could play the hum in the next day's broadcast, so that the world could listen.

Brody secured his audio recorder in his satchel, hit Record, just in case the hum started up again, and hurried back the way he came, back toward the first fence he'd climbed.

Panting (he was an audio guy, not an athlete), Brody reached the fence. He put a hand on it and felt his arm spasm uncontrollably in one long, sustained, hot pulse.

The same type of electric shock that had knocked him off the second fence was once again rushing through his fingers and into his arm. He crumpled to the ground with a new, yet familiar, scream on his lips. Luckily, he fell backward, and the weight of his body jerked his hand away from the fence, breaking the electrical current.

Lying in the snow, his arm shook violently for several seconds, and Jesus, his heart—it was skipping beats like a rock skimming a lake. He looked back at the fence. It was just fifteen feet high, and slouching in parts where the support poles were bent, or in some cases missing. It was old, a relic of a bygone era. Totally unassuming.

Or so he'd thought.

Somehow, there was now electricity coursing through it, electricity that hadn't been there when he'd first scaled it, just minutes earlier.

Someone had turned on the juice, and that meant someone was watching him.

When he first parked his car, he'd counted two fences from the road.

Two fences between him and the rumored Soviet installation.

No problem, he'd thought. The fences were falling apart—he could easily climb them. But now here he was, stuck in between them. Like a rat in a cage.

With his stomach in his throat, Brody cradled the audio recorder.

Okay, so he'd recorded a sound that just might change the world, but as several headlights appeared in the road just beyond the now-electrified fence, as dark silhouettes of bulky Russian men poured out of the cars and hurried through the snow toward him, he found himself asking a much more personal question:

Was it also a sound worth dying for?

PART ONE

MOTHER RUSSIA

ONE

JAKE'S HEART SEIZED UP the moment the Russian cop jerked open the freezer door. He'd seen his fair share of bodies, of course, the majority having been when he was in his twenties, covering the police beat for the *Baltimore Sun*. But he'd never seen a colleague's body, and he'd certainly never seen a childhood friend's.

Brody White was sitting upright in the freezer, an impressive feat considering his condition. Bugs and scavengers and inclement weather had ravaged his skin and much of his muscle, yet his Beyerdynamic Pro headphones were still clamped around his skull, and what was left of his fingers were still clenching his portable audio recorder, as if tweaking the levels to capture the cleanest possible sound.

That was Brody for you. The consummate soundman. He was always working, even as a corpse in a Russian morgue.

No.

No, this had to be some sort of mistake.

This near-faceless corpse wasn't Brody—he was some other poor schmuck's soundman. *Jake's* Brody was still on assignment in Dagestan, a mountainous region a thousand miles south of Moscow. *Jake's* Brody had been attempting to record the "Dagestan Hum," a mysterious low-decibel vibration sometimes heard by the locals—who, as so-called terrorist sympathizers, were often at odds with the Russian government. The locals claimed the hum was military in origin, and the source of insomnia, brutal migraines, and the rampant diarrhea plaguing the local populace.

But this corpse, this dead Brody-wannabe, had been found in a rock quarry two hours north of Moscow, so it couldn't have been Jake's Brody, right? Dagestan was a day's drive south of Moscow. Two hours north was a big detour. Brody would've called to check in, if not with Jake, then surely with—

Claire.

Oh, God.

If this *was* his Brody, how in the hell was he gonna tell Claire?

By being brutally honest, he quickly decided. Claire was young, sure, but she loathed being handled with kid gloves. He'd just have to come right out and say it: Claire, the love of your life, your fiancé is—

"Скажи ему, чтобы определить парень уже. Мои яйца холодные."

The words came from the cop who'd escorted Jake into the morgue, a member of the Russian *politsiya*. The man was standing inside of the walk-in freezer, just to the right of the body. He reminded Jake of a potato—knobby, hard, and in the absence of a heaping spoon of butter entirely fucking bland.

"What's he saying?" Jake asked his translator, an acne-scarred Russian who was lighting his tenth cigarette that morning. Jake couldn't stand cigarette smoke, but in Russia nicotine seemed to be synonymous with oxygen.

"He says he's freezing his ass off," the translator said quickly. "He'd like you to hurry up and ID the body. So would I."

The translator had grown nervous and irritable recently, especially after Jake had turned his nightly reporting into a referendum on what he scathingly decried as: "Putin's post-Soviet police state."

Not exactly comfortable words to be broadcasting about the ex-KGB-officer-turned-president, especially while still in Moscow. After all, Putin was a man who assassinated his enemies with polonium-210—a man who once imprisoned an all-female punk band for a simple protest song—a man who harbored fugitives like Edward Snowden, who picked wars with Ukraine, and sold arms to the Syrians. In other words, a real asshole on the world stage.

"Ask who found him."

"Huh?"

"Ask who found the body."

The translator asked, then turned back to Jake and said, "He says a couple of school kids stumbled across the body at a nature preserve."

"Nature preserve?"

"Yeah, he's saying it was for birds, mostly. Siberian cranes are the big draw. Maybe your friend was trying to record them when he fell into the quarry? You know, he had his eyes…and ears…on the sky?"

"Why in the hell would he want to record birds?"

The translator shrugged. "They're endangered?"

Jake looked back at the body. It was difficult, if not impossible, to stomach the man's face (it wasn't a face anymore, just a tattered stretch of gray flesh), so he focused on the corpse's body, which had been frozen stiff by at least three weeks of exposure to a brutal Russian winter. Most coroners kept their corpses in body bags, but here they'd staged this poor schlepp on a chair against the back wall of the freezer. They hadn't had a choice. His knees were frozen at ninety-degree angles. The body would have to thaw before anyone could bag him.

"Ask him why he thinks he died with his knees bent like that."

"With all due respect, Mr. Boxer, the sergeant looks cold. I mean this is just a formality, right? They already matched his fingerprints. They know it's Brody White. Shouldn't you just ID your friend so we can get the hell outta here?"

"I will. Just as soon as you do what I'm paying you to do."

The nervous translator sighed and lit a fresh cigarette before posing the new question.

The dour faced cop barked back, "Вот так мы эту сволочь и нашли."

"He says that's how they found him."

"Sitting up?" Jake asked incredulously. "I'm supposed to believe that this man stumbled across a nature preserve, fell into a fifty-foot rock quarry while recording birds, broke his neck, and then took a seat on a rock before he died? With his headphones still on?"

"Maybe not exactly in that order—"

"I'm not asking you," Jake interrupted, then jabbed a finger at the pota-to-cop. "I'm asking him."

The translator exhaled a big black cancer cloud Jake's way, then turned to the sergeant and asked if the dead man had been sitting on a rock when they found him.

"Да. Ноги у трупа так и были согнуты, когда мы его нашли. А это блядь еще кто?"

"He's saying yeah, he had his earphones on when they found him," the translator interpreted, "but he was lying down, not sitting up. His legs were just bent. He's saying it happens. That the dead do funny things."

Funny things.

Jake stared at the corpse and waited for it to tell a joke.

It was possible, he supposed, that Brody had made a detour to the quarry on his way to Dagestan; it was even possible that he'd fallen into the quarry and broken his neck while trying to record the Siberian cranes. Brody was a self-proclaimed audiophile—a freak about it, really—and he recorded damn near everything in the name of sound preservation. But if it were true, wouldn't there be nature sounds on his audio recorder?

A recorder that was still clenched tightly in the dead man's hand.

The sergeant started talking again.

"Okay, now the sergeant's saying that he's seen your show—*Bullseye*. That they stream it here on the Internet. He's getting a kick out of the subject matter—Soviet-era conspiracy theories. He's saying he finds it very *entertaining*."

Jake saw red. *Bullseye* was *hard* news—hell, some of his viewers might even call it *life*-changing news. It was not "entertainment."

He started to say as much but bit his tongue. Jake made a living interviewing people, and he, more than anyone, knew the truth was usually in what someone *didn't* say, not what they did. This policeman hadn't complimented his show—he'd threatened it.

In fact, this whole gruesome show-and-tell at the morgue had been one big threat.

Now you've seen what we did to your soundman. Keep pushing, and you'll see what happens to the rest of your crew.

Jake studied the cop. The man was cool. *Too* cool. Too well trained and too arrogant to be a simple police officer. No, this guy was more dangerous than that.

Jake's entire crew was American and that put them squarely in the realm of the Federal Security Service, or FSB—heir to the now-defunct KGB. If the potato-cop *was* FSB, *Bullseye* had successfully kicked over the hornet's nest. And as brash as Jake was, even he knew he'd better get the hell out of that morgue, and quick.

Jake turned his attention back to the body.

He squeezed both eyes tight and swallowed, an involuntary tick that had only grown worse the past couple of weeks.

Forcing the harsh vision of his dead friend from his mind, he stepped back into his emotional castle—a fortress where, as an investigative journalist, he could defend himself from the pesky dragons of guilt and grief. It was the only way he could do his job. Otherwise Brody's death would consume him. He knew that now was not the time to be consumed. Their story hinged upon the contents of Brody's audio recorder, the one that would either contain the squawks of endangered Siberian cranes, or the ominous near-silence of something more.

Something like the Dagestan Hum.

Had the FSB murdered Brody while he'd been trying to record it?

There was only one way to find out.

"Okay, yes," Jake said finally, and as somberly as he could, "that's my soundman, Brody White." He pointed to the recorder. "And that belongs to my production company. If you don't mind, I'd like to take it with me. I need the audio to finish up a couple of episodes."

The translator translated. The potato-cop considered the audio recorder, then looked back to Jake. And in perfectly plain English said, "Why not?"

And smirked.

TWO

"THAT FUCKING COP SPOKE ENGLISH, CLAIRE! But he let me ramble on with our translator like an idiot. You wanna know why? Because he *wanted* me to say something revealing—something the FSB could use against *Bullseye*—well I'm not that dumb!"

"Who *cares?*" Claire said, burying her hot, tear-stained face into his chest. "He's gone. Oh, God, he's gone!"

Claire was a babbling mess. Okay, sure, she'd only just found out that her missing fiancé was dead, but Jake still hadn't been expecting the Chernobyl-sized meltdown. After all, this woman had arranged interviews with death row inmates, horse-swapped sources for smack with meth-heads, and bribed the proper Russian authorities for visas to film in Moscow. The Claire O'Donnell that Jake knew had brass balls, and Jake had to force himself to give this weeping, babbling incarnation of her time.

While Brody's death had turned Claire into a puddle, it had galvanized Jake. He couldn't wait to get on camera. To tell the world about this grave injustice. He needed to smell pancake makeup beneath his nose and feel tungsten studio light on his face. He needed to stare down the unflinching black eye of that camera lens, a lens that would beam him into the one point two million households who'd been tuning in nightly as the frantic search for the missing *Bullseye* soundman unfolded. And after signing off for the night, he would watch the wrath of his audience play out by way of blogs, Tweets, and Facebook posts. Jake knew that he'd never win a direct confrontation with Brody's murderers, not with Putin, but he could win the war of public opinion.

He really needed Claire to get her shit together, though. He was already down a soundman; it would be a hard slog to go on without a producer too.

"Listen to me, Claire. I know you're upset, and of course you have every right to be. But we need to broadcast. Those Russian cops wiped Brody's hard drive, completely erased it—I promise you, I swear to God, whatever he recorded got him killed, and we need to tell the world. For Brody."

She wasn't listening. Her long body was still collapsed against his, her cascade of red hair twisted into knots, her fists still pounding his chest, as if it were a drum.

The glint of her engagement ring caught his eye (he couldn't help but observe that it was a rather wimpy diamond). Apparently, Brody had proposed and Claire had said yes over strawberries and whip cream mere hours before the *Bullseye* team boarded a 747 from Dulles to Domodedovo International. Admittedly, the romantic development between Brody and Claire had stung, but not because Jake was jealous. He was just protective of her. He'd personally recruited Claire straight out of journalism school, in no small part by acknowledging that *Bullseye* was probably her worst paying offer, but pointing out that his show was different—that he didn't give two shits about ratings. He used his bully pulpit to hold men and women of power responsible—that was his measure of success. *Bullseye* was unlike anything else on TV, and if she accepted his offer, she'd be in on the ground floor. It was just the sort of bullshit an idealistic young woman—who'd graduated magna cum laude from Columbia—wanted to hear.

In the end, Claire came on as a research assistant, but by the following season, she was an associate producer, and when his lead producer got cancer, she took his place.

Somewhere along the way, Claire and Brody had started their torrid love affair. No sweat off Jake's back. Yes, he was attracted to Claire, but he'd already done the serious girlfriend thing and had decided he was better off being married to his show. And in his mind, there was absolutely no cheating on *Bullseye*. He simply didn't have time for it, and besides, he'd been sincerely thrilled for his best friend.

Well, *mostly* sincerely thrilled.

The workplace disruption had been difficult. And in his opinion, Brody and Claire didn't really go together. Physically. Claire was tall, only a few inches shy of Jake (a towering man himself), while Brody stood maybe five foot eight. Hell, Claire *never* could've wept into Brody's chest like she was doing into Jake's now. Instead, she would've been weeping all over the top of Brody's head. And Brody had been an introvert, more comfortable listening to interviews through his headphones than actually conversing with another living, breathing human being. Claire was a producer. Engaging with others was her job, much like Jake's as an anchor.

And now, as morbid as it was, Brody was little more than a frozen corpse in a Russian morgue.

But Claire was still amongst the living, and Jake needed her.

Taking her by the hand, he led the grieving woman to their hotel's bed. She collapsed, curled up, and sobbed, only taking a break to fish out a cigarette—a Sobranie Black. Back in the States, she'd only been a casual smoker, but Brody's disappearance had cultivated the habit into full-blown addiction.

"Listen to me, Claire. His legs were bent," Jake told her. "He was sitting upright in the freezer because they couldn't fit him in a body bag. He *died* sitting on a chair."

She lit the Russian cigarette. Jake coughed. Her voice quivered. "A chair?"

"Yes, a chair. I've been trying to tell you: Brody partitioned his hard drives. He kept multiple copies of the same file across the partitions, just in case a sector went bad—but they were all empty. Someone deliberately erased the entire drive. And I bet that same someone, probably the FSB, tortured him to death in a chair.

"But why? Why would anyone want to torture Brody?"

Jake had not been looking forward to this part of the conversation. "Do you remember Buck Masterson?"

"Buck Mast..." Her voice whiffed into vapor. "You mean that old death row inmate?"

That was the one. *Bullseye,* Season 3, Claire's first as lead producer, had brought them to the Texas State Penitentiary at Huntsville, a dreary place where they executed inmates by the bucketful. They'd shot an interview with Buck Masterson, an elderly death row inmate, guilty of murdering a young Soviet dissident couple back in the '70s. Three decades passed before newly discovered DNA evidence put Buck at the scene of the crime. Once apprehended, Buck Masterson admitted to the murders, but he also claimed he'd been employed by the CIA at the time. He claimed that he'd intercepted and deciphered encrypted plaintext proving the Russian couple were spies—a dire threat to national security—and that the order to kill them had come directly from George H.W. Bush, then director of the CIA.

Buck's accusation, considered "highly unlikely" by the mainstream media, was pertinent to his defense and central to *Bullseye*'s story.

"Yes," Jake said, "The old death row inmate. Do you remember his interview?"

"I remember it was long, Jake. He was showing signs of dementia and didn't always make sense."

Jake nodded. In fact, half of the interview had ended up on the editing room floor.

"Buck claimed that at the height of the Cold War, the CIA was quite concerned with American companies doing business with the Soviets, that a Soviet economic victory was a bigger threat than her nuclear arsenal. He claimed an American telecommunications company had been helping the Soviets develop an advanced communication system to give them a military edge. Supposedly these experiments required massive amounts of energy, energy that was marked by a vague and periodic hum. Well, the local populations in Dage…Dagestanian—"

"Dag*estan*," Claire corrected.

"Right. Dag*estan*—the locals there, near Gimry, have been complaining about migraines and diarrhea, and, you guessed it, they're blaming it on a mysterious hum."

"So you sent Brody to record it? A hum that's been around since the seventies?"

"It's a *periodic* hum, Claire, in a remote mountain region—a spot that's fenced off from the public, it's not exactly easy to get to. It's protected. Get it?"

Claire blinked a couple of times. "Yeah, I get it. Brody is dead because you listened to that crazy old death row inmate?"

"Not crazy, Claire. *Right.*"

She shook her head. "Jesus, Jake. *Why* didn't you tell me about this before he left? I'm your goddamn producer!"

"I wanted to," Jake said quickly, "but Brody wouldn't let me."

Claire's mouth pinched up. "Why not?"

"Because he knew that if we went there, like all of us, as in the *Bullseye* team, we would've drawn too much attention. The Russians are trying to stop us from reporting on this, and that's exactly why I have to get back in front of that camera. We can put international pressure on them, Claire—we can bring the truth to light—but *only* if we take this live."

He waited for her to stub out her cigarette.

He waited for her to wipe away her tears, to put on her game face, to pick up the phone and call their boss at AT/AW (Anytime / Anywhere) News.

So why hadn't she?

"You know what I think?" Claire asked, studying Jake closely, no longer crying. "You're becoming as paranoid as your audience. There's no conspiracy here. FSB agents aren't following us. We're a second-rate news show, Jake—nobody gives a shit about us." She stood and grabbed her keycard. "If you really want to find the guy who killed Brody, take a long hard look in the mirror. And then get the guy looking back at you a fucking therapist."

She didn't wait for his response. She just stormed out of the room, slamming the door hard enough to make Jake's teeth ache.

Mike and Tim, the remaining members of the *Bullseye* crew, had been watching quietly from two chairs flanking the room's only window. The team was staying at, and broadcasting from, the fourth floor of the Napoleon Hostel, a cramped but tidy place less than a mile from Moscow's Red Square. The room's window offered a plum view of St. Basil's candy-striped spires, the Kremlin's dollhouse facade, and, just a few blocks beyond, the massive Lubyanka—a tiered bureaucratic building that once housed both KGB headquarters and the infamous Lubyanka prison. It was now home to the FSB. Jake was sure that just as he was looking out at them, they were looking in at him.

Contrary to what Claire said, he *had* seen tails since they'd arrived—civilian cars following their taxi from Domodedovo International. Bums who hopped into subway trains right before the doors closed. Jake had seen glints of light following them from high in the sky more than once—Dozor-3 Russian combat drones armed with cameras and for all he knew, ballistic missiles.

Before they'd left the States, Jake had been all too sure that Claire's admirable skills had secured the proper filming visas, but now he was beginning to think differently: Had Putin lured them within his borders to make it easier to kill them off? Was this all because *Bullseye* was targeting Russian corruption on the global stage? It sounded like a wild conspiracy, but was it really that unbelievable?

Jake looked at Mike and Tim. "We have to broadcast. Quickly. Before anything else happens to the rest of us. You guys agree, right?"

Mike swallowed heavily, his worried gaze on the Lubyanka. "To tell you the truth, my back is killing me, man. I've been lugging this camera all over creation—"

"I'm sorry. You're going to let a couple of stiff vertebrae get in the way of exposing Brody's killers?"

"It really hurts."

"And Brody is really dead."

Tim spoke up. "You're right, Jake. We have to broadcast this, but we're kind of behind enemy lines here. Would it hurt to wait until we're back in the States? We can get a flight out tonight."

"That's exactly what they want! For us to leave! Now c'mon. I understand why Claire can't see this rationally—her fiancé is dead—but what in the hell is wrong with you two?"

Tim looked at Mike pleadingly. "Are you gonna tell him, or is it going to be me?"

"Tell me what?"

Mike sighed. "We can't help but think you're doing this for other reasons."

"Other reasons? What other reasons?"

"Well, since Brody went missing, we've had our highest ratings ever—"

"This is *not* about ratings," Jake barked. "It's about our colleague. It's about our friend. Am I understood?" He looked at Tim. "Get me a satellite link with New York." He looked back at Mike. "And you, quit whining about your back and set up your camera."

Mike reached stiffly behind him, gesturing futilely. "But Jake, it really hurts."

"Now."

THREE

This is a rush transcript from the January 18, 2013, episode of Bullseye. *This copy may differ from the actual final broadcast.*

JAKE BOXER, HOST: Good evening. I'm Jake Boxer, and for the next half hour, I'll be more than just your host—I'll be your guide through the darkness of conspiracy and murder. Just remember, my faithful viewers: I can merely hold the light aloft. *You* must find your own way through. Now, as most of you know, Brody White, our audio engineer here at *Bullseye*, disappeared three weeks ago, shortly after our arrival in Moscow. In previous broadcasts, I told you that he vanished after traveling to Dagestan some thousand miles south. That much is true. What I didn't tell you is that he traveled to Dagestan to record audio evidence of a secret intelligence project being carried out by the Russians and several prominent international telecommunication companies, a project that spans decades. Now, we can only assume such a collaboration—and the secrecy surrounding it—has military applications and perhaps, ultimately, is critical to the Russian government's obsession with regaining its status as a world superpower. Tonight, with a heavy heart, I must report that this theory has been substantiated. Earlier today, I identified the body of Brody White, our friend and colleague, who not only disappeared but also was tortured and murdered while in the hands of Russian intelligence. We believe this was done to deter our reporting here in Moscow, but I can promise you this: It has only emboldened us. We here at *Bullseye* stand in solidarity. We will not leave Russia until Brody White's murderers are held accountable. If the American government pressures us to return, we'll tell them to go to hell. If the Russians revoke our visas, we'll hide in basements, in rental cars, in subways and trains. If they take our equipment, we'll upload video from our phones. And if they kill the rest of us? Well, they'll have to deal with you—my loyal audience—a legion that will stop at nothing until the secret that Brody White so nobly gave his life for is revealed to the world. So come, dear viewers, and follow me into the darkness, for this light I hold came from my best friend, and now I hold it for you. And as for Mother Russia? All I can say is watch your back; I've got you in my crosshairs. *This* is *Bullseye.*

PART TWO

WHITE ALICE

FOUR

THREE YEARS AFTER BRODY'S DEATH, with her red hair spilling down the back of a simple white shift, Claire O'Donnell vowed her eternal devotion, until death did they part, to a man who was once the unlikeliest of spouses imaginable. Moments later, Jake Boxer, former host of the now-disgraced news show *Bullseye*, vowed the same to her, and the couple, who'd somehow survived a tumultuous, gravity-defying courtship, were pronounced husband and wife.

However, they wouldn't be going by Mr. and Mrs. Boxer. Claire was keeping her last name.

In the wake of *Bullseye*'s sensational implosion, Jake had retreated into obscurity, mostly to tend to his mental health and to reflect on the spectacular on-air rant that had ended his professional career as a newsman. Claire had kept working, though not in hard news. She'd taken a job writing the travel column for the *American Post* soon after leaving Moscow. Over the years, she'd built a loyal following under the name Claire O'Donnell, and she didn't want to confuse—or lose—her readership by changing her last name.

The newlyweds simply couldn't afford it.

Unlike Jake, Claire had been all too happy to leave the dog-eat-dog world of twenty-four-hour cable news behind. For her, writing came naturally, and before long, she'd cranked out several widely praised articles about sun-drenched resorts, Americana in the heartland, and the best places to score handcrafted beer in Mendocino County. She traveled frequently (often with Jake, when he wasn't too drunk or disagreeable), visiting far-flung corners of the country like Marfa, Texas, or Blind River, Alaska, which also happened to be their current honeymoon destination.

A ski resort for the adventurous well-to-do, the quaint town was nestled in the crook of the Denali National Park, amidst the truly awe-inspiring Alaska Range some three hundred miles north of Anchorage. It would be a working honeymoon; at least that's how Claire had pitched it to Jake. The newlyweds could spend a week away from Washington, D.C. in joyous, if frozen, marital bliss, and the *American Post* would float the bill.

Besides, Claire's article was part of her most popular series, "Extreme Honeymoons," and if she hadn't included her own, her readers would've crucified her for it. She figured she could squeeze in enough writing time while Jake groused about the "good ole' *Bullseye* days"—a hobby he'd taken quite a shine to as an unemployed ex-newsmaker.

In the years since *Bullseye*'s spectacular on-air implosion, he'd been sobered by therapy and had even acknowledged that most of what had gone wrong could be attributed to his obsessive and paranoid behavior. His psychiatrist had treated him with careful doses of Risperdal and Valium—brain scramblers, as he liked to call them. A year into therapy, he'd kicked the Risperdal. The year after that, the Valium. Now, even his tick—an involuntary blink and swallow reflex that began plaguing him in Russia—had subsided, and he only medicated with over-the-counter stuff. Herbal teas for the occasional freak-out and a couple of Advil for the periodic headaches.

He'd certainly come a long way since that time in the morgue, a painful moment he'd rather forget, even though his therapist insisted he "learn from it." The month after Claire stormed out of their Moscow hotel had been disastrous. She didn't return, not even to pack her things. Instead, she took a taxi straight to Domodedovo International and booked the next flight back to the States. Mike and Tim had hung on for a couple of months, but eventually Mike's back went out for good, and Tim missed one too

THE GOOD SPY DIES TWICE 25

many of his kid's piano recitals. They, too, took a taxi to Domodedovo International. That left Jake alone in Moscow getting an earful from anxious AT/AW News executives back home. As producer, Claire had been his de facto editor. Without her, his nightly broadcasts suffered. His ratings plummeted. His budget for the season evaporated. And despite repeated trips to Dagestan's rugged terrain, he'd failed to capture the mysterious hum that might have pointed to a broader conspiracy, the evidence of which Brody had died attempting to record.

By then, Putin had even issued a public statement lamenting Jake's loss of his colleague and friend, and promising to extend his visa "for as long as it took."

As far as his network was concerned, it was time for Jake to come home. But he didn't. He stayed on, hiring local crew until his budget was truly busted. And then, when his humiliation had been all but complete—and live on *Bullseye*—he declared that Brody's death was the result of a conspiracy cooked up by Russian intelligence and top executives at AT/AW News. Why? To destroy *Bullseye*, of course. To stop him from reporting the truth. He'd even claimed to have seen President Putin himself on his tail while making his way past the Lubyanka back to his hotel. Putin, he asserted, had been carrying an umbrella gun, ready to inject him with a pellet of polonium-210.

Yes, he had gone that nutso.

But even after that disastrous on-air rant, he'd kept on, maxing out credit cards and borrowing money from a shrinking pool of supporters back home.

Months later, on his therapist's sofa, he would discover that he'd been subconsciously killing his show.

Why?

Because his show had killed his best friend.

But now, ascending a mountain in a wobbly ski lift on his honeymoon in Blind River, Alaska, he was pretty sure there'd been a different reason. That reason was nestled next to him on the lift chair, wearing a sparkly new wedding ring with a diamond, Jake noted, that was conspicuously larger than the one Brody had given her.

Jake hadn't killed his show because his show had killed Brody. He'd killed it because Claire had been watching back home. Because Claire was gauging the moral fiber of his character back home. Because Claire was just maybe forgiving him back home. And when Jake finally *did* return home, bankrupt, unemployed, and in serious need of emotional help, Claire had answered her phone. She'd become his lover, his best friend, and his career counselor—why not build a second career as a lawyer? He was a zealous interviewer and, if he believed in a case, would be a warrior in the courtroom. Jake had told her that at thirty-eight he was too old for law school, but he'd still signed up to take the LSAT, right after their honeymo—

"Oh, my God. They killed him."

Jake ripped his gaze from the hypnotic blanket of snow beneath him and looked at his bride. She was staring at her phone. Again. Since their arrival in Blind River the day before, Claire had been glued to it.

"Oh shit. I'm sorry," she said, catching his gaze. "We shouldn't be talking about this on our honeymoon."

She slipped her phone back into the pocket of her neon green ski jacket and zipped it tight.

"You can't do that."

"Do what?" she asked, innocently enough.

"Say they killed him and then not tell me who they killed. Or who did the killing."

Claire looked at the colorful tasseled hats zipping down the mountain below, at the streaks of red and blue through the falling snow. Blind River's guests were packing it in while they could—in just one week's time, the mountain would close for the winter, and it wouldn't reopen until March.

"They executed Buck Masterson," she said softly.

Buck Masterson.

The elderly death row inmate who claimed he'd been an assassin for the CIA. The guy whose interview had sent the *Bullseye* team to Moscow all those years ago.

Before therapy, the mere mention of Buck Masterson would've made Jake's stomach churn, and he would've spent several seconds swallowing back bile. But now the name was simply irksome—like hearing about an old girlfriend who'd not only gotten away, but also had a beautiful family and thriving career.

"We were kind of expecting that, weren't we?" Jake asked. "He was on death row."

"Yeah, but he still had several appeals pending. Someone must have expedited them."

Jake groaned.

This was another shining example of what he called "the crazy switcheroo." Back in Moscow, when Jake had torpedoed his own career by chasing Brody's ghost, Claire had been all too sure that there was no conspiracy. But in the past couple of years, she'd inexplicably picked up the torch he'd dropped. She'd even traveled to Huntsville recently to meet with Buck Masterson. Jake found this switcheroo more than just annoying. It was self-destructive. Yet he hadn't confronted her about it. He was hoping her renewed interest would simply run its course. Everyone went through phases, right? Even in their thirties?

The wind picked up. Their chair, now a good fifty feet above the earth, rocked. Jake grabbed the old iron double-seater's support pole with a gloved hand. The cold he could deal with. And the altitude? His migraines were worse, but at least they were sufferable. No, it was the wind that cut like a thousand knives that bothered him, that kept him hunched deep inside of his red-and-black North Face ski jacket like a dog burrowing for warmth; it was the grating squeak of the old chairlift as it rocked to-and-fro, so high above the face of the mountain that terrified him.

Who the hell had the big idea to dangle people way up here without seatbelts, anyway?

Sweat percolated across his forehead. Vapor clouds burst from his lips. But then he felt Claire's calming hand on his thigh, and he turned and saw her smile reassuringly as she said, "It's supposed to rock. If it didn't give, the wind would knock the lift right over."

God, how he hoped she was right.

Jake looked upward. A steel knuckle gripped the haul line. It had, indeed, been built to slip about the twine of steel rope. After a few seconds, the wind ebbed and the rocking eased, and Jake looked ahead of them again, hoping to see the end of the line. But it was a dismal November day, and the snowy gray sky had yet to open her curtains.

He could, however, pick out a ridge of black granite slashing through the packed snow like a dorsal fin. He was pretty sure the granite spines were near the peak.

They had to be close.

"You okay?"

Claire.

"Yeah. Fine."

"What are you thinking about?"

He didn't want to cop to his first thought—that they were about to die. And he didn't want to cop to his second—Buck Masterson—either. So instead, he nodded to the pocket where she'd slipped her cell phone. "I'm thinking I can't believe you get a signal up here."

Claire's mouth drew a hard line. "Oh, I don't. Austin sent me the text when we were back in the hotel. I just remembered to check it."

Austin Foley. Her boss at the *American Post*. Jake was no fan. Despite the fact that Claire was his best writer and had a background in hard news, Austin had kept her writing the travel column. He didn't *want* to see her switch departments but then again who would?

Everyone loved Claire.

The wind picked up again. Their chair swayed and then jerked to a sudden stop.

"Jesus Christ!" Jake swore, grabbing the lift's support pole with both hands and dropping his ski poles in the process. They plummeted to the mountain below where they disappeared in a deep drift of snow like a magic trick.

And once again, he felt Claire's gloved hand on his thigh. "Calm. Calm. Breathe."

"Is this supposed to happen?"

"Yes. They stop the lift if someone is having trouble getting on or off. Everything's going to be fine. Just close your eyes and picture us at the ending."

Us at the ending?

Yes.

Us.

As in Jake and Claire.

As in husband and wife.

Jake closed his eyes and imagined himself and Claire disembarking from the lift. They did it smoothly and confidently, and not without a little grace. The lift operator gave him new ski poles, and, together, they tipped over the nearest slope and skied effortlessly back to the Hotel Ascent far below.

When he opened his eyes, the lift was once again in motion, and he could even make out the lift's turnstile up ahead of them. A tall concrete support pole featuring a yellow bull wheel that churned the steel haul cable up the mountain and then back down the opposite way.

The end of the line. Thank God.

"Better," he said, breathing easier now, rediscovering his lost confidence.

Claire smiled and gave him a kiss on his stubbly cheek. "There's the man I married." He'd lost his ski poles, so Claire gave him hers. "Here, take these."

"What are you going to do?"

"They'll have extras at the lift house. Just keep the tips of your skis up."

She gestured to Jake's skis. He had them crossed at the back, and the tips were pointing down. He straightened them so that they were parallel and lifted the tips, as instructed. Jake was a big man. Back in high school his towering frame had been a major advantage, especially on the basketball court, but as an out-of-shape man pushing forty, his large frame was burdensome, at best. Any activity requiring precision took extra effort.

"Try to hold your body like him."

Jake followed Claire's finger to a bearded man riding solo in the chair ahead of them. The skier was also sizable, but where Jake's girth was more or less evenly distributed, this guy was packing it all solely in his paunch, which was the size of a small moon. Jake also couldn't help put notice that he was wearing a gaudy souvenir ski jacket that read, "I Wolfed-Out in Blind River."

As he prepared to depart the lift, the man held his skis parallel to each other, the tips slightly up, his poles angled to the ground. And he hopped off the lift with ease.

Well if moon-man could do it, Jake could too.

Moments later, the lift was whisking Jake and Claire over a raised platform of snow. Claire popped out of her seat and glided effortlessly toward a small ski shack. Jake, however, launched himself a little late, did his best to keep his ski tips up, but still ran roughshod down the slope with one ski straight, the other angled sharply to the right.

He slid to an ugly, yet successful, stop.

He didn't fall.

"Hey honey! How was that?" Jake shouted above the stinging wind, proud for not wiping out—he hadn't been skiing since college. "It's like riding a bike—just like you said."

"I'm always right!" she shouted back, collecting new poles from the ski shack. She gestured toward the slopes just beyond them—white slides cutting through thick trees. "Now, all you have to do is get down the mountain!"

The lift had taken them within a couple hundred feet of the summit. Blind River's mountain was no Denali, the tallest peak in North America, and just a hundred miles to the west, but at twelve thousand feet, Jake was dizzy. The wind wasn't cutting as sharply as it had on the lift, but up here the air was much colder, and it was sitting on him like a stone.

Jake considered his position. To his right, he saw a large snowy bowl— steep but mogul-free, and filled with snowboarders. Directly ahead, there was a ski run zigzagging down a gentle decline. To his left, in the direction Claire was headed, he saw a difficult run. A mogul-filled trail plunging steeply into a thick thatch of pine. It was also flanked by the ruins of several precariously perched concrete buildings—buildings that were old and empty and crumbling. A few still had roofs intact, roofs that featured rusted, circular mounts. They almost looked like the remains of the World War II artillery turrets that could still be seen up and down the West Coast—defensive measures taken against an Axis threat that had never arrived. But Blind River was a good eight hundred miles inland, far out of range from attacking Japanese submarines.

Claire, now poised near the top of the difficult run, plugged earbuds into both ears (Patti Smith, her favorite artist, was always blaring). She nodded in the general direction of the concrete ruins, and Jake noticed that the burly man with the moon-paunch was already there, plotting his own course down the mountain.

"Easy or hard?" she asked, though her body was facing the more difficult, mogul-filled run, not the smooth, snowy bowl.

It was a challenge—one Jake did not fear.

But probably should have.

"When have I ever taken the easy way?" Jake shouted back, angling his skis toward the moguls.

Claire grinned, dug her poles into the snow, and pushed off toward the moguls. Before Jake knew it, he was plodding haphazardly after his new wife, building up a decent head of steam as he approached the treacherous slope. He was so focused on the minefield of moguls that he barely registered the wooden sign ranking the run with two black diamonds, the most difficult slope in all of Blind River, and the name of the run, carved into the wood and embossed with glaze.

White Alice.

It took a good thirty minutes to tumble down the slope. When he was finally at the bottom of the run, muscles throbbing, caked in snow from spill after spill, he flopped down in the snow and caught his breath, just in time to notice a glint of light in the gray sky.

A glint he hadn't seen since his days in Moscow.

FIVE

BACK IN THE EARLY 2000s, the United States operated a fleet of fifty unmanned aerial vehicles, better known today as drones. In 2016, that fleet stood in excess of seven thousand with nearly two thousand drone pilots. Two branches of the military, the U.S. Air Force and the Marine Corps, operate drones, and they're also a mainstay in operations within the CIA and Homeland Security. They operate out of places like the Creech Air Force Base in Nevada, or the Holloman Air Force Base in New Mexico, as well as CIA offices in the Washington, D.C., suburbs, but the exact location of the drones themselves, usually flying sorties over Afghanistan or Syria, remains top secret.

Their use over American soil was finally acknowledged by the Obama administration back in 2011, an admission spurred in no small part by *Bullseye*'s sixth episode of Season 5, titled "The Drones Above Us." At the time, Obama's administration claimed drones had been used over American soil no more than ten times in the past seven years, and only in the limited capacity of reconnaissance, such as hunting a fugitive, tracking kidnap victims, or following drug trade routes. But Jake's investigation turned up a source deep inside of Homeland Security who claimed that Vice President Dick Cheney had secretly authorized Langley to run "domestic drone checks" at their discretion in the aftermath of 9/11. According to the source, Langley didn't use innocuous drones armed with cameras either. They used Reaper drones armed with Hellfire missiles, the same laser-guided missile system that had meted out justice to terrorists across the Middle East. Only now they were flying over America.

Of course, there were plenty of other explanations for the flash Jake Boxer saw in the sky that afternoon in Blind River. It could've been a small aircraft, a weather balloon, lightning from a distant rainstorm...

Well, whatever it was, it's gone, Jake thought.

Planting his poles, he pushed himself upright from where he'd flopped down in the snow, then scanned the gray sky again, hoping for a second glimpse of that glint of light—hoping to verify it *had* been a drone—but no such luck. He found himself repeating a familiar refrain from his therapist, "Don't let your thoughts run wild," and willed himself to focus his gaze on the mountain, hoping to see his one good thing: Claire. But she wasn't there either.

Don't. Let. Your. Thoughts. Run. Wild.

Taking a deep breath, he stilled his thoughts and tugged his jacket tightly, a lame defense against the cold. It was November in Alaska, which meant daylight, and warmth, were scarce commodities. And though it was only four in the afternoon, dusk was already bleeding across the sky, and the black clouds on the darkening horizon were dumping snow on top of Denali Park's saw-toothed mountains. The little town of Blind River sat a good ways east of Denali, but sooner than later, those same clouds would circle back across Highway 3 and pass over Blind River.

Jake planned to be under a duvet, and between his new wife's legs, long before that, assuming, of course, he ever saw her again.

Jake had lost Claire early in their run. One minute, he'd been swooping after her like an honest-to-God Swiss skier; the next, he was a tumbling ball of powder. By the time he'd located his jettisoned skis, Claire was long gone, oblivious to his wipeout, in no small part thanks to Patti Smith's *Horses,* which had been blaring through her earbuds, he was sure. Jake was a little irritated that she hadn't waited for him before going back up the lift for

another run (at least, by then, he'd assumed she'd gone back up). But then
again, maybe she thought he was still stuck on White Alice, maybe even in
trouble. It *was* a double black diamond. The lift was the fastest, not to mention only, way back up the mountain. It was entirely possible that she'd gone
back for him.

After thirty minutes or so, he poked around the crowded base, thinking
maybe Claire was waiting on him, but he didn't see her, and his feet were
sore, so he made his way to the mountain's small ski shack, popped out of
his skis, returned them to their locker, then slipped into his tennis shoes before venturing back outside. Walking away from the ski shack, Jake eyed the
foot traffic between the mountain and their hotel, on the lookout for Claire's
neon green jacket, thinking there was one other place Claire could've gone.

Blind River's Main Street, just beyond their hotel, was walking distance
from the lifts. All one had to do was cross over an old wooden train trestle
that connected the hotel to downtown. He thought about the news she'd
gotten on her cell phone—that Buck Masterson had been executed. He
thought about how they were on a "working honeymoon." Had she gone to
town to get a proper cell phone signal? To quiz that dickhead Austin about
Buck Masterson's execution?

Jake looked beyond the twisting ribbon of river to Main Street and its
rows of pastel-colored box stores. They'd been built to mimic the clapboard
storefronts of an Old West boomtown—a pleasing and nostalgic aesthetic.
From such a distance, the pedestrians on the street were the size of ants, but
he bet he'd be able to spot Claire's shock of red hair…unless, of course, she
was hiding it from him. Maybe bunching it up beneath her knit hat *knowing*
he'd be looking for her—

"Not easy being married, is it, Mr. Boxer? The wife always keeps you
waiting."

Jake turned to the booming voice. The words of wisdom had come from
Albert Bridge Tulane, Jr., the only black man Jake had seen since touching
down at Ted Stevens Anchorage International.

Yes, Inuits aside, Alaska really was that white.

The elderly man was laboring away in the hotel's "Winter Garden," just
shouting distance away. Al was wearing a forest green coat with big brass
buttons. Clean-shaven and meticulously groomed, it looked as though he'd

licked every last strand of white hair into place—even the ones sticking out of his enormous ears.

Al was the long-time concierge for the Hotel Ascent. Jake and Claire had met him the day before, when they'd first arrived in Blind River. Al had escorted the newlyweds up to the Honeymoon Suite, rambling away 'til he was blue-in-the-face, telling them all about the history of the hotel, as well as Blind River.

But at the moment, Al wasn't tending to his concierge duties. Instead, he was carefully pruning a ten-foot flowering shrub, the centerpiece of the Winter Garden, and the only other plant besides fir that seemed to grow in such bitter cold. Besides the shrub, the garden consisted of several large spherical boulders standing some eight feet tall. Each boulder had been split in two like orange halves. The massive stones encircled the bush, flat sides up, and made for a damn fine sight.

Art in the Alaskan mountains.

"What do you think, Mr. Boxer? She look okay?" Al adjusted his bifocals and hooked a thumb to the bush. "The witch hazel. Just thought I'd get your take. Eyes aren't quite what they used to be."

Jake wiped his runny nose and looked at the plant. Al had done a terrific job. With the dead and extraneous limbs lovingly snipped away, the witch hazel's thin arms twisted from the ground with a satisfying reach, thin enough to appear elegant, and with more than enough yellow flowers to surprise.

"Looks great."

Al's natural born smile grew even wider. "That's a relief. Gotta take care. Only a couple of plants in the world bloom in the winter, and this is one of 'em. It's very fragile. If it gets too heavy, either with snow or dead limbs, it sags and that's that. Never straightens again." He looked at Jake. "You're lucky you gotta wife, Mr. Boxer. A man needs to be pruned too."

Al laughed at his own joke—a rich, beefy baritone that practically shook the snow off the mountain.

"And you shouldn't worry so much. She'll be back."

"You're pretty perceptive, Al."

"It's my job. Reading people."

"Used to be mine too."

"Oh yeah? And what did you do, Mr. Boxer?"

Jake hesitated. "I interviewed people."

"For a newspaper?"

"No. I had my own show."

Jake immediately regretted saying it, especially when he saw Al's face brighten.

"On the TV?"

"That's right."

"Ooh, a celebrity! Well what was it? Which show?"

"*Bullseye.*"

"*Bullseye*...?" The concierge thought hard. "Uh, what was that one about again?"

Jake cringed. The only thing more irritating about having to talk about his failed show was conversing with a stranger who'd never even heard of it. It made him feel like a total loser.

"It was a news show," Jake said, stomping his feet—they were growing numb. "We were the number two ranked cable news show back in 2013."

"Huh."

Jake could see Al trying to place him inside of a television set. It was no easy feat. Jake hadn't been camera-ready in years, and he certainly no longer looked like the imposing, athletic man who'd hosted *Bullseye.*

"Sorry, Mr. Boxer," Al said. "Can't say I recall *Bullseye,* but don't take it personally. Never did pay much attention to the kitten-drowning type. Not the press, mind you. The politicians. Oh, we get 'em out here from time to time—the politicians, that is—and I always try to avoid them. Not only are they in love with their own reflections, they're lousy tippers. The Kidd, though...he likes 'em enough. Thinks their presence makes this place, how does he put it? *Desirable.*"

"The Kidd?"

"Christopher Kidd. His daddy was Walter Kidd. The Alaskan oil baron? The Kidd bought this place—bought all of Blind River—from the Feds back in the nineties. Without him none of this would exist. Sunk his entire fortune into this town and...Mr. Boxer, I'm sure she's fine."

Huh?

Jake looked back to Al. The old man was making a careful study of him, as if considering which dead ends he should advise Claire to prune.

"Excuse me?"

"*Mrs.* Boxer," Al said.

Jake blinked, only then realizing that he'd lost himself in the skiers swishing down that mountain again. "Mrs. O'Donnell, actually, she's keeping her last name. For professional reasons. I guess she's still up on the mountain. I lost her up there."

Al must have heard the worry in Jake's voice because his face softened and then he said, "Okay, Mr. Boxer. The clinic's in the downtown square off Main, but if anyone gets hurt on the mountain, they take 'em to the first aid shack first." Al pointed to a small one-story building with a red cross painted on the roof, just beyond the lift. "And if a guest goes to the shack, the first thing they do is call the hotel on the walkie." Al pulled his heavy green cloak aside to reveal a cheap walkie-talkie. "Now mine's been quiet all day which means your wife's A-OK. She ain't hurt."

"Of course she's not hurt," Jake mumbled, but he was unable to mask his emotion. After all, the last time he'd lost track of someone in the mountains, they'd ended up dead.

"I met her," Al said with a smile. "Your wife. Beautiful lady. Tall redhead, mid-thirties and Irish-white, right?"

"Yeah."

"So describe what she's wearing and I'll have Mountain Rescue find her lickety-split. Or I can call Sheriff Grout if you think she might've taken a stroll into downtown?"

Jake considered the old concierge with the walkie-talkie, and then imagined Mountain Rescue plowing up White Alice on their snowmobiles, informing Claire that she needed to catch a ride back down the mountain. That her new husband was worried sick, even though he'd only been waiting an hour.

God, she would think he was still nutso.

So, what should he do?

No. That wasn't the right question.

What would *Brody* do?

Brody, his always-cool, unflappable best friend who'd had no problem cavorting about Russia alone. Brody, who'd been Claire's first love—Claire's first *everything*. Shit. Brody would let Claire be Claire, that's what he'd do. And Claire? Well, Claire was a fiercely independent woman who, most likely, was just trying to get in one last run before dark.

"Thanks for the offer," Jake finally said. "But let's wait a few before calling the cavalry."

"Fair enough. In the future, the two of you might want to set a meeting place, just to put your minds at ease. Cell phone service stinks out here, and it'll be dark more often than light until we close next week, which will make it harder to find each other on the mountain."

"Close next week?" Jake asked, looking to the black storm clouds. "You'll be lucky if you don't close down in a couple of days."

"Oh, we don't shut down because of the weather," Al said, almost amused. "We shut down because of the wolves."

The wolves?

Really?

The words stuck with Jake as the concierge finished his work in the garden, then ambled back to the hotel, offering friendly greetings to passing guests.

Beyond the concierge, the hotel staff was lighting what appeared to be an endless supply of hanging oil lights, reminding Jake that it would soon be dark.

Jake pulled out his phone. It was what the kids called a dumb phone, but it was still smart enough to send texts, not that he could type on the phone's little keyboard with his gloves on. He pulled the right one off, and the cold sapped the warmth from his flesh almost immediately. Trembling, he quickly tapped out a message before stuffing his hand back into the glove.

Waiting in garden. Going inside if don't hear from u in 10.

SEND

Jake ended up waiting twenty minutes, not ten, but she still didn't text back. She was probably out of range, he told himself. Or, maybe his phone didn't send the text? He was in a nether-region of sorts, lingering between no bars and no signal—he'd probably have better luck inside of the hotel.

As he made his way to the Hotel Ascent, he couldn't help but scan the Alaskan sky for another flash of light, for the telltale glint of a drone dipping beneath the clouds for a better view.

Stop it, Jake. Your paranoia belongs with your first wife—*Bullseye*—*not* with Claire.

He shook the pesky feelings off with the shake of a wet dog, sure that the conspiratorial thoughts would vanish just as soon as she texted him back.

SIX

WHY IN THE HELL wasn't she texting him back?

She was hurt! She'd been raped! She was dead—

Jake. *Chill.*

You're not the host of *Bullseye* anymore. You're a *reasonable* man now. A *husband.* Studying for the LSAT...so that you can go to Columbia and get a degree with a bunch of snot-nosed rich kids...and graduate with a mountain of debt...so you can defend scumbag criminals from a system that eats the poor and helpless for breakfast.

Christ.

Jake didn't know which was crazier.

His paranoid obsessions as the onetime host of *Bullseye*, or his future as a functioning member of society.

Well. The latter was a life, he supposed. A life with Claire—and that's what he wanted.

Wherever Claire was.

Jake's cell phone had maxed out at three bars on the fifth floor of the Hotel Ascent, exactly ten man-sized steps to the right of the Honeymoon

Suite.

Standing in the sweet spot, he'd called Claire several times, and each time?

Voicemail.

Hi, you've reached Claire O'Donnell. Leave a message.

He didn't leave a message. He left several.

There was no reason to freak out, of course. Like Al had said, reception was for shit in Blind River. For all he knew, Claire was just a few floors below him in the crowded lobby looking for him—hell, she was probably thinking that *he* was missing. That *he* was still up on the slopes. That *he* was out of cell phone range. That he was the one diddle-daddling about, for whatever reason.

Yes, it made perfect sense. They were looking for each other—and since they were both moving about, they kept missing each other. Well, when they did finally catch up with each other (and they would shortly, he was sure), he'd make sure they had a prearranged meeting spot next time, as that concierge had suggested. That's what people did before they had cell phones, right? Set places and times to get together?

He couldn't remember for sure, but it sounded right.

Trying to get his mind off Claire, Jake took in his surroundings. He was standing in the hallway on the fifth floor of the Hotel Ascent, just outside of the hotel's Honeymoon Suite. The air there was warm and redolent with the pleasant smell of burning pine. On the other side of the hallway's banister, a tall chimney stabbed upward from an enormous fireplace, set dead-center in the spacious lobby below. The stone hearth, which was open on both sides, was currently burning what looked like several six-foot-long lengths of pine, and the raging fire inside was hot enough to heat the entire hotel. Just to be sure, aluminum ducts radiated from the stone chimney at the ceiling, like spokes on a wheel, dispensing waves of heat throughout all five floors of the hotel.

According to Al, the lobby was relatively new, an expansion dating back to the late nineties. Before then, the rooms had opened motel style to the outdoors—hence the wooden bannister along the hallways.

Jake peered over the bannister and took in the lobby below. He saw a sea of balding heads and bulging waistlines. He also saw middle-aged women

with dyed hair and fur stoles. The affluent guests were lounging about casually, sipping whiskey from snifters, and swigging martinis. Their boisterous
laughter soaking into the dark cherry wood walls. There was something
strange about the crowd, but he couldn't quite peg it…at least not until he
spied a man in a white cowboy hat who had his arms around two younger
women, the sort of women a man like that could get on lease but never
buy. The three didn't look like extreme skiers. At all. For that matter, neither
did the rest of the crowd. But if they weren't there to ski, why had they
bothered to come to a place as far-flung—not to mention as nauseatingly
cold—as Blind River, Alaska?

Jake's phone buzzed.

Claire!

With his stomach in his mouth, he jerked it from his sweatshirt pocket,
expecting a text.

But it wasn't a text.

It wasn't even a missed call.

It was a voicemail, just catching up now that he finally had a signal.

Still, maybe it was a *message* from Claire?

Nope.

Not even.

*Jake! Tabitha Fox here. Hey, amigo, heard through the grapevine you got married
and thought, Jesus—who in the hell could put up with his shit? I mean besides me, of
course. Listen, NewsFlash is in D.C. covering the election—I've got fashion covered, but
I need someone in scandal. And no, I'm not talking about which interns Bill is screwing.
I want real stuff. I want hard news—I want the stories Jake Boxer would chase, and I'm
paying. A lot. I'm telling you, this is your big chance to re-launch* Bullseye—

Jake hit delete.

Tabitha Fox was the owner, and face, of NewsFlash, a sleazy, sixty minute gossip show dedicated entirely to celebrity gossip, celebrities in bikinis,
celebrities cheating on each other and, just to round it out, celebrity crime
stories. Needless to say, it was a ratings bonanza and catnip for advertisers,
but as successful as she'd been, Tabitha Fox was still anathema amongst her
colleagues—the woman was as unethical as she was ruthless—but she also
happened to be a true believer in Jake Boxer—one of the only true believers
left. She'd been very vocal, both on and off the air, that AT/AW's canceling

of *Bullseye* had robbed America of its sole truth-seeker. Tabitha, of course, had a fix—Jake's own segment on NewsFlash. *Bullseye Redux*. Together they could put the corrupt politicians back in Jake's crosshairs and make about a gazillion dollars in the process.

Claire had been adamantly opposed to the idea. Jake was healthy again, yes, but the slightest misstep could knock him back into a tailspin. The last thing he needed was to plunge back into the world of twenty-four-hour news. And besides, *Bullseye* had been broadcast on AT/AW, a top-rated cable news network, why would Jake want to be associated with tabloid-trash like NewsFlash? With yellow journalism that hocked celebrity smut and time traveler conspiracies in the same breath? Law school was a much better fit.

Of course, the fact that Tabitha Fox was also Jake's one and only serious ex-girlfriend didn't exactly endear her to Claire either.

Slipping the phone back into his pocket, Jake's thoughts returned to his missing bride. She was AWOL, yes, but was that unlike her? No. Back in their *Bullseye* days, he'd frequently lost her to the work. Whether it was hiring crew, locking down interviews, or finding locations, she was easily swallowed by production, and sometimes Jake wouldn't hear from her for days. Technically, they were in Blind River on a job. So maybe she was off writing her travel article? Arranging interviews with staff?

Sure, but they were also there on their honeymoon—maybe she could think about her new husband for a change.

Breathing deeply, he decided to have a look around. She wasn't on the fifth floor, and he'd already checked out their Honeymoon Suite, so Jake headed to the elevator for the fourth floor, padding across the hotel's thick carpet, patterned with stark red- and-white chevrons. The fourth floor was a bust, totally Claire-less. The third floor was likewise, but it did have a dark north wing that, apparently, was under construction. He considered hopping a rope and exploring the corridors, but a woman from housekeeping told him that the yet-to-be completed wing was off-limits, that this was the unfinished Phase II of Christopher Kidd's remodeling plan. The second floor started off more promising than the others; there were two conference rooms to explore, but Claire wasn't there either. Disheartened, Jake abandoned the second floor, eschewing the elevator for a staircase straight out of *Gone with the Wind,* complete with red carpet and gilded handrails, which spilled into the lobby like water.

The lobby was crowded with guests—a bit claustrophobic—but it was also warm and comfortable. The fireplace was flanked on all sides by chaise lounges, comfy leather chairs, and several benches, all close enough to the roaring flames to defrost frozen toes. The front desk was to his left, manned by the same pretty blonde who'd checked them in the night before. Her name was Summer—easy to remember because, outside, it was so *not* summer. Al's concierge station was just beyond the front desk, a beaming beacon of goodwill to guests passing through the hotel's wide, revolving front door.

Claire wasn't in the lobby either. But all was not lost. The lobby's north wing was under construction, but the south wing appeared to be finished, and after shoving his way through a throng of carefree guests, he spied a brass placard screwed into the wall that read:

To Pool.

To Hot Tubs.

To Business Center.

Hot tubs…

Hadn't Claire mentioned them that morning? Something about champagne?

He followed the signage down a stuffy hallway and eventually reached a rear exit that led to a back slope of snow. The hotel's guests were lounging about in skimpy swimsuits, the older men with bulging crotches and the not-quite-as-old women with droopy boobs in tiny bikinis, soaking up the queer dichotomy of the freezing weather and near-boiling water. Which was probably swirling with Viagra.

An ambivalent reservations clerk sat outside, handing out towels. No, he hadn't seen Claire, though he might have seen her the night before. (Night before? Hadn't Jake been with her all night?) The clerk offered to make the newlyweds a hot tub reservation, but Jake declined.

Instead, Jake made a careful study of the mountain. It was nighttime. The slopes, now lit by tall lights, looked like white tears running down the mountain's otherwise dark face. Jake's gaze drifted to the rickety old chairlift he and Claire had taken to the summit. A long line of skiers and snowboarders were still queued up, even at this hour, eager to get to the summit, eager to blast down the slopes in a spray of snow and adrenaline, and who could blame them with only a week left of skiing before the wolves came?

He tried, but he didn't spy Claire's shock of red hair amongst them.

Jake traced the lift's haul rope up the mountain. It plunged into darkness halfway up, but he spied it again near the summit, just a couple hundred feet from the old hollowed-out concrete boxes that lined White Alice. His gaze drifted to the circular mounts on top of the structures.

Not gun turrets, he thought. You don't mount artillery on top of buildings that fragile. Besides, Blind River was far too remote a place from which to fire on submarines or passing ships, and he doubted if there'd been any hostile flyovers in the region, at least not low enough to shoot at—not even during the Cold War when the Soviets frequently penetrated Alaskan air space.

The Cold War...

Hadn't Alaska been rife with intelligence operations spying on the Soviets? Maybe the mounts had been used for radar arrays?

A cold finger traced his spine, and it wasn't because of the wind.

Where in the *hell* was Claire?

Jake rushed back into the south wing of the hotel. It had been three hours since he lost her on White Alice, and true worry, not the paranoid sort, began to take root.

At least it *felt* like true worry.

Okay, so let's say she did sneak back into town to call Austin about Buck Masterson—how long could that have taken? An hour? At most? But wouldn't she have at least checked in afterward? Wouldn't she have known I'd be worried?

Of course, she would've known.

He pulled out his phone. He texted her three more times, just as fast as his trembling fingers could find those annoying little buttons on his stupid fucking "dumb" phone.

Where r u???

R u hurt???

Write back or I'm calling cops. Serious.

She didn't reply.

And why should she?

Just because he was her goddamn husband?

He closed his eyes. He rubbed his temples, trying to squash a migraine before its onslaught. Bile bubbled up his esophagus, and he swallowed heavily, fighting the acidic tide.

Psychosomatic ticks, his therapist had told him.

Precursors to a psychotic breakdown, his therapist had told him.

Breaking into a near-run, he shoved past offended guests. He stuck his head into any door that opened. He knew he was shouting "Claire" every time he did, but at the same time he *didn't* know. He wasn't himself anymore. He was outside of that guy looking down at someone new. Everything had changed when he'd said, "I do." Now, he was a husband without his wife—a new concept that scared the holy living shit out of him.

He found the indoor swimming pool. He saw Speedos, bikinis and, yes, a thong or two but no Claire. The business center, immediately adjacent to the pool, was likewise Claire-less, and Jake—now sweating like a marathoner—saw no need to explore the unfinished north wing of the hotel before ordering Al to radio the cops.

Claire was surely dead.

Jake had called the hotel on the six-hour drive from Anchorage, just to check on road conditions; the number was still on his Recent Calls menu. He punched it up and after a few rings, Summer's pleasant voice answered. "Thank you for calling the Hotel Ascent, how can I be—?"

"Concierge's station."

"Of course. Are you a guest or—?"

"Just put me through!"

He heard a little harrumph, then, "Please hold."

It was an excruciating hold, featuring a tourism sales pitch, complete with acoustic guitar, periodic eagle caw, and a man's deep, thundering voice.

So, whether you're rafting the river's roaring rapids, skiing our one-of-a-kind mountain, or relaxing in the Hotel Ascent's world class dining hall, there's no greater adventure than Blind River, Alaska. Come discover the magic—

"Concierge's desk. This is Al. How may I help you?"

"Call the police."

"The who? I'm sorry, is this—"

"Jake Boxer. You said you'd call the police if I didn't find her, and I didn't, so I want you to call them, and I want them to find her. Something's wrong."

"Yes, sir, Mr. Boxer. Right away. Come meet me in the lobby."

Jake hung up.

His heart gave a few mighty knocks as he saw Claire anew in his mind's eye, her long freckled body beaten and raped and abandoned on the frozen bank of the mountain's dark river. But who'd killed her? The same men who'd murdered Brody? Or some gap-toothed backwoods Alaskan hillbilly?

Jake clenched his jaw, and ran.

Wending through narrow cherry wood corridors, he rounded a T and broke right, toward Al. He entered the sprawling lobby, his tennis shoes slapping across the stone floor, drawing every eye, including Al's, who was just hanging up a landline. Jake ran to the elderly man, who turned slowly, his dark face drawn and pinched, and in his baritone voice, he said, "I just spoke to the sheriff. Everyone's looking—"

Jake's phone buzzed.

With one swift draw, he pulled it from his sweatshirt pocket.

It was a text.

And it was from Claire.

Best skiing ever. U still on the mountain? xoxoxox

The text took several moments to process, and when it did, his nausea was replaced by a white-hot ball of fire.

Claire O'Donnell.

Lost in her work…with *zero* consideration.

His phone buzzed again.

Poking around for article. Where ARE you?

Jake looked back at Al.

"The sheriff will be here any minute, Mr. Boxer," Al said.

"You can tell him not to bother. It's Claire."

Al's face broke into a grin that rivaled the Grand Canyon. "Well, Mr. Boxer, that's terrific!"

Jake had always imagined that he would be the neglectful partner in a marriage, but apparently his wife was the one with other things on her mind.

The tiny part of him that still longed for the unflinching black eye of the camera understood, but a larger part of him wanted his new wife to understand that, work or no work, this sort of behavior would not fly.

They were married.

He came first.

She came first.

That's how it worked.

Right?

Given their history, Jake wasn't so sure, but he did know that if he want-ed to get his point across, cooler heads would have to prevail.

So, instead of texting out a scathing dress-down, he opted for some-thing terse and uninspired and soon to be entirely true.

drunk in bar

SEND

SEVEN

"THREE *HOURS*, CLAIRE," Jake slurred, counting them off on his fingers. "*One. Two. Three.* That's *Uno. Dos. Tres.* Just in case you don't speak English." Jake leaned back on his barstool, teetering briefly before regaining his balance and finishing with an entirely unnecessary, "*Three.*"

Claire, sitting on the bar stool next to him, quietly hissed, "Jake. Please. You're embarrassing yourself."

There was no arguing with that.

By his fourth drink, Jake's efforts to play it cool had completely evaporated, as had his argument.

Drinks number one and two had gone a little better. He'd mostly gotten his point across, up until he'd used the term "man and wife," of course.

"Husband and wife," she'd corrected, explaining that she understood her responsibilities perfectly well, and that this little lapse was *his* fault, not hers. She hadn't even realized she'd lost Jake until she'd reached the bottom of White Alice. Blame it on Patti Smith blaring in her ears, fine. But was losing her husband on a ski slope a marital sin? No. She'd waited a long time at the base of the run before finally deciding that he must have been stuck somewhere on the mountain. So she took the lift back up. But she didn't see him on her second run down White Alice either. She had, however, spied a few well-worn trails through the trees, trails that led to easier slopes—maybe Jake had taken one of those? Well, before she knew it, a couple of hours had passed and it was dark—and nearly five o'clock—their prearranged meeting time with Christopher Kidd.

"Christopher Kidd?" Jake had asked. This had been between drinks number two and three. "You mean *the* Kidd?"

"Who?"

"The concierge told me that that's his nickname...the Kidd."

"Huh," she said and added the nickname to a long list of research notes she had stored on her iPhone.

"Why were you with Christopher Kidd?"

"I told you this morning."

"Told me what?"

"That we were meeting him at five in the ballroom—the Glass Hall?"

He remembered seeing a sign for the Glass Hall, but he hadn't gone in. At the time thinking why in the hell would Claire be in the ballroom?

"The Glass Hall?" he asked.

She nodded and her eyes widened. "It's unbelievable. By far the architectural achievement of this building. The entire wall is one huge glass collage. The kitchen and service hallways all attach to it, so it's like the heart of the hotel—at least that's how Christopher Kidd described it."

Jake had never met Christopher Kidd but he already hated him.

Claire must have picked up on his mood because she shook her head, then smiled thinly. "I tried to call you, Jake, but there was no signal and your voicemail was full."

Tabitha Fox *had* left a long-winded message.

"When I couldn't get a hold of you, I figured our five o'clock appointment with Christopher Kidd was our best meet-up point...or did you forget? Or were you just not listening when I told you about it?"

Would she stop it with the Christopher Kidd meeting already?

Jake drained drink number three and ordered number four. Chilled Belvedere. If his tenure in Moscow had given him anything, it was a taste for vodka.

The meeting with the Kidd sounded vaguely familiar, yeah—but him forgetting or *not* forgetting wasn't the point. It was around then that he reminded her she'd gone three full hours without bothering to check in.

Uno. Dos. Tres.

And that was *not* how newlyweds behaved.

"Behave?" she asked, lighting up a Sobranie Black, causing him to cough. "I'm sorry but since when does *the* Jake Boxer actually care about newlywed behavior?"

"What's that supposed to mean?"

"It means you're Jake Boxer, the guy who never wanted a wife on his arm, only some corrupt politician *in your crosshairs.*"

Hearing his show's old tagline made him want to puke, and she knew it.

"When did marriage become this sanctimonious institution?" she asked. "All of the sudden, we have to be in constant, minute-by-minute communication, or you think I'm off screwing someone else or dead in the river somewhere?"

"Oh c'mon, Claire, we're on our honeymoon. I just want to be with you. And I would think that you'd want to be with me."

"Jake, this is a—"

"If you say 'working honeymoon' one more time, I swear to God, I'm gonna go up that lift and jump off the mountain."

Claire sighed, and he felt her eyes on him, as if considering what to say next. And then it clicked.

"You're not working on a travel article," Jake said, his words revelatory. "You're writing something else…something bigger."

"What?"

"*That's* why you're being defensive! That's why you lost me on the slopes—it's a story you don't want me to know about because you're afraid I can't handle it. That I'll regress."

"Jake!"

"You're using our honeymoon…you're using your travel article…" He scooted closer to her. "Jesus Christ, Claire, you're using *me* as a cover."

"I ditched you because I was thinking about Brody. Alright?"

She said the words sharply and without remorse, just a little intake of air to go along with the plain, unaffected facts.

She was a reporter.

And now she was reporting on herself, as if she were somebody else.

But she wasn't.

She was Claire.

She was his wife.

Jake leaned back on his bar stool, shell-shocked.

"Brody?"

"You're a shitty skier," she said quietly, explaining. "Brody wasn't. He was a good skier, and after I lost you on that run, it made me think about him and, well,…I spent two hours sitting on a rock up on that mountain, bawling my eyes out. By the time I came around, it was five o'clock and I had to meet Christopher Kidd. I really did think you'd be there."

Claire pulled out a fresh Sobranie Black, but she didn't light it. She just tapped the filter against the mahogany bar, as if considering her addiction, but she was clearly considering something else.

"I love you with every ounce of my heart, but…" Her voice dropped. "You married a widower, Jake. A widower who never got to enjoy her first marriage—who doesn't even have fond memories to look back at—and now that I'm on my second." Her words fell away. When they came back, they finally cracked with emotion. "I didn't think it would kick me in the ass, but it did. Do I have to keep going or do you get it?"

Wow.

There it finally was.

Candid Claire.

Jake considered his wife. In truth, this was the end of a conversation he'd tried to have with her a week *before* the wedding, a conversation she'd ended with a dismissive chuckle and waive of her slender hand. Now, sitting in that bar, her words stung—jealousy could be a monstrous bitch—but still, he was thrilled that she was finally articulating what he knew she'd been feeling. Jake had always assumed that by marrying Claire, he was also marrying Brody's ghost, but maybe this was a proper step in coming to terms with his death?

"So…" Jake said, taking a sip of his Belvedere. "You're *not* using me as a cover?"

"Jesus Christ. *No.* I'm here on a crappy travel article because we're too poor to honeymoon on our own."

"Until I graduate."

"What?"

"We're poor, but we won't be after I finish law school. Even public defenders do pretty well in D.C. And who knows? Maybe I'll open my own firm someday? Land a big case? Defend some rich-shit celebrity accused of murdering his lover?"

That got a smile out of her. It was small, and a little sad, but a smile nonetheless. "You would hate that."

Jake shrugged his big shoulders and gestured to the bartender for two more drinks. As the bartender mixed them, Jake lit a fresh cigarette for Claire and studied the woman perched on the stool next to him.

When they'd first announced their engagement, no one understood why she'd want to marry a guy like Jake, especially her father. But she'd gone on about how he'd been a lion before Moscow, and how he'd be a lion after graduating from Columbia. She was willing to overlook the broken middle, when he was a lame wildebeest. But no one had ever bothered asking Jake why he would want to marry a woman like Claire. They'd all assumed this gorgeous, successful redhead was marrying down. And she was, in every way but one: Claire was still drowning in grief. And time after time, Jake Boxer—Brody's oldest friend—had been the only one who could save her.

Claire took a long drag off her cigarette and stared at the martini the bartender had just poured, took a sip, then conceded, "I should've checked in with you. I was being selfish. I'm sorry."

Jake nodded, wanting to say, "It's okay," but not feeling it yet. So, instead, he gestured for another Belvedere, saying, "Do you need to work anymore tonight?"

"No."

"Then why don't we just forget about today and agree that our honeymoon starts now?"

She nodded and then considered his kind, stubbly face. "You know Christopher Kidd used to watch *Bullseye*? He's a huge fan."

"Really?"

Feeling better, she nodded again and even gestured for another martini. "Yeah, he went on and on about how we broke the Tom Delay corruption story. He's dying to meet you. He even wants to buy us dinner. I think he's busy tomorrow night, but maybe the next if we're not doing anything?"

"The Kidd," Jake muttered, his dark eyes taking stock of the bustling patio bar, as if realizing for the first time they weren't alone. "You might think he's your MPP, but I bet he's not."

A smile crept across her face. "And I suppose you're going to tell me who is?"

He shrugged.

Of course he was.

MPP was Jake and Claire's shorthand for *Most Powerful Person* as a source. The newlyweds had a long standing journalistic debate—was the MPP a person of stature, say a senator? Or was it the person who *served* that person of stature, like an aide or someone on staff? A story's best MPP, in Jake's opinion, was someone who had a score to settle and had the means, or access, to do it. Like Edward Snowden, who stole troves of data from the NSA. Someone with both the motive and resources to make news. Claire, on the other hand, tended to go after the person of power, but Jake had to admit that she chased them with a tenacity that could loosen the most reluctant of tongues.

Claire had obviously decided that the Kidd was her MPP for the honeymoon story. She'd already met with him, and there was potential for dinner later that week. But Jake wanted to prove her wrong, and not just because he was admittedly jealous. This was a game they'd often played in their time together at *Bullseye*, and he still enjoyed the challenge.

"So who is it?" Claire asked.

"Hang on. I'm looking."

The patio was small and crowded. Heat lamps kept things toasty enough, and transparent plastic flaps, which could be rolled up during the day, allowed the guests to gaze out at the mountain, still lit by the low-glare lights for night skiing. The drinks were flowing, and the picnic tables were packed. A three-piece country band was performing on a small stage opposite the bar. It was a boisterous place and had only grown more so in the hour since the newlyweds had arrived. In fact, it was so packed that Jake could no longer see everyone from the bar.

"Looks like I'm gonna have to do a walkabout," Jake mumbled, sliding off his stool. "Five minutes and I'll have your MPP."

All sorts of people were in the bar. The rich lazy ones he'd seen in the lobby and the snow-dusted daredevils he'd seen on the slopes. As drunk as he was, they all seemed to leer at him, and he immediately regretted leaving his perch on the stool next to Claire. He was overwhelmed.

Oh, who in the hell was he kidding?

He wasn't overwhelmed. He was rusty.

"Boxer," he muttered to himself. "You've got these bastards in your crosshairs."

Steeling himself, he pushed into the crowd. He made a careful study of every face—as careful as a drunken man could. His gut didn't bark, at least not right away, so he turned his attention to the band, which was ripping through a cover of "On the Road Again." A tall couple nearby was doing their best to two-step along, but they were failing miserably.

The tall couple…

Now here, his gut told him, was something to watch. They were trying a bit too hard to fit in, especially the man, who was dancing listlessly on his two left feet. He was tall, besting even Jake by a couple of inches, and sported a bushy mustache. The woman was no shirking flower either. She had a face chiseled from granite, and her long black hair poured over shoulders that were better suited for a football player than a woman. The couple clearly didn't belong, but were they his MPP?

Maybe…or maybe they were just really bad dancers.

He pressed on, shouldering deeper into the crowd, and that's when he saw him. A strange looking man in a raking fedora sitting at a corner picnic table. He was wedged in with the rest of the crowd, but he wasn't with anyone.

Lone wolves always piqued Jake's interest.

The man's skin was tight beneath the brim of his hat, almost to the point of translucence. He had cool gray eyes, and his nose ended suddenly at the tip, as if some drunken plastic surgeon had accidentally sliced it off. It was impossible to gauge his age with all the work he'd had done, but Jake did notice an old gnarled hand as the man tipped back a pint of wheat beer, quelling a persistent and dry cough.

Now here was a man who looked like he had a story to tell. What he was doing in Blind River was anyone's guess—and would most likely make for a fascinating article, or at the very least, an interesting aside.

Jake grinned, proud of his detective work. Surely this guy was a much better MPP than the Kidd. He actually looked like he had something to say.

He turned back to Claire to claim victory, but the crowd had thickened, and by the time he got back to the bar, Claire was gone and other guests had taken both of their stools.

Jake's heart knocked mightily against his ribs, just as it had that afternoon.

Again?

His cell phone vibrated.

It was a text…well, a sext. Claire had sent him a selfie. And in it, his bride was lying naked on the Honeymoon Suite's heart-shaped bed, her red hair cascading about her small pale breasts, exposing a single pink nipple.

The text attached to the photograph read,

found ur MPP

EIGHT

JET-LAGGED AND STILL REELING from losing his show, Jake had called Claire shortly after touching down at Dulles from Moscow. It had been late in the afternoon, and Claire was getting ready for Nerd Prom—aka the White House Correspondents Dinner—an annual gala featuring not only the biggest players in print and television media, but President Barack Obama himself.

Jake's invitation had been "lost" in the mail, probably around the same time he'd accused his bosses at AT/AW News of murdering his best friend to sabotage *Bullseye*. But Claire, who'd already accepted a position with the *American Post, did* have a ticket, and it allowed her to bring along a guest as well.

Wouldn't it be a great opportunity for Jake? To prove to his colleagues that he wasn't as crazy as he'd appeared on that final disastrous episode of *Bullseye?*

But Jake declined—he was in no shape to face his peers. Claire still showed up at his apartment after the gala, just to check up on him. It was there that she admitted she'd watched *Bullseye* every night until AT/AW pulled the plug. She'd seen Jake chase the conspiratorial ghosts he blamed for Brody's death. She realized that it wasn't Jake's fault that Brody had traveled to Dagestan alone.

It was Brody's.

She wanted to make it up to Jake. She felt responsible for the show's implosion. If she hadn't left, she could've stopped him before he burned the whole thing down. Also, Jake was the only person on earth who knew Brody, *really* knew him, like *she'd* known him. And wouldn't it be nice, if just for the night, they could both be with Brody together?

The sex was good. It was really good.

And it *stayed* that good.

When Claire was slumming it through yet another travel article, when Jake was staggering through another trough of depression, drifting through the seedier bars of Foggy Bottom, sex was the glue that kept them together, and things hadn't changed now that they were husband and wife.

Of course, Jake wasn't gonna get *any* action tonight if he couldn't figure out how to unlock their Honeymoon Suite. The damn keycard reader…it kept *moving* on him.

He finally got the keycard in. Pulled it out. And opened the door. Inside, the lights were out, but Claire had drawn the drapes so that moonlight was seeping through the large picture window, flooding the room with a milky glow.

His wife was naked on the bed, on top of the covers, her long thin body a thing of freckled beauty. He staggered across the room for her, and she reached for him, her fingers taking him by the waistband. Pulling him on top of her. Helping him out of his sweatshirt. Unzipping his jeans with her thin fingers. Those fingers, those fingers. God, all of the marvelous things she could do with those fingers. He looked down at her mouth and thought about all of the marvelous things she could with that too. And she did them. Right then and there and without prompting. Kissing him, biting him, whispering how sexy he was, despite the new mats of grey hair on his back, despite a body that had gone soft in his nearly forty years, a body now bulging in all sorts of decidedly nonsexy ways.

He rolled her over and pulled her against him—she liked it like that—when she suddenly stopped him with a look.

"My phone…" she said, her eyes widening.

"What about it?"

"I forgot to charge it."

She rolled away from him and even managed to get a foot on the cold floor before he hooked an arm around her thin waist and pulled her back onto the bed.

"No phone tonight," he said. "Just me.'"

She relented and slid on top of him, her thin pale legs wrapping about his waist. His hands found her hips, and he moved her back and forth. He felt her wiggle and listened to her moan—no, listened to her *burst*—what an incredible, melodic thing, and for a split second he found himself wishing that Brody had been there with his audio recorder, capturing the sound of his wife, his beautiful Irish bride, on their honeymoon. He grunted through his own orgasm perfunctorily, and Claire rolled off him, panting, her long hands flopping on her sweaty stomach that one day soon might carry their baby.

His big body depleted, Jake closed his eyes and tried to stop his world from spinning.

Mr. Belvedere, I swear to God: Never. Ever. Again.

It was cold in the room, even with the fire in the lobby pumping heat through the vents. Despite the chill, Claire slipped out from under the covers, grabbed her purse, and fished out a cigarette. She offered one to Jake, but he waved it off, of course. It annoyed him a little. She knew he didn't care for smoking, and she knew he was nauseous.

He heard the soft strike of steel against flint and caught a whiff of tobacco. Then her voice.

"Christ, Jake, how much did you have to drink?"

Jake squinted, trying to remember. He was pretty sure he'd ordered two more vodkas after Claire's sext, fully intending to bring them both back to the Honeymoon Suite—one for him and one for Claire—but he was also pretty sure he'd arrived on the fifth floor empty-handed. He vaguely recalled drinking at least one of them as he staggered up the hotel's enormous staircase, where he'd stopped, transfixed by the view of the mountain through one of the hotel's windows. Had he drunk both vodkas as he gawked at the dark rigid outlines of those crumbling buildings with their radar turrets, still clinging to the side of the mountain after all those years? He couldn't remember, but he did remember thinking, "What in the hell was Blind River like forty years ago?"

"Cold," Claire said with a shrug, taking a drag off her cigarette.

Jake looked at her, confused, until he realized that he must have spoken his thoughts aloud.

"And crawling with spooks," he muttered.

"Spooks?"

"*Spies*. This place was a listening post during the Cold War."

Claire trimmed the ash off her cigarette and groaned.

"White Alice," Jake said drunkenly, his words slurred.

"The ski run?"

"Not just a ski run. It's the name of a spy network that was peppered across these mountains. You know, our early warning system in case the Soviets lobbed a nuke over the polar icecap. Those buildings up there on the mountain housed some of the radar installations...I also saw a drone."

Claire rubbed her temples. "This isn't my idea of pillow talk."

"I'm just saying. I saw a flash of light."

"Do you really think you'd see a flash if a black drone was flying at thirty-five thousand feet?"

"Well, it probably had to fly pretty low to get under the cloud cover. The sun was setting and..."

He closed his eyes. The darkness spun as it only did for drunks and, holy shit, did he need some Dramamine.

"Are you going to throw up?"

"Nope," Jake said curtly. It was all he could get out.

He was gonna throw up.

"C'mon. I'll help you to the bathroom."

He felt her hands on his arms, pulling him upright, but he didn't dare move. He'd rather go outside and bury his dick in the snow than get sick in front of Claire.

"No...please...Claire...just...*just* let me die here."

"You mean *lie here*," she corrected.

"Uh-huh."

Relenting, she let go of him, and then laid her head against his broad chest. "Okay," she said softly. "For argument's sake, let's say you're right. That this place was used as an eavesdropping installation to spy on the Soviets. Why would the American government send a drone to spy on it's own listening station forty years later?"

"Who says...who says the drone was American?"

Claire closed her eyes.

Shook her head.

Smoked her cigarette down to the butt.

"Jake," she said softly. "I wasn't in Moscow to stop you from destroying *Bullseye*, but I'm here now, and I will stop you from destroying our marriage."

"Destroy it?" he mumbled. "C'mon, Claire, I'm going to law school... Remember? No more crazy for me."

She hesitated, as if suddenly reconsidering what she was about to say, but then plowed ahead anyway.

"I don't think you're crazy. I wouldn't have married you if I did."

"Then why," Jake mumbled, "why won't you tell me why we're *really* here?"

She took a deep breath, and Jake, even at his drunkest, saw the old widow return, peering down at him through his bride's emerald eyes.

And then she said it.

"Because I'm afraid you'll fuck it up."

Okay.

He wasn't sure if she'd *really* said that, or if she'd simply inferred it with a judgmental cast of her eyes, but either way, it didn't matter. The point had been made.

The real reason she wanted him to go to law school?

She didn't think he could hack it as a journalist anymore.

"Tabitha Fox called."

"What?" Claire asked, confused.

"*Tabitha Fox*," Jake repeated, louder this time.

Claire shut up.

Mentioning Tabitha *always* shut her up.

But in Jake's drunken mind, he hadn't muttered Tabitha's name to shut up Claire. He'd said it to remind her that yes, he may have put *Bullseye* in the rearview mirror, but it wasn't because he couldn't do the job anymore. It was because he loved her. It was because he was getting older, and if he was going to change careers, it was now or never. It was to remind her that going to law school was for her, not him—a decision he could live with so long as he could have her until death did they part.

None of that meant he couldn't do the job anymore.

And she *had* said that…right? That she was worried he was going to blow her story?

Yes, he was sure she'd said it…at least with her eyes.

Pretty sure.

Regardless, he knew she'd gotten the point because her face grew flush against his bare chest as he said, "She's in D.C. covering the election—she does fashion and all that stuff but she needs someone with a head for hard news. She wants to relaunch *Bullseye*. I'm gonna tell her no way, of course." Jake was trying to sound rational, trying not to slur. "But when I fail the LSAT…I mean *if*…maybe I should take her up on it? And if I do, maybe you should quit your job, come work for me, just like…like old times. Like *Bullseye* times. Would you…would you like that? *I'd* like that…I like…I like you *with* me…do you like you with me?"

It was about then that his stomach informed him that he had two options: get sick or pass out.

He chose the latter, falling into a stone's sleep.

If Claire ever answered, he would never know.

NINE

A WOMAN'S VOICE slipped into his slumber.

A woman who wasn't Claire.

"Hello? I'm sorry to bother you, but are you awake? Mr. and Mrs. Boxer?"

A sharp knock followed. Okay. The voice he could dismiss, but the knuckles rapping against the door? The sound split his skull like hot points of light.

Jake wrapped his pillow around his head and promised God his first born if He would only make her stop.

But God must have had His music up too loud because the voice, and the knocking, continued.

"Hello?" the mysterious, and rather annoying, woman shouted, "Mr. and Mrs. Boxer?"

"It's O'Donnell!" Jake barked. "She's keeping her maiden name!"

"Oh. Mr. Boxer? Gosh, I hope I didn't wake you. It's Summer. From the front desk? You missed your prepaid brunch this morning. It wasn't cheap. I thought I'd stop by to make sure that everything was—"

"Everything's fine," Jake blurted.

A partial truth at best.

Mr. Belvedere was still tossing firecrackers around inside of his skull, and his churning guts felt as though they'd been filled with grease from a McDonald's fry vat.

"Okay," she said hesitantly. "Well, if you need anything, just dial zero."

Jake listened as her footsteps walked away and, for a second, thought he might actually be able to fall back asleep.

Fat chance.

His body felt as shriveled as a dying man's in the desert, and dying men did not sleep. They suffered.

Agua, he thought. *Need. Water.*

He cracked an eyelid but immediately regretted it.

The drapes were still open from the night before, and the cold November sun was barnstorming the room. After a brief struggle, Jake once again found himself squinting at the bright face of that God-awful granite mountain he'd tumbled down the day before (was there a muscle, or bone for that matter, that *wasn't* sore?).

"Claire," he muttered, burrowing back under his pillow. "Close the drapes and I'll buy you that pony you always wanted as a kid."

She didn't answer. He snaked a foot over, expecting to find her skinny legs. But he didn't. The lump beside him was nothing more than her pillow.

Maybe she was already in the shower?

No. He didn't hear the water running.

He listened for a pee or a fart or whatever, but nope. She wasn't in the bathroom. She wasn't in the Honeymoon Suite.

She was gone.

Again.

"Oh God," he groaned.

Unlike the day before, he was too hung-over to worry. Besides, wasn't she trying to plow through her article so that they could enjoy their honeymoon? Yeah, sure. So she was probably interviewing guests or sucking down double shots of espresso on the Ascent's patio, hammering out drafts of "Cold Love" (a working title) on her laptop…a laptop that was still sitting on the Honeymoon Suite's breakfast table.

Really?

Yup, it was right there. He could see it through a cracked eye.

Jake sat up and immediately clutched his throbbing head, feeling as though his brain had come untethered overnight.

Moving slowly, he found his pants wadded up at the foot of the bed and fished out his cell phone. One bar. Enough. He called her. Her phone rang—so she was within cell range—but she didn't answer.

Hi, you've reached Claire O'Donnell. Leave a message.

"What did you…" He hacked and cleared the phlegm. "Sorry, what did you give me to drink last night? I can't get outta bed. Stop working on that stupid article and get up here. I need my wife—I need some TLC."

He hung up. Then sat there a moment, replaying his message in his head. He'd sounded casual, right? Very Brody-like, meaning *not* paranoid? After all, there was no reason for him to *be* paranoid. Just because he'd woken up without his wife? Because they'd missed an expensive champagne brunch? Because she didn't have her laptop and therefore couldn't be working on her article?

Lightning struck behind his eyes.

He told himself to slow down, that there was no point in getting worked up over Claire *again*. He'd catch up with her soon enough. In the meantime, he'd hydrate, brew some coffee, eat a little toast with jam, and enjoy a little Jake-time. Maybe he'd even go through a lesson or two in his long-neglected LSAT prep book.

Sure, just as soon as he shit his brains out.

Tiptoeing across the chilly hardwood floor, he miraculously made it to the bathroom without having an accident. He plopped down on the toilet and emptied his bowels in a single fast, and surprisingly refreshing, forced exile.

Good riddance, Mr. Belvedere.

He cleaned himself up, washed his hands, soaked a washcloth in cold water, and draped it around his neck. Leaving the bathroom, he walked over to the kitchenette and drank two glasses of crisp water and brewed a single cup of French roast. It was then that he noticed that both of their coffee mugs were still clean.

Claire hadn't made coffee that morning.

He dialed her cell phone again.

Hi, you've reached Claire O'Donnell. Leave a message.

"Hey, it's me. Where are you? I thought you were done with your disappearing acts. Call me back. Let me know you're okay."

Coffee in hand, Jake sat down at the little breakfast table and drained half of his mug in one gulp. The throb in his head ebbed, thank God, and his gaze drifted to Claire's laptop, which had slipped into sleep mode. He tapped the spacebar and the login page popped up asking for a password.

He deliberated, but not for long. Yes, this was an invasion of privacy, but wasn't she his wife? Hadn't she given up her privacy at the altar? He knew Claire's password and quickly typed it in: *aroyall*.

The password referred to Anne Royall, a woman, born in the late seventeen hundreds, who was widely considered to be the first American female journalist. An old anecdote told of her catching up to then-President John Quincy Adams while he was bathing naked in the Potomac. Supposedly, Anne Royall took a seat on his clothes and refused to move until he answered her questions—thus the first presidential interview ever given to a woman. There was a time, before Claire began writing travel articles, that Jake could've seen her do the same to Obama.

The laptop screen blinked out of the login page, and Jake found himself staring at a word document. Most of Claire's articles were around five hundred words. "Cold Love," a work in progress, was right around three hundred. Still, what she had put down on the page was certainly well written. He'd even call it polished. In fact, it read much more like a sales pitch, he thought, but what did he know about writing travel articles? He was about to close the laptop when his gaze stuck to her last sentence.

There's no greater romantic adventure than Blind River, Alaska. Come discover the magic, you might just leave here enchanted.

Adventure…*Magic.*

He'd heard Blind River described like that before…from Claire? It must've been—she'd probably read him the article while he was dozing off the night before.

He was about to logout of her account when he saw an open Safari window behind the word document. Curious, he clicked on it and got the surprise of his life.

She'd been reading NewsFlash's website, of all things. Tabitha Fox's tabloid. And apparently she'd taken an interest in a story with the headline:

Who Is Buck Masterson?

11/04/16. Huntsville, Texas. "CIA CONTRACT KILLER" EXECUTED. Buck Masterson, a convicted murderer who made headlines a decade ago for the defense that he was a contract killer for the CIA was executed at 10:36 this morning after several pending appeals were abruptly denied. Masterson admitted to a spate of murders across Texas in the late 1970s, including those of two Russians living in Pflugerville, Texas. Masterson, who represented himself, made the sensational claim in the final days of his trial that he'd been in the employment of the CIA at the time of the murders, though he offered no evidence, and the Central Intelligence Agency denied his existence. Still, the claim set off a firestorm of speculation. Public records show that Masterson was employed as a "low level analyst" for the CIA in the early 1960s, but that he had quit in 1963 for personal reasons. The Huntsville warden said Mr. Masterson's last meal consisted of fried chicken, mashed potatoes, and two bowls of mint chocolate ice cream. His last words were reported to have been, "The good spy dies twice."

So what do you think? Was Buck Masterson a CIA agent, or wasn't he? Share your thoughts in the talkback below.

Jake scanned the talkback. It was long and profane and filled with enough conspiracy theories to write a dissertation. Everything from the Supreme Court's Justice Anthony Scalia's death to rampant fraud in the 2016 presidential election. Jake, himself, had been mentioned in several of the comments. A few trolls had called him a pussy and a hack, but most of the commenters lamented the cancellation of his show—the country needed *Bullseye*. Now more than ever. There would be a new president in office in just a few months, and God only knew how that would work out.

A gunshot interrupted his thoughts. It was distant and, to the untrained ear, might have been confused with a sharp crack of thunder, but Jake had worked the police beat in Baltimore.

He knew a gunshot when he heard one.

Hunting was popular in Alaska, and if the advertisements he'd seen at the front desk were any indication, the sport was particularly popular in Blind River. With the right permit, you could even bag yourself a grizzly, not that grizzlies were out that time of year. They were hibernating. Still, there was plenty of other big game. Moose. Caribou.

Wolves...

Jake thought about what the old concierge had said, that in Blind River, the winter belonged to the wolves, and he found his gaze drifting to the large picture window, scanning the dramatic and rugged landscape for a pack of snarling four-legged beasts. He didn't see any wolves, but what he saw instead was far more impressive.

He and Claire had driven into Blind River at night. The following day, spent tumbling down White Alice, had been gray and overcast. But today was crisp and clear. The storm he'd seen over Denali must have blown the other way. Jake could see for miles. And he'd never seen anything like it. The picture window framed Blind River's mountain like a snow-swept Matisse. A series of vertical granite spines dotted the mountain's crisp, white peak... the dorsal fins he'd seen from the lift...long spines of black rock jutting through the snow.

The mountain looked as though it had been carved into the sky itself— like a great artisan had spent millennia painstakingly detailing every nook and cranny. The pine trees and rocky outcrops. The rickety chairlift and White Alice's abandoned concrete platforms. Even the skiers were picturesque, daredevil guests enjoying their last week on those treacherous slopes.

He spotted a couple of neon green jackets, but one belonged to a man, and the other belonged to a short and stocky woman, certainly not his lissome bride.

Jake looked at the clock on the bedside table. One o'clock. She hadn't canceled brunch. She'd left her laptop behind. Her cell phone charger hung in the wall.

She'd clearly meant to return, probably long before he woke up.

Jake, sore from tumbling down White Alice, groaned as he pulled on his clothes—blue jeans and a flannel. He pocketed his cell phone, found his wallet, and was looking for his keycard when he noticed a crooked photograph on the wall. It was one of several—a series of photographs meant to present a history of Blind River. The oldest of the photographs—from the early nineteen hundreds, Jake guessed—were black and white and featured swarthy miners, some hard at work with pickaxes and shovels. Other photos featured men playing Ping-Pong or holding up hunting trophies (yes, wolves). As the years dragged on, the subjects, and Blind River residents, changed. Naturalists took the place of the miners. Adventurers took the place of the naturalists. There were shots of brave men and women riding Blind River's rapids or climbing the inverted wall of the mountain's perilous northern face.

Abruptly, however, the adventurers gave way to politicians. Jake recognized Eisenhower and Kissinger to name just a few. Later, when the Kidd remodeled the Ascent into a five star hotel sometime in the nineties, celebrities like Kim Basinger, Tom Cruise, and Harrison Ford appeared. The most recent photograph showed the beloved former Alaskan senator Ted Stevens, who'd died in a plane crash back in 2010 after attracting scrutiny for supposedly taking payoffs in office—a story, Jake recalled, that *Bullseye* helped break.

The photographs hung perfectly straight, with the exception of the one to the right of Kissinger's, the crooked one Jake had noticed. Interestingly, the subject of that photograph wasn't a politician, but an artist. The woman was waifish and underdeveloped; in fact, Jake would've confused her for a teenager had her face not been so drawn. Crow's-feet framed her narrowly set eyes, and she wore her black hair in a tight bun, like a stern schoolteacher. One eyebrow was cocked, and her mouth was sort of slack, as if she'd just been shot with a bullet, not a camera. As if the photographer had taken her by surprise. She was holding a thin paintbrush. The back of her easel was facing the camera, so her painting was hidden from view, but the position of the easel, and her proximity to the Honeymoon Suite's large bay window, made her subject obvious.

She was painting the mountain.

Jake looked back at the woman's face. It was familiar, as was the name inscribed in a simple brass placard screwed into the frame: *Ana Turov.* But he couldn't quite place it.

Another female professional with a name that started with an *A*, like Anne Royall. Claire had probably taken it off its hook to admire her. Maybe she'd carelessly rehung it? Maybe because she'd gotten a call? Or maybe she realized she was late for an interview with the staff? Maybe that's why she left without saying good-bye or taking anything she might have needed to work on her article?

Jake straightened the photograph and made a mental note to ask Claire about Ana Turov just as soon as he found her, and then picked up his phone and called again.

Hi, you've reached Claire O'Donnell. Leave a message.

He didn't leave a message.

He hung up, closed his eyes, and willed his burgeoning migraine away.

Where was Claire?

Where in the *hell* was his wife?

TEN

"MR. BOXER! WHAT ARE YOU *DOING?* Did you just...you *did*...you broke into Mr. Kidd's office!"

Jake, holding the charred butt of one of Claire's Sobranie Blacks, looked behind him, toward the office door. He wasn't surprised to see Summer standing there. Someone had been bound to hear him shatter the Kidd's office window. Fortunately, Jake already had what he'd come for, and he held up his prize as if it were the only explanation needed—a mostly smoked Russian cigarette he'd just fished from the Kidd's ashtray, amongst an ocean of stinky cigar butts.

"You told me Christopher Kidd hasn't been in today."

"He *hasn't* been in today," she said defensively.

"Then why is one of my wife's cigarettes in his ashtray? Or are you going to tell me that someone else smokes Russian cigarettes in Blind River?"

After inspecting Ana Turov's crooked photograph, Jake had left the Honeymoon Suite, determined to find his magically disappearing wife. He'd bumped into Summer in the elevator. No, she hadn't seen Claire, which was why she'd woken him up, and she was pretty sure she wasn't with her boss—

it was Christopher Kidd's day off. After the two split, Jake had snuck into the hotel's administrative wing, tracked down the Kidd's office, and peered through the door's narrow window.

Which was when he'd spied a black cigarette butt in an ashtray.

He'd tried the doorknob before breaking the window, of course—he wasn't a maniac—just hung-over and short on patience. But the door was locked, and there was a baseball-sized rock in a nearby planter that would smash glass nicely.

"I'm calling the sheriff," Summer said, stepping back.

"Go ahead. You lied to me, and I'll be happy to tell him as much."

Taking umbrage, Summer wrinkled her nose. "I *didn't* lie. Mr. Kidd hasn't been here all day—and I have no idea how that cigarette got in there. Maybe your wife was in here with Mr. Kidd before I started my shift?"

"You're on the day shift. You start early."

"So maybe she was in here sometime last night."

Jake chuckled. "It's our honeymoon. I think I would've noticed if she'd had a late-night rendezvous with your boss."

Actually, Jake had blacked out relatively early the night before…*not* that that was any of Summer's business.

Jake looked back at the Kidd's desk. Besides the ashtray, the only other item he saw was a small, framed photograph of two men fly-fishing. The handsome one with a thick head of wavy hair had to be Christopher Kidd, because the other fisherman, who was mid-cast, was Dick Cheney. Yes, *that* Dick Cheney.

Right about then, a new voice boomed out from around the corner.

"What in the heck is going on back here?"

Jake recognized the rich baritone immediately.

Al.

The concierge appeared behind Summer, clearly flustered. He was breathing heavily, his wrinkled face flush, cheeks huffing in and out like a blowfish. Apparently, they'd interrupted his lunch break—either that or the ketchup-stained napkin, still tucked in his collar, was a fashion statement Jake simply didn't understand.

Al looked at the broken window and then at Jake, who was still standing inside of the office.

It didn't take a genius to put it together.

"Go call Sheriff Grout, Summer. Go do it now."

Summer nodded and hurried off. Al stepped into the doorway, filling it up, blocking Jake's escape. Jake was much taller than the elderly concierge, and being forty years his junior, could've easily taken him, but that, of course, would have meant assault and battery on top of the breaking and entering charge.

"What's going on here, Mr. Boxer?"

Jake held aloft the cigarette butt. "My wife has been meeting with your boss behind my back. She's out and about, probably with him now, and I want to know where. I want to know *why*."

Al considered the cigarette butt, then shook his head like a disappointed schoolteacher. "I don't know whose cigarette that is, but I do know that your wife isn't with my boss."

"She's *disappeared* again, Al. She was gone when I woke up, and she isn't answering her phone."

"I just left her twenty minutes ago, Mr. Boxer. She's walking to Main Street in downtown. Alone."

Jake blinked. "What?"

"I spent three hours with your wife this morning, gave her the tour of the hotel, inside and out—even missed brunch and lunch to do it," he said, only then remembering the napkin. He snatched it from his collar and dropped it into a small waste bucket. "She wanted every detail—for her article."

Jake shook his head. "Claire would've told me if she was with you."

Al offered a sympathetic smile. "Yes, well, I kind of beat around the bush on that one, knowing it's your honeymoon and all. Even asked her where you were. She said you were sleeping it off—that if I saw you, I should tell you she's fine, she just forgot to charge her phone last night. She's taking a quick stroll around downtown for her article and then she'll be back."

"Her phone *rang*. It *was* charged. My calls went through."

"I prefer not to meddle with our guests private affairs, but..." He lowered his voice. "More than one guest saw you two bickering on the patio last night and, well, your wife bristled this morning when I mentioned you. You two having yourselves a lover's quarrel?"

"No."

At least he didn't think they had.

Sure, they'd squabbled the night before, but they'd also buried the hatchet with mind-blowing sex.

Hadn't they?

Because I'm afraid you'll fuck it up.

Her words came back to him, as if from a dream.

Hadn't that been an admission that she was in Blind River on a different story?

No. Not necessarily. If he was recalling things right, Jake only *thought* he'd heard her say that. But she had *definitely* said she'd been up on that mountain, crying over Brody. Now whether that was true or just a cover story was something he'd have to get out of her when he found her again. If she *had* lied to him, it was something she would need to apologize for, just as he needed to apologize for bringing up...

Tabitha Fox.

Oh crap.

In his drunkenness, he'd told Claire about Tabitha's voicemail, hadn't he? But that wasn't all he'd done—he'd also told her that...

He wasn't planning on passing the LSAT.

And that he wanted her to quit her job to come work for him at *Bullseye*.

Jake.

Boxer.

World.

Class.

Schmuck.

What in the hell was wrong with him? Was he that determined to blow up everything he cared about?

Okay. Well, all was not lost. Undervaluing what she did for a living—when he couldn't get a job to save his life—was certainly a dick move, but it wasn't irredeemable. They'd certainly been more awful to each other in the past, and they'd always kissed and made up. So was this spat really bad enough for her to pull yet another disappearing act?

He thought about Claire's hero, Anne Royall. He thought about the woman sitting on John Quincy Adams's clothes until he granted her an interview. Teaching a lesson to a sitting president of the United States.

Yes, Claire could be teaching him a lesson as well—not that Jake cared to learn it.

"Sheriff's on his way, Al."

Summer. She'd poked her head into the office long enough to quickly inform them, then dashed away just as fast. After she left, Al returned his big, sad eyes to Jake—they'd grown kinder, as if he'd been reading Jake's thoughts.

"You love her very much, don't you, Mr. Boxer?"

"Yes."

Al, more relaxed, nodded. "Well, call me a hopeless romantic, but I hate seeing the two of you getting off on a bad foot—especially here at the Hotel Ascent. This is a place for lovers. Your wife might be a bit teed off, but there's no doubt she has the big stuff for you in her heart—I could see it in her eyes." He looked at the broken glass at his feet. Then spoke very slowly. "Accidents happen, Mr. Boxer. So do misunderstandings. I don't see anything here that can't be remedied, so long as you offer to pay for the window. I can even charge it to your room, if that suits you."

Jake nodded, and even felt a bit relieved. "It does."

"Good. I'll tell the sheriff as much when he gets here, and I'll also make sure Summer understands that this was all one big misunderstanding. But in exchange, I want you to do something for me."

"What's that?"

"Find your wife and apologize for whatever cockamamie thing you said to her last night. That woman's a catch. Take it from a guy who's been waiting eighty-three years for Mrs. Right—you ain't ever doing better."

ELEVEN

HALF A CENTURY AGO, the Trans-Denali Railroad stretched from Anchorage to the mouth of the mine that led deep into Blind River's mountain. Mining equipment and rations came in, and carloads of gold, silver, and other precious ore went out. The mining operation was shuttered decades ago, but the impressive wooden trestle bridge forging the river still stood. The railroad line had been converted into Blind River's downtown Main Street. Its terminus was no longer the mouth of a mine, but a large circular driveway that serviced the Hotel Ascent.

Bundled up in his North Face jacket, Jake studied the dark perpendicular imprints where the steel railroad tracks once ran along the trestle bridge. If the railroad still existed, it would've run straight through the Ascent's impressive revolving door.

That was one way to close a mine, he supposed. Build a world-class hotel right on top of it.

It was a cold but clear day, without much wind, and many of the guests were strolling the mile or so to Main Street's colorful storefronts, the same route Claire would have taken. He didn't see a point in calling her again.

Either her phone really had run out of juice or she was simply too pissed to answer.

Al was probably right. He had to find her and tell her he was sorry, that even if he did reboot *Bullseye*, she wouldn't have to come work for him. She could waste her God-given talent and write her lousy travel articles until she was a hundred and ten for all he cared.

But there was still a small part of him that didn't believe it: the part that told him that Claire, even at her most petulant, wouldn't ditch him on their honeymoon, not unless she absolutely had to. And that same part told him she wouldn't ditch him unless she was in danger.

Or else she was out there somewhere bawling over Brody again, wishing she were still with her first love.

Jake pushed the thought away. It was simply too painful.

More determined to catch up to her than ever, Jake was preparing for what was sure to be a scrotum-shrinking walk into town when he heard an animal whinny.

Turning, he saw two skeletal Clydesdales clomping around the hotel's snowy circular drive, pulling a kitschy and brightly painted sleigh behind them. The driver, a fist of a man with unwieldy mutton chops, was whipping the reins and steering his once-impressive, now-haggard horses toward Jake, who, with his bare hands beneath his armpits, surely looked like an easy fare.

"There's gold in 'dem hills!" the driver shouted with a heavy drawl. He pulled even with Jake and tipped his top hat. "Those words were spoken back in 1867, when the first white men set foot in this valley. And yes, they were prospectors." The driver pointed at the mountain. "You're lookin' at more than a couple o' good ski runs. The Gold Rush started in California and ended right here in Blind River. Ten bucks gets you a blanket, a ride into town, and the best tour in all of Denali, all right here on the Sleigh of Good Fortune. Whaddaya say?"

Jake considered the offer. Claire had a head start, so why not make up a little time, and glean a bit of the local wisdom too?

He pulled a hundred dollar bill from his wallet—one of only two hundreds he had left.

"Okay, but I'm looking for a real tour," Jake said. "Not the one you do for entertainment."

The driver looked at the Benjamin and immediately lost his hammy accent. "And what sorta 'real' tour are you looking for, mister?"

"Let's start with my wife. A tall redhead, mid-thirties, lots of freckles.
You didn't by chance give her a ride today, did you?"

The man cocked a bushy eyebrow, then plucked the hundred dollar bill
from Jake's hand. "And here I was hoping she was single."

As it turned out, the driver, who introduced himself as Peter Lancaster,
had given Claire a ride into town just thirty minutes earlier. She'd given Lancaster the same line she'd given everyone else, that she was researching Blind
River for a honeymoon article and had asked to be dropped in the most
romantic spot in town. So Lancaster had taken her to the little town square
on the opposite end of Main Street where the ice-skating rink and hot cocoa
stand were decorated with enough mistletoe to get the entire town laid.

Jake asked to be dropped at the same sexy spot.

The sleigh slid slowly down Main Street, away from the Hotel Ascent.
The two horses were clearly miserable, their nostrils flaring with clouds of
vapor, their skeletal shanks shuddering in vain, unable to rid themselves of
the bitter cold.

"They don't look good," Jake observed, hunching down in one of the
sleigh driver's complimentary blankets. "It's gotta be close to zero out here."

The driver turned around and gave Jake a proper view of his squashed
nose and fuzzy cheeks. "They've got *fur.*"

"So do you," Jake said, gesturing to the man's sideburns, "but you still
have a blanket."

The driver looked down at the heavy blanket across his lap and grinned
broadly, displaying a row of dark yellow teeth. "Got yourself a point. I'll
find 'em something back at the stables."

The sleigh bumped as the horses plodded onto the trestle bridge. Jake
looked down at the river beneath them. The current was pulling the dark
water like black thread on a loom, weaving it through the narrow canyon
that wound through town. Ice encroached from the riverbank. Another
week and Jake figured the river would be frozen solid.

"So what gives?" the sleigh driver shouted over his shoulder. "Your wife
didn't tell you where she was going?"

"Must have slipped her mind."

He chuckled. "Thought womenfolk played hard to get in order to *find* a hubby, not lose one. And certainly not on your honeymoon."

Jake looked up. "I never told you we were on our honeymoon."

The driver took a moment, whipped his reigns, then said, "She must've then. Talkative fare, your wife. Blabbed all about her big article and how it's gonna drive tourists to this town by the bucket. But in this cold?" He shook his head. "Good luck with that, I told her."

The sleigh bounced as it came off the bridge and slid back onto Main Street's icy macadam. From a distance, the storefronts had appeared brightly colored and well maintained, but now that he was closer, all Jake saw was peeling paint and missing roof shingles. That the buildings weren't well maintained was something of a surprise. Especially when compared with the Hotel Ascent, an exquisite building that had been meticulously doted over, down to the very last nail. Except for that north wing, of course—the part of the hotel still under construction.

Jake studied the deteriorating storefronts, then looked back at Lancaster's deteriorating Clydesdales.

"Tough times in Blind River?"

Lancaster shrugged. "Been better."

"Hotel seems to be doing alright."

"Sure."

It was a nonanswer, and for the first time in years, Jake felt the old interviewer stir inside of him. Nonanswers were the catnip of journalism.

"Sure?" Jake said, leaning forward. "And what exactly is that supposed to mean?"

Lancaster turned back around, showing off his bulbous nose. "It's supposed to mean *sure*."

"Seems like the fact that the hotel is doing just fine, but you can't feed your horses, might bug you. Sure as hell would bug me."

"Then it's a good thing you're *not* me."

Jake took note of the man's powerful shoulders and stony hands. Lancaster was in his fifties, but he still had the musculature of a young man. Jake had met people with that genome before, back when he'd done a story on Appalachian Big Coal. But this man with a miner's body was driving a tourist sleigh—why?

"You been doing this your whole life?"

"Doing what?"

"Pulling a sleigh."

"Seems like it."

"Not much money in that."

"I thought you wanted a tour about the town, not me."

"You ever mine the mountain?"

He groaned. "No."

"Well you sure are built for it. How about your father?"

"You always ask so many questions?"

"Sorry, bad habit. I used to be a reporter."

Lancaster sighed, and then his gaze shifted to the mountain. "Department of the Interior shut down the mines in '63, right after the collapse. My old man was only twenty."

It was all he had to say.

Not only was Peter Lancaster a Blind River native, but he was also the son of a miner. It also meant that Lancaster had spent his fifty-odd years eking out a living in the shadow of the very mountain that had killed his old man. Yes, Lancaster made ends meet by driving a sleigh, but surely he longed to plunder the mountain, a mountain Christopher Kidd now owned.

Those two facts together made Lancaster a perfect MPP.

"Was my wife with anyone else?"

Peter Lancaster whipped his reigns again, saying, "Whaddaya mean? Like with another man?"

"Like the Kidd."

"The Kidd?" He chuckled. "Christ, man, aren't you two on your honeymoon?"

"She ditched me for a couple of hours yesterday. I know he was one of the people she met. When I woke up this morning, she was gone again. I haven't seen her since."

"Rest easy, son. She was alone."

"Then why won't she answer my calls?"

"Beats me. Maybe because cell service is for shit in Blind River?"

"If she's not sneaking around with another guy, the only reason she wouldn't call back is if she were in trouble. But I'm her husband. If something was wrong, seems like I'd be the first person she'd call."

"Sure. Unless, of course, she was trying to keep the trouble away from you."

Jake fell quiet. It was something he hadn't considered.

Was Claire dodging him to keep him safe?

The thought threw him, and Lancaster saw it.

"Oh, don't listen to me," he said quickly. "I'm sure she's just fine. Probably picking out the right bunch of mistletoe for your Honeymoon Suite right now."

Sure, Jake thought. Because picking mistletoe was such a Claire thing to do.

It was only four in the afternoon, but the sun was already behind the mountain. A gloomy dusk settled across the storefronts. Jake saw signs for a caramel factory, a health spa, a yoga studio, a kitschy pan-for-gold store, and even a juice store. So when did Yuppie Heaven crash-land in the mountains?

"This place change much over the years?" Jake asked.

"Oh yeah. None of this was here in my father's day. Back then there was a general store, a whorehouse, and everything else was part of the mining facility—rock busting, filtering, and sorting. After the collapse, the Feds closed the mine and decided this would make a damn fine place to spy on the commies." He jerked a thumb toward the square concrete buildings, just visible near the mountain's summit. "Spent the sixties and seventies looking for Soviet nukes. They never came."

"White Alice," Jake said, his gaze on the old structures.

"That's right. Radar arrays. Government built 'em all over Alaska. Sputnik changed everything. This place used to have enough spooks to fill the *Titanic*. People don't realize it—when you say Cold War, they always think of the Berlin Wall—but you're looking at Ground Zero. If Soviet nukes *had* come, they would've struck this place first."

"You around during all that?"

"Some of it. I was born in sixty-two, a year before my father died. Mom used to cook and clean for the miners—then went to work for the spooks. Don't remember much about 'em besides they were an unfriendly bunch. I came of age in the seventies and eighties, right around the time this place was becoming an artist retreat. Things were pretty good 'round here until the Kidd bought the place and turned Blind River into fuckin' Alaskaland.'"

Jake was listening to Lancaster, but his eyes were on the pedestrians, searching for a flash of red hair. No luck. He did, however, see a couple of men with rifles slung over their shoulders, entering a taxidermy store. Their pickup truck was parked at the curb, and in the back of the bed, Jake spotted a lump of gray-and-white fur, mottled with blood.

The gunshot he'd heard earlier...

It *had* been a wolf.

"That legal?" Jake asked.

Lancaster glanced at the wolf's cadaver. "Oh sure. Not only legal, but the state of Alaska *pays* you to kill 'em—hundred and fifty bucks a pelt."

"I heard that winter in Blind River belongs to the wolves."

Lancaster chuckled. "It's a ghost story, pal. It sounds mysterious and dangerous, and it helps the Kidd book rooms. But wolves don't attack people, everybody knows that."

"I didn't know that."

"Well you do now. And truth is, there aren't many wolves left around the mountain. Sheriff damn near shot 'em all. Said they were a nuisance."

"Eating the livestock?"

"Scaring the scientists."

"Scientists?"

"Yeah, studying climate change or some bullshit. We had a whole slew of 'em spend a winter up here a couple years ago. Jumpy bunch. Didn't care much for the great outdoors, I gather."

"So, if they killed all the wolves, why shut down for the winter? The weather?"

"Nah. I spent every winter out here growing up. Christopher Kidd's just too big of a pussy to stick it out, and when that hotel shuts down, *everything* shuts down, so what's the point in the rest of us staying? There's no money in it."

"But there's still money in Blind River, isn't there? There has to be a reason you've stayed on all these years."

The man's head turned to the mountain. "Sure there's a reason. *Ningakpok Iggik*. Means *angry mountain* in Inuit. The Kidd owns this town, but he doesn't own the mineral rights—Feds still do. So a few years ago, me and a couple of other guys put in for a new mineral survey. We were poking around the mountain for a new entrance when the Department of the Interior called and informed us the mountain's too unstable to mine. I told them, yes, the mine that killed my old man was unstable, which was why we needed to dig a new one. But Interior didn't see it my way; *no one* at Interior saw it my way. Come that November, who did I see at the Kidd's annual end-of-the-year auction? The secretary of the Department of the Interior. You see, a new mine would interfere with the tourists, and the Kidd's dropped an awful lotta coin into this town. But I'm not going anywhere. One of these days I'm gonna get inside that mountain. And I'm gonna finish what my old man started."

The town square came into view. Jake saw an ice-skating rink and an adjoining one-room coffeehouse. A low wooden fence draped with Christmas lights and wreaths of holly enclosed the park. Streetlights, the sort you might find in London, bathed the entire square with a soft amber glow, though Jake noticed that at least two bulbs needed changing.

The driver stopped the sleigh at a tall arch, the entrance to the square. The arch was made entirely of caribou antlers, meticulously hooked together by their thorny tines.

"Mistletoe's mostly on the porch." Lancaster nodded beyond the arch to the cozy coffeehouse. "That's the last place I saw your wife."

"Right."

Jake took off the blanket, stood and turned to step off the sled, but Lancaster caught him with a beefy hand. "Here, take this." He handed Jake his business card. "Give me a jingle when you catch up to your wife. That hundred bucks bought you a ride back to the hotel, too."

"Thanks," Jake said, slipping the card into his wallet. "It's been an education."

Lancaster nodded, cracked the reigns, and the skinny Clydesdales trudged away with the closest thing to a moan a horse could muster.

Jake strolled around the park, ordered a cappuccino in the coffeehouse, and scrutinized the ice-skaters. Claire wasn't there. Assuming she'd left by foot, she was most likely patronizing one of the surrounding businesses. Toward the bottom of the square, he saw the less touristy establishments, tucked away in the settling darkness. An auto garage, a horse stable, a small clinic, and a fire and police station. Beyond that, Main Street twisted back and forth through the narrow valley, stretching all the way to Highway 3. That road ran all the way to Anchorage. It was dark, and he could see the warm glow of houselights throughout the valley. The locals had built their homes on the riverbanks. Tremendous for salmon fishing, he was sure, but it also meant that the homes were very well hidden. Jake flashed on Claire, bound and gagged in some backwoods wacko's house.

He called her cell phone again, and this time it went straight to voice-mail. Her phone had run out of juice, or else she'd turned it off.

Or someone turned it off for me.

No way, Claire. You wouldn't put yourself in that situation. You aren't stupid.

The police station sat at the bottom of the town square, just a couple hundred feet away. Several F-150s were parked in a back lot, and Jake could see the gold stars emblazoned on the doors with the initials BRPD. He felt the itch to call them—yes, the cops were probably irritated after yesterday's false alarm, but this time things were different. It was nearly five o'clock in the afternoon. She'd been gone all day. He had no doubt that, by then, Claire would've called, no matter how badly he'd pissed her off.

Ignoring a dull throb behind his eyes, he strolled back through the antler arch to the sidewalk. He didn't even have to call the cops. He could just walk across the street and tell them. But as he started in that direction, he spied a familiar figure dashing through the spill from the street lamps on the opposite side of Main. The man was hunched against the bitter wind. The thick collar of a heavy sheepskin coat mostly obscured his face, but Jake still recognized him. It was the handsome son of a bitch who'd been fly-fishing with Dick Cheney—Christopher Kidd, owner of the Hotel Ascent and, according to his misanthropic sleigh driver, the man responsible for turning Blind River into Alaskaland.

The Kidd was hurrying toward the dark blue door of what looked like a café, and he was carrying a bouquet of witch hazel, its surprising yellow flowers in mid-bloom and on full display.

Yeah, but a bouquet of flowers for who?

Jake saw red.

And followed.

TWELVE

———

JAKE WAITED A FEW MINUTES before pushing through the dark blue door of the Café Beaujolais. He wanted the Kidd and Claire to be seated before making his big entrance.

He wanted to catch them red-handed.

Once inside, he stomped his tennis shoes on a tongue of red carpet that led into a moody dining room, a room with hardwood floors and rich mahogany walls. Christopher Kidd was sitting in a far corner booth, alone. The man was, however, wearing an eager look on his boyish face, nervously fiddling with the bouquet of witch hazel. Waiting for someone.

Claire? Maybe she wasn't there yet?

"Will it just be you tonight, sir?"

The hostess. Jake turned and saw that she had a menu in hand.

"I hope not," Jake said, then nodded to a small espresso bar. "My wife must be late. I'll wait for her over there."

Jake hurried to the espresso bar, all too sure that the Kidd had already seen him. And hadn't Claire told him that the Kidd was a big fan of *Bullseye*?

He had to be careful.

Jake plunked down on a stool and a bored barista, as thick as prime rib, looked his way. Behind her, he saw a sign showing a cartoon wolf scarfing down an enormous steak.

"That's right," she said, sounding bored out of her mind. "Eat a seventy-two-ounce steak in an hour and you get it free, as well as one of our souvenir jackets."

Jake followed her finger to a heavy gray jacket hanging in a glass case and sporting the words, "I Wolfed-Out in Blind River."

Suddenly, the bitter wind chapped his face, and he was back on that rickety ski lift, his gaze vacillating between the spine of glistening black granite below and the man riding in the chair just ahead of them.

A man who'd been wearing the exact same jacket.

A man who Claire had followed onto White Alice, the most difficult slope on the mountain.

A man who Jake had lost sight of on that very same run where he'd also lost sight of Claire.

"A lot of people win?" Jake asked, trying to keep his cool. Trying to remember how to quiz a potential source.

"Yeah, maybe one a month."

"How about this month? How about this week?"

"Yeah, I think someone won."

"Bearded guy? Big potbelly? Hey, you got a registry? Something where you write down the winner's names?"

"No."

She was clearly lying, but she also was clearly annoyed. He considered slipping her his last hundred—it had bought him valuable information from the sleigh driver—but his gut told him this woman wouldn't be quite so garrulous.

Better to save the cash.

"I thought this was a French café," Jake said finally. "What are you doing serving up steaks?"

"You're in Blind River," she said dryly, more comfortable now that they were talking about food. "We serve steaks everywhere. Can I get you one?"

"I'll just do a cappuccino."

Then, behind him, the Kidd suddenly stood. Jake did too, ready to catch

Claire at the door. Ready to dish out the wrath beholden to his new role: Jake Boxer, jealous husband. But it wasn't Claire who entered.

Yes, it was a woman, but not the beautiful redhead who'd recently told Jake *I do*, though she did have a familiar face. It was gaunt. Dark circles ringed her narrow eyes. A nob of black hair was pulled into a tight bun, accenting her harsh look. She was a twiggy little thing, so much so that he might've mistaken her for a—

Teenager.

It clicked.

Ana Turov.

He was looking at the artist in the photograph from the Honeymoon Suite, the one Claire had left crooked on the wall.

But that was impossible. That photograph had clearly been old, probably from the seventies. The woman who'd just entered the café couldn't have been older than thirty.

She wasn't Ana Turov, but she sure as hell did look like her.

The Kidd gestured to the other side of the booth, and the Ana lookalike walked briskly over. Once there, she pushed the bouquet of witch hazel aside and flashed the Kidd a reluctant smile. Jake was too far away to overhear their conversation, but it was obvious that the dinner was not a date—it was about something other than romance.

Not that Jake cared.

Bogged down with worry, he sank to his stool with an unbearable realization—he was still no closer to finding Claire.

He pulled out his cell phone and was about to call her for the millionth time when an authoritative voice froze his fingers.

"Mr. Boxer. Mind if I have a word?"

He was asking…but he *wasn't* asking.

Jake turned and saw a thin but well-muscled young man, starched khakis for pants, and a forest green button up for a shirt. A gold star was pinned into the breast pocket, and a 9mm semiautomatic rested comfortably in the leather holster of his utility belt.

"I'm Deputy Travis Benson," he said. "I was one of the men who went looking for your wife yesterday when the Ascent's concierge called to report she was missing?"

"Thank God," Jake said. "Look, she's still missing. I think I need your help."

"Right…" Travis rubbed a hand across his clean-shaven face, looking slightly embarrassed. "Do you mind stepping outside for a moment, Mr. Boxer? It might be better to discuss this in private."

"I don't think anyone around us is listening," Jake said, suddenly wary.

The lawman smiled, glanced at the barista, and then at a couple of patrons in the vicinity, who were sipping their hot caffeinated drinks.

"Okay," he said, then lowered his voice. "We'll do this here. Now, I know you and your wife are reporters, but we like to think that Blind River is a private place, a place where anyone can come and relax, ski the mountain, and enjoy the wildlife. That goes for guests and locals alike. Hell, our city's motto is, *To each his own*." He smiled, then leaned in close, *uncomfortably* close. "Means we don't stick our dicks in each other's business. Get it?"

"What did she do?"

His face squished up. "*She?*"

"My wife."

"Oh no, Jake, I'm not talking about her. I'm talking about you breaking into the Kidd's office this afternoon."

Jake blinked, wondering what, exactly, Al had told the police about the incident. "That was an accident."

"Uh-huh. And how exactly did you 'accidentally' end up in the employee-only hallway when you 'accidentally' broke that window?"

"I got lost. I was looking for my wife. I knocked on the window, thinking someone was inside, and it shattered. It must have already been cracked."

"Al told me that the two of you broke it playing catch. Said you two were passing the time until your wife came back. You really think I believed that? Catch?"

Jake wanted to bury his head in the snow. Playing catch? Really? That was the best that the old concierge could come up with?

"Listen," the deputy said, "I know who you are—"

"A student?" Jake asked, interrupting. "Well, I hope to be. I've got to pass the LSAT first, but if I do I'm going to Columbia."

"Okay," the deputy said, "then maybe I should say I know who you *were*, and I know that most reporters have a penchant for being…nosy. I don't want to involve the sheriff in this. The last week in Blind River is always a circus—the man's got enough on his mind. But I am going to have to get him involved if you keep following around the Kidd." The deputy nodded to the Kidd and his mystery date, then leaned close. "Yes, he is a lady's man, but believe me, he is not fooling around with your wife."

"Christopher Kidd?" Jake said dumbly. "Why I didn't even know he was here."

The lawman grinned. "I can't prove you broke a law, so I'm letting you off with a warning. We appreciate that your wife wants to write an article on our little town. Sounds like a real nice piece—"

"How do you know?" Jake asked quickly.

"Know what?"

"That it sounds like a nice piece?"

The deputy looked at Jake as if he were an idiot. "Well, she told me all about it."

"Told you? When?"

"When I had this exact same conversation with her about ten minutes ago. Found her in the square taking photographs of the skate rink. I just gave her a ride back up the hill—we had our little chat about privacy along the way."

"Did she say anything about me?"

He held up both hands defensively. "Let me preface this by saying my job is to keep the peace, not dish out marital advice, but as a man on the other side of ten years of marriage…" He lowered his voice, as if clueing Jake into some secret club. "You don't tell 'em to quit their job for your own personal ambitions, Mr. Boxer—not in this day and age, not even out here in Blind River."

So that was it! Claire *was* pissed at him for telling her to quit her job, and she was making him pay for it by her silence.

"The woman wants to write travel articles," the lawman said, "so, *let* her write travel articles. I mean it pays, right?"

Jake didn't answer. Instead he stood, started to leave, but the deputy caught his arm.

"Where are you going?"

"Back to the hotel."

"She's not at the hotel. I took her to the slopes."

"Why?"

He shrugged. "Said she had to meet someone up there about her article."

Someone on the slopes? Well if it wasn't the Kidd, who?

A heated exchange drew their attention back to the Kidd's booth. The Ana Turov look-alike had stood abruptly, knocking over a champagne glass on the way. Jake watched as she stormed for the door, a trail of yellow flower pedals fluttering in her wake. Behind her, the Kidd was burning up, clearly unaccustomed to such insubordination. He hopped to his feet and hurried out after her, barging out the door without paying—almost as if he owned the place. And he probably did.

Jake turned back to the deputy. "You dropped Claire off at the mountain? That's where she is?"

"I dropped her at the locker room."

Jake started for the door, but the deputy stepped in front of him.

"*To each his own*, Mr. Boxer, or we're gonna have a problem. Am I clear?"

"Crystal."

"Good. Now listen. It pains me to see a perfectly good honeymoon go to waste, especially for a man who, I must admit, has me a little star-struck." He grinned and made little guns with his fingers. "You might even say that *you've got me in your crosshairs.*" Much to Jake's chagrin, the deputy fired off his finger guns and then slapped him on the back, as if they were thick as thieves. "C'mon. It would be my honor to escort *the* Jake Boxer up the hill to save his marriage. If we hurry, you might even be able to catch her before she reaches the lift."

Jake's gut turned.

Right.

The lift…

THIRTEEN

CLAIRE'S SKIS WEREN'T IN THEIR LOCKER, which could only mean one thing: she was already on the mountain.

But his own skis were there, of course, right where he'd left them, leaning upright in the back of the locker. He pulled them out, along with his poles and lift pass. Kicking off his sneakers, he quickly stepped into his ski boots, and then stepped onto the ski's bindings, locking them in. He hadn't had time to run back to their room for long underwear or wool socks. So his North Face jacket, blue jeans, and bare hands would have to do.

The wind fought him as he pushed outside.

Gloveless, Jake dug his poles into the ground and duck-walked through a nascent snowfall toward the mountain's only lift. He'd only gone a short ways before his thighs screamed and lungs burned as they sucked down the frigid air.

It was cold.

Frostbite cold.

Neon green vest, he reminded himself. All that matters is the neon green vest.

Skiers and snowboarders were whooshing down the mountain in a blur of vibrant color, illuminated by the tall lights. A flash of neon green caught his eye. He nearly fell as he swiveled to the right, instinctively following the color.

But then he lost her.

But then he found her!

A tall woman, her hair tucked underneath a knit hat, some fifty feet away, queuing up for the lift.

It wasn't her.

It *was* her.

He couldn't be sure, but he did know one thing: something was wrong.

He couldn't explain it—he just knew it.

Claire, his wife, was in danger.

Digging his poles into the snow, he shoved off with renewed urgency, duck walking and skidding in short stretches to the lift.

"Claire...CLAIRE!"

The wind blew his voice right back at him. He caught sight of her again as she entered the lift's loading zone, and this time he saw her profile. This time he saw her high cheekbones and freckled face. It *was* Claire. He was so close.

"CLAIRE!" he screamed, but only succeeded in bursting the eardrums of the man directly in front of him. "Sorry, that's my wife. It's our honeymoon. That's my...CLAIRE!"

But she still didn't hear him.

One of the lift operators gestured for her to get on the lift. She was alone. Jake exhaled. Well, at least there was that. At least she wasn't cheating on him.

As Jake lined up at the back of the queue, Claire stepped toward an empty chair rounding the turnbuckle. And then something happened. The lift operator waved for the snowboarder, standing behind her, to load into the same seat—apparently he, too, was riding stag. They both caught the chair, sitting down as it scooped them up, the haul rope yanking them away from the loading zone. And then they were gone.

He hadn't seen the snowboarder's face, just the back of his head, and he'd only been able to process a tight black skullcap.

Had Claire been planning to board the lift with him? Had these two deliberately queued up as strangers in order to avoid attention? It was roughly fifteen minutes to the summit, plenty of time for two people, say a reporter and her MPP, to speak discretely without fear of anyone else eavesdropping.

Board as strangers. Pass information. Depart as strangers.

All in the cover of snowfall and darkness.

Something he would've done back in his *Bullseye* days.

Jake burst into action.

"Excuse me," he said, shoving past skiers. "My wife is up there, my *new* wife…excuse me, I'm terribly late…so sorry…I really appreciate it…I'm in enough trouble as it is."

Jake managed to cut his way to the loading zone. Above him, he could still make out Claire's neon green ski jacket in the darkness, but just barely.

"Sir? Sir, I'm sorry but you can't cut in line."

The lift operator. A young bearded guy who was surely skipping PSYCH 101 to work there.

"I'm sorry," Jake said, "I can't ski very well, and my wife…" He slipped on his skis as he said it, "My *new* wife, she's sick—mentally and emotionally—she's looking for me, goddammit. She thinks I'm up at the summit. She's there, right there, in the green jacket—and I'm way back here!"

Jake pointed even though he couldn't see her anymore.

"I'm sorry, but you're going to have to go to the back."

Jake punched one of two black buttons on the support pole. The lift stopped, the skiers behind him groaned, and the lift operator nearly developed an aneurysm.

"Sir! Operating this lift without a license is against the law!"

"My *wife* is *sick*!" He held up his ski pole and puffed up his considerable frame. "And this pole *will* fit up your ass if you don't let me on this fucking lift!" He took several breaths before saying, "*Please.*"

The lift operator studied him, then…

"Wait a second. I know you. You're that guy who flipped out on live TV. God, that was epic. The whole Putin thing? With the umbrella gun and the polonium-210? Jesus. Me and my parents, we thought you were kidding."

"That's right, that's right. I'm Jake Boxer and I've got you in my crosshairs. Now please. I need my wife."

The operator, more confused now than anything, looked at where Claire was dangling, just barely out of view. And then he looked at the two women Jake had just cut in front of.

"It's fine. Just let him on," one of the women said.

Jake grumbled his thanks and pushed himself into the loading zone.

The operator punched the other black button, the bull wheel turned, the haul rope caught, and the next empty chair swung around and hit Jake in the back of the knees, scooping him up like a helping of Jake Boxer ice cream.

"Putin's not at the summit, but it is ten below up there," the operator shouted as Jake whisked passed. "Hope you don't freeze."

Mere seconds into the ride, Jake realized he'd freeze well before reaching the summit. Digging his hands into his armpits, he tried to ignore the biting cold so that he could concentrate on the situation at hand. He could see two chairs ahead of him, but beyond that, everything was dark. The chair in front of him was empty—his antics in line had caused the operator to miss loading it, but there were two skiers in the chair just ahead of the empty one, and Claire and her mystery snowboarder were probably two or three chairs in front of them. So Claire was probably only four or five chairs in front of him, too far for him to shout and be heard, but close enough that he could catch her at the summit.

The summit…

White Alice came back to him, the double black diamond lined with concrete buildings that had once been Ground Zero in the war against the Soviets. High-tech eavesdropping stations… *listening* stations—

Brody.

His best friend.

His *audio* man.

For one hot second, Jake saw Brody riding the chairlift in front of him. The back of his head—those earphones still clamped around his bone-white skull—just *listening*.

But to what?

A Blind River Hum?

And if so, why hadn't he heard it?

His chair approached the last light before a long stretch of darkness. Brody disappeared in the final light. Then Jake passed through, and left it far behind, which was when it *really* got cold. His jeans did nothing to cut the wind, a wind that blew in howling gales that rocked his chair and gripped his heart with panic. The chair was gonna tip. Throw him right the hell out. Abandoning his armpits, he hooked his right arm around the support pole and then looked up at the knuckle gripping the thick haul rope—a steel snake moving slowly above him. What had Claire said? The knuckle was designed to give. If it didn't, the wind would blow the lift right over.

It made him feel a little better.

What else had she said?

Close your eyes and picture us at the ending.

A distraction technique.

Get your mind off the present and into the future.

Of course, when Claire had said it, she'd been sitting right next to him, and he'd had the comfort of her arm threaded through his. Now he was alone, his arms (and in particular his hands) going numb. Jake closed his eyes anyway, even though every time he did it, he saw Brody's vermin-eaten face.

Jake thought about the ending, and in his mind's eye, he saw himself reaching the top of the lift, and he saw his beautiful bride waiting for him. He saw himself wrap his arms around her, and he felt her strong body against his, and he saw himself put his mouth to her ear, and he heard himself say, *You can write travel articles for the rest of your life, so long as I have you,* even though he now knew beyond any doubt that this honeymoon was not about a travel article.

He opened his eyes.

There was a hazy glow in the distance. The lights of the lift's upper turnstile. The end of the line. Another five minutes, maybe, and he'd be at the summit.

But then the lift jerked to a stop.

His body swayed forward, and for one perilous moment, the earth rushed to greet him. He slid back into the safety of the chair, which was swaying gently on the haul line.

The lift had stopped the last time he was on it too. Claire had told him someone was probably having trouble getting on or off the lift. Hell, he'd stopped it himself just ten short minutes ago when he smacked that black button. It would start again at any second, of that he was sure.

No. Not sure. *Freezing.*

He was going to *die.*

Stop.

Count down from twenty.

Nice and slow.

Slow. Slow. Slow.

But by the time he reached zero, the lift still hadn't revved back to life, so he counted down from fifty. He took in the sights as he counted, and guessed they were above one of the vertical granite spines that gave the mountain its idiosyncratic look—black granite that would surely kill them if the haul line snapped, *if* they fell.

But they weren't gonna fall. He was sure. Claire said this happens all the time. Right?

"Hey!" he shouted at the two skiers in the seat beyond the empty chair just ahead of him. "You know what's going on?"

"What?" one of them shouted back—a woman. Her voice was muted and scared. At least he wasn't alone. She wore a puffy snowsuit and was having a tough time turning around to face him.

"I SAID, WHAT'S GOING ON? CAN YOU SEE ANYTHING?"

"NO!" she shouted back. "DON'T KNOW WHAT'S HAPPENING!"

Jake squinted, but he couldn't see beyond them. In theory, Claire was just in front them, riding with her mystery man. Was this little stop some-how planned? Could Claire have paid one of the operators a couple of bucks to halt the lift? To score a bit more time with her source? Or, more Machiavellian, to scare him into talking?

"CAN YOU SEE ANYONE IN FRONT OF YOU?" Jake shouted. "A WOMAN IN A GREEN SKI JACKET? SHE'S MY WIFE."

"YOUR WHAT?"

"MY WIFE! IN A GREEN SKI JACKET! IS SHE OKAY?"

Jake watched as the skier leaned forward, as she squinted into her own darkness before turning back to Jake. "CAN'T TELL! IT'S REALLY DARK!"

"CAN YOU PLEASE TRY YELLING TO HER? CAN YOU TELL HER IT'S OK? THAT I'M RIGHT BEHIND HER?"

"WHAT?" the skier asked.

The other skier, a man, turned to Jake and shouted, "IT'S REALLY HARD TO HEAR YOU!"

"JUST TELL HER IT'S OKAY! THE WOMAN IN FRONT OF YOU! THAT HER HUSBAND'S RIGHT BEHIND HER!"

The skier turned and looked in Claire's direction, then turned back. "SHE'S NOT GONNA HEAR US, MAN!"

"JUST TRY!" Jake urged. "SHE *HAS* TO HEAR YOU!"

"WHAT?"

"I SAID SHE *HAS* TO HEAR YOU—"

The lift jerked forward, then came to a halting stop again. Off balance, Jake grabbed for the lift's support pole and lost both ski poles to the darkness below. The metal was freezing and the wind bit his naked knuckles like a pack of angry dogs.

Or wolves.

He scooted back into the seat, his breath ragged and desperate. His heart, once again, knocking about his ribcage.

Oh, Jesus.

Oh, Jesus.

Oh, Jesus.

Ahead of him, the two skiers were likewise inching back into their seats. Something was wrong. Really wrong. They were all going to die.

No.

This is all in your head. It's just a routine stop. Deal with it.

Jake dug into his jacket pocket for his phone and felt around with numb fingers. Maybe he could text her. Maybe she'd get it. Maybe they were in some weird freaky signal zone—like the spot ten steps to the right of their Honeymoon Suite where he got three bars. Trembling, he looked at the phone's screen.

The bad news was that he had no bars.

The good news was that it didn't say, No Signal.

He doubted if he could make or receive a call, but maybe a text would slip through.

Maybe.

R u ok? Right behind u on lift.

SEND

Jake waited for what felt like an eternity. She didn't write back.

I'm sorry I told u to quit. Stupid. Txt me back. Let me know ur ok.

SEND

I don't care what ur really doing here. I love u. Let's do it together.

SEND

He hesitated, his frozen fingers hovering over his phone's keyboard, and then he typed out the only possible reason why she'd been behaving so poorly.

Even if its about Brody.

SEND

That was it.

There was nothing more to say.

There was nothing more to do, for that matter, but to wait.

The haul line jerked forward. Stopped. And this time the whip was hard. *Very* hard. Jake nearly lost his phone. Hell, the skiers two chairs in front of him nearly lost each other—he could tell by the panicked screams—but they somehow managed to hang on. He knew that this was no longer just "in his head." Below, he saw small bouncing lights, but only vaguely registered them as snowmobiles. Surely, they were emergency snowmobiles racing up the mountain, a futile act unless they had fifty-foot ladders.

Jake thought about dying up there in the dark and in the cold and quite alone, and he felt scared. Back in his *Bullseye* days, he'd done plenty of stupid things that could've, and probably should've, gotten him killed. But back then, the thought of dying didn't bother him. The thought had even been glamorous—the intrepid journalist dying for his story.

But now things were different. *Bullseye* was in the rearview mirror, and he was a married man, a married man with an emotional future, if not a vocational one. He had a wife to live with and to love, and he wanted to have kids and grandkids. Goddammit, he didn't want to die, he *couldn't* die, not like this, not right now. Not alone. *Claire* couldn't die alone.

Claire wasn't alone, he realized dully.

That snowboarder was with her.

His phone buzzed. He looked back to his glowing screen.

The Good Spy Dies Twice

Claire.

She'd sent the text.

He'd seen the words before. He knew them. Buck—

A tremble rippled the steel cable above. He felt a small but noticeable lift, as if a giant had plucked the haul line. And then, in the distance, he heard a sharp metallic pop, as if the gears attached to the bull wheel had come apart. Somewhere ahead of him, a woman shrieked.

Claire?

Then the skiers ahead of him were thrown ten feet straight up before plunging back down. Down, down, down toward the black granite spine. The skiers were still in their chairs, and the chairs were still attached to the haul rope, but the haul rope had come undone. The haul rope was *falling*.

And then it was Jake's turn.

He saw the rope come loose above him and grabbed the chairlift's support bar, holding on for dear life. He plunged for the earth, his chair rolling forward so that he was soon falling headfirst, but his descent stopped suddenly when, high above, the haul rope inexplicably jerked to a stop. The steel line had been caught by something high overhead. He felt relief, but it was short-lived. The sudden stop bucked his chair sharply, tossing Jake, who was by then upside down, forward. He tried to hang on but his momentum was too great, his numb fingers of little use. He lost his grip and tumbled into empty space. As he fell, he passed a blur of empty chairs— chairs that had apparently bucked their riders as well—and it registered that one of them had been Claire's—*and she was no longer in it*—and then he felt a thousand scratches across his face. Then several loud cracks as he smashed through a pine tree and broke God-only-knew which bones, and then he was twisting and flailing again, hitting the granite spine beneath him feet first before falling backward, finally striking his head.

He saw a starburst, like when the filament pops in an old light bulb, and staring at the sky, he experienced the sort of hyper-clarity he'd heard sometimes accompanied severe trauma. The clouds above him were no longer a gray smear—they were gates—gates that revealed an infinite universe— gates that opened just wide enough to let a soul through. Then they closed and the show was over and Jake saw only darkness.

Like ink.

PART THREE

RED FURY

FOURTEEN

THE BAHIA HONDA STATE PARK, a stopping point along the A1A bridge on the way to Key West, sported one of the finest beaches Jake had ever seen: stretches of bone-white sand melted into aquamarine water that was as quiet and as flat as a sheet of glass. The island was largely undeveloped, but it still had a hotel and a bar, and Jake and Claire had spent the past three days lounging about in their swimsuits, indulging their newlywed bliss.

That morning, however, had been a little bit different. Jake had woken late, only to discover that Claire had already left their room. At first he panicked, but then he remembered what she'd told him the night before.

"Sleep late, honey. I'm going to get up early and work on the article. Get it out of the way."

See? Nothing to worry about. She was just working on her latest travel article, one she'd titled, "Love In The Sun."

So, after a leisurely breakfast, Jake strolled through the rolling sand dunes between the hotel and the beach. They were covered with golden ammophila, and he took great pleasure in running his fingers through the plant's brushlike tips along the way. He heard the call of several birds overhead.

He looked up, expecting seagulls, but they were much larger. They were also stark white and flying in a V-shaped flock typical of migratory birds.

Weird.

He couldn't place them, but he was sure he hadn't seen such birds on the beach before, that the type stuck to northern, colder climates.

He found Claire on a lawn chair beneath an umbrella, her long fingers click-clacking across her laptop's keyboard–it could have been a piano, and she could've been Mozart.

Damn, could she write.

He stopped before she knew he was there, just to admire her in her green bikini and sheer cover-up. Then he cleared his throat. She looked up and when she saw him, saved what she'd been working on, closed the computer, and powered down her cell phone.

They were on their honeymoon, after all.

Work could wait.

She stood and turned to him, but Jake couldn't see her expression—in fact, he couldn't see her face at all. She was wearing a wide sun hat. It cast a shadow as black as tar across her face. Still, she stripped off her cover-up and ran across the fine white sand to the waterline. Jake followed. She slipped when she got to the wet sand, still a little awkward in her long body after all those years, but Jake caught her from behind, and they splashed into the warm water together, laughing and flirting. But he still couldn't see her face beneath that hat; the shadow it cast was just too dark. Up to their chests, their legs intertwined, Jake suddenly found her shadow's hot mouth on his, kissing him, moaning, and speaking in susurrations. "I love you, Jake. I love you more than I ever loved Brody. You know that, don't you?"

"Yes," he said, "I know." And then he reached into the black shadow to take her face, to pull her close, but when he touched her cheeks, he felt stubble. And when she tilted her face to the sun, he saw Brody. But not for long. Soon, Brody's eyes rolled back into their sockets and his skin began sloughing from his face like a snake's. His ears peeled off, and he was wearing those headphones again. The tide pulled against them. The ocean yawned revealing a mouth of granite teeth, a bottomless stone quarry where those Russian school kids had found him. Brody's bone white jaw came unhinged as he hissed, *"Picture us at the ending."* Brody shoved him hard, his skeletal palms connecting with Jake's chest. The black magic of Jake's nightmare was suddenly very real.

He tumbled backward into the pit. He fell, landing on jagged stones, and then his back snapped, and he saw the flock of birds again.

White Siberian cranes, he realized.

That's what they were. Flying in a V formation across the gunmetal sky. Somewhere in the back of his head, he recalled a news story about Vladimir Putin donning a white jumpsuit and piloting a mechanized glider in an attempt to lead a flock of the endangered birds to a sanctuary.

To a nature preserve.

Which was surely just beyond the quarry into which he'd fallen.

He saw several schoolchildren perched on the lip of the quarry some thirty feet above. They were pointing at him, speaking to each other in Russian, eyebrows arched and mouths slack—*Oh my God, do you see that?*

He tried to call out to them, only to discover that he had no breath. He tried to sit up, but the Devil grabbed his spine with a thorny, hot hand, and pain boomeranged the length of his back.

And then he heard the hum.

The Dagestan Hum—a low-decibel vibration that moved through stone and flesh alike. Jake heard the undulating sound through Brody's Beyerdynamic Pro headphones, now clamped to his own skull. Brody's audio recorder was suddenly in Jake's own decaying hands.

He closed his eyes and the hum grew louder. Just as it threatened to burst his eardrums, he heard a beep.

A steady, rhythmic beep.

He opened his eyes.

Instead of white Siberian cranes, he saw white ceiling tiles, old and mottled with water stains.

Not on the beach with Claire.

Not in the quarry with Brody.

But the Devil still had a grip on his spine and...

Dear God. What had happened to his back?

The pain, it was...excruciating!

The steady pulse of beeps. The stink of disinfectant.

He was in a hospital, an *old* hospital, and not very well maintained, if those ceiling tiles were any metric.

But why?

And why couldn't he move his head?

He tried his fingers. Those moved—all ten—but they stung. He could feel a million little cuts on them. His right hand, in particular, felt burned, as if he'd plunged it into the Hotel Ascent's enormous fireplace.

No, not fire—it had been cold.

So very very cold.

He tried to move his legs, but the Devil didn't like that. Pain radiated from his lower back in pulsing currents—electric fire. Jake discovered that the rest of his muscles worked in one spastic jerk of recollection, prompting a hoarse scream.

Seconds later, he heard a door open, then soft footsteps. Someone in tennis shoes approached. Then he saw a beefy and tired-looking nurse in a crumpled white uniform.

"Mr. Boxer," she clucked indifferently. "You're awake."

"*Claire...*" he muttered. "Where...is...*Claire?*"

God, it hurt just to talk.

The nurse smiled wanly, then turned to an IV stand at the edge of his vision. She replaced an empty bag with a full one. The drip started again and the Devil loosened his grip. Jake felt the soft white sand between his toes. He felt the warm Florida sun on his face. He saw the sheet of never-ending ocean glass.

The next time he opened his eyes, he was once again staring at those off-white ceiling tiles, and the bag on the IV stand was once again empty.

And the pain...Jesus Christ, *the fucking pain!*

More, he thought primitively while he fumbled for the nurse's call button—*more drugs*—but a voice stayed him before he could push it.

"Don't worry about calling a nurse, Mr. Boxer. I promise, you're in good hands—as good as you're going to get in Blind River, anyway."

Blind River?

No.

He was on the beach with—

"*Claire.*" Jake choked up the name in another spasm of pain. It felt as though his throat had been packed with ice.

"Yes, your wife. We'll get to her, but first—*you.*"

Jake heard a chair squeak as it was rolled across the floor, and then a heavily bearded man in his mid-fifties appeared beside him.

"Mr. Boxer, my name is Elmore Wallace. I'm the physician in these parts. You were in a terrible accident. Do you remember what happened up on the mountain?"

The bitter cold chapped Jake's face.

The herky-jerky motion of the lift made him nauseous.

Ningakpok Iggik.

The angry mountain.

Yes, he remembered.

"I took you off your pain medication," the doctor continued. "I need you lucid to assess your condition. How would you rate your pain on a scale of one to ten?"

"CLAIRE!"

That outburst drained him. He sank back into his bed, closed his eyes, and willed the doctor, the hospital, the Devil's hand…*everything*…to just go the fuck away.

But they didn't.

The doctor did, however, cease his line of questioning. Instead, he poked him with needles and made notes on his chart, all while looking more or less pleased. And when he was done, the beefy nurse wheeled Jake out of the room, across a very small lobby, and into another room, this one with an MRI machine. They prepped him and rolled him into the machine, which was shaped like an enormous doughnut. The machine's clicks echoed in his ears, and Jake couldn't help but to wonder if he'd just been sterilized. With the battery of tests over, they returned him to his room where he once again found himself staring at the off-white ceiling tiles, though now he could move his head. They'd removed the neck brace before his MRI, but they hadn't bothered to put it back on.

His foggy brain told him that this was probably good, that it meant his neck wasn't broken.

"How would you describe your pain now?" the doctor asked. "On a scale of one to ten?"

"Around twenty," Jake muttered, surprising both himself and the doctor. It was the first sound that wasn't a grunt, groan, or CLAIRE! that had come out of his mouth, and the first indication he was feeling better, if only a bit.

"Well, that's a significant amount of pain but, trust me, it's better than *not* feeling. Can you turn your head toward me?"

Jake turned his head a few inches but did most of the work with his eyes. He saw the doctor's laptop sitting on a rolling dais. There were twelve photographs on the screen, each with a different cross-section of Jake's spine. Dr. Wallace pointed at the upper-left-hand scan.

"Your cervical vertebrae look fine," his finger drifted to a lower scan, "and your thoracic vertebrae do as well, but when we get to here…" He tapped an even lower scan featuring Jake's thick lumbar vertebrae. Two of them looked squished together, the fluid between them jettisoned, and a tiny hairline crack through the lower one was evident. "The MRI confirms that there was no damage to the spinal cord, but we are looking at a ten percent compression fracture of the L5 vertebra. That may sound bad, but below thirty percent, we don't do surgery. The only remedy is rest, relaxation, and, well, painkillers. It's good news, really. As good as we could hope for."

"Doesn't feel like good news."

"Trust me, it is. You'll be walking again in a few days. Seems the tree that broke your back also broke your fall."

His fall…

"Claire…where is Claire?"

"Yes. Claire."

The doctor leaned back and took careful stock of him. He had such a friendly face—a face seemingly made to deliver bad news.

"What I'm about to tell you won't make a lick of difference now, but later, it might provide some small measure of comfort." And then he said it, "She didn't suffer."

FIFTEEN

JAKE'S HEART HEAVED. Hot tears splashed down his cheeks.

He tried to say something, but the news of Claire's death had awoken a monster, and that monster was deaf, blind, and stupid, and all it could do was wail.

"Please, Mr. Boxer. You *have* to calm down. Your spine…"

Fuck his spine.

The monster *wanted* it to snap.

It wanted to die and go to Heaven and be with Claire, where it belonged.

At some point, the stocky nurse rushed in with a shot and stuck it deep into the monster's flailing arm, and the beast calmed and slept and became Jake again.

Hours later, the sedative dulled, and Jake awoke.

The monster did not.

The nurse wheeled in a steel trolley with a tray of red Jell-O, buttered toast, and orange Pedialite, but Jake didn't eat or drink. He'd become transfixed with the reflection of himself in the trolley's warped aluminum siding.

He was covered in a thousand tiny scratches—damage from the pine tree that supposedly broke his fall. His face was puffy and purple and several blood vessels had burst in his left eye.

The nurse carted out his untouched food, and Jake heard her call someone from a phone, saying, "I think he's ready."

He spent the next hour staring out his window at the small snowy parking lot—his dull brain replaying the scream he'd heard as the chairs fell—wondering exactly what the nurse thought he was ready for.

The answer came by way of a Ford F-150 with a gold sheriff's star embossed on its door. It parked just outside of Jake's window. A few minutes later, the door to his room swung open and an oak of a man, dressed in a Blind River police uniform, appeared in the doorway. The officer was holding a thin valise in one hand and his Stetson in the other, revealing a head of tousled brown hair, touched by gray at the temples.

"Mr. Boxer," he said in a surprisingly slow and high-pitched voice. "My name's Sheriff Wilson Grout. Mind?"

He gestured toward a rolling chair.

"No," Jake said, his voice catching in his throat.

The lawman moseyed across the room, took a seat, and rolled himself over toward Jake's bed, setting that valise down next to him. He drummed the brim of his hat a couple of times before saying, "I spoke to your doctor. He says you're out of the woods, so to speak. That you might be up for a quick chat, if it's not too much trouble." He paused briefly before offering, "About the accident."

As if there were a zillion other things he could've been there to talk about.

"I thought you might want to know why the accident happened."

Of course Jake wanted to know why. The Why was one of the Six Ws of journalism, the others being Who, What, When, Where, and hoW, but the Why was always the most important. The Why was the *reason* something happened.

Claire had died for the Why.

"Rest assured, Mr. Boxer, our investigation began last night, the moment the ski lift left its track. Insurance investigators arrived this morning, as did representatives from the Department of the Interior, geological specialists." He leaned forward. "I'm treating this as a *criminal investigation* until we know otherwise. That being said, at the moment, everything points to this being an accident. Seems that one of the bolts inside the sheave train—that's a fancy word for the metal wheel assembly—snapped, immediately engaging the emergency brakes, which is why the lift stopped. Unfortunately, the excess pressure from that one busted bolt snapped the others, causing the sheave train to come apart and the haul rope to fall. The safety caught it, but you, your wife, and eight others were on the section of the lift *between* the safety and the upper turnstile, the section with that busted sheave train. The haul line never broke per se, but there was enough slack in the rope for the chairs to fall a good ways down and flip the lot of you out of 'em." Wilson flipped his hat in his hands, as if to demonstrate. "At any rate, that's the initial Why as it stands right now. But I wouldn't presume to sign off without first talking to you. If you'd like to tell me about the events of the past couple of days, this is my invitation. I'm all ears."

All ears indeed.

Big ears and bushy hair—bushier even than Jake's. Matched with a broad nose and heavy brow. The sheriff had a stupid and slow look about him.

But it would be a mistake to dismiss him as such, Jake thought. He was a cautious individual, and caution in a lawman was usually a mark of intelligence. Maybe he was even someone who could help Jake make sense of what had happened to Claire.

Jake told Wilson nearly everything, only leaving out the flash of light he'd seen in the sky, fearful that the sheriff wouldn't take him seriously if he did.

After he finished his story, Wilson took a moment to review what he'd scribbled down, and Jake, leaning forward, gamed a quick look at the man's yellow legal pad. The Devil squeezed as he moved—a harsh fire burned a line up his spine—but the pain had been worth it. The pad was covered in messy handwriting, but the lawman had underlined one name several times, and Jake had seen it.

Ana Turov.

And here Jake had nearly left out the part about the crooked photograph—he'd only mentioned it as an aside, thinking it wasn't very important.

"Just writing down what you said," Wilson muttered, noticing Jake's gaze on his notes.

"Ana Turov. Who is she?"

"The concierge didn't tell you?"

Jake shook his head.

"Well, that figures. Al sometimes has a hard time talking about her." Wilson lowered his pen. "She came to Blind River as part of a cultural exchange with the Soviets. This was back in, what, '73? After the mine shut down and the Feds moved in and, well, an observant man such as yourself probably saw the remnants of White Alice up on the summit, right?"

Jake nodded.

"White Alice was the *reason* she came. Ana was the Soviet's hotshot artist at the time, and she was going to paint our mountain. In return, the Feds would shut down their radars here at Blind River. White Alice was a big network, and Blind River was just a small part of it, but that wasn't the point—the point was the gesture. The symbolism. This was in the middle of the Cold War, mind you, and people were scared shitless. Sputnik had flown over our heads, we were testing thermonuclear weapons, and we'd nearly gone to war during the Cuban Missile Crisis, not to mention that a communist sympathizer had assassinated Kennedy. Ana Turov's presence on this mountain was meant to chip away at all that fear and hate. To foster goodwill. No one thought it would make things worse. No one expected Ana Turov to just up and disappear."

"Disappear?"

"She defected, and she took the painting she was working on—a painting everyone around the hotel had hailed as a masterpiece—with her. The U.S. gave her a new identity, and she hasn't been heard from since. Oh, it pissed those commies off to no end, nearly triggered World War III. But it didn't, and Ana Turov managed to escape the evil empire, and we helped her do it, right here in Blind River. The good guys won."

"So what does she have to do with my wife dying on that ski lift?"

Wilson shook his head. "Haven't the foggiest, but if there is a connection, I *will* suss it out."

Jake wasn't sure what surprised him most—the fact that he believed the earnest sheriff, or that for a brief few seconds, he hadn't thought about Claire.

Somehow, he'd put his grief aside and listened, really listened, to Ana's story. After all those years, he'd returned to his castle, a place where nothing mattered but those six precious Ws—a stone fortress where he didn't need a wife, children, or even love—only the story.

His sudden return to that frame of mind was at once refreshing and terrifying. Sure, it was a defense mechanism, probably the only way he could turn off the spigot of grief gushing from his heart. But whatever. At the moment, he needed to be there, no matter what his therapist would say. It had already jarred something loose that he'd completely forgotten to tell the sheriff.

"*The Good Spy Dies Twice.*"

Wilson, who was slipping his legal pad and pen back inside his valise, looked up. "Excuse me?"

"Claire texted that to me right before the lift fell. *The Good Spy Dies Twice.*"

"Huh. Any idea what it means?"

Jake thought back to the NewsFlash article he'd read on Claire's laptop. "Buck Masterson…those were his last words before he was executed."

"Buck Masterson?"

Jake nodded. "An old death row inmate down in Huntsville. He was convicted of murder—which he never denied committing—but he did say he was employed by the CIA at the time. That he was a spy."

"And what kind of spy dies twice?"

Jake licked his cracked lips. "One time, when I was interviewing him, he told me that a good spy dies when he becomes one, at least the stuff inside of him. You know…the *good* stuff. The stuff that would make him think twice before pulling the trigger. And then, I guess, that same spy dies a second time at the end of it all. In Buck's case, when the state of Texas spiked his vein with a lethal dose of potassium chloride."

"Huh. Well, any idea why this death row inmate's last words would also be your wife's?"

Jake shook his head, though only slightly, so as not to aggravate the crack in his spine.

Wilson scratched his jaw, then stood and placed his Stetson back on his head. "Well, if it comes to you, you've got my number: 911. Rest easy now. The good news is that the doc sees a lot of compression fractures. If he says you'll be up and at 'em in no time, he means it."

"I want to see her."

Wilson, who'd already turned for the door, froze. "Sorry?"

"You need someone to identify the body."

"Not really. She still had her lift pass around her neck. We're sure it's your wife, Mr. Boxer. Rest a couple of days. Grieve. Then look. You've been gravely injured."

"I thought you said I'll be up and at 'em in no time."

"*In no time* isn't now."

"If it were your wife, wouldn't you want to see her as soon as possible? Wouldn't you *have* to see her?"

"Don't know," he said, sounding annoyed. "I'm not married, Mr. Boxer. But I'd like to think I'd do whatever my doctor thought was best."

"Then you don't mind sticking around while I ask for permission?"

"I'll tell you what I wouldn't mind sticking around for, someone telling you to lie still. You broke your goddamn back. Get it?"

Sure. Jake got it. The sheriff wasn't all Andy Griffith after all.

"I'm sorry," he said, breathing hard. "I shouldn't have used that word. I'm just not accustomed being talked to like that."

"Like what?"

"Like I'm on your TV show."

Jake hadn't spoken like that in quite some time either, not that he told Wilson. Instead, he lowered his voice and said, "I'm a journalist. I need to see to believe. And right now I need to see Claire. Please..."

Wilson bit his lip, considering him. "She's down in the basement. I wouldn't even know how to get you there. You can't walk."

Jake looked at a wheelchair, folded up in the corner. "I think they call those wheelchairs for a reason."

SIXTEEN

"UNZIP HER," JAKE SAID, licking his dry lips and shifting uncomfortably in the wheelchair.

Despite his recent dose of oxycontin, he was in quite a bit of pain.

Sheriff Wilson Grout hesitated. The journey from Jake's room to the morgue in the clinic's basement had gone smoothly, but now that they were facing Claire's body bag, and now that Jake was hyperventilating, his face ashen, his eyes hollow, the lawman was reconsidering, and rightfully so.

Jake was not well.

"*Unzip* her," Jake demanded, trembling.

"Mr. Boxer, I think this was a mistake."

Wilson, standing behind Jake's wheelchair, started to pull back, but Jake grabbed the chair's steel push ring and held tight. The muscles across his broad back tensed, and a numb, nauseating wave flowed from his cracked vertebra—a wave, that if not for the drugs, would've killed him.

"*Unzip* her," he said through clenched teeth.

There were two body bags in the basement, both lying on steel gurneys against the back wall. As the sheriff reluctantly walked over, Jake flashed on the last time he'd identified a corpse—it had been Brody's, of course. And now he was about to identify Claire's.

A pang of jealousy shot through his heart. The old lovers were finally reunited—enjoying the honeymoon they'd never had.

Wilson reached the body bags and inspected the tags. Finding Claire's, he carefully unzipped the bag.

The last time Jake had seen Claire she'd been flush with sex, naked and pressed up against him on a heart-shaped bed. A big part of him wanted that mental photograph to be the last one in his album. Slipping in a shot of her corpse would ruin the collection, but if he left it out, wouldn't it be a disservice? They'd been husband and wife—didn't he have a responsibility to see her?

Wilson got the zipper down under her chin, and the gray tip of her nose appeared. Jake's white-knuckled grip tightened on the arms of the wheel-chair. As the bag slipped down around her face, Jake, who'd been on the verge of a complete neural meltdown, breathed a huge sigh of relief.

It wasn't his wife.

It wasn't Claire.

At best, it was an old black-and-white facsimile of her. After all, Claire was Irish white, *not* cadaver gray. Claire had vibrant red hair, not a clumpy flat mess of it, blackened by dried blood. Claire was beautiful and funny and God, she was smart—*incredibly* smart—but the woman in the bag was none of those things. The woman in the bag was dead.

"Sit down, Jake…*Jake*."

Jake wasn't exactly standing, but his feet were on the cold concrete, and he'd pushed himself up on the armrests so that his butt was off the seat, in a half-standing position. He hadn't even been aware that he'd done it. Jake eased himself back into the chair. He blinked hard several times. He swallowed back bile. His tick—it had returned. *Of course* it had.

He wasn't sure how long he stared at her face, but however long it was, the sheriff's demeanor never changed. He never hurried him; he never asked how he was doing—and somewhere inside of Jake's castle, the old reporter jotted down a note. The sheriff had done this before. He *knew* not to rush things. And that meant people had died violently in Blind River before.

"Can you unzip her a little more?"

"She's unzipped enough. All I need is a yes, this is my wife, or a no, she isn't."

"She had a mole on her right hip. I want to see if it's there."

Wilson sighed, then unzipped the bag the rest of the way.

Jake grabbed the cold push bar and inched closer. He began his inspection where it would be easiest—her feet. Claire had big feet in life, and they were no different in death. They were gray, like the rest of her skin, but they were also skinny and perfect. His gaze traveled up her long legs—the bottoms of which were dark with coagulated blood—past her mound of pubic hair to the brown mole on her right hip, just below and to the side of her belly, the same belly he'd dreamed might one day carry his baby. His gaze went to her small breasts and then to her freckled shoulders, where the deep black bruise of a broken neck could be clearly seen.

Unable to look at it, he adverted his gaze, and instead followed her arms down to her hands, to her fingers.

Her *naked* fingers.

"Where's her wedding ring?"

"We didn't find one."

Jake looked up. Wilson's face was inscrutable.

"What do you mean, you didn't find one?"

"It was a long fall. Maybe it came off on impact?"

It was bullshit. Both men knew it.

"The only jewelry she was wearing was a necklace."

"A necklace?" Jake asked. "What did it look like?"

"Thin silver chain," Wilson said. "Small diamond."

Not a small diamond, Jake realized.

A puny diamond...*Brody's* puny diamond.

She'd made a necklace out of the engagement ring while they'd been dating—it was her way of giving up on Brody, but it was also a way for her to always remember him. She'd promised never to wear it again after they married. But, apparently, on the last day of her life, Claire had ditched his wedding ring for that necklace.

"Where is it?"

"With her personal belongings," Wilson told him. "I'll be sure you get it back along with the rest of her things."

Jake looked at the body bag next to Claire's, half expecting old Brody's corpse to unzip it and say, *"See? She's mine."* But he didn't. Brody had been buried three thousand miles away in a family cemetery outside of Charleston, West Virginia.

No, inside the other body bag held the only other casualty of the accident—the mysterious snowboarder who'd been sharing the chair with Claire.

Jake looked to the tag on the body bag and saw, in neat blocky handwriting, the words, *FARRIS, SEAN. 2/16/1972.*

Gears that Jake hadn't used in years began to turn.

The guy was forty-four.

Just a few years older than himself.

Wasn't he kind of old to be on a snowboard? Especially on a mountain as treacherous as Blind River's? He must have known the slopes…he must have known them well.

He was a local.

"Can I see him?"

"Who?"

"Sean Farris."

"No."

"Why not?"

"Because you're not family."

"Can you at least tell me who he was?"

"He managed Blind River's visitor center."

"How long had he been there?"

"At the visitor center?"

"No, Pluto."

Wilson glared at him. "Why I imagine ten years or so. He transferred over from Fairbanks to become manager."

"The visitor center is run by the state, right? That makes him a state employee?"

"Yes, it does. It's actually run by the Alaskan Forest Service; and yes, I already contacted them, and yes, yesterday was Sean Farris's day off."

"It was his day off and he went skiing?"

"Everyone skies on their day off, Mr. Boxer. It's the only reason anyone lives here. They're adrenaline junkies, and Sean was no exception. Now listen, the only time anyone saw Sean and your wife together was on that lift. There's absolutely nothing to indicate that they were anything more than random lift buddies."

"Sure. Except for a missing wedding ring. How do you explain that?"

Wilson couldn't. But he understood the implication. "Okay. Let's assume for a second that she *was* doing something suspicious with Sean here. You said that she didn't return your phone calls all day. If she was having an affair, wouldn't she have had the common decency to lie to you? To make something up? To at least let you know that she wasn't going to be around so that you didn't worry? You guys were on your honeymoon, right?"

"She was mad at me. And I never said she was having an affair."

"Well, if she was mad enough to not call back, maybe she was mad enough to take off the ring?"

"Or maybe she took it off to help cajole a source, a source that put her in danger. A single woman is gonna get a lot more out of a man than a married one."

"Or maybe she did it because she didn't really want to be married. People do get buyer's remorse, you know."

Wilson's face scrunched up almost as soon as he said it.

"I'm sorry. I shouldn't have said that. It isn't my place to make assumptions."

But it was too late. The poisonous words had merely been thoughts before, thoughts Jake really hadn't given much weight, but now that the sheriff had vocalized them, they were stones.

Looking back to her body, Jake saw his wife, his lover, and just maybe a liar who had never truly gotten over Brody.

It was definitely Claire.

SEVENTEEN

———————

TWO DAYS LATER Jake took his first step post-accident.

Holding onto the doctor's shoulders, with a stiff brace hugging his lower back, he slowly slipped off the bed and touched the cool tile floor, first with his toes, then with his heels. The Devil squeezed, but the pain dissipated quickly, like a tuft of black smoke from a candle. Dr. Wallace gingerly led him during those first shuffling steps, then let go, and Jake managed to take a single small step all on his own. But that's all that it was—a single step—before he slumped back into the doctor's arms, tired and sore.

"Very good," the doctor said, struggling under Jake's tall and cumbersome body.

"It was just one…just one step," Jake panted.

"Yes, just one step, but a good one. You need to exercise for your back to properly mend. The faster you walk, the faster you'll heal."

The doctor's bearded face was inches from his own, and Jake noticed that the man's quick eyes seemed to be assessing more than just his physical state.

"How would you feel if I told you that I think you can leave soon?"

"I don't think I have a choice. Doesn't Blind River close in a few days?"

"Yes, but I think you can leave even sooner than that. Like today."

"Today?"

"Yes. Today."

The doctor led Jake to his wheelchair. Over the past forty-eight hours, and in spite of a right hand that was still raw and bandaged from exposure, he'd learned to maneuver the chair quite competently.

"Your wife needs to undergo an autopsy," the doctor explained. "I'm not a pathologist, and we're not outfitted for anything like that here, but we have a medical transport that can take her to Providence Alaska in Anchorage this afternoon. The sheriff thought you might want to accompany her, *if* I give it the okay."

The thought of escaping Blind River was more than exciting, it was liberating. For the first time in days, Jake felt as though he could breathe again.

"And are you? Giving me the okay?"

The doctor shrugged. "You can operate your wheelchair, and we can manage your pain with medication. If you feel up to it emotionally, I don't think a five-hour drive to Anchorage will hurt. You've got a couple of hours to think about it. There's room in the van. It would just be you and your wife."

Dr. Wallace left him to his thoughts, which were many, mostly along the lines of, would Claire even *want* him to go with her? The sheriff's observation two days earlier had really stuck: maybe she'd regretted getting married.

It wouldn't have been unlike her to simply take off her ring and throw herself into work rather than face the fact that her new husband—a man she didn't really love—had told her to quit, not just her job, but also a budding career. Another thought also struck him—if she *had* quit her job and gone back to work for him, in addition to already being *married* to him, they never would've been apart. That begged the question, had he really wanted to reboot *Bullseye*? Or had he simply wanted to completely own Claire O'Donnell?

Like his old pal Brody White had completely owned her?

If true, Claire's poor behavior, this whole Blind River mess, could be chalked up to simple buyer's remorse. And if it had been buyer's remorse, the conspiracy he'd been circling, that someone sabotaged the lift to stop her investigation, wasn't true. Maybe it had been as the sheriff said: a snapped bolt in the sheave train and foul rotten luck.

Even if Claire had decided that marrying Jake had been a mistake, they'd both still said *I do*, and as her husband, Jake was duty-bound to stand by her side. That meant that if Claire was on her way to Anchorage, so was he.

Jake gripped his chair's cold push ring. His spine protested as he rolled to the phone, but the oxycontin made it manageable. He put the receiver to his ear, dialed zero, and informed the nurse that he wanted to take the doctor up on that ride to Anchorage.

Great. She would be by shortly to help him gather his things.

He hung up but left the phone off the hook, a tactic he'd resorted to after Sheriff Grout had confirmed to the *Anchorage Daily News* that Claire O'Donnell, travel writer for the *American Post,* had been amongst the dead in the accident, and that her new husband, Jake Boxer, ex-host of the now defunct show *Bullseye,* had suffered a serious spinal injury as well.

After that, his cell phone had blown up (including about a zillion calls from Tabitha Fox), but he only took two calls. One from Claire's father, who, in tears, had made Jake swear to get to the bottom of what had really happened, and the other from Claire's editor, Austin Foley, her prick of a boss who was still sporting an enormous hard-on for his wife, even in death. Jake had only taken Austin's call to grill him.

Why was Claire in Blind River? Was it really to work on a honeymoon article? Or was she just using the story as a cover to investigate something else?

Austin swore up and down that he'd only sent her there for her travel column, but that it was also no secret that Claire belonged in hard news. It was then that he admitted to having a standing offer with her—if she brought him a story, a *big* story, he'd see what he could do about securing her an editorial column, the most prized real estate in print journalism.

That was news to Jake, but he hung up convinced that Austin was telling the truth, and also with the hunch that he'd given Claire such a long leash that he hadn't really known *what* she'd been up to.

An hour after Jake told the nurse he was ready to leave, she came in to help him get dressed. It was the first time he'd worn street clothes in three days, and though he needed the nurse to help him with his socks, he managed to pull on his shirt, boxers, and pants all by himself and with only a modicum of pain.

Of course, taking double the recommended dosage of oxy might have had something to do with that, but the doctor had conditionally approved it, so long as it was short-lived and Jake didn't experience any side effects. And except for a pleasant numbness, he hadn't.

The day after he'd identified Claire's body, two deliveries had shown up, along with a sympathy card from Christopher Kidd, owner of the Hotel Ascent and much of Blind River. Jake had trashed the card, he didn't have to pack that, but now he considered the deliveries: their luggage from the Honeymoon Suite and Claire's personal effects, removed from her body by the police.

The personal effects fit into a cardboard box no larger than a container of Chinese takeout. When these things had first arrived, Jake asked the nurse to stow them all away—he just couldn't bring himself to look at them.

The thought of unpacking her suitcase and smelling her laundry and perfume and deodorant and Sobranie Blacks…well, it made his heart ache.

But now he was leaving, and the nurse had pulled both the suitcase and the box of her personal items out of the room's small closet, lest they be forgotten.

Jake, staring at the little box, suddenly felt an overwhelming urge to confirm what the sheriff had told him, that Claire had been wearing Brody's necklace when she died.

He signed his discharge papers and asked for a moment alone. The nurse complied, reluctantly, and then told him he should hurry. Claire was already in the back of the medical transport.

Jake thanked her, and when she left, he angled his wheelchair toward the bed and rolled himself over to the box, which opened easily from the top as he undid two cardboard tabs.

And there it was.

Looking right back at him like a black eye.

Brody's necklace.

The tiny inlaid diamond twinkled, as if winking at him, and Jake could see old Brody with his face peeled off and those headphones on his skull where his ears used to be as he flashed a toothy grin and said, *'My diamond was on her when she died, not yours. Fuck you very much."*

Jake picked it up. His diamond had been four times as big, but in the end, Claire hadn't cared about size. She'd only cared about who'd given it to her.

He dropped the necklace back into the box. Looked at the rest of the contents: just her lift pass, some loose change, a cracked tube of Chapstick, and her cell phone.

God, that cell phone. Her constant companion for all those years.

Fishing it out, he saw that the glass display was shattered—not entirely surprising after such a fall. He didn't expect it to work, but he tried the power button anyway and was surprised when the Apple insignia popped to life.

He unlocked the phone with a swipe of his finger and was startled to find himself staring at Claire, wearing the simple white shift she'd worn on their wedding day. Jake was in the selfie, too—his arm wrapped tightly around her, and his lips pressed firmly on her left cheek. Her left hand outstretched as she'd snapped the photograph.

Despite her lingering feelings for Brody, there was joy in it, *real* joy, and though that happy day had been less than a week ago, it already felt a dream.

His finger hovered above the text message button. He wanted to tap it, but he was afraid if he did, he'd see a slew of his ignored texts, and he didn't feel like suffering another such indignation. At the same time, he was deathly curious about who, if anyone, she'd been communicating with. So he tapped the button anyway, despite his reservations, and a list of correspondences filled the screen. His unanswered texts *had* been read, though she'd only sent one in return, that inexplicable, *The Good Spy Dies Twice.* It was her last text, and there was nothing suspicious above or beneath it.

He saw a text thread with Austin's name, tapped it, and found himself staring at the texts she'd read to him on their first day in Blind River.

Executed Masterson @ Huntsville. 10:32 am

Her response was simply:

No

To which Austin wrote:

Call me when u can

Jake punched through her recent call log and saw that she'd phoned him just an hour later, right around the time Jake had been turning the hotel inside-out looking for her.

A time she'd supposedly been up on the mountain bawling her eyes out over Brody.

But if she'd successfully called Austin, she couldn't have been on the mountain. Right? The signal up there was only strong enough to send texts.

He looked at the phone's current signal strength.

Five bars.

Jake hadn't gotten five bars on his own phone since leaving Anchorage.

Jake turned his attention back to Austin's texts.

How's the article?

He'd texted it the following day. She'd replied:

Good - this is it

And that *was* it, at least while Claire had been alive. Austin had texted her again later, but not until the day after the lift accident.

Word count?

And, after not getting a response…

U ok?

Finished with her texts, Jake tapped over to her Dialed and Received calls, but they were dead ends, as were her voicemails. She'd made a few local calls to a couple of stores, but there was nothing suspicious, which, Jake had to admit, was slightly suspicious in and of itself.

Jake was about to return the phone to the box when he noticed that he'd missed something—white earbuds.

Along with the phone, they were one of Claire's near constant accessories, more popular even than earrings. She'd had them in when he'd lost her on White Alice; he even remembered seeing her wearing them when she approached him on the patio bar. And though he'd been too far away to see them, he'd bet his last dollar that they'd been plugged into her ears on that final lift ride up the mountain.

A morbid thought struck him: What had been the soundtrack of her death?

He picked the soft plastic cord from the box and plugged it into the phone. Fitting both small speakers into his ears, he tapped the iTunes app and made a guessing game out of what band would pop up while it loaded. Claire was thirty-five when she died. She'd grown up with bands like Green

Day and Blink 182, but the classics were what turned her on. Led Zeppelin. The Who.

Patti Smith.

Of course.

Jake studied the album cover beneath the phone's cracked screen. A black-and-white photograph of the seminal female punk rocker stared back at him. Strangely, he felt comforted knowing that Claire had died listening to her favorite artist. He opened the album and hit play on "Gloria," the first track, Claire's all-time favorite. He closed his eyes and waited for Patti's languished opening lines, but then something strange happened.

Patti didn't sing.

Instead, he heard voices—a man's and a woman's. It sounded as though they were casually conversing. And then a soft knock interrupted, and he heard a muffled voice say, "Room service." A door creaked as it opened. A cart squeaked as it was wheeled into the room and a platter lid clinked as it was removed.

Room service.

Room service in a hotel.

His first thought was that one of Claire's podcasts had been digitally scrambled up with Patti Smith's album, but that was probably impossible, right? And besides, there was no story. No interview. No podcast. He was listening to people...*real* people...in real time?

The woman who'd intruded on Patti Smith's opening track thanked whoever brought her food, shut the door, and resumed her quiet, but pointed, conversation with the man in the room; it was a conversation that made Jake feel like death warmed over. Not because of what they said, but because of how they said it.

In a different language.

Claire's disappearing acts suddenly made perfect sense, and the revelation hinted at the darkest and most dangerous of conspiracies.

Claire hadn't ditched him because she'd been experiencing buyer's remorse, she'd ditched him because she'd been conducting surveillance on this couple at the Hotel Ascent.

A couple that was most definitely conversing in Russian.

EIGHTEEN

"THE VAN IS READY, Mister Boxer."

Jake felt the nurse's hot gaze on his back. She was waiting impatiently in his doorway, practically leaping out of her skin.

She *really* wanted him out of there.

She couldn't wait to roll him out of the clinic and to the medical transport that would take him the hell outta Blind River.

Forever.

A scant two minutes ago, leaving Blind River had seemed like a splendid idea, but now, with the Russians conversing softly in his ears, Jake couldn't imagine a worse fate.

I'm afraid you'll fuck it up.

She *had* said it—at least with her eyes—and she'd been talking about the Russians. She'd been talking about *bugging* the Russians! Russians staying inside of the Hotel Ascent.

God only knew who else she'd bugged.

He couldn't leave Blind River. And he certainly couldn't go to Anchorage. Not before he knew why she'd done it.

Bugging a source was illegal, sure, but the practice within his old vocation wasn't exactly new. "Rupertgate," the scandal that brought down Rupert Murdoch's *News of the World,* had made headlines after it was disclosed that their reporters tapped cell phones of everyone from the British royal family to the parents of a poor slain thirteen-year-old girl. Jake himself had asked Brody, his audio expert, to bug the occasional room.

Was it such a stretch to imagine that Brody had taught Claire how to do it? They *had* been engaged.

Claire wouldn't have taken such a risk for a travel column. She would've taken it for a big story—say one that involved a death row inmate who claimed to have been a contract hitman for the CIA, or for a prominent Soviet artist who defected to America at the height of the Cold War.

She would've done it for a story that was going to make an enormous splash on the front page of the *American Post.*

And I would've kept it a secret if I ran the risk of my new husband screwing things up, or regressing to the paranoia he'd experienced in Moscow, years earlier.

I could've handled it, Claire. You should have *told* me.

If I'd gotten you back into the game, there was no way you would've gone to law school.

And what do you think is gonna happen now?

I don't…I don't know.

Well at least she could admit that.

"Mr. Boxer." It was the nurse again. "The van?"

"Can you give me a minute?"

"Your wife has been waiting. You should hurry."

"Why? Because she's itching to get to her autopsy?"

She glared at him.

"Look," Jake said. "I just want to give the room a dummy check to make sure I got everything."

"Well I can help you with that," she said, walking briskly into the room.

Why did she want him out of there so badly? Why wouldn't she leave him alone? And why did Claire's cell phone get five bars when the most he'd ever gotten was three?

Back in his *Bullseye* days everyone carried satellite phones. So maybe this was an iPhone that also worked as a satellite phone. Satellite phones needed a direct line of sight with the sky, but there were antennas that allowed them to work indoors. Perhaps someone modified Claire's iPhone to do so?

The nurse looked down at him as she passed. Jake flipped the phone over, hiding the cracked face against his lap and popped the earbuds out of his ears. For a couple of seconds before he was able to turn down the sound, he heard the Russians, still conversing. Tinny and distant but audible.

"Только чтоб там была эта картина! Если на самом деле у Кристофера Кидда ее нет."

Had the nurse heard it? It wasn't likely, but even if she had, who cared? For all she knew, he was listening to a *How to Speak Russian* podcast.

Except, of course, that Jake had just met this nurse a few days ago. She could've been anyone. Hell, maybe the Russians who murdered Brody had planted her there to spy on him, to make sure that he…to make sure that he did what?

To make sure you get into that van.

Right, Claire. So *that's* why she won't leave me alone—she wants me out of here.

Jake watched as the nurse double-checked the drawers of a small dresser. With her back to him, he noticed that years of lifting patients into and out of their beds had erased her feminine curves, blessing her instead with stretches of muscle. Before the accident, Jake could've handled such a woman, but now, with a compression fracture through his L5 vertebra, he doubted if he could wrestle a child to the ground, much less this bull of a nurse.

Don't over think it, Jake. Just buy enough time to listen to my phone.

Claire was right. Claire was *always* right.

"Well this could've been bad."

The nurse. She was standing in the bathroom holding a small plastic pouch with his toothbrush, toothpaste, and dental floss, the toiletry kit Claire had packed for him before leaving D.C.

"You nearly forgot your toothbrush." She strolled over to his luggage next to the door. She zipped the toiletry bag into an outside pocket, then hefted the suitcase up by its handle. "I'll take this down to the van. And then I'll be back for you."

Jake nodded. As soon as she left, he pushed the earbuds back into his ears and turned up the volume.

"Мы должны выиграть эту картину—сколько бы ни пришлось заплатить, кого бы ни пришлось убить."

Jake didn't know what they were saying—and found himself longing for his translator back in Moscow.

They could've been plotting Obama's assassination or bickering over who had left the toilet seat up. At one point, he could've sworn that he heard the woman say "Khristofor," as in Christopher Kidd, but she was talking so fast that he couldn't be sure. The phone beeped. Looking down, he saw the battery status bar was in the red, and that there was a warning on the screen: *Battery Life at 5%*.

Great.

Where was her charger? Probably in the suitcase the nurse just took down to the van.

He didn't have much time. With the thought that if Claire bugged one room, she probably bugged more, he quickly swiped over to Patti Smith's next track, "Redondo Beach," a song that began with a chiming keyboard, as he recalled. But not this time. This time it cut abruptly to what sounded like an infomercial on a television. *"So whether you're rafting the river's roaring rapids, skiing our one-of-a-kind mountain or relaxing in our world class dining hall, there's no greater adventure than Blind River, Alaska. Come discover the magic."*

Jake had heard the same pitch before. On the phone, when the hotel had put him on hold, but somewhere else as well.

Claire's article.

The document on her laptop. She'd practically written the exact same thing as a rough draft for her article.

Jesus Christ…she'd plagiarized it? She was a tremendous writer, why would she…?

To fool him, he realized. She'd written it just in case he took a look while she was out bugging hotel rooms. The fact that she had deliberately deceived him like that was humbling.

Who the hell had he married?

Jake looked at his own television, screwed into the wall opposite the bed. He rolled over to the remote control, turned it on, and channel-surfed until the same infomercial he was listening to on Claire's phone popped up on his TV. The audio sync was nearly perfect. Jake was definitely listening to real-time audio. This wasn't something Claire had prerecorded on her phone. It was then that he realized he could hear more than just the infomercial inside of that room. Someone was moving about on a bed. He heard the periodic squeak of a mattress, and the soft swipe of a pant leg against a duvet. And then, suddenly, the infomercial was interrupted by a dry and endless cough. An image came to him—a man in a fedora with translucent skin, skin as tight as a drum.

The man Jake had guessed was the hotel's real MPP on the patio bar... the night before Claire died...hadn't he been plagued by the same dry cough?

Jake swiped to the next song, "Birdland." He no longer expected music, just voices, and that's exactly what he got.

"*. . . not getting screwed by this,*" a man was saying, clearly agitated. "*Yes, I own it, but your company built the goddam thing.*" There was a pause, and Jake could hear a rhythmic thump, as if the man was nervously bouncing something on his desk. "*We did perform a maintenance check, just two weeks before it fell.*" Another pause. More thumps, faster now. "*Of course they're going to file suit. What planet do you live on? Now listen, your company made basic warranties when I paid ten million dollars for you to install that thing, and I am NOT paying out for two wrongful dea—*"

The man's voice ended suddenly.

The battery drained.

The phone powered down.

Dammit.

Jake was sure that last voice had been Christopher Kidd's, the owner of the Hotel Ascent.

So *that's* why he had found one of Claire's cigarette butts in the man's office—she'd been planting a bug.

He tried not to think about what she might have done to gain access.

He looked back to the now-silent phone. Its cracked display was black. Out of juice, yes, but far from out of secrets.

Jake sensed eyes on him and looked up to find both the nurse and Dr. Wallace staring at him. How long had they been there?

He pulled the earbuds from his ears and did his best not to wilt. Yes, the journalist was back in his castle, but he hadn't cast a spell for some time. He wasn't sure if he could still do it—bullshit, that is—and the hovering dragons seemed all too aware.

"I was just listening to some of Claire's old music," he explained, lying through his teeth, summoning up a bit of emotion to go with it. "She loved Patti Smith."

"Yes, well, I just wanted to stop by to wish you the best of luck." The doctor handed Jake his completed discharge papers. "You're officially discharged. I've already made arrangements with Dr. Brooke Fryer at Providence Alaska, a wonderful spine specialist. We've arranged for a room in their recovery ward. You can stay there until your wife is ready to go back to D.C." He paused, scratched his beard, then pulled a medication sample from his pocket. "Oh, oxycontin, so that you can manage your pain on your way to Anchorage."

Jake eyeballed the blister pack. "There's only six."

"More than enough to get you through the drive. Dr. Fryer will reevaluate your pharmaceutical needs once you've checked in at Providence."

The nurse stepped forward. "I'll help you to the van."

Jake grabbed the cold metal push bar, holding himself in place. He looked at the bearded doctor. "I don't want to go to Anchorage."

"Excuse me?"

"It's an autopsy. I don't want to be there for that." He tried to summon the emotion again, but found that he couldn't. He was too deep inside of the story. "I'd like to remember Claire how she was."

"Which is why you wanted to identify her body so badly?"

"That was a mistake," Jake falsely conceded.

"Mr. Boxer, you won't actually be *in* the autopsy room. Your presence is more of a symbolic gesture."

"But the hospital in Anchorage will keep her until Sunday, right?"

"It's Thursday," the doctor said, ignoring him. "They'll be done with autopsy by Friday night. If you leave now, you could be back in D.C. by Sunday." He lowered his voice, maybe a little too much. "I know you have funeral arrangements to make, as well as friends and family who will want to be with you in this difficult time."

"I'm not ready to leave."

"Mr. Boxer, I don't think you understand. Dr. Fryer runs the best physical therapy center in the state. We don't specialize in that sort of rehabilitation here. You may not *feel* as though you're ready to leave, but you really *need* to. For medical reasons."

"Listen, my wife came here to write an article for the *American Post*. I think it would honor her memory if I finished it for her."

"That's very noble, but like I said, we can't keep you here."

"No problem. I already paid for the Honeymoon Suite through the weekend."

"The Honeymoon Suite? At the Ascent? In your wheelchair?"

"Why not?"

"Mr. Boxer, in my professional opinion, you aren't ready to leave a medical facility."

Jake held up the discharge papers the doctor had just signed. "Then why did you just give me these?"

"I only discharged you because I was under the *impression* that you were going to a superior rehabilitation center at Providence."

"And I appreciate the offer, but I'm going to pass."

The throb in his back reminded Jake that the doctor was right. He should be in a medical facility. But there was no way he was leaving Blind River now, not after what he'd just heard on Claire's phone.

"If you aren't going to consider your own health," the doctor said finally, "I urge you to consider Claire. She's preparing to undergo one of her final journeys. If the situation were reversed, I'm sure she'd be in that van with you. Please, don't do something you'll regret. Think about your wife."

"Believe me," Jake said, plucking the blister pack of oxy out of the doctor's hand, "I am."

NINETEEN

MAIN STREET, ALSO KNOWN AS EXIT 47 off Highway 3, was the only way in or out of Blind River. As Jake watched the driver load the medical transport with Claire's body, he wondered what would happen if one of the road's old truss bridges collapsed, or if a rockslide made it impassable. Main Street was the only road that connected with Highway 3. So how would anyone get in?

Maybe more importantly, how would anyone get out?

Jake, who was sitting in his wheelchair at the clinic's front doors, watched the van pull away with a heavy heart. Not only would he miss Claire's autopsy, but he'd also lost his best, and possibly only, chance to escape Blind River.

Blind River. A place that was feeling less like a ski resort and more like the ninth circle of Hell.

Outside, giants patrolled the dark skies, shaking the snow from their hides, the wind from their lips blowing cold and hard. It didn't take long for the night to swallow the van's taillights, and like that, Claire was gone forever.

Searching for comfort, Jake squeezed Claire's cell phone, which he'd stashed safely away in his sweatshirt's big front pocket.

Yes, Claire was in the back of that van, but her story was still here, in Blind River, and Jake wasn't about to leave without it.

The approaching clomp of several animals drew his attention away from the highway and back toward the downtown square, where he saw Pete Lancaster's Clydesdales trotting gloomily toward the clinic.

At least now they were wearing blankets.

The stubby sleigh driver yanked back on the reins, prompting annoyed and tired snorts, then hopped to the icy road and hurried to the clinic's lobby through a hypnotic snowfall. When he threw open the doors, a draft of cold air punched Jake in the face like a heavyweight boxer.

"Hell of a snow tonight," Lancaster said, stomping his boots. "You sure you don't want to…"

He was probably going to say, "wait until the morning," but he didn't finish his sentence. He was gawking at Jake, the battered and wheelchair-bound widower. Lancaster's words followed his smile right off his face.

"Holy shit. You really fell." Then, as if only just remembering, he doffed his top hat and shook his blocky head, saying, "Oh, uh, and I'm sorry about your wife. I…I just can't imagine it…and on your honeymoon."

"Thanks," Jake said interrupting. "Now, if it's okay with you I'd like to get the hell outta here."

After refusing the doctor's ride to Anchorage, Jake had mercifully rediscovered Pete Lancaster's business card in his wallet. As it turned out, the sleigh driver could accommodate a wheelchair. Ferrying skiers with freshly broken legs was unfortunately commonplace in Blind River.

Lancaster had been happy to help out. Jake had never cashed in on his free ride back up to the Hotel Ascent—and a deal was a deal.

So Lancaster wheeled Jake out of the clinic and up a rickety, wooden ramp to his sleigh. He secured the wheelchair with several ropes and tucked a heavy blanket around Jake's legs before pulling himself up onto his perch. He cracked the reigns. The horses strained against their harnesses. The sleigh slowly slid across the frozen asphalt, then back onto Main Street, where the driver plotted a course back to the Hotel Ascent.

Before the chairlift accident, Main Street's most obvious flaws appeared to be peeling paint and loose shingles. But Claire's death had changed things.

The luster had left Jake's lens, and he saw the town for what it truly was, shabby and deteriorating. Jagged cracks lined the storefront facades, stretching from floor to rooftop. Chimneys crumbled, threatening to topple over. Rotting porches were missing planks and railings. Elsewhere, dumpsters overflowed in dark alleys. Bloodshot eyes peered back at him through dingy windows—eyes obscured by the folds of filthy, flimsy jackets.

As they made their way toward the Ascent, Jake noticed several proprietors boarding up their windows for the winter. They worked in pairs, one man holding a large sheet of plywood while the other hammered it into place, reminding Jake that Blind River would soon be closed.

Lancaster shouted something and jerked the reigns to the left. One of the horses stumbled but found its footing, and the animals took the sleigh out of the claustrophobic lower stub of Main Street and into the open town square. It was there, looming high above the small ice-skating rink, that Jake laid eyes upon the mountain for the first time since the accident.

With the lift in ruins, there were no skiers on the slopes, but the lights were still on, and the runs were still lit. Jake found himself transfixed by the white slopes, like tears on the mountain's otherwise black face.

Squinting, he picked out the ski lift and followed it up the mountainside. He lost sight of the haul rope halfway up but rediscovered it near the same granite spine that had taken Claire's life. That portion of the lift was dark when it fell, but was now illuminated by work lights, set up in the old concrete bunkers that lined the ski run—bunkers that were once part of White Alice.

Jake closed his eyes and looked fifty years into the past. He saw bearded NSA men receiving word that the Soviet's premier artist, Ana Turov, would soon be arriving to paint the mountain. In return, Blind River's listening station would be shuttered and dismantled as a gesture of goodwill.

The Blind River spooks, Jake imagined, would not have taken the news well.

So what had they done? Had they somehow retaliated? Or had they lied to the Soviets and simply never shut down?

Opening his eyes, Jake saw ant-sized workers attempting to repair the devastated lift. The task looked Herculean in the gut-wrenching cold. They were laboring in the shadow of the upper turnstile, the one with the sheave train that had supposedly failed. As he watched, he felt the cold wind on his chapped face. He *felt* the lift drop. He heard the woman's scream—he heard *Claire* scream—and he pulled his blanket tighter around himself.

He picked out the fallen haul rope again. It was dangling lamely in a loose loop, the empty chairs still gripping it by their knuckles, carrying no one but ghosts. All of that destruction, eight injured and two dead, for the failure of a single bolt. A bolt that had supposedly passed a visual inspection. A bolt that was probably inside of someone's evidence box…or was it?

Jake looked at the piles of snow on either side of the black granite spine. If a bolt had snapped, it would have fallen, in pieces, to the mountain below. It would've sunk into the deep snow. And a bolt that was what? Six inches long, at most? *Maybe* as thick as a Sharpie? The odds of anyone finding such a bolt were slim; maybe when May rolled around, when the snow melted, but in just three days? And in the middle of November?

Forget about it.

Even if someone *had* found the bolt, surely they hadn't found both pieces, and without the entire bolt, how could the sheriff, or anyone for that matter, be sure it hadn't been tampered with?

The sleigh finally left downtown and bounced onto the wooden railroad trestle that forded the widest part of the river and led to the Hotel Ascent.

The sleigh bounced off the trestle, and Jake caught sight of the warm and inviting hotel—a Christmas card compared with the downtown they'd left behind. Where Main Street was poorly lit, hundreds of gas lamps bathed the Hotel Ascent in ethereal light. Where the storefront facades were cracked and peeling, the Hotel Ascent was pampered and primped like a trophy wife. Where the locals were silent and gaunt with wiry beards, the Hotel Ascent's guests were clean-shaven and in high spirits. Where Blind River's downtown stank of stale piss, the air here was redolent with roasting meat, baked sweets, and burning pine. And, of course, the Hotel Ascent bore another accessory that wouldn't be found anywhere on Main Street—the beaming smile of Al Bridge Tulane, Jr., concierge extraordinaire, standing just inside of the hotel's large revolving door.

Lancaster pulled back on the reigns. The horses whinnied and came to a thankful stop—Jake's back was killing him. Jake fished his last hundred from his pocket as the driver climbed into the payload to untie the wheelchair.

Lancaster saw it, blushed, and said, "Mr. Boxer, I can't accept that. You already gave me one…"

"Who's Sean Farris?"

Lancaster's face darkened. "Why does it matter?"

"He was sharing a seat with my wife when the lift fell. The day you gave Claire a ride into town…did she mention him?"

"No."

"Did she mention meeting someone who worked at the visitor center?"

"No. Now Mr. Boxer, you really should be going."

Lancaster looked at the Hotel Ascent's revolving door. Al was standing just inside, waiting for Jake to enter. They didn't have long before the old man would venture outside to offer a helping a hand.

"Look at me," Jake demanded.

Lancaster, taken back, did as ordered.

"You think you should be pulling gold out of that mountain, not a sleigh down Main Street. You told me as much, and I think you told my wife the same story."

"And why, exactly, would I do that?"

"Because she's a reporter with a big megaphone—the *American Post*."

"Working on a honeymoon article."

"Is that what you really think?"

Lancaster considered the hundred dollar bill, still in Jake's hand. He took it. "Okay, so she asked me."

"Asked you what?"

"Why I've stuck around this place for so many years. So I told her about my dream of shoving Christopher Kidd's face into a heaping pile of horse-shit."

"You told her about the gold in the mountain?"

"I told her about the gold."

"And what else did she ask you?"

"If there was still a way to get into the mine."

The words stuck in Jake's ears. "Why would she ask you that?"

"Beats me."

"And what did you tell her?"

"The truth. That the Feds sealed the mine in the sixties, then built that hotel on top of the entrance. The only way to get into that mountain now is to dig a new tunnel."

"Why didn't you tell me about this on our first ride together?"

"Because she asked me not to repeat our conversation. Being a gentleman, as well as a man of my word, I swore I wouldn't, but now that she's gone I figure my word no longer applies."

"But you two never talked about Sean Farris?"

"No. Neither one of us."

"Any idea why she'd want to meet him in secret on a chairlift? Why someone might have wanted to kill them?"

Lancaster licked his thick lips.

Jake leaned toward him and grunted as the Devil's thorny hand squeezed tightly. "You know who I am?" Jake asked, his back throbbing. "You know I used to have a news show?"

"Sure."

"Well someday soon I'm going to *have* that show again, and when I do, I can use it to shine a spotlight on your little mining problem with the Department of the Interior. I can make the controversy surrounding your mineral survey so hot, the Feds won't have a choice but to grant you new mining rights. Do you understand what I'm telling you?"

Lancaster eyed him cautiously, then pointed at a quaint log cabin built on the riverbank opposite the hotel. The single-story building was Blind River's visitor center.

"You been in there?" Lancaster asked. "Where Sean Farris used to work?"

"We stopped by to pick up a couple of trail maps."

"They've got those. They also keep Blind River's municipal paperwork. Articles of incorporation. Property records. Geological studies. We don't have a city hall, so it's all kept under lock and key in the back room there, and Sean Farris was the only one who had that key."

"You think Claire could've been after a property record?"

"Your wife was asking an awful lot of questions about the mining operation inside of that mountain. It sounded to me like she wanted to get inside and take a look around. There are old maps inside of the visitor center, maps detailing the entrance of the mine. Sean Farris was the only man with access to those maps."

Jake looked to the Hotel Ascent. "But the hotel was built on *top* of the entrance."

"That's right," Lancaster said, following Jake's gaze. "But that doesn't mean you can't get inside. It just means Christopher Kidd won't let you in."

Jake considered the hotel and then looked back to the visitor center. "What would it take to get me that map?"

"Sorry. Are you asking me to steal something?"

"I'm asking for a photocopy." He pulled out Brody's small, one might even call it puny, diamond. "Would this cover your troubles?"

Lancaster took Brody's diamond necklace. "Tiny. Worth maybe three hundred bucks."

"A down payment until I knock down the Department of the Interior's door with a camera and get your story up on *Bullseye*."

Jake didn't think he was going to bite, but then Lancaster stuffed the necklace into his pocket, saying, "I'll see what I can do."

Jake looked past Lancaster at Al, who had ventured outside and was now standing between the sleigh and the revolving door, his great green cloak pulled tightly around him.

"Mr. Boxer!" Al shouted, waving affably. "We weren't expecting you, but welcome back—welcome back to the Hotel Ascent!"

Jake nodded and offered a small wave before looking to the dark mountain beyond—a murderous mountain full of secrets, and his to lay eyes on for the duration.

Welcome back indeed.

TWENTY

———————

"WE'VE HAD ACCIDENTS BEFORE, Mr. Boxer, even the occasional death, but what happened to your wife? Up on that lift? And on your honeymoon?"

Al, who'd been unpacking Jake's suitcase, fixed his eyes on the wheel-chair-bound ex-newsman. "Well...I don't know what to say."

No one knew what to say. Probably because there was nothing *to* say. It was just shit all around.

"Yeah, it's awful," Jake confirmed while reacquainting himself with the room.

The ex-newsman hadn't expected his return to the Honeymoon Suite to be an emotional experience. After all, it was just a room, a room that had been thoroughly scrubbed. Lemon Lysol had been used to clean the floors. Jake could smell it. What he could no longer smell were Claire's Sobranie Blacks. What he could no longer see were the coffee stains she'd left on the counter, the phone charger she'd forgotten in the wall. He was sure the strands of red hair she'd left in the shower drain were gone.

It had only been a few days, but housekeeping had already scrubbed every last bit of Claire from the room—it was as if she'd never even been there at all.

But she had.

They'd made love on that heart-shaped bed, he'd watched adoringly as she brushed her teeth in that bathroom, he'd leaned down and kissed the top of her head as she drank her coffee at the breakfast table next to the picture window that framed that terrible mountain. He swore to hold onto those memories, to lock them up in his castle and defend them with his life, even though he knew that time—that master thief—would eventually steal them all.

"You okay, Mr. Boxer?"

"Fine," he said, having to fight past the lump in his throat. "And it's not as uncommon as you think, you know."

"What's that?"

"Honeymoon tragedies. They're in the news all the time. An Italian bride gets run over while honeymooning in Venice Beach, a British couple in Antigua is murdered in a botched robbery, a South African couple is killed in a car accident while driving to their honeymoon destination, just a day after their nuptials."

"That's why I don't read the news."

The concierge turned back to the task at hand, folding Jake's boxer shorts and placing them in the dresser drawer.

"But," Al said, "I did go back and watch some of your old *Bullseye* clips on the YouTubes. *I've got you in my crosshairs.*" He chuckled heartily. "Heckuva tag, Mr. Boxer. I enjoyed them for the most part. That last episode, though, the one when you talk about the new, uh, what did you call it? New World Order?"

"*Old* World Order, actually."

"Right. Gotta admit, that one scared the pants right off my ole rear end. Especially when you got all worked up."

" 'Getting all worked up' was why I lost my show."

Al nodded gravely. "Hope you don't get that worked up again—what with the way your back is and all."

"I won't," Jake said, forcing a smile.

"Mr. Boxer, your wife is gone, and that's a scary thing, but when you get to be my age, you start to realize that scary things don't exist unless you put them there. Unless you go *looking* for them. And I can guarantee that if you look hard enough, you're bound to find something horrifying, but that doesn't mean it's real. It just means you're looking."

"You think I'm making up the fact that my wife died?"

"No, Mr. Boxer. What I'm saying is that we all want to explain away our tragedies, but, sometimes, you just can't. Oh…" He clapped his hands. "Just so you know, I did try to pay my respects to you in the clinic, but Dr. Wallace said you weren't seeing visitors. I hope you at least received Christopher Kidd's sympathy card, on behalf of the entire hotel."

"I did," Jake said.

And I threw it in the trash, he thought.

"He's mighty torn up over what happened. I'm sure he'll show up in person tomorrow to tell you himself." Al finished unpacking the suitcase, then moseyed over to Jake. The elderly man looked out of breath. "I've seen quite a few guests come through with broken legs and fractured vertebrae, enough to know that sitting for such a long spell must have your back a screamin'. Let's get you into bed so that you can rest."

Jake wasn't interested in the bed. He was, however, interested in another oxy.

"Mind getting me a glass of water first?"

Al hesitated, but then said, "Sure," and turned for the bathroom.

The old man had yet to look him in the eye, not that Jake blamed him. It was impossible to look upon his battered face without seeing the bloody business that had killed Claire.

Jake heard the faucet in the bathroom, then Al shouted, "Say! Did I tell you the water around here's glacier water? Even the stuff from the faucet."

Al kept rambling, but Jake tuned him out as he pulled a blister pack of oxy from his pocket. He popped out a sixty-milligram tablet and held it between his trembling thumb and index finger. The pill was red and circular, and he couldn't wait to get it inside of him. The fire was creeping up his back again.

"I'm sorry…"

Al again. Suddenly apologizing. But for what?

Jake looked to the bathroom. Al was standing there, holding the glass of water, but his eyes were on the floor. As if shamed.

"Don't be sorry," Jake said. "Just bring me the water."

He wanted...no, he *needed* to take that oxy—*now*.

But Al didn't move. Strangely, the man was on the verge of tears. "I lied to you, Mr. Boxer. It's not really glacier water. It's from the river, which is sourced from a spring, so ecologically speaking, its spring water. Mr. Kidd makes us say its glacier cause he printed it all over the latest batch of brochures." Al nodded to a small card propped against the ice bucket. It read: *Go Ahead, Drink from the Faucet. Taste a Glacier.* "He doesn't want to pay to *re*print 'em, of course, even though a lot of us objected, but I always feel bad about lying, especially to you, given what's happened to your wife and..."

"What's going on, Al?"

"I shouldn't have said it."

"This isn't about the water."

"*No-No-No*," he admitted. "Not the water." He took a deep, brooding breath. And then he said it. "It's about what I said to your wife."

For a moment, Jake forgot about the oxy. "What did you say to my wife?"

"When I gave her the tour of the hotel," Al said guiltily. "The day that she died, she told me all about your argument the night before—I didn't pry, Mr. Boxer, so help me God. I get that sorta thing from my guests all the time, emotional vomiting. Mr. Kidd says it's because I'm a familiar face, what was the word he used? Aven...Avon...No, no. Avun—"

Avuncular.

Not now, Claire.

"What did you say to her?" Jake asked.

"Well, when she told me you asked her to quit her job, I told her it must be tough to be married to an ex-celebrity—somebody trying to claw his way back into the limelight. I told her she should put herself first. That if I were her, I wouldn't call you back for a while. I'd let you stew, to make sure you knew just how valuable she was." He fell silent. But not for long. "Don't you see, Mr. Boxer? If I hadn't said anything...if I'd kept my big mouth shut... maybe she would've answered your call. Maybe she would've let you catch up to her. *Maybe* she wouldn't have been on that lift when it fell."

So that's why he hadn't been able to look Jake in the eye.

Jake's first instinct was to leap out of the wheelchair, wrap his hands around the old man's neck, and squeeze. But then Claire piped up again.

Calm, Jake. Calm. Remember: You're stuck in a wheelchair. You're going to need the eyes and ears of someone who can walk. Use this...use him.

Claire was right, of course.

Claire was always right.

Angry, Jake rolled the oxy pill between his fingers and considered the concierge, then said, "Give me the water, Al."

The concierge shuffled forward and proffered the glass, head bent, as if offering treasure to a king. Jake popped the oxy and chased it with spring water that really did taste as if it had come from a glacier.

"You didn't have to tell me that," Jake said. "I never would've known. But now that I do, the way I see it, you owe me."

"Anything," he said, emotional. "Just name it."

"What do you know about Ana Turov?"

Al cocked his head. A vein flared in his temple.

"Ana Turov?"

"The sheriff told me she wasn't your favorite subject. Why?"

Al sighed. "Oh, I don't know, Mr. Boxer. She's an old story, is all. Not much to it really. Not nearly as much as what's going on today, right now, in this hotel. Christopher Kidd is doing some marvelous things."

"Like allowing Blind River to fall to pieces?"

"Sorry?"

"Why hasn't he finished remodeling the north wing of the hotel?"

"There's been a worldwide shortage on cherry wood."

"Cherry wood?"

"That's right. Been going on for a couple of years, I suppose. Besides, it really hasn't affected the hotel. There are plenty of other amenities for our guests to enjoy, beside the north wing."

"But the Kidd, he owns the stores on Main Street too?"

"Most of 'em."

"Well is there a reason why they're falling apart? They don't look like they were made out of cherry wood to me."

"I'm just the concierge. I don't have access to Mr. Kidd's municipal plans, but if you're questioning his attention to detail—"

"I'm questioning the amount of money in his bank account. Your little ski town is falling apart, and he can't finish the remodel on the one building he seems to care about. If you don't want to talk about Ana Turov, maybe you can tell me about that?"

"What I can tell you, Mr. Boxer, is that in the twenty years since Mr. Kidd took over, he's never bounced a paycheck, and I've never seen him waste a penny. He's a thrifty man who gives generously to all sorts of Alaskan nonprofits, and if you had any idea how difficult it is to maintain buildings in sub-zero weather, you'd know why some of Main Street needs a little love. Besides, it doesn't make a whole lot of sense to fix 'em up now, not with a harsh Blind River winter coming."

"A winter that belongs to the wolves?"

"That's right."

"I was told that most of the wolves were dead."

"Most. But not all." Al considered Jake harshly. "If this was what it was like to be on your TV show, Mr. Boxer, I feel sorry for your subjects."

"Don't be. Feel sorry for Claire. Feel sorry for those wolves. They're the ones who are dead."

All affect left Al's face. "That's true. And, unfortunately, death isn't all that uncommon in these parts. Mr. Kidd doesn't advertise it, but we lose two or three a season, if not right here in Blind River, then out near Denali. Usually mountain climbers going too high, or skiers going too fast. The chairlift accident and your wife, though…well, that was preventable, which makes it a tragedy. If I were in your shoes, I'd be feeling a whole lot of anger right now."

"You have no idea what I'm feeling right now."

"I'm quite a bit older than you, Mr. Boxer. I've experienced a lot—"

"But you've never been married."

"But I *have* been in love."

Jake had been pushing Al's buttons on purpose. It was an old interviewing technique. If you wanted something from a person, but you didn't know exactly what, strike a match, light a fuse, and see what blew out of them.

Before Jake knew it, the concierge had taken the photograph of Ana Turov (which was crooked again) off the wall. He held it gingerly, as if it were the artist's delicate hand.

"I'm from Greenville, South Carolina," Al said. Slowly at first, but then he picked up steam. "Ran away from home when I was sixteen, found myself in Blind River by the time I was eighteen."

"Why'd you run away? And why'd you run so far?"

"Because my daddy was a killer. I saw him murder a man in our basement, a man he referred to as a commie. He did it with a hammer. Split the poor man's skull right open—I saw his...*I saw his brains*..." Al froze, clearly haunted, even all these years later. "This was back in '59, when Sputnik was flying overhead and chirping on our radio, when the entire country was scared silly of nuclear war." He considered Ana's photograph. "You can imagine what I thought when I heard a commie was coming to Blind River. She was here for six months. Had Soviet handlers who followed her everywhere. The only time they left her alone was when she was here, in this room, working, and the only American who was ever allowed inside of this room was her bellboy. Me. Back then the hotel didn't have a concierge. I did most everything, including weekly runs into Anchorage to buy whatever she might need: paints, brushes, canvases." Al closed his eyes, lost in the memory. "And every morning, I'd bring her breakfast: black coffee, hardboiled egg, toast with blackberry jam, and those yellow flowers from the garden. I'd spend fifteen...thirty minutes a day with her, laying out her spread and stealing glances at her painting while she ate. Eventually I figured out that I wasn't spending time with one of those awful commies Daddy had cursed up and down, but with a splendid talent, and I knew in my heart she thought the same of me. Oh, you might not believe it, Mr. Boxer—a young black man and a white Soviet painter falling in love...why we didn't even speak the same language. But those commies, they kept her like a pet. I was the only free man she knew, and she loved me for it. Al and Ana," he said wistfully. "We just went together." Al's face suddenly hardened. "Ana coming here was a big deal. You've probably heard that Nixon even agreed to close down this bit of White Alice because of her visit? Now think about that, art bringing peace. It could've been something—it almost *was* something—until both Ana and her masterpiece disappeared."

"You mean defected."

"I mean disappeared. There are those who claim that Ana Turov defected through Blind River, but there are others who say she never left."

"You think someone murdered her?"

The old man shrugged, then held up Ana's photograph, showing off the artist's dark and startled eyes. He hung it back on its nail and straightened it.

"Mr. Boxer, there are only so many times a man can straighten a photograph before he begins to believe."

TWENTY-ONE

JAKE SPENT THE REST OF THE EVENING with two ghosts instead of one. Claire stretched out next to him in the heart-shaped bed, while Ana Turov, his new mistress, worked furiously on her masterpiece near the Honeymoon Suite's picture window.

"They couldn't have been more different," he muttered later, speaking the words to himself, filling the lonely room. For years, his voice had entertained millions of viewers, but in that moment, maybe for the first time ever, it actually kind of entertained him. He cleared his throat and tried it again, stronger this time.

"The two women couldn't have been more different."

Not bad.

Then something funny happened. He smelled pancake makeup beneath his nose. He felt the heat of the studio lights on his face. He saw the unflinching black eye of the camera staring right at him.

And then a voice burst out of him with a strength and confidence he hadn't felt in years.

"Ladies and gentlemen, thank you for tuning in. My name is Jake Boxer, and this is *Bullseye* on NewsFlash, where you can watch any time, download or stream, and most importantly, where you can share your thoughts with your friends and the *Bullseye* community right here on NewsFlash.com. Tonight's story begins with two dead women, women whose lives couldn't have been more different. Claire O'Donnell, an American journalist, strong in both mind and body, and Ana Turov, a Soviet painter, sickly and tortured. Claire was born twenty years after Ana died, but their lives unexpectedly intersected in one room: the Honeymoon Suite at the Hotel Ascent, the premier lodge of a sleepy little ski town named Blind River, Alaska. It was here, in this room, that Ana painted her masterpiece, and it was here that Claire O'Donnell began a journalistic masterpiece—a story about a secret underneath a mountain used to eavesdrop on the Soviet Union at the height of the Cold War. So come with me my faithful viewers, let's illuminate these women's lives and finally put their ghosts, real or imagined, to rest. *This* is—" The Devil squeezed. Jake groaned, spat out, "*Bullseye*," and quickly realized, with more than a passing terror, that the bearded doctor had been right. He had no business being alone. Even resting on that soft heart-shaped bed, even on the oxy, fire was suddenly spewing from his cracked spine in agonizing flares.

Al had turned off the lights before leaving, but the drapes were still open, and moonlight was seeping into the room, enough for Jake to make out the blister pack of oxy on the sheets nearby. There were five pills left. He couldn't take another until the morning, not if they were going to last until Sunday—no easy feat.

Desperate for a distraction, he pulled Claire's cell phone from his pocket. He still hadn't charged it, which made it about as useful as a pair of dull scissors. But Jake had informed Al that it was dead, and he urgently needed a few numbers off it—to inform friends and family of Claire's passing. The concierge had promised to look for a charger. If worse came to worst, Al would have someone pick one up first thing in the morning.

But Jake needed the charger before morning, and a distraction from the pain was just one of many reasons why. Stakeouts like the one he was trying to conduct were both long and tedious, and they demanded time if any useful information was to be gleaned.

It was Thursday night. Check out time at the Ascent was Sunday morning at eleven o'clock sharp. That gave him seventy-two hours to make sense of Claire's story or, at the very least, gather enough information to lead with it when he launched the online version of *Bullseye* with Tabitha Fox.

Bullseye...

To Jake, the name meant news and news meant politics and politics meant power struggles and ideologies and politicians—oh, Jesus, *politicians*. Jake hated them. Back in the day, nothing gave him more pleasure than lining them up in his crosshairs and pulling the trigger, story after story. Breaking the Tom DeLay corruption scandal had been a career highlight, as had the story of Senator Larry Craig's infamous solicitation for gay sex in an airport bathroom. As far as Jake was concerned, any politician at the national level was a narcissist. And most of them were stupid. What made them uniquely qualified to govern? To tell other people how to live their lives? They gamed the system, manipulated the masses, spied and backstabbed and waged war, and when they were done with all that, they became lobbyists and cashed in for millions.

Oh, God!

Was he really jumping back into the game?

He wasn't ready, he knew that, but what else could he do? It had taken three years of soul searching to become a good husband, but the chairlift accident had stripped him of that role in the blink of an eye. The only sanctuary for the naked, quivering, abandoned man left behind was his castle, and Jake's castle was *Bullseye*.

Every minute he spent with the dead cell phone was a minute lost, and nighttime minutes were far more valuable than day. Deals weren't struck in broad daylight. Extortions weren't plotted and ski lifts weren't sabotaged during the day. Those sorts of plans were hatched under cover of darkness. Jake needed to be listening. Now, of course, with only seven hours of daylight, November in Blind River was dominated by darkness, a notion Jake clung to as the minutes crawled by.

Jake popped a second oxy around one a.m. Four left.

Not the end of the world. Not yet.

He'd just have to wrap up his investigation a little early.

With the extra oxy kicking around his system, the Devil loosened his grip, and Jake was actually able to concentrate on the sounds of the hotel.

Coquettish laughter drifted through the walls. Drunken guests staggered by, shouting over that wooden railing to the cavernous lobby below. Jake listened for the telling cough of the strange old man with the tight skin, or Christopher Kidd and his foul-mouthed temper, or the Russian couple speaking their native tongue, but he didn't hear any of them, and he wouldn't, he realized. Not without Claire's iPhone. It struck him that he'd found one of her cigarette butts in the Kidd's office, a butt that had been extinguished sometime in the middle of the night while he'd been passed out in the Honeymoon Suite. Under what pretense had she gained access to his office? Of course, he already knew the answer to the question. There was only one reason a man met a woman in the dead of night. The image of Claire seducing the Kidd stuck. Her mouth on his neck, her hands on his back, her tongue on his—

"Mr. Boxer? Mr. Boxer, are you awake?"

Summer, he realized, groggily opening his eyes. Shouting at him through the locked door.

Wait a second, Summer worked the day shift.

Had he fallen asleep?

"I've got your charger. Al said it was important. Are you well enough to come to the door?"

It was still dark in the room, though the clock read eight thirty a.m.

Had he really slept for seven hours?

"Mr. Boxer?"

"I'm coming," Jake croaked. "Hang on."

Without thinking, he slid his legs out from under the bed covers and reached for the floor. The pain was unbelievable, like someone slicing his spinal cord in two with a scalpel. His entire head washed to white and he cried out—a strained and anguished scream before collapsing in a heap.

"Mr. Boxer?" Summer shouted, clearly concerned. "Are you okay?"

Sure, he thought. Fine. I'm just face-first on the cold hardwood floor with a broken back, is all.

Get up, Jake.

I can't, Claire.

The doctor's keeping tabs on you through the staff. They will *make you leave the hotel if they think you're a danger to yourself.*

Jake cursed Claire, then groaned as he willed himself to his feet. Using the bed for support, he wavered uncertainly before he was able to inch his way over to the wheelchair. Grabbing the armrests, he slowly lowered himself down. Once sitting, he grabbed the cold push rings and rolled himself to the door. He opened it and looked up. He peered at Summer through eyes he knew were drunk and dizzy with pain. He prayed she wouldn't notice.

"Do you need a doctor?"

"No. Thanks."

"Are you sure?"

"The charger."

She studied him a moment, then reached into a pocket and pulled out a soft white cord with a plug. But she held it back. "I want you to call Dr. Wallace."

"Fine," Jake said, wiggling his fingers.

She hesitated a moment longer before giving it to him.

The chore done, her face softened. "Oh, and I'm supposed to let you know that the van got to Anchorage just fine. The autopsy is scheduled for this morning."

"Thanks," he said, even though the word *autopsy* completely eviscerated him. He shut the door on Summer and sat for a good while, battling the brutal image of his precious bride and her date with a nameless pathologist and his bone saw. He took another oxy—he had no choice—there was simply too much pain to numb.

Three left.

And then what?

He couldn't think about it.

Maybe he'd get Claire's story that very day? Maybe he'd be in Anchorage that very night?

Sure, and maybe space aliens would reverse time, giving him the chance to talk Claire into honeymooning in Key West?

The oxy kicked in. He remembered that he now had a cell phone charger. Major coup. All he had to do was plug the charger into Claire's phone, and then the wall. Reaching into the saddlebag on the left side of the wheelchair, he felt around for Claire's phone. Its cracked glass cover bit his thumb. He pulled it out, plugged in the charger, and slowly rolled his chair forward until he was even with an electrical outlet. Taking great care, he leaned down, plugged the charger into the wall, and held down the phone's silver power button.

Nothing happened.

It was broken.

Unfixable.

Fu—

The Apple insignia popped up. The phone flickered to life. And Jake found himself staring at the selfie of Claire and him in their wedding clothes, their loving arms wrapped around each other, before they'd ventured to Blind River.

Weren't those the days?

TWENTY-TWO

———————

"So what was he doing when you got to the Honeymoon Suite?"

A man's voice—*Christopher Kidd's* voice.

"*Sleeping.*"

Summer's.

"*Then why did you wake him up?*"

"*Because Al left a note saying he needed an iPhone charger ASAP—so I bought him one and brought it over.*"

"*Al left you that note?*"

"*Yes.*"

Even over Claire's iPhone, Jake could hear the gears turning in the Kidd's head.

"*I told you not to listen to Al. The old son of a bitch has lost his mind. And last I heard this Bullseye asshole was going back to Anchorage. Any idea why Al didn't tell me he came back to the Ascent?*"

"*Maybe he didn't think it was a big deal?*"

"*Not a big deal? There's only one reason a newsman would stick around a hotel when his bride's body is undergoing an autopsy three hundred miles away—to stir up a wrongful death suit! And if he can't put together a wrongful death suit, he's gonna dig up some trash on this hotel and put it on national fucking TV, and that's the* last *thing I need. I'm losing way too much money on this town as it is."*

An awkward silence followed, interrupted only by the same strange *thump-thump-thump*ing Jake had heard in the man's office the day before.

The Kidd was thinking.

Finally, he said, *"Had I known his cunt of a wife was married to the Jake Boxer—wacko guru of the conspiracy nuts—I never would've agreed to that honeymoon article. The auction's tomorrow…I want you to keep a close eye on him. I want you to make sure he doesn't meddle."*

"And how, exactly, am I supposed to do that?"

"You're a good-looking woman. Use your imagination."

"Mr. Kidd, I don't think that I—"

"You don't have to screw him. Just don't let him wander around the hotel alone. Shouldn't be hard if he's stuck in a chair. And when you do see Al, tell him I want to talk to him. Immediately."

"Yes, Mr. Kidd."

Jake heard a door open and close. Summer had left. The Kidd sighed whimsically before muttering, *"and when you're done comforting Jake Boxer, get that sweet little ass back here to comfort me."*

Jake, who was once again lying on the heart-shaped bed, earbuds in place, was scribbling down notes on a small pad of the hotel's complimentary stationary, transcribing as much as he could.

He kept listening to "Birdland," Christopher Kidd's track on the Patti Smith album, for at least an hour after Summer left. The Kidd passed most of that time placing courtesy calls to his wealthy guests, assuring them that the long shadow of the chairlift accident wouldn't ruin the rest of the weekend. Yes, downhill skiing was a bust, but they still had Blind River's notorious Saturday night auction to look forward to, so talk pretty to your bank accounts, iron your best Alaskan duds, and brace your asses for a boozy-doozy. You're not going to *believe* what's for sale this year.

At a little past two in the afternoon, the sun was already low in the sky, and several empty bags of nacho cheese Doritos were strewn about the bed. Jake was craving real food but refused to eat room service. He had no desire to become the next headline: Ex News Host Dies in Hotel Room After

Mysterious Brain Aneurysm.

He'd taken another oxy just before lunch. He hadn't had a choice. It was either listen to Claire's satellite phone or be rendered useless as the crackling flames devoured his spine. Yes, that meant he only had two pills left and, yes, at his current rate, those too would be gone by the end of the day, but for the moment life was sweet and his ears were full of unsuspecting voices. Jake was filling page after page of story—*Claire's* story. The notes were strewn about on the red duvet. He would have to make sense of them later—the pressing issue at the moment was transcribing as much as possible. His hand was cramping and his ears ached, but the work made him feel worthwhile again, as if he was waking from a dark dream.

His day had been filled with a hodgepodge of voices. The track "Gloria" featured the Russians, whom he'd dubbed *Ivan* and *Ivana,* if only to give them a little personality. They spoke only in Russian, so their conversations were impossible to decipher, but he was still able to infer much about the couple by the *way* they spoke, and soon his little pad of paper was full of notes like: *Lovers. Moody. Ivana speaks perfect English—Ivan does not. Probably has accent.*

The track "Redondo Beach" brought him the man with the thin smoker's cough. He'd filled page after page about this guy as well: *meticulous, confrontational, smokes incessantly.* Jake even managed to glean the man's name— Mel Perkins—after he made a call to a plastic surgeon about a chin tuck on his return to Los Angeles. So Jake dubbed this one *Plastic Mel.*

Jake had already learned plenty from the Kidd's track. The Kidd had a choleric temperament and was all about money—making it, not losing it. And, yes, the Kidd was a womanizer (who'd spent time with Claire, he reminded himself), but perhaps more worrisome, he sounded paranoid, especially about Jake's presence at the hotel.

Not that his paranoia was entirely misplaced—after all, Jake was eavesdropping on the man.

The fourth track on the Patti Smith album, "Kimberly," had been quiet all day. Jake thought the room might now be empty. Looking out his picture window, he'd seen several guests leaving the hotel with packed suitcases— maybe the occupant had left? But as the sun dipped beneath the horizon, Jake heard the soft clicks of a keyboard in the mysterious occupant's room.

He heard a door open and close and a shower being turned on. Jake listened for a very long time. The hypnotic sound of the shower, coupled with the burden of eavesdropping all day, soon had Jake's eyes growing heavy. He needed a break, a little catnap, another oxy pill, and then he could go at it again.

A cell phone rang. Startled, Jake jerked awake and a bolt of lightning shot up his spine. He crumpled like a pinned bug and somewhere in his feverish mind he realized that the phone wasn't ringing inside of the Honeymoon Suite, but in the room he was eavesdropping on, the one with the unknown occupant.

Jake waited for the person to turn off the shower. To answer the phone. To say hello so that he could at the very least determine if he was eavesdropping on a man or a woman. But the phone went to voicemail. Jake's eyelids grew heavy again. Suddenly there was sand between his toes. Claire was in his arms with that terrible black shadow across her face. A door slammed, and Jake, once again, was startled from a restless sleep.

Whoever had been in the shower had just left the room.

Ah, shit, did he miss something?

Who knew?

Upset with himself for dozing off, he edged off the bed toward his wheelchair. He wasn't going to fall asleep again. Hoping a little discomfort would keep him awake, he placed both hands on the wheelchair's armrests, stood, and turned his body until his butt was over the seat. As he lowered himself, the pain from his bending spine scorched its way into each and every nerve ending.

Who would've thought the simple act of sitting could hurt so goddamn bad?

Jake spent the rest of the day in his chair, pushing himself in lazy circles as voices buzzed in his ears. Later, he practiced standing and, eventually, took slow walks around the spacious room. It hurt, but he was acclimating to the pain, growing stronger, and most importantly the discomfort, and movement, were keeping him awake.

The last room Claire had bugged before dying was on the track "Free Money."

Jack quickly ascertained the sex of this guest, not from the timbre of his voice, but from the severity of his flatulence, which was both copious and ear splitting. The man was drunk, and Jake learned that his name was Nick Gold as he listened to him entertain a steady stream of equally intoxicated guests. The conversations ranged from the folly of England's "Brexit" to who was going to win the 2016 presidential election, just days away. The singular thread throughout multiple conversations seemed to be that Obama's big government was a disappointment, and that private industry had to do more to influence the world. It was also here that Jake caught his first whiff of a real conspiracy—in the names of organizations that made his hackles rise: *WMF. John Birch Society. The Carousel.*

Those names were commonplace in New World Order conspiracies. Those names spun webs between intelligence agencies, investment banks, and international corporations. Jake had investigated those names during his stint with *Bullseye*, including on a certain trip to Moscow, where he'd stayed in the shadow of the Lubyanka, headquarters to Russia's foreign intelligence service, the FSB.

"Why do you think these assholes come to this godforsaken mountain year after year? For the skiing? Ha! There are easier places to ski, believe me."

Nick Gold was mumbling to some poor drunken woman who'd stumbled into his gaseous presence. His words were slurred and stilted, and he sounded as though he was on the verge of passing out.

"This joker Christopher Kidd, he caters to rich middle-aged dudes looking to get laid. You seen the photographs he has in his office? Siberian billionaires. Arab sheiks. Freaking Dick Che…" He belched. *"Dick Cheney."* He paused, and for a moment, Jake was sure he'd passed out. But then he heard a long inhale—he'd either taken a long drink or a deep toke.

"Where was I?"

Arab sheiks, Jake urged silently. Siberian billionaires. Dick Cheney.

"Oh, yeah," he finally said, *"The assholes who show up to ski on this mountain. I mean look—I'm a lawyer. A damn good one. Believe me, I know how wealthy clients operate. In a hotel with a hundred and sixty-six rooms? And in the middle of nowhere? That's a hundred and sixty-six closed doors—a lotta real estate for a lotta hush-hush business in a place the rest of the world barely knows exists, you get me? Yeah. You got me, I think. You're smart, I think. But not as smart as me. I'm only here one time, missy. I'm smart enough not to get involved with these assholes—not after this weekend—not*

after this auction—say? Mind if I lie down?"

Nick Gold didn't wait for his lady-friend to answer. Jake heard a heavy plop and then the squeak of a straining bed. Then one last lingering belch that took its own sweet time dissipating, like the sound of a distant foghorn.

Jake thought that was it—the grand finale before a drunk and stoned black sleep, but then the woman's voice finally piped up.

"You are *smart, Nick. Far smarter than anyone else here in Blind River."*

She had an accent. It wasn't Russian—it was European.

"Fuckin' rightsss…rightssssss yous are…and I'm a patriot…my client is a patriot…and I swear to…I swear to God…I'm gonna win *that commie painting."*

TWENTY-THREE

JAKE'S GAZE DRIFTED to Ana Turov's photograph.

The missing woman's startled eyes looked right back at him, silently confirming what he now knew.

Somehow, the Kidd had gotten his hands on her missing masterpiece, and he was going to sell it at Blind River's annual auction.

Had the Kidd killed Claire because she'd found out? And if so, why? How much money could the sale of an obscure and long-dead Soviet artist really bring in? A couple hundred grand?

There was a knock at his door, followed quickly by a familiar voice. "Mr. Boxer? Mr. Boxer, are you awake?"

Summer.

Again.

He didn't have time for her. His mind was racing, not only because of what he'd just heard, but what he was still hearing. Nick Gold had passed out. With Claire's earbuds still firmly in place, Jake could hear the lawyer (who'd proven a sterling example of why Jake *didn't* want to go to law school) snoring—but the woman with the European accent was still there, and Jake could hear the telltale chime of a computer booting to life, and then the click-clack of fingers on a keyboard. She was on Nick Gold's laptop. But why? Who was she?

"Mr. Boxer. Dr. Wallace called. He wants me to make sure you're okay."

Bullshit.

He'd overheard Summer's conversation with Christopher Kidd. She was there to make sure that he wasn't snooping around, which, of course, he was.

"I have a key," she said, "if you don't answer, I'm coming in."

Irritated, Jake pulled the earbuds from his ears and stuffed them, along with Claire's phone, into his wheelchair's saddlebag.

"Yeah…sorry. I was in the bathroom. Hang on."

Jake rolled toward the door but stopped short. The bed was still covered with notes, notes summarizing conversations from numerous bugged rooms, including Christopher Kidd's office. There was no way he could pick them all up before Summer became suspicious. There were too many, and his back was pulsing with fire again. But it was dark. The sun had set long ago and the only light came from a floor lamp opposite the bed. Maybe she wouldn't see them?

No.

They were on a heart-shaped bed, a bed that drew Jake's eye every time he entered the room. There was no way she'd miss them.

"Mr. Boxer," Summer's voice, still there, behind that door, "are you feeling okay?"

"Fine," Jake said. "I'm fine. I'm just…look, this medication is making stomach go crazy. I had to go, you know, number three, and it's gonna take a while to get my pants back on. Do you mind coming back in a few minutes?"

"Number three? That sounds bad, but…Mr. Boxer, Dr. Wallace wants me to check up on you. Now."

"My *pants* are down, Summer. I just took a terrible shit."

"It's no problem. I can wait."

Of course she could.

"I don't think you're listening. I want you to go away. Tell Dr. Wallace I'm fine. I don't need help, and I don't feel like seeing anyone right now."

Turning her away was dangerous. Surely she'd report back to Christopher Kidd. But what else could he do?

"Okay," she said finally. "I'll go. But I'm going to have to tell Dr. Wallace you refused to see me."

"Tell him whatever you want."

Jake held his breath until her footsteps retreated. He quickly stuck Claire's earbuds back into his ears and waited to hear what the woman in Nick Gold's room would do next, but all he heard were the raspy ins and outs of a drunkard snoring.

The mystery woman had left while he'd been arguing with Summer.

Frustrated, he swiped back to "Birdland," Christopher Kidd's office, expecting Summer to already be inside, mouthing off to her boss. But when he landed on the Kidd's office, it wasn't Summer's voice he heard. It was a new voice, a deep baritone, and the man sounded choked up. *"...just a Saint. First you throw the party to end all parties and now this pledge."* He took a moment to suck in some tears. *"Thank you, Mr. Kidd. This is gonna keep the kibble in the bowl for at least another year."*

"Well, Sam, I sincerely believe that Operation Sled Dog is crucial to one of the richest traditions in our great state. We can't allow these animals to go without food."

Operation Sled Dog?

The Kidd politely, but definitively, ended the conversation, and Sam took his leave. Jake heard the rhythmic *thump-thump-thumping* against the desk again, and then the Kidd's door opened, and Jake heard another sniveling voice, this time a woman's, say, *"Oh my God, Christopher, dearie, you and that rubber ball are just too cute!"*

"Alexis," the Kidd said coolly. *"So good to see you. Please, have a seat. I want to hear all about the orphanage."*

As the hours ticked by, Jake listened as the Kidd held court with guest after guest. They paid their respects to this Alaskan Godfather, and in return, the Kidd doled out financial pledges like candy to trick-or-treaters.

There was an oil executive after lobbying money to drill in the Arctic National Wildlife Refuge. The congressman from Fairbanks, looking for his vote in the upcoming election...and a little super PAC money, if the Kidd could spare it. There was even a research scientist out of Anchorage looking to fund an artificial intelligence project.

But something didn't sit right. If the Kidd had all of that money to hand out, why was Blind River's downtown dominated by peeling paint and shoddy workmanship? Why was the north wing of the hotel still under construction? Why was the Kidd pledging a fortune when his own backyard was crumbling?

Around midnight the last of the Kidd's guests, a man trying to start a nonprofit for Alaska's homeless, took his leave, and Jake heard the proprietor sigh loudly, then grumble, *"bloodsuckers."* The word was followed by the distinctive sound of a cork being pulled from a bottle. Listening to the Kidd get drunk was about as stimulating as watching paint dry. Jake's eyes grew heavy, and he would've fallen asleep if he hadn't noticed that Ana Turov's photograph was once again crooked.

There are only so many times a man can straighten a photograph before he begins to believe.

Al's words knocked around his head as his gaze lingered on Ana's startled black eyes. Al clearly believed that his old love had been murdered in Blind River, and that her ghost was too stubborn to leave. So what? She spent her days floating around the Hotel Ascent, cocking pictures of herself to creep out the guests?

It was preposterous, though Jake couldn't help but to wonder how it *had* moved. Suddenly, he had the unmistakable sensation that he was not alone. Real or imagined, he didn't know which; it certainly *felt* as if someone were breathing the same cold air that he was.

Ana and he, they were both trapped in the Honeymoon Suite. Jake in a wheelchair, Ana Turov within the frame of the crooked photograph, startled, he realized, by whomever had snapped her picture.

The photographer...

Had it been Al?

Jake wheeled himself over to the picture.

Someone had gotten past her Soviet guards. Someone had surprised her while she'd been working.

Someone she hadn't been expecting? Someone who'd also killed her? From his castle, Jake could see the storm clouds of a story on the horizon. Was it a big story? Sure. But was it a story that a newlywed woman would risk her life for?

No. At least not yet.

Jake took the photograph from the wall. He ran a finger over the walnut frame. It hadn't been weighted, at least as far as he could tell. He placed it back on its nail, making sure it was absolutely straight, and then turned back to the bed where his nearly depleted blister pack of oxy lay.

Two more.

He'd taken one six hours ago, but his hands were already trembling, and his back was taking on a sharper, more sinister pain.

He should take another oxy now, he thought. It would probably last until morning. And then, if he took the last one at breakfast, he'd have all day to hunt down more drugs.

He could call Dr. Wallace, he told himself, as he wheeled to the bed and picked the blister pack out from amongst the stray notes. He'd convince him to hand over just one more sample—surely the doctor wouldn't let a patient suffer.

Jake pushed the second to last oxy through the blister pack, popped it into his mouth, and swallowed.

"Where the hell have you been?"

Startled by the words, Jake nearly fell out of his chair. It was the Kidd, and from the sound of it, he was quite drunk. Someone else had finally entered the Kidd's office.

"Entertaining the guests," Summer said back. *"Isn't that what you wanted me to do?"*

"I wanted you to check on Jake Boxer."

"I did that too."

"And?"

"He's up there working on his wife's honeymoon article."

"That's it?"

"I'm guessing so. His place stunk—like he hadn't left it for a few days."

Jake sniffed the air self-consciously. She was right. But she was also lying. She hadn't come inside, so how could she know what his room smelled like?

"So you saw him?"

"Of course I saw him. You told me to check in on him."

Jake heard the Kidd bounce what he now knew was his little rubber ball.

"*Good. How about a drink?*"

Jake heard the gurgle of liquor leaving a bottle.

"*No thank you, Mr. Kidd. I'm tired. I think I'll head home.*"

"*I had to have Terry track you down,*" the Kidd said sharply. "*And now you want to leave without so much as having a friendly drink?*"

She hesitated before saying, "*I guess one wouldn't hurt.*"

"*That's the spirit.*"

He heard the Kidd pour a second drink.

"*Summer, do you have any idea how important tomorrow is for me?*"

"*The auction is always the highlight of the season—*"

"This *year, Summer.* This *auction. Do you have any idea?*"

"*No.*"

He heard Summer inhale sharply, as if she'd just been grabbed. "*I built this place to make money, a lot of money, and by God, this year I'm gonna get my money.*"

"*I'm sure you will.*"

"*I won't if my own staff lies to me.*"

"*Lie?*" She said, terrified. "*I…I don't know what you're talking about, Mr. Kidd.*"

"*No? What do you see over there?*"

"*A computer.*"

"*And what do you see on the computer?*"

"*Room numbers?*"

"*That's right. I monitor the electric locks on every door in this hotel, which tells me a number of things, including how many times each door has been opened. Guess how many times the door to the Honeymoon Suite opened today? Zero.*"

Summer replied quickly and quietly, with no small amount of fear in her voice. "*Okay. I'm sorry. I tried, Mr. Kidd, really, I did, but he told me to go away.*"

"*Why didn't you tell me he told you to go away?*"

"*I know that you have certain expectations.*"

"*And?*"

"*And I didn't want it to be like the last time I let you down.*"

"*It doesn't have to be, Summer.*"

Jake heard a smack and then a wet sucking noise, as if the Kidd had spanked her and was now chewing on her neck.

Oh, God.

This was all Jake's fault.

If he hadn't have told her to go away she wouldn't have lied to the Kidd and...

Don't just sit there, Jake. Do something.

I'd love to, Claire. But I'm in a wheelchair. What the hell am I supposed to do?

"You know I've wanted this, Summer. It's gotta be now. Come Sunday the season will be over. We'll never see each other again."

"There's always next season, Mr. Kidd."

"Ha. Right."

"Please...Please don't."

"Shhh..."

"Don't."

"You lied to me, Summer, and now you're gonna make up for it—you owe *me."*

Jake couldn't stand it. Grabbing his chair's push bar, he shoved himself to the landline, grabbed the receiver, and dialed zero. The phone rang several times before a young man answered. "Front desk, this is Terry, how may I help you?"

"Christopher Kidd's office."

"Umm. It's three in the morning. Mr. Kidd went home a long time ago."

"Just transfer me."

"I'd be happy to send you to his voicemail, Mr. Boxer. I'm sure he'll call back first thing in the morning."

In Claire's earbuds, Jake heard a zipper peel open. He heard the Kidd grunt.

"Okay, Terry, listen. I have Sam with me, from Operation Sled Dog?"

"Oh, sure."

"Your boss pledged half a million in support tonight."

"Christopher Kidd *is* a generous man."

"Right, well this is a bit embarrassing, and Sam didn't think we should call, but he's got me worried."

"Worried?"

"Yes, Sam seems to think that your boss might be in trouble. He was more than a little drunk when he made the offer, you see. He was drinking scotch, a lot of scotch, and he threw up in the trashcan, right in front of Sam. He was supposed to meet him later but he never showed—Sam's worried that he might have passed out in his office."

Terry chuckled. "Oh, I doubt that, Mr. Boxer."

"Terry. Did you ever see him *leave* his office? "

The night receptionist fell silent. Over the earbuds, Jake heard the Kidd grunting regularly. God, was he raping the poor woman?

"No, I didn't see him leave, and I did bring him a couple of bottles at his request," Terry finally admitted. "He had his meetings tonight, and he wanted to imbibe with his guests, if so desired."

"Terry. Just check on him. Please!"

Hurry…Hurry…*Hurry!*

Finally, Terry said, "Oh, alright, Mr. Boxer. You win. I'll take a peek and make sure he's gone."

Terry hung up. Jake turned his full attention back to his earbuds. What only took a few seconds felt like hours of Summer saying, *"No, please,"* and the Kidd saying, *"Just relax,"* but then Jake heard the soft click of a keycard, the creak of a door opening, and the shriek of the Kidd as he jerked his fly up so fast that he probably drew blood.

"Oh, God," Terry stammered. *"I'm…I'm sorry."*

"Don't be," Summer said brusquely, and Jake exhaled a sigh of relief as he heard her scurry out of the room.

"What are you doing?" the Kidd shrieked. *"Get out of here! Get out!"*

"Yes, sir, Mr. Kidd. Sorry. Sorry. I didn't know. Jake Box—"

"Out!"

"Yes, sir."

Jake heard Terry start to close the door, but then the Kidd said, *"Wait. What did you say?"*

"Jake Boxer called," Terry explained. *"That's the only reason I'm here. He told me he thought you might be passed out drunk in your office."*

"Did he?"

"Yes, sir. Yes, he did."

Jake jerked the earbuds out. He didn't have time to listen to anything else. He knew he only had minutes, if not seconds, before Christopher Kidd was in his room.

TWENTY-FOUR

"MR. BOXER?" THE KIDD called from the other side of the door. "I'm sorry to bother you at such an hour, but Terry told me you're concerned about my well-being? I thought I'd take the opportunity to say hello, finally, and to assure you that I'm perfectly fine...Mr. Boxer, are you awake?"

Yes. Jake was awake...and totally screwed.

After realizing the Kidd would be paying him a visit, he'd pulled the duvet—covered with eavesdropping notes—from the bed and hid it in the bathroom. Most of the notes had stuck to the blanket for the ride, but a few had drifted to the hardwood floor. Jake was still rolling from page to page, straining to pick up the notes between fingertips, wishing to God that the fifth oxy would hurry up and kick in because his spine barked each and every time he reached for the floor.

"Jake," the Kidd shouted, "are you awake?"

"Yeah," Jake said. Panting. Training his gaze on the last note in sight. "Glad to hear you're okay."

He rolled for the final note.

"I'm fine, thank you. I would like to express my condolences for what happened to your wife. I tried to pay them at the hospital, but the doctor turned me away."

Red in the face and out of breath, Jake reached the last note, stretched, and *snagged* it, just as the Kidd said, "So I hope you're decent. I'm letting myself in."

The electronic keycard reader clicked. The door opened. And Jake crammed the wad of stray notes beneath his ass.

He was sure the Kidd had seen them but reconsidered when the disheveled millionaire staggered inside, a bottle of twenty-year-old brandy in one hand, a couple of crystal snifters in the other.

Maybe he'd been too drunk to notice?

Jake had been listening to the man for nearly twenty-four hours straight, but it was the first time he'd actually seen the Kidd since the Café Beaujolais. The Kidd was wearing blue jeans and a plaid button up, though he'd lost the shirt's top button, presumably while forcing himself on Summer.

Despite the Kidd's disheveled appearance, Jake knew that his own face looked far worse, and he wasn't surprised by the Kidd's raised eyebrows when he muttered, "Christ! And here I was expecting to find the man I watched night after night on TV."

The Kidd closed the door and shuffled over to the suite's kitchen table, where he set down the brandy, snifters, and a manila envelope, which he'd had tucked beneath one arm. As he uncorked and poured the brandy, he said, "Can you roll over to the table or should I roll the table over to you?"

"I'm on medication," Jake demurred, "I'm not supposed to drink."

"Well, if you didn't die in that horrific accident, a drink won't kill you. C'mon. This is some of my best stuff."

He pushed a full glass to the spot where he wanted Jake to sit. But Jake didn't move. Unfazed, the Kidd took a nip from his own glass, then took a cigarette out from behind his ear.

"Your doctor have a problem with secondhand smoke?"

"No. Just me."

"I see. Well, I suppose if it were your hotel, you could stop me."

The Kidd lit up, inhaled deeply, then allowed the smoke to seep from his nostrils, as if there were a lazy fire burning within.

"I met your wife on the mountain the day before she died. Did you know that?"

"She told me."

"I'd agreed to help her write her honeymoon article, figuring the publicity might help put this place on the map. But do you know what she wanted to see? Not the hotel, but the old hollowed out eavesdropping stations up on the ridge. Doesn't that strike you as strange? For a honeymoon article?"

"Claire moved in mysterious ways."

"Yes, I suppose so. I knew she was here on her honeymoon, so I naturally asked where her new husband was." He chuckled. "Can you imagine my surprise when I found out she'd married the one and only Jake Boxer, ex-host of *Bullseye*?" He leaned forward, a genuine smile on his face. "Oh, I'm a huge fan. I watched your show religiously. Naturally, I wanted to meet you, but Claire said maybe later, that you were up in the room taking a nap. She wanted to take me to dinner and chat one-on-one about the hotel. Did she tell you about that, Jake? That we dined together?"

"No," Jake said breathlessly.

"*Hmm.* I suspected as much. You weren't napping either, were you? I mean a man like you? A man who has America in his crosshairs? You don't have *time* to nap." The Kidd leaned back, considering Jake. "I've been dying to ask you something. Season 1 of *Bullseye* was all hard news, but by the end of Season 6, you were spewing nothing but conspiracy after conspiracy. Which got you the better ratings?"

"If you're implying I'm inventing some sort of a conspiracy here—"

"You've met the sheriff," he interrupted. "You've seen with your own eyes that we're conducting a *thorough* investigation." He hooked a thumb toward the window where Jake could just make out the work lights near the top of the lift. "How would you even get a whiff of conspiracy?"

"I don't."

"Then why in the hell are you still here?"

"My wife came to Blind River to write an article. I'm going to finish it."

"The honeymoon article?"

"That's right." Jake grabbed the cold push ring and rolled his chair toward the table, toward that drink. "Listen, it's my turn to clear the air. I know you sent Summer up here to check on me—that Dr. Wallace wanted to be sure I was okay—but I didn't open the door. The truth is that Summer's a beautiful woman, and…with it being so close to Claire's death…I just couldn't, well…"

"Couldn't what?"

Jake shrugged. "Celebrity has its perks. Especially for an unmarried man."

The Kidd winced. His face darkened. "Somehow I don't think you're her type."

"Too tall?"

"Too crippled."

"Then who is her type? You?"

The cold air grew thick between them. The Kidd's smile widened to the point of being grotesque.

"Quit beating around the bush, Mr. Boxer. If you have something to say, say it."

"Forgive me. Sometimes I imply too much—comes with being an investigative journalist."

"*Ex*-journalist." The Kidd stabbed his cigarette out on the table, as if putting the period on the conversation. "You strike me as a naturally suspicious man. No longer a journalist, but maybe you still have the head for it. Well, if you're suspicious of me, let me open my heart to you. I wouldn't *dream* of trying to slip something past the all-powerful Jake Boxer, the man who spent one of the most embarrassing months ever to be broadcast on national TV." He refilled his glass and chuckled. "I'll never forget that line: *Our* Planet. Earth!"

The Kidd was imitating the most widely mocked portion of Jake's very public meltdown, a moment that had been replayed over and over again on YouTube.

Even Jake had to admit he'd sounded overly dramatic.

The Kidd went on, saying, "One would think you would've learned your lesson by now, that you really shouldn't go around inventing stories where none exist. It destroys careers, as you very well know, and in your wife's case, it ended her life."

"In my defense, I never knew honeymoon articles could be so dangerous."

"Mr. Boxer, you and I both know why she was really here." The Kidd took a drink. Raised a finger. "You're sneaking around for no reason. Yes, the auction is invite only, but after the accident, we had several cancellations. There's plenty of room if you'd like to attend, just remember it's Alaskan formal."

"Attend?"

The grotesque smile returned. "That's what your wife was really here to write about—the fact that I'm selling Ana's painting, right?"

Jake opened his mouth to respond, but then he closed it.

His gaze drifted to Ana's photograph.

It was crooked again.

"Al tell you his little ghost story?" the Kidd asked, noticing Jake's eye-line. "About how Ana's ghost slowly cocks the photograph?"

The Kidd stood, removed the photograph from its hook. And then, without warning, smashed it against the table, shattering glass and splintering the walnut frame. A thin piece of copper in the debris caught Jake's eye.

The frame *had* been weighted.

"Ghost stories sell, Mr. Boxer. Not quite as well as the conspiracy shit you peddled on *Bullseye*, but beggars can't be choosers. Ana didn't die here. She *defected* through here."

"How can you be so sure?"

"I looked into it." He held up the manila envelope he'd brought along, opened it, and pulled out a newspaper clipping. "My people found this in an old issue of the *Boise Gazette*."

He handed the clipping to Jake. It was an obituary for a woman named Phyllis Rose. It didn't say how she'd died, but it listed her age as thirty-seven, and featured a black-and-white photograph of a woman who looked exactly like an older Ana Turov.

"Phyllis Rose," the Kidd said with no small hint of gaiety. "Sounds like the G-men who helped her defect also let her pick her own name, right?" He reached into his pocket and pulled out a red rubber ball, like one a kid might buy from a novelty machine. He bounced it against the tabletop as he spoke.

Thump-thump-thump.

"Before Ana defected, she stashed her masterpiece in a basement wall of the hotel. I don't know why—maybe she planned to come back for it—

but she didn't. I found it ten years ago when we started renovating the hotel. It took that long to prove that Ana Turov really was Phyllis Rose, a woman who never married and never had children. A woman who has no relatives or trust that dictates what should happen to her painting." He reached into the envelope again. This time he pulled out a piece of paper embossed with Alaska's state seal. "It's a painting that the state of Alaska has deemed legally mine to keep, *or sell*, as the owner of the hotel in which it was discovered."

Jake studied the decree. It certainly appeared authentic.

"It's mine. But tomorrow, after the auction, someone else will own Ana's painting, legally and without lien." He tucked the certificate and obituary back into the envelope, then stood. But he didn't leave. Instead, he stared down at Jake and bounced his silly ball a couple more times. "My only regret is that your wife died for nothing. This is a fifty-year-old story. Old news, no—*ancient* news. Nobody but art enthusiasts and history buffs even care. Tell me something: Do you think she would've been up on that ski lift interrogating the director of the visitor center if she knew I legally owned the painting? What a shame."

The Kidd grabbed his bottle and moved toward the door, leaving Jake alone to ponder the meaninglessness of Claire's death.

"You know," he said, pausing at the door. "Fans often say they're disappointed after meeting their favorite celebrity, that no one can live up to the idea they have of them in their heads. I think they're onto something."

The door closed softly behind him.

TWENTY-FIVE

_____

Lift Collapse Ruled an Accident

11/05/16. A federal investigation into the November 3 chairlift disaster in Blind River Valley was declared an accident late last night. After a faulty bolt in the lift's guide track snapped, several chairs fell injuring eleven and killing two. The deceased were Sean Farris, the director of Blind River's visitor center, and Claire O'Donnell, columnist for the *American Post*. When the tragedy struck, Mrs. O'Donnell had been honeymooning with her husband Jake Boxer, of the once-popular news show, *Bullseye*. Mr. Boxer escaped with moderate injuries and is expected to make a full recovery.

"IT'S HOGWASH, Mr. Boxer."

Jake, once again lying in bed, lowered his issue of the *Anchorage Times*.

Al, who'd just delivered the newspaper and was still in the room, was looking slightly embarrassed, as if he'd written the article himself.

Jake shifted—a futile attempt to get comfortable. It had been six hours since his last oxy, and the crack in his back was once again spewing lava.

"And why, exactly, do you think it's hogwash?"

A familiar look of dread crossed Al's face. "Things happen on this mountain, Mr. Boxer—things that can't be explained." His oh-so-serious gaze drifted to the mountain, which was only then brightening in the late morning sun. "They look like accidents, but they're decidedly *not*—"

"Your boss rigged Ana's picture frame," Jake interrupted.

Al's brow furrowed. "Mr. Boxer, I know you're a journalist, and that it's your job to explain the unexplainable."

"Al, look on the table."

After the Kidd had taken his leave, Jake had placed the thin strip of copper, used to weight the frame, next to its splintered walnut remains. Al studied it, then picked it out from the debris.

Jake spoke softly. "There was only one reason he told everyone that Ana Turov was murdered here: a good ghost story sells. He put the copper in the frames to add a little color."

"No...no. Ana died here."

"Did you ever see her body?"

"She *died*," Al said, fuming. "Her ghost cocks her pictures."

"She changed her name to Phyllis Rose. She died in Boise, Idaho, in 1982. I saw her obituary. Christopher Kidd showed it to me."

Al shook his head. "Mr. Kidd would've told me if she'd defected."

"You sell the story better if you believe it, and as head concierge, you're the one interacting with the guests."

"It *can't* be true," Al said, his voice cracking. "If she didn't die here...*if she didn't*..." He took a deep breath. "It means she...she left me."

And like that, Al broke down on the kitchen table like an old Model T—nuts and bolts skittering all over the place. It took Jake by surprise, and it was then that he realized there was more than just Claire's story at stake. There was also a lonely old man who'd been living with the romantic notion that the woman he'd loved had died in this place, that her restless spirit still wandered these halls, and that by taking care of the hotel, he'd been taking care of her.

"Don't be so hard on yourself," Jake said, doing his best to comfort the man. "Your girlfriend was caught between two superpowers. The Soviets were using her for her talent, and the Americans were using her for a cheap political win. She was under tremendous pressure, Al. She had no good choice."

Jake's words fell on deaf ears. Al was no longer there. He was in nineteen seventy-three, watching a timid artist throw paint on a canvas in the corner of the room.

Jake was about to tell Al that the Kidd had rediscovered her masterpiece and was planning to hock it at the auction, but before he could, Al found his feet and stumbled for the door, blathering, "Nine years. If she didn't die until nineteen eighty-two, I could've been with her for another nine years."

And then he was gone.

It took a while for Jake to remember exactly why he'd asked Al to his room in the first place—and then he saw the basket of chips and cookies on his bed. "Breakfast." He pulled the blister pack of oxy from the wheelchair's saddlebag and sighed longingly—one pill left. The directions on the back read, *Take with food.* He pushed the pill through the foil, popped it into his mouth, and swallowed, then opened a bag of Doritos and ate.

Ten minutes later, the volcano in his back cooled. Relaxed, he sank back into his bed, his eyelids sagging to half-mast. He slept only sparingly after the Kidd left his room the night before, and he hadn't dreamed at all. The sand…the beach…the yawning ocean with the mouthful of granite—none of it mattered anymore. Claire had been chasing a nonstory. Worse than that, she'd *died* for a nonstory, a fact that made Jake viscerally ill.

What had Al said?

We'd all like to explain away a tragedy, but sometimes you can't.

After all those years, Claire had sacrificed herself in a vain attempt to explain what had happened to Brody, and what had Jake done? He'd given Brody's engagement diamond, a jewel Claire had died wearing, to a sleigh driver for a couple of mining surveys. What a deplorable act. Who *cared* if she loved Brody more than him? As if it mattered anymore. And at the very least, didn't he have a duty to bury her with Brody's diamond? At the moment he had about as much use for those mining surveys as he did for Blind River.

I've got about six hours before the last oxy wears off, Jake thought, and Providence Alaska in Anchorage is what, five-and-a-half, maybe six hours south? So, if I move quickly, I could get Brody's necklace back and then get over to...what's the name of that physical therapist? Dr. Fryer?...before my spine starts spewing lava again.

Rolling to the bedside table, Jake pulled Lancaster's card from his wallet and dialed the sleigh driver's number. The phone rang, but nobody picked up, and for just a second, Jake was dialing Claire again, getting her voicemail, calling her back, getting her voicemail, calling her—

Light split his skull. He blinked hard, swallowed back a bit of bile, and told himself that his tick, that the headaches, would ebb just as soon as he left this nightmare. Still, he couldn't keep a parasitic question from burrowing into his brain—would Claire, the smartest person he'd ever known, really have behaved the way she had if she'd been chasing a nonstory?

Then...

"Hi-Ho! There's gold in dem hills and there's only one way to get it: Blind River's Sleigh of Good Fortune. Leave a message and I'll show you the money."

The voicemail beeped. "Pete, it's Jake Boxer. Listen, forget about mineral surveys. I don't need them, but I *do* need that necklace back. I'll still pay you—just give me your address, and I'll write a check as soon as I'm home. Oh, and I'm leaving today, hopefully in a few hours. So call me back, I'm in the Honeymoon Suite."

He hung up and rubbed his temples. Now that Jake had made up his mind to leave again, the urge to get the hell outta Blind River was overpowering. It was all he could do to keep from calling Dr. Wallace and beg for an immediate lift back to Anchorage. But he knew if he left without Brody's diamond, he would never see it again.

An hour passed, and Lancaster still hadn't called back. Jake wasted the time by slowly walking to the bathroom, where he painstakingly gathered the notes he'd hidden the night before. If what the Kidd had told him was true, that he could legally auction Ana's masterpiece, the notes were worthless, but he still didn't want anyone else to find them. He preferred Claire's good name not be sullied by revealing her illegal eavesdropping operation.

After carefully packing the notes into his suitcase, he called Lancaster again, got his voicemail again, and left another message. Jake decided to give it another ten minutes. Ambling over to the coffeemaker, he poured in a couple of cups of water, spooned some coffee into the filter, and hit Brew. As the pot gurgled, his gaze drifted to the mountain outside of the picture window.

Ningakpok Iggik.

The angry mountain.

Bathed in gray light, he could make out men in snowsuits dismantling the work lights they'd erected on top of White Alice's hollowed out buildings. Elsewhere he saw other employees collecting the orange flags that had been used to demarcate the ski runs. Near the mountain's base, several snowmobiles chugged toward the Hotel Ascent, towing what looked like supplies that had been used at the lift stations, probably packing everything up for the long winter. Tomorrow, Blind River would be closed. From his perch in the Honeymoon Suite, Jake also had a good view of Main Street, where things were also shutting down. Most of the storefronts sported plywood on their windows already. Jake didn't care about the storefronts, of course—he was looking for Lancaster's Sleigh of Good Fortune. Figuring this was a high dollar day (there was no shortage of guests and locals alike moving up and down Main Street), he'd assumed Lancaster hadn't called back because he was busy, but the man's sleigh was nowhere in sight.

Jake was about to give up and call Dr. Wallace when he noticed something near the railroad trestle, on the opposite side of the riverbank from the Hotel Ascent. At first he thought that it was simply a pile of dry leaves, but then slowly changed his mind—no way they were leaves, or even dry pine needles.

They were legs...*brown* legs.

The legs of a woefully skinny animal.

A woefully skinny horse.

TWENTY-SIX

He squinted at the brown shapes in the snow—God, how he would *kill* for a pair of binoculars.

Rubbing his eyes, he blinked several times and then picked out the skinny brown shapes again. This time he also made the shape of a long brown body. It was definitely an animal, and it was definitely dead. He was pretty sure wolves weren't that shade of brown, and the grizzlies were all denning—so it had to be one of the Clydesdales. Right? Lancaster had owned two horses, of course. If he *had* found one of them, the other was likely nearby.

He spent the next thirty minutes studying the twist of the riverbank and determined that what he'd first mistaken for a fallen tree, just a few feet from those brown legs, was the second horse. They'd died together. That meant the sleigh was most likely inside a thatch of nearby fir.

Was Peter Lancaster's body still on the sleigh? Perched like a garish scarecrow, stiff and waiting for the wolves to get him?

If someone was trying to hide the bodies, they couldn't have picked a better spot. That particular twist of river was far from Main Street. The animals would only be visible from the slopes—the *empty* slopes—and the Honeymoon Suite, of course.

Jake looked at the upper turnstile at the top of the lift, and the long scar of granite where Claire had died. And like that, he felt the wind sting his chapped face. The support bar freeze the naked grip of his right hand. The haul rope jerk. His guts were suddenly in his mouth. He was falling, and a woman who sounded like Claire was screaming and the darkness was spinning like he was in zero G—

Lancaster, Jake. Think about the sleigh driver. Not about me.

Right.

Claire was always right.

Jake called Lancaster's phone again, hoping against hope that he'd see the man stumble out from the thatch of fir, his feet leaving tracks in the pine duff as he made his way to the riverbank in search of a better signal. He hoped against hope that the would-be miner he'd paid to steal an old mineral survey was still alive. But Lancaster didn't answer.

Jake squeezed his eyes shut and swallowed. In truth, there was no way to know if the driver was dead or alive. It was infuriating. All he wanted was a straight answer. He was exhausted; Claire was still gone; and God-oh-God, he'd been so *relieved* to be leaving that mountain, but now...

How could he go?

He needed to think. He needed to *pace*.

Back in his *Bullseye* days, Jake had burned up miles of carpet breaking stories; pacing really got his blood pumping. So, using the table for support, he eased himself out of his chair and slowly strolled the Honeymoon Suite, his thoughts a tempest of pointed questions.

Why had the horses died on the riverbank directly opposite the visitor center? Had they died *after* Lancaster had stolen the mineral surveys? Or before? Had the Clydesdales been murdered? Or had the starving horses, pushed beyond exhaustion, finally given Lancaster one last panicked ride before death? Or even more likely, had someone *murdered* Lancaster and attempted to hide him, and the horses, out of sight?

In his mind's eye, he watched Lancaster break into the visitor center, photocopy those surveys, then hurry through curtains of snow toward the hotel. So what had happened next? Had he hurried upstairs for the Honeymoon Suite? Had he raced to give Jake his spoils?

No. Of course he hadn't.

Jake didn't *have* the mining survey. Now think, goddammit. What *might* have happened? Maybe he *did* try to get to Jake's room, but he'd been stopped somewhere along the way.

By Sheriff Wilson Grout?

That didn't sit right. If Wilson had caught him, Lancaster would be in jail right now, not dead beneath the firs. Had he'd been stopped by a customer? By someone wanting a sleigh ride back to town?

Yes. That made more sense. This mystery person, this *murderer*, who'd probably knocked down the chairlift as well, had wanted to stop Jake from getting that mining survey, to stop him from getting inside of that mountain.

So, Lancaster and this murderous fare had loaded themselves into the sleigh for what turned out to be a final ride. Someone would've heard a gunshot…slitting Lancaster's throat would've been a more likely way to dispose of him. Maybe on the bridge between the Hotel Ascent and downtown? Maybe, after killing him, the murderer had taken Lancaster's ridiculous stovetop hat and hopped into the driver's seat, fooling any passersby, while the real Lancaster bled out in the bottom of the sleigh? *Maybe* the killer drove the horses into the thatch of fir to conceal the crime. And then slit the horses' throats as well?

Okay, and after that?

The killer would've taken the photocopied mineral surveys from Lancaster's pocket and burned them. Or dropped them into the river. Or, for all he knew, used them for toilet paper.

Jake looked out the window toward the visitor center. It was in plain view of the hotel, meaning anyone could've seen Lancaster break in.

Christopher Kidd.

That Russian couple.

Plastic Mel.

Nick Gold.

Or the mysterious showering guest.

Any one of them could've killed Pete Lancaster.

Any one of them could've killed Claire.

Jake thought about calling the sheriff, but he only had twenty-four hours before Blind River closed for the winter. If the police got involved, they'd take up every last second, precious time he needed to uncover Claire's story…assuming there was a story to uncover, of course.

Whether he liked it or not, Jake was now facing an inescapable truth—he wasn't leaving Blind River.

Not yet.

Weary, Jake eased his stiff body back into his wheelchair. He heard a crinkle of paper. Oh yeah, the notes he'd stashed beneath his ass the night before. Pulling a few pages out, a written summary of what he'd heard from all five rooms that night caught his eye. He had a hard time reading his own messy scrawl—he'd been writing fast—but, eventually, he muddled through it: *Guests prepping for auction. Kidd too. Probably why Claire was here.*

Talk about inescapable truths.

TWENTY-SEVEN

THREE SHORT HOURS LATER, Jake Boxer, his back brace secure around his waist, dressed in as close to "Alaskan formal" as he could manage (tennis shoes, new blue jeans, and a plaid flannel that Claire had packed for him at the last minute), left the Honeymoon Suite for the first time in days.

As the door opened, he found himself hoping that he was opening the front door of the brownstone he'd shared with Claire back in D.C. That he'd see her working on her laptop at the kitchen table with her coffee and her English muffin and *All Things Considered* droning on from somewhere in the living room. That she'd look up at him and fix him with the same look she always wore when he stumbled in after a bender. "Again?"

"I wasn't drinking," he'd explain. "I got lost in this shithole of an Alaskan town and you were dead and I was trying to catch the guys who did it and Claire…" He'd pause here for dramatic effect because this next part was so very important. "Claire, I never want you to leave the Travel section. Who cares if its not hard news? Never. Ever. Leave it."

But then he saw the red-and-white chevrons on the Hotel Ascent's thick carpet and the long hallway that ended in an elevator that would take him down to the busy lobby and maybe, if he was lucky, to the story that Claire, Sean Farris, and likely Peter Lancaster, had died for.

He peered over the banister. The lobby was packed, though the guests were sprawled about haphazardly, as if an earthquake had shaken them out of their rooms. Jake studied the bald spots, the dyed hair, the cowboy hats, of course. He thought about how he'd been listening to five of what must have been two hundred people.

How had Claire chosen them? Had they been marks? Or had she simply bugged the rooms she knew she could talk her way into? Speaking of which, how, exactly, *had* she talked her way in?

Claire was too deliberate to improvise. She'd chosen her five victims. Made a study of them. Hell, she probably knew how she was going talk her way into their rooms before they'd even arrived in Blind River.

So why them? Why the five?

Somehow, he would have to find out.

Jake leaned heavily on the wood banister, then slowly made his way to the elevator. He'd left his wheelchair behind, wanting to draw as little attention to himself as possible during the auction, but when he was halfway to the elevator, his back began throbbing. He cursed his own stupidity.

So Lancaster's horses were dead—who gave a shit? He shouldn't have ever left his room. He should've had Dr. Wallace send the van to pick him up and take him to Anchorage. Now, not only was he *not* with Claire, he was out of oxy. It was enough to send him scurrying back to his room with his tail between his legs. He was about to turn when he felt the unmistakable heat of someone else's gaze upon him.

Looking down, he caught the flash of a face, turning away. The man had averted his gaze, but he couldn't hide his fedora, nor could he hide a dry, persistent cough that wracked his thin frame.

"Redondo Beach"—*Plastic Mel.*

Jake took him in, reacquainting himself with the man's slight profile and the strangely tight skin stretching across his cheekbones. Just seeing the man was rejuvenating.

So long as Claire's marks were still here, Claire was here too.

By the time the elevator reached the lobby, the guests were moving en masse toward one of the few rooms Jake had yet to explore, the hotel's ballroom. The room's ornately carved double doors had always been closed when Jake had passed—the room was only open for dinner—but they were open now. Standing at the mouth of the elevator, Jake caught his first glimpse inside.

The crowd obscured it, but he could still discern a motif of darkly stained wood. A waitstaff in black tie distributed champagne flutes and caviar on silver platters. But it was the centerpiece of the room that drew his eye, a collage of glass covering the entire far wall. The installation gave the room its name—the Glass Hall.

Summer stood at the hostess station just outside the ballroom, checking in guests and wearing a smile so phony that it might as well have been a mask. Hoping not to draw unwanted attention, Jake waited until the crowd had entered the Glass Hall before leaving the recess of the elevator's alcove, shuffling over just as Summer was closing the large double doors.

"Mr. Boxer," she said as he approached, a wan smile on her pretty face. "Glad you could make it. Have you downloaded the app?"

"The app?"

"Yes…to bid?"

She handed him a pamphlet with instructions. Apparently, the Kidd had developed the app specifically for the auction.

"First I've seen of it."

"Huh. Everyone going to the auction should've received one of these in their rooms."

"Yeah, well I didn't get my invite until very late last night." Jake extended an elbow. "Help me to the door?"

She considered him for a moment, then slipped her thin arm through his and helped him walk the final few feet to the Glass Hall. A petite receptionist helping a hefty man a full foot taller was comical but necessary. Not because of his back (though it helped), but because Jake didn't want anyone else to hear what he was about to say.

"You know you don't have to come back next season."

He felt her blue eyes on him, and for one hot moment, this whole ordeal—his broken back, the death of his beautiful bride—would be worthwhile, so long as this young woman escaped Blind River.

So long as Jake could save her from that rapist Christopher Kidd.

"But I like it here," Summer said quietly, and with no small measure of put-upon calm. "It pays better than the other resorts, and I get to ski whenever I want."

"I *heard* what happened last night. Easy money or not, you should decide what you really want out of your life, and I doubt very much that it's Christopher Kidd. I understand you're scared, but he can't hurt you if you're not in Blind River. At the very least stay away from him tonight. I imagine he'll be drinking again."

"How do you know about what happened last night?"

"It doesn't matter. What matters is that you leave, and that you never come back."

Several hotel employees passed behind them. Both Jake and Summer straightened and did their best to behave naturally.

"I'll see about that," she said, struggling to get out her next words. "Glad you're back on your feet again, Mr. Boxer."

Summer unhitched herself from his arm and opened the ballroom's doors. Jake's farewell to her was lost in an uptick of applause. Inside, the guests were on their feet, clapping and whooping as Christopher Kidd rang in the year's annual Blind River auction.

Not that Jake was paying attention. How could he in the presence of such an astounding glass installation? He had a clear view of it now, and what an amazing view it was.

The ballroom's entire eastern wall was a pastiche of glass panels, from floor to ceiling. The panes were cut in differing sizes and shapes. There were no perfect circles, no perfect rectangles, but rather curves, like waves, and corners cut in both acute and obtuse angles, some pointed, others rounded. There must have been more than thirty panes of glass in all, held together by an iron web that had been meticulously crafted to hold each individual pane in place. And then, of course, there was the view. There was the mountain. That impressive sight never got old.

"Thank you...thank you! Thank you all so very much."

The Kidd's voice was coming from the front of the ballroom. The crowd was still up on its feet, still clapping, but Jake was taller than most and could easily see the handsome son of a bitch—the same man he'd overheard calling Claire a cunt—smiling broadly and bouncing his little red rubber ball at a dais set up in the front of the room.

As a journalist, Jake had never believed in villains—his worldview was too nuanced for that—but he certainly believed in them now.

"Please," the Kidd said. "My guests...*friends*...have a seat and let's begin."

The crowd sat. Jake, however, had been late to the party, and he didn't know where he was supposed to sit. There were maybe thirty circular tables staggered throughout the ballroom with what looked like ten spots per table. There were name cards at each seat and more than a few empty chairs. One was meant for him, he was sure, but he didn't want to draw attention to himself by staggering around from seat to seat. A man of his size, and hobbling, got noticed.

And he wanted to keep a low profile.

Instead, he made his way to a small bar near the kitchen where he'd seen a couple of empty stools.

The Kidd kept doing his thing. "Now I'm very conscious of the fact that Blind River wouldn't be here without your annual support, and as you all know, I consider this fundraiser the highlight of the year. For the past decade, we've gathered in this room to bid on the best of what Alaska can offer. This year, like the last, we'll be conducting the bidding by phone. If you haven't downloaded our app, please do so now. You should all be able to connect to the hotel's wireless for the download."

The crowd pulled their phones from their pockets, almost in unison. The ones who'd yet to download the app studied their brochures, the same brochure Summer had handed to Jake on his way in. Jake had no intention of bidding, but he still pulled Claire's phone from his pocket, hoping to fit in. At that moment, he was struck by a sudden thought.

Whoever knocked down that ski lift was right here in this room.

He studied the sea of suspects, trying to identify Claire's marks.

"And please, don't forget to enter your bank account information. The program automatically verifies your funds. Once we get started, your screen will display the items up for auction, as well as the current high bid for each."

"What are you having, sir?"

It was the bartender, a young bearded guy (did any man in Alaska *not* have a beard?). Jake ordered a beer, even though his doctor had expressly forbidden him to drink on the oxy…but *I'm not on oxy anymore*, he reminded himself. *I'm out.*

It had been nearly twelve hours since his last pill, and his skin was beginning to itch.

"All we have is IPA on tap. That okay?"

"Fine," Jake said, and then did a double take. Not because of the IPA, but because of the woman who was sitting just a few stools down. It was the woman who'd angrily confronted Christopher Kidd at the Café Beaujolais—the Ana Turov look-alike. She was perched on her stool, her thin back to Jake, her dark and narrow eyes fixed on the Kidd.

"Eight dollars."

Jake looked back to the bartender, then to the pint sitting before him.

"Put it on my room," he said loudly, or at least loud enough for the Ana Turov look-alike to hear. "Jake Boxer. Honeymoon Suite."

The woman cocked her head…and gave herself away.

She knew who he was.

Yes, it was possible she recognized him from *Bullseye*, but it was far more likely that she knew him through Claire. Claire, who'd somehow talked her way into this woman's room and planted a listening bug. Jake flashed on Claire's naked freckled body twisted up in this dark-eyed woman's sheets.

Stop, he told himself. *It doesn't matter. What* does *matter is that you're sitting near the guest Claire tagged as "Kimberly" on Patti Smith's album. It's the mysterious showering guest, and if your hunch is right, the same woman you heard hack into Nick Gold's laptop.*

She must have felt his gaze on her back because she looked back at him suddenly. Jake raised his beer in toast, saying, "To Ana Turov." She didn't reciprocate. Instead, she grabbed her Campari, slid off her barstool, and hurried away, most likely to her seat amongst the sea of tables.

"Now, of course, we're celebrating tonight in the shadow of a tragic accident. Two people lost their lives. Scores more were injured. As the owner of the Ascent, I will tell you that this has been the worst five days of my life, but I am humbled and grateful that the husband of one of the deceased is here with us tonight."

Jake's gaze flew back to the Kidd. The man was staring at him. Even worse, the rest of the crowd was staring at him too.

What was he doing?

"Some of you may know him as the host of *Bullseye*, one of the best hard news shows ever to have graced TV. He and his wife, the esteemed *American Post* reporter Claire O'Donnell, were here on their honeymoon when she was taken from him. Mr. Boxer, please, allow me to personally extend the condolences of the entire town. I am so sorry for your loss."

And like that, Jake had been exposed. Any shred of anonymity, gone. Everyone inside the Glass Hall knew his face and that meant they knew *not* to talk to him—of if they did talk, to lie. Jake reluctantly waved to the crowd, then looked back at the Kidd, who was still staring at him. Was that a smirk on his chiseled mug?

Yes. It most definitely was.

"Now," the Kidd said, turning back to the crowd, "about tonight. Many of you have heard the story of Ana Turov, the Soviet artist who traveled thousands of miles to paint our mountain way back in 1973, a time when we were but a nudge away from nuclear war with the Soviet Union. Many of you know that Ana disappeared. Some say she defected. Others say she was murdered. But whatever happened, there is one aspect of the story that has never been disputed—her last painting, her *masterpiece*, disappeared with her." The Kidd raised a finger. Shook it. "Well, we now know that's not true. While remodeling the hotel, I rediscovered this lost masterpiece. I've had the pleasure of secretly admiring it for a decade, but now one of you will have that chance, not just to view the painting, but to own it."

With that, he gestured to a long display table sitting before the ball-room's wall of glass. Every head turned that way. Not that they could see anything. A silk screen covered each item up for auction. One of them, the item dead center, was obscured by a four-foot-tall screen, just big enough to hide a painting.

"Now Ana Turov disappeared before properly naming the painting, so I took the liberty of doing so myself." The Kidd dramatically walked through the sea of tables toward the item. On reaching it, he took a hold of the screen. The crowd collectively inhaled as he whipped it away saying, "Ladies and gentlemen, I give you, *Red Fury*."

TWENTY-EIGHT

ANA'S PAINTING WAS SMALL, maybe two feet by three feet, but it was truly a masterpiece—just as the Kidd had proclaimed moments earlier.

A stunning experiment in light, it felt both defined and impressionistic. She'd used dabs rather than brushstrokes, but by utilizing the smallest of brush-points, Ana Turov's rendering of the mountain still held a crisp, stark shape. She'd captured the mountain at a bloody dusk, the sun having just set beneath the horizon. The snow covering the vertical northern face was tinged with a dark red. And while she'd dabbed her way through much of the painting, she'd used bold and angry strokes to paint the vertical granite spines that encircled *Ningakpok Iggik's* summit. Like knives slitting through the painting's canvas. Knives that had murdered Jake's poor Claire.

Sweat dampened Jake's forehead. In his mind's eye, he saw the flash of light in the sky—one of the drones, looking down at Blind River. Looking at the painting?

Breathing hard, he took in the two hundred faces around him. They were distorted and smiling, obese and sniveling—and then it struck him—they were *all* here for the painting—they were all here to *murder his Claire.*

Calm down. I only bugged five of them, Jake. Five.

And why? Why did you bug them? Goddammit Claire, give me *some-thing*—

Jake had abandoned his bar stool shortly after the Kidd revealed the painting. The back of a wooden chair he was now using as a support snapped in his grip. Jake moaned as he fell. Thank God there were several men right there to catch him. They helped him straighten, asked if he was okay, and after Jake assured him that yes, he'd be fine, they returned to their business of eyeballing *Red Fury*. Jake, panting, looked beyond the painting to the Glass Hall's collage of windows. To the mountain. For a moment, Jake couldn't tell the difference between the real thing and Ana's interpretation. She'd somehow captured it exactly as he was seeing it now: dangerous, fore-boding, and entirely indifferent to his plight.

Claire's phone buzzed. He'd downloaded the auction app, and beneath the web of cracks on the display, he saw an icon for each item up for sale. Currently, each item showed $0.00 as the high bid. There was also a two-hour countdown at the top of the screen. The time was flashing—the rea-son for the buzz—and, as he watched, it began counting down from two hours.

The auction was afoot.

Jake looked back at the app's icons. Ana's painting—the big prize—was the first icon in the upper-left-hand corner of the screen, but there were several other hot-ticket items right next to it, including an ivory statue, a gold compass, and a depiction of the hollowed-out concrete shelters still lining White Alice. As Jake watched—just a few seconds into the auction—the first anonymous bid popped up. Surprisingly, it wasn't for *Red Fury*. It was a fifty-dollar bid for the ivory statue. Someone immediately upped the bid to one hundred dollars.

Jake looked at the crowd. Who was bidding? Half the room was staring at their cell phones—it could've been anyone.

At the front of the ballroom, the Kidd was introducing a stodgy, gray-haired woman with heavy rimmed glasses. She was his art expert, hired on to validate the painting's authenticity and ownership. She was currently dis-playing the certificate the Kidd had shown to Jake the night before.

"Ana had been known as a 'promising student.' Her earlier work had been heralded in Soviet circles, particularly her skill at Socialist Realism. This was the style that aimed to depict Stalin's ideals, the struggle and victory of the working class, in a valiant light. *Red Fury* is a radical departure from that theme. Though it's a landscape, her contemporaries—had they ever seen it—would've surely labeled it rebel art, if only due to its lack of nationalism."

"*Red Fury*? Sounds like a…like a comic book character—"

The words were cut short by a wracking cough.

Plastic Mel.

"Redondo Beach."

Turning, Jake found himself face-to-face with one of the guests he'd been eavesdropping on for the past forty-eight hours.

And the old man knew.

Jake could see it in his milky white eyes.

He'd found Claire's bug and he was here to confront him, to kill him—

Stop it, Jake. He doesn't know anything. I bugged this guy for a reason. Please, try to keep it together until you find out why.

Jake, who was standing near one of the circular tables, considered the odd man. His face had been nipped and tucked by a plastic surgeon until it had taken the shape of an expressionless mask. The skin was stretched taught across his fine cheekbones, and paper-thin. He had dyed the few wisps of eyebrow that still remained black. Along with the fedora, it was an unsettling combination, as if he'd just stepped out of a Stanley Kubrick film.

"I don't believe we've met," Jake said. "Jake Boxer."

"Mel Perkins." He shoved a bony hand into Jake's. "You're the *Bullseye* fellow. Just wanted to offer my condolences. Your wife…." *cough-cough…*"on your…" *cough…*"on your honeymo—"

Cough—cough—cough.

"Yeah, it's tragic," Jake muttered.

The old man cleared his throat and shook his head. "The world can be…a real bitch, can't it?"

Jake shrugged, then looked at *Red Fury*. "Are you here for the painting?"

"That *thing*?" He said it as if they were looking at road kill. "Might throw a few dollars at it. But if you want a real piece of Alaskan art, I'd go for that." Mel pointed to the bone white ivory statue on display next to *Red Fury*. "The *Diomede Ivory*," he said with a whistle, "carved out of a walrus tusk. Probably took some poor Inuit a year to make."

The tusk was about two feet long and more-or-less straight. It had been carved to depict the choppy waters of the open sea. On top of the water were two intricate islands; the island on the right was quite large with tall cliffs around its perimeter. The second island—the one on the left—also had cliffs, but was much smaller.

"You know the Diomedes?" Mel asked.

Jake knew a little. "They sit right in the middle of the Bering Straight. International dateline goes through 'em, right?"

"That's right." He pointed to the larger of the two islands. "The big one there is Russian, the smaller one's American. Back in the Cold War, we called the two-mile stretch between them the Ice Curtain." Mel fell silent, then leaned toward Jake, his thin face glowing, his cloudy eyes wide. "Can you imagine what those two islands were like during the Cold War? KGB on one side, CIA on the other, staring at each other with binoculars, rifles at the ready, each side waiting for a defector or a spy to sneak over? Kennedy, Johnson, Nixon, all of 'em saw those two islands as the most likely place to spark a war—either by spy or by submarine or some hot-headed soldier who woke up one morning and decided he wanted to paddle over and kill himself a commie. What those presidents *didn't* know...and *had* they known they would've squashed the program immediately for political reasons... was that two men—two *private* citizens—one an American, one a Soviet— set up a direct line between the two islands. So when tensions rose, if one side suspected the other of some goddamn tomfoolery, the soldiers could at least call each other first. For a while, those two islands were the only place on earth where you could make a direct phone call from America to the Soviet Union. *Communication...*" Mel stressed, putting his skeletal face in Jake's, stifling a cough. "*Communication* is the only thing that keeps us from all-out war."

"Who were they?" Jake asked.

"Who were who?"

"The two men, the private citizens, who set up the phone line between the islands?"

Mel's face darkened. "What the hell does it matter?"

"They must have had quite a bit of sway to go around the president. How did they even put a phone line between two islands in the 1960s? Must have cost a fortune."

"So what if it did?"

The man fell into yet another coughing fit. Jake spied a glass of water on a nearby table, handed it to him. Mel drank thankfully. Jake noticed flecks of blood on his lips.

"I'm sure you know…" Mel tried again. "That the rich play by their own rules."

"What I *know* is that you met with my wife shortly before she died."

He cocked a nearly hairless eyebrow. "And what brought you to that conclusion?"

Because she bugged your room, Jake thought, and that means you *must* have invited her in.

"She told me," Jake lied. "Just before she got onto that lift. I didn't think much of it at the time. But I'm sure you can understand why I'm curious now."

"She told you before you two got on the lift?"

"That's right."

Plastic Mel licked his thin lips and adjusted his fedora with a swollen, arthritic hand. "I'm curious, Mr. Boxer. How is it that she died, but you survived?"

Jake offered a sad smile. "We weren't sitting together. We'd had an argument."

Mel took in the words and nodded. "Lucky you."

The comment could have been biting, but there was no sense of irony, or joy, on Mel's tautly drawn face.

"I'll consider myself lucky if I find out *why* she died, and that starts with you telling me what you two discussed."

"You don't think it was an accident?" he asked, ducking Jake's demand. "Do you?"

Mel considered the question with a wheeze, and Jake could hear his lungs rattle like an empty can of spray paint. "Have you ever heard of the book *Fifty Bricks*, the best selling novel of 1969?"

"Sure. Written by Mel…" Jake clammed up, making the connection, "…Perkins."

Mel nodded.

Fifty Bricks was a true crime novel about a Vietnam vet who returned to the States with forty-nine kills. His PTSD, an illness hardly acknowledged at the time, drove the soldier to murder his wife in order to reach a clean fifty. It was considered one of the best narratives that chronicled the country's shoddy treatment of Vietnam vets. As a journalism student at FSU, Jake had written several essays on the book. It was brilliant, and Jake found himself shocked to be engaged in a conversation with its author, all these years later.

"Half a century ago, I was part of a cultural trade meant to ease tensions between our countries," Mel explained. "Ana came here. After the success of *Fifty Bricks*, the State Department sent me to Moscow to write about the Soviets. But when Ana disappeared, the Soviets accused me of being a part of a conspiracy—"

"And they detained you," Jake said, remembering. "For what? Ten years? Nixon…Ford…Carter—they all tried to get you back. But it took Reagan, right?"

"Good ole Jelly Bean Ron," he concurred. "I spent a decade in the Lubyanka with the KGB's boot heel on my throat." He leaned in close enough for Jake to smell his halitosis. "Your wife knew who I was, Mr. Boxer. She came to my room for an autograph. I knew who she was too, and I told her in no uncertain terms to leave Blind River immediately. She didn't listen. I hope you do."

The old writer turned away, but Jake grabbed him. Spun him back around. "Who murdered my wife?"

"You're asking the wrong question." Mel's milky eyes tracked over to *Red Fury*. "Who killed Ana Turov?"

"No one. She defected."

"Sure she did, Mr. Boxer." His gaze drifted to the wall of glass behind them. "And it only took a couple hours to build that window too."

Falling into yet another coughing fit, the once-great writer shuffled back into the crowd.

Jake watched the Lubyanka survivor tap his phone, then looked down to his own, and saw the first bid hit Ana Turov's *Red Fury*.

TWENTY-NINE

THIRTY MINUTES LATER, Ana's painting stood in third place with a high bid of just over eleven thousand dollars.

The *Diomede Ivory*, on the other hand, was in first place with twenty-five thousand, while several Cold War relics mined from the White Alice installations were in second place, the leading bid a solid thirteen grand. The guests, by and large, were dismissing *Red Fury* as a moody painting by an obscure Soviet artist.

It came as little surprise to Jake, but the fact that Christopher Kidd was still chatting breezily with the guests, seemingly unconcerned, made him nervous. For Christ's sake, his big splash had just belly flopped.

Jake, of course, hadn't taken Plastic Mel's admonition too seriously. He couldn't leave the auction, not without knowing who won *Red Fury*. Besides, for all he knew, the once-famous author might have knocked over the ski lift himself.

Maybe he was just trying to throw Jake off his trail?

Not that the Kidd had made staying on anyone's trail particularly easy. The guests weren't just staring at Jake anymore; they were approaching in droves, and Jake found himself spending more time fending off sympathetic drunks than he did observing the bidders.

All according to the Kidd's plan, Jake was sure.

He did his best to keep his gaze on the Kidd's art expert, who was still working the room, buttering up guests, and showing off *Red Fury*'s "Certificate of Authenticity."

He also scanned the bidders for the rest of Claire's marks. Plastic Mel had found the bar, and despite his cough, he was chain-smoking cigarettes while staring at his cell phone, periodically pecking out a bid. The Ana Turov look-alike was standing just a few feet from *Red Fury*, where she'd been rooted ever since its big reveal. Was she plotting to steal it? The woman *was* a thief. He'd heard her break into Nick Gold's laptop the night before.

Nick Gold...

Jake spotted the flatulent attorney at a table near the front of the room.

The hefty man—who'd "wolfed-out" on seventy-two ounces of steak earlier that week—had already polished off a salad and two lobster tails. It also appeared that the attorney had been the only guest to screw up "Alaskan formal" by squeezing himself into an honest-to-God tuxedo. The attorney was conspicuously bored by the affair, and Jake read the man's aloofness as superb confidence, like he had the resources to win whatever he wanted. And if he could win, Jake had no choice but to engage him.

By the time Jake worked his way through the sea of empathetic bidders, Nick Gold was working on his third lobster tail, his fingers covered in butter sauce.

"Mind?" Jake asked, gesturing to the empty chair beside him.

"Kind of, yeah," he said, sucking down some of the white meat. "But go ahead. If I gotta be nice to anyone, I suppose it's you. "

Jake thanked him and gingerly sat, using the table for support.

"Compression fracture in the L5 vertebra," Jake explained. "As long as I don't move faster than a snail, I'm alright."

"Huh?"

"As long as I don't move—"

"Yeah, yeah, I heard you. Look, to be perfectly frank, and I know this ain't PC, but I'm more ripped up about *Bullseye* than your wife." The attorney fired off a couple of finger guns and chuckled. "God, I loved that shit.

The episode when you took on the Obamacare roll out? Classic."

"It's always nice to meet a fan."

Nick Gold scratched an itch and got butter sauce all over his face. "*Mostly* a fan. I didn't care for that drone episode. Obama's a hack, but he's gotta keep us safe, and drones are the one way he's doing it right." The attorney leaned back. "What if Cheney put a program in place to keep a couple flying over America? Who cares, so long as they're looking for bad guys."

Jake's first inclination was to counter with the fact that Obama had used drones to assassinate American citizens overseas, and Cheney's domestic drone program was a huge black eye on the average citizen's right to privacy, but he reminded himself that this conversation wasn't about a stance he'd taken on an old episode of *Bullseye*. This was about the new episode.

This was about *Claire's* episode.

Jake smiled and raised his hands in mock surrender. "You make a good point."

Nick considered Jake, then muttered, "Like I said, besides that one drone episode, I loved your show." He extended his hand, as if Jake had passed some sort of asshole test. "Nick Gold."

Jake looked to the man's buttery hand and passed him a napkin.

"Thanks," he said, wiping it down. "So. You know you got yourself a helluva payout coming to you. When the dust settles, you might be down a wife, but you won't be hurting, *financially* that is."

"Do you think a financial settlement matters to me, Mr. Gold?"

Nick's eyes went wide. "It fuckin' well better. Money won't bring your wife back, but a big settlement will make the idiots running this mountain think twice about letting it happen again."

"Sounds like you know a thing or two about lawsuits."

"I'm a businessman. Unfortunately, lawsuits go with the territory."

He was lying, of course. The man was an attorney. And he'd been passing his time in Blind River blind drunk, entertaining his guests with talk of the Carousel and a New World Order. Jake also knew that the man was there to win Ana's "commie" painting, as he'd put it.

"Did you ever meet my wife, Mr. Gold? Claire O'Donnell?"

"Can't say I had the pleasure. Haven't had a lot of time to socialize. I'm only here to wrap up a little business with the Kidd before the season ends."

"What sort of business?"

Nick Gold set down his lobster. "You're a pushy bastard, aren't you?"

"It's just a question. You don't have to answer."

"Why *wouldn't* I answer?"

"Maybe you're hiding something."

"And maybe you got paid entirely too much money to ask stupid questions."

"I believe you're referring to the legal field, not journalism. Reporters seek the truth. Lawyers seek a paycheck."

Nick Gold's face burned. "*Do* they?"

"In my experience." Jake placed both hands on the table and began to stand. "Well, thank you for your time, Mr. Gold. I'll let you get back to your lobster."

"*Sit,*" Nick said, putting a greasy hand on Jake's arm.

Jake slowly, and thankfully, sat back down.

Don't think about your back, Jake. Think about the asshole I followed off the ski lift when we first arrived in Blind River.

Nick wiped his mouth with a napkin and said, "I'm a soda pop distributor, if you have to know."

Apparently, Nick Gold wasn't comfortable talking about his real vocation, which meant that his clients were most likely less than reputable, and therefore, so was his cash.

Mossack Fonseca immediately jumped to mind, the law firm at the center of the infamous Panama Papers scandal. In what was the largest document leak in history, journalists were able to demonstrate that the law firm had possibly helped a global Who's Who list of billionaires and world leaders launder their fortunes.

Just because someone knew the law didn't mean they followed it.

"Soda pop?" Jake asked.

"Mostly specialty drinks. You can't do Coca-Cola out here. We're in Blind River, the great West. You gotta go grape pop, vanilla cream, sarsaparilla…Christ, nothin' better than a good head of foam on a cold glass of sarsaparilla."

Jake nodded to Nick's cell phone, sitting next to him on the table.

"And what's a pop distributor doing here at an auction?"

"Ah, I'm just lowballin' the cheap shit. I'm here for the lobster."

"Mr. Gold—"

"Call me Nick."

"Okay. Nick. This is a small town. I find it hard to believe that you didn't bump into my wife. Maybe a photo of her would jog your memory?"

Jake fished out Claire's cell phone, tapped the Home button, and showed off the selfie of Claire in her wedding dress.

"She's hot," Nick said, then looked back to Jake. "No wonder you're all ripped up."

"Did you see her?"

He pursed his thick lips, then adjusted his glasses. "Yeah, sure, I think so—on one of the runs."

"White Alice?"

"White Alice—yeah, that sounds about right. I was at the top of the mountain when she came up behind me. I remember now, because she was just on one ski."

"One ski?"

"Yeah. One ski. She said she'd lost the other over the side of a ravine. She also asked if I would follow her down."

Jake bristled. "And did you?"

"Hey," he said defensively. "If a hot ginger needed your help getting down a double diamond, would you do it? It took forever, though. She must've fallen a dozen times."

In his mind's eye, Jake saw Nick's greasy hands catching her. He saw him holding her upright. He saw her arms around his sloped shoulders, her body smashed up against the attorney's man-tits.

"And what happened when you two reached the bottom of the mountain?"

"Nothing. She thanked me and hobbled off on her one ski to get a replacement."

"What did you do after she left?"

"I went back up the lift to get in a proper run."

"And that was it?"

"Yeah. Well…almost. Later in the day, I realized that my wallet was missing. At first, I thought your wife stole it, but I checked with Lost and

Found and someone had discovered it up on the mountain. Whoever turned it in didn't fit your wife's description, so I must have legitimately lost it."

Or, when she was done with it, Claire had just left it in plain sight somewhere.

"I see," Jake said, feeling better.

At least Claire hadn't slept with the man to gain access to his room.

Of course I didn't. I stole his keycard and snuck into his room while he was still skiing the mountain.

And while I was turning the hotel inside out looking for you, worried sick.

"What about you guys? Either of you meet his wife?"

Jake snapped out of his reverie. Nick was speaking to the couple across the table. Jake hadn't noticed them when he sat down, but once he did, he recognized them immediately—it was the mustachioed man and the husky dark-haired woman—the awkward couple he'd seen dancing on the bar patio the night before Claire died. There were nametags next to their plates, but the tags weren't facing him. He couldn't read them, but they did bring the other nametags at the table to his attention.

There was *Nick Gold*, of course. And he could also read two others. At the moment, both nametags sat before empty seats. One was for *Mel Perkins*, and the other was for *Mila Noël*.

Mel Perkins was Plastic Mel, of course, author of *Fifty Bricks.*

Mila Noël? Could that have been the name of the Ana Turov look-alike? The woman who was currently on the other side of the Glass Hall, standing just a few feet from *Red Fury*?

Jake looked back to the couple across the table.

Could they be Ivan and Ivana? The Russian couple he'd heard instead of Patti Smith's "Gloria"?

Jake suspected that Claire had bugged these guests because they were the only ones with advance knowledge of the auction. They'd come to Blind River with a singular purpose: to win *Red Fury*. If true, seating these guests at the same table certainly made sense, financially speaking. The best way to drive up the price was to increase competition, and there was nothing more competitive than watching the person seated across from you launch bid after bid for an item you desperately want.

Or need.

"Oh, *you're* Jake Boxer?" the husky woman (Ivana?) with the lank dark hair exclaimed. "We are just so sorry about your wife. I can't even *imagine* it. And on your honeymoon?" She turned to her hulking husband. "Can you imagine such a thing, darling?"

The mustachioed brute shook his head and took a drink.

Wordless, Jake noticed, and for good reason.

After eavesdropping on the couple, Jake had noticed that Ivana was always the one to call the front desk or order room service. She had a perfectly passable American accent. Ivan, on the other hand, couldn't mutter a word without sounding like a Russian.

"And your face!" she said, gawking at Jake's injuries. "What a terrible fall—"

"Awful," Jake interrupted. "Thank you. And I'm sorry, but your names are?"

"Heather," she said pleasantly. "Heather Platt. And this is my husband, Tom."

The knuckle-dragger nodded without a word.

"So what are you guys bidding on?"

It was Nick Gold, and the question was telling.

Nick didn't know who they were, which meant they probably didn't know him either. Jake wondered if anyone seated at the table knew the other.

"Oh," Heather said, "well, the cruise looks nice, and that ivory statue is exquisite. And what about you?"

"Oh, I'm just here for the lobster. Probably won't bid on much."

Jake watched Ivan during the exchange. The bearish man had been transfixed by his phone, a meaty index finger hovering over the bid button. And as soon as Nick was done talking, Ivan punched in a bid, and Ana's painting jumped from twenty to twenty-one thousand dollars. Nick Gold's jaw quivered, and then the attorney tapped his own icon, and the bid jumped to twenty-*three* thousand.

It was an awkward moment, like two men on a double date who just realized they were after the same woman.

Jake considered grilling the couple across from him but decided that it would only bring unwanted attention. They were definitely Ivan and Ivana, and that meant he'd identified all of Claire's marks. Claire, he realized, had probably identified them while she'd been inside the Kidd's office. After all, the Kidd had invited all of them to the auction. He knew they'd bid on *Red Fury*. He probably had their names written on a ledger or a calendar or something, and Claire must have seen them. Now that Jake knew who they were too, the only thing left to do was sit back and watch to see which of them won the painting.

The winner, Jake knew, would almost certainly lead him to the "Why."

THIRTY

With just fifteen minutes to go, the energy in the Glass Hall suddenly swayed. The raucous laughter tempered to nervous chatter and almost everyone took a seat. The few still standing, including Mila Noël, eyed each other cagily, as if gauging whom amongst them would make the mad dash to steal *Red Fury* first. The obscure Soviet painting, which had been largely ignored at the beginning of the night, had suddenly captured the room. There was a reason, of course.

Money.

The high bid for *Red Fury* currently stood at six hundred and thirty-six thousand dollars, and it was still rising. At eighty-six grand, the *Diomede Ivory* was now a distant second, and the Cold War relics from White Alice hardly registered at all.

At first, Jake was surprised that a high six-figure bid had such an effect on the affluent crowd—surely they had bank accounts with much more. But this was no longer about a dollar figure—this was about heat.

When the high bid leaped to seven hundred grand, the room audibly inhaled. It was suddenly clear that this was no longer a friendly auction, and that a little healthy competition amidst a couple hundred wealthy narcissists was primed to do just one thing—make the Kidd money.

A lot of money.

Jake thought about the crumbling storefronts in Blind River's downtown. He thought about the Ascent's unfinished north wing. He thought about the millions of dollars in donations the Kidd had pledged to various Alaskan organizations—pledges that helped him maintain a certain societal standing out here in America's final frontier.

And then it hit him. The Kidd was broke, and this night, a night that had been God-only-knew how many months—or years—in the making, was his golden parachute.

The double doors to the lobby burst open, and Jake, who'd abandoned Nick Gold's table for the bar, where he had a clear vantage point of Claire's marks, saw Summer hurry inside. The young woman glanced his way, caught his eye, and for a moment, Jake thought she was going to run over to tell him he was right—she was leaving Blind River, and Christopher Kidd—immediately. But she didn't.

Instead, she ran straight to Christopher Kidd, who'd been entertaining a steady flow of guests at the front of the room. Jake watched her gesture for him impatiently, and then noticed that her other hand was closed in a tight fist.

She was holding something.

Something that she seemed intent on giving to the Kidd.

Jake realized exactly what she'd found and felt the lump of betrayal rise in his throat.

Sweating, he glanced at his watch. Ten minutes left in the auction.

I can't leave, he thought. The bids are anonymous. I have to be here at the end to study their faces—it's my best, maybe *only*, chance to identify the winner.

Across the room, the Kidd finally excused himself from the line of fawning guests and traipsed over to Summer, who immediately whispered in his ear. She handed the Kidd whatever it was she'd been holding, then pointed right at Jake. The Kidd looked his way, and his gaze burned a line between them. Jake thought briefly about running until Claire piped up, her voice loud and clear in his mind.

Who in the hell are you kidding? You can barely walk, much less run. Besides, there are only eight minutes left. You have to stick around.

Well, if he was gonna stick around, he also had to make the inevitable confrontation with the Kidd as difficult as possible.

The effects of Jake's last oxy had worn off. The Devil had his spine, but Jake did his best to ignore the bastard as he slipped off his bar stool and staggered through the tables of guests, all of whom were glued to *Red Fury's* exponentially rising price.

The bidding now topped a whopping two million dollars.

Jake found Mila where she'd been hanging out for the past couple of hours, standing just a few feet in front of *Red Fury*. She hardly blinked as her gaze vacillated between the painting and her cell phone, her thumb constantly tapping the bid button, raising the price by a thousand bucks anytime she was outbid.

"Careful, you'll wear out your thumb."

She glanced back at him for the briefest of seconds before returning her attention to her cell phone, all but ignoring him.

"I think you met my wife Claire O'Donnell. She was killed in that ski lift accident."

"In eight minutes I'll talk to you for as long as you'd like," she said, her voice draped in her European accent—he still couldn't quite place it.

Jake saw the Kidd moving toward him with purpose.

He didn't have eight minutes.

"You're related to Ana Turov, aren't you? That's why you look like her and that's why you're paying a fortune for the painting."

"I'm the curator for the Brussels Museum of Modern Art. And, yes, I happen to be Ana's granddaughter. Now would you kindly piss off?"

"I saw you and the Kidd arguing at the Café Beaujolais," Jake went on, ignoring her. "You were trying to buy the painting before it went up on the auction block, weren't you? You *knew* he was going to sell it."

"I know that I want you to leave me alone."

"You're not going to win it. You *can't* win it. Do you see that man in the tuxedo over there?" He jerked his head to Nick Gold. "He has unlimited financial resources. The painting is his for the taking."

She finally turned to face him, saying, "We will see."

Those three words, coupled with her smirk, told him everything.

But before he could dwell on it, he felt a hand on his shoulder—the *Kidd's* hand. It was strong and it was determined and it jerked him hard to his right. With his feet planted, Jake felt his spine twist. The blue ocean rolled back, and he was suddenly falling toward the stone-toothed maw of the granite quarry where Brody had died. When he hit the rocks below, he wished he were dead, too. Slumping with a yelp into the Kidd's arms, he felt the man's smooth lips in his ear as he purred, "You broadcast a word of what you heard and I'll slit your fucking throat."

The Kidd pressed something small and sharp into Jake's palm, then sloughed him off into an empty chair like so much dead skin. Hours passed. Years came and went. Decades...*centuries*...lumbered by. And then he finally heard the Kidd shout from the front of the room, "Five minutes, everyone. Five minutes."

Not years, Jake. Only minutes. You haven't missed the ending yet. There's still time.

The crippling pain had tightened Jake's hand into a fist. Willing it to open, he saw the small sharp object that the Kidd had pressed into his palm. It was a pronged circuit, no larger than a fishing fly—one of Claire's listening bugs.

Jake looked at Summer, who adverted her eyes.

Jesus Christ.

He'd tried to help her; he'd tried to get her away from her rapist of a boss and what had she done in return? Combed the Kidd's office and found Claire's bug.

Forget about her, Jake. What's the high bid on the app?

North of three million. And less than four minutes to go.

Keep watching or you'll never get the story.

Claire was right.

Jake took several breaths and did what he could to ignore the hot ember climbing his spine. But the room was blurry. The guests' faces were grotesque. The mountain a dark smear of snow, and the painting...*Ana's* painting...became not just the center of the room but the universe. He felt his back muscles spasm, and he screamed involuntarily. A woman sitting nearby exclaimed, "*Oh, my God*," and grabbed him before he tumbled out of his chair. She mopped his brow and asked if he was okay before turning and shouting for a doctor, but Jake told her to shut up. To help him back up. He *had* to ride out these final few minutes.

Look around, Jake. Where are my marks?

Mila. Nick Gold. Plastic Mel. Ivan and Ivana. The Kidd…

The high bid for *Red Fury* jumped a whopping five hundred grand. The room gasped, then held its collective breath as the high bid leapt another five hundred thousand, and then a full million. Tom Platt, the Russian Jake knew better as Ivan, was now standing as he tapped his phone, keeping pace with the rest of them. And why not? For all Jake knew, Ivan had Putin's limitless coffers to spend on the painting. But where in the hell was Plastic Mel? By the bar, he realized, hearing the man's dry cough. Also with his finger on the bid button.

With just sixty seconds to go, the auction was no longer between two hundred guests. It was between four. The four Claire had bugged. The four who'd arrived with enough money to win the painting, no matter the cost. The four who had known *Red Fury* was going to be for sale.

Just as Claire had known.

Jake did his best to keep the pain at bay, to concentrate on the matter at hand. He felt dwarfed by the ballroom's impressive wall of glass and the black mountain looming outside, a mountain with impossible intelligence, as if it had somehow orchestrated this entire drama.

Ten…Nine…Eight…Seven…Six…

With seconds left in the auction, the price skyrocketed. Claire's marks were bidding as if their lives depended on it, and Jake couldn't help but to think that they probably did.

Three…Two…One…

THIRTY-ONE

"AL? AL...C'MON! Open the door—please!"

A sweat-inducing thought dashed through Jake's head.

What if Al had already left town?

He couldn't go to Dr. Wallace for drugs. The physician would force him to leave town immediately, and that couldn't happen. Not yet.

But if he didn't get some sort of relief soon, well...

As Jake kept pounding on Al's door, the final few minutes of the auction played out over and over again in his head. The winning bid had been astronomical. And the winner...the winner had been...

Mila or Nick Gold or Ivan and Ivana or Mel Perkins or—

Shit!

He didn't know.

He couldn't *think!*

The pain in his cracked back was too intense.

All he knew was that, after the auction, he'd somehow managed to stumble out of the Glass Hall, through the lobby, and down the maze of corridors to Al's room—yes the elderly concierge lived in the hotel.

Al was the only one who could alleviate his pain, or so he hoped. A concierge could find anything at any hour, right? Wasn't that his job? So why wasn't he opening his goddam door?

"C'mon, Al!" Jake screamed, just as the door finally opened. But not all the way. It caught on a chain lock, revealing a three-inch vertical slice of Al Tulane, Jr.

It was the first time Jake had seen the concierge looking anything less than impeccable, yet there he was, bloodshot eyes peeping out from under a head of thin tousled hair, wearing boxer shorts and an undershirt that showed off his once-strong, now-saggy biceps.

"Mr. Boxer," he mumbled. "The hell you doing here?"

"Just get me…get me to your bed."

Al didn't move. Instead, his barrel chest rose as he took a deep breath and said, "Spent the day lookin' up Phyllis Rose of Boise, Idaho, on the computer, the woman you say was Ana Turov."

"*I* didn't say it. Your boss did. Now let me in."

"This woman in Boise, she'd been a school teacher. Biology. You know I couldn't find one darn thing that said she'd painted a day in her life."

"Al—"

"Even if Ana *did* defect, do you really think she would've given up painting? It was a talent—a *true* talent."

"Do you have any idea what just happened in the ballroom?"

He blinked his sticky eyes. "Blind River's annual auction."

"That's right. And do you know what your boss just sold for twenty-three *million* dollars?"

Al's head tilted back and his eyes grew wide.

No. He hadn't known.

But he did now.

Jake didn't even have to say it. There was only one thing in Blind River that could've sold for such a sum, and Al Tulane, Jr., had been in love with the woman who'd painted it.

"What?" he asked, unable to mask his surprise. "Do you mean—"

"Let me in, Al. Let me in and I'll tell you everything."

The concierge pursed his lips and closed the door. Jake heard the chain lock clink as it slipped from its housing, and then the door opened all the way. Jake, who'd been clutching the door frame with both hands, swooned as he stumbled inside. Al caught him, though it wasn't easy. Jake had a good five inches on him, and at least thirty pounds. As the two men limped over to Al's bed, the concierge asked the obvious: "The Kidd…he sold Ana's painting?"

"Yes."

"He *had* it. You *saw* it?"

"Yes. And it was just as you described. A masterpiece."

A spasm rippled across his back. Jake screamed and slipped through Al's big hands, then crumpled to the cold hardwood floor. Another spasm came, this one crippling, and Jake was sure it would land him on the next transport to Anchorage.

Al, his face awash with concern, was saying something above him. Something about the painting. Something hot and passionate—expressing disbelief, Jake was sure. The Kidd had hidden the painting from Al, and Al was justifiably pissed.

But Jake was simply in too much pain to care. Another spasm jolted his body—Jake screamed louder than Al had been swearing—and through blurred vision, he watched Al stop his blue streak and turn for the phone. The old concierge was undoubtedly aiming to call up the sheriff or doctor, and from deep inside of Jake, a single word bubbled to the surface and popped.

"*Stop!*"

Al, holding the phone, a finger poised to dial, considered him. "Mr. Boxer. I ain't ever seen a man look as bad as you. You need help."

Al started dialing.

Jesus Christ.

Jake closed his eyes and fought for his next few words. "Wait. The *Kidd*…he betrayed you."

Jake felt Al's hot gaze on him. His finger hovering over the final number of whomever it was he was calling.

"He knew you loved her," Jake said, finding his voice. "But he didn't tell you about the painting before he sold it. He didn't even let you look at it, and he'd been hiding it for ten years! What kind of a person would do that to you…after all these years of loyalty?"

Exhausted, Jake closed his eyes and focused on breathing.

One breath at a time.

"Don't call the doctor...help me get it."

He couldn't say anything else. Al would either call the doctor and Jake would lose his final twelve hours in Blind River, or Al would help him to his bed, and Jake would still have a chance to present Claire's story to a waiting audience.

Jake heard a soft click. The concierge had reset the receiver on the phone, and then he heard Al's baritone voice say, "Get what, Mr. Boxer? The painting?"

Jake nodded. "*Red Fury.*"

"*Red Fury?*"

"That's what the Kidd calls it."

"Huh. I kinda like that."

Then Jake felt Al's hands underneath him. His broken body roared in protest, but he allowed Al to heft him to his feet. Once again, they were moving toward the bed.

Al's room was laid out just like the others—a bedroom, kitchenette, and small dining area—only there was fifty years of life inside of it, too. This was Al's home, and once upon a time, the furniture might have been top of the line, but it was now old and well worn. A rickety bookshelf opposite the queen-sized bed held hundreds of history books, everything from the Civil War right up to America's struggle against ISIS. Al had dedicated an entire shelf to the Cold War. At first glance, Jake saw titles like *Signals Intelligence* by the U.S. Marine Corps, *The Cold War* by John Gaddis, and *NORAD and the Soviet Nuclear Threat* by Gordon Wilson. He wasn't exactly surprised to discover that Al was a history junkie—if anyone was living in the past, it was Al. But he was somewhat surprised by the academic nature of these books. Al was better educated than he'd let on.

On top of the bookcase, Jake also saw several framed photographs, including a photo of a black man, probably in his thirties, surrounded by his children. The picture was fading—undoubtedly old—and Jake had no doubt as to the identity of the man in the center of the adoring horde.

"That's Daddy," Al said softly, confirming Jake's suspicion.

Daddy, the guy who'd crushed a man's skull with a hammer because he thought he was a commie.

"Looks like a nice enough guy," Jake said.

"The nicest, 'til his head got sick." The two reached the bed. The next step, one Jake wasn't looking forward to *at all*, was to lie down, an act that would include bending Jake's back. Al must have picked up on Jake's trepidation because he said, "Keep your eyes on me now, son. Don't think about what's gonna happen next."

Al slowly sat Jake on the bed. Jake's spine had no choice but to bend, and he moaned loudly, but once his butt was on the mattress, Al was quick to lay him flat on his back. The pressure ebbed and the pain dissipated.

"Thought you were getting better," Al said worriedly.

"Your boss…" Jake groaned, "*undid* things."

Al looked away. "Are you sure he sold Ana's painting?"

"Positive. He even…certified it. He screwed both of us, Al. He sold that painting out from under you, and I think he killed Claire when she got too close to understanding what he'd planned to do with it."

Al cocked his head. The old man was soft, his muscles had atrophied long ago, but they still hung from the same powerful frame he'd had in his twenties. Jake couldn't explain it, but in that brief moment, he was sure the concierge was going to pick up a pillow and smother him—it wouldn't have been difficult given Jake's condition.

"That's a mighty big accusation," Al said finally. "I hope you have some mighty big proof to back it up."

Jake groaned as he shifted. "It's all around you…downtown's falling apart…the hotel's construction has been delayed for how long now? And he pledged millions of dollars over the weekend to various bullshit causes. To top it all off, he's a rapist—a real piece of shit!" Jake shook his head and softened. "Al. He wants *power*. And he buys it by giving away money. But he's up against a wall. He needs cash, *that's* why he's selling Ana's painting."

"Mr. Boxer, you were a heckuva reporter back in the day—had your own TV show and everything—but I just don't see how you came to all this. It feels as though you're swatting at flies."

Having no choice, Jake reached into his pocket and pulled out the buglike transistor Claire had used to eavesdrop on the Kidd.

"My wife bugged your boss's office. She also bugged four other rooms.

She bugged them because she knew they were here to buy Ana's painting."

Al took the eavesdropping device from Jake and pushed it around on his palm. "This is what you've been doing for the past couple of days? Eavesdropping on the hotel?" His face darkened. "Eavesdropping on me?"

"No, not you. Just the bad guys. Now listen, the auction was anonymous. I don't know *who* won the painting, but at some point, the Kidd has to deliver it to the winner. I don't know how he's going to do it without anyone else seeing, but you work for the hotel. You can get behind the scenes. *You can find out.*"

The concierge still didn't look convinced. Jake wondered if the Kidd's grip on Al was as strong as it was on Summer. He wondered if Al's next move was to tell the Kidd what Jake was confiding to him.

"Al," Jake pleaded, "this is Ana Turov's masterpiece. You loved her. Now do you want it hanging over some rich guy's mantel? Or in a museum?"

Al considered Jake's words and then walked to his closet. He opened it, revealing rack after rack of forest green Hotel Ascent uniforms.

He pulled one from the rack while saying, "The Kidd keeps a first aid box in the basement. Last time I was down there, we had some codeine. Now it's no oxy, but it'll do you up a heck of a lot better than aspirin. I'll get it for you and then check in on my boss. In the meantime, try to get a little shut-eye. I'll wake you just as soon as I'm back."

Al finished buttoning his shirt, then pulled on his pants and stepped into his perfectly shined shoes before leaving his room.

Jake did his best to ignore the fact that he saw the concierge turning to the right as the door closed behind him, when he knew damn well that the basement with the codeine was to the left.

THIRTY-TWO

———————

The photograph of Al's murderous father stared down at Jake from the top of the bookcase.

Al Tulane, Sr.—the bastard—had murdered a man with a hammer in front of his son.

Christ, what would that *do* to a kid?

In Al's case, it had made him rebel. He'd fallen in love with Ana Turov, a prominent "commie" herself. A woman he was *still* in love with—and that love was, apparently, still in bloom.

While the photograph of Al's father had been relegated to a tiny frame across the room, an eight-by-ten photograph of Ana Turov sat on Al's bed-side table, a spot usually reserved for a wife or mother. Just next to the photograph sat a small tube of hand lotion and a vase of freshly cut witch hazel. Apparently, Ana was the last face Al looked upon before drifting off to sleep, and the first thing Al saw on waking up. At first, Jake thought it was the same print as the one hanging in the Honeymoon Suite—the one the Kidd had smashed to prove it wasn't haunted. But after studying the photograph for a good twenty minutes, Jake concluded that while the framing was the same—and while Ana was wearing the exact same startled look—it wasn't actually the *exact* same picture. The photograph in the Honeymoon Suite had been muted, its color sapped to sepia, and in some parts, practically black and white. As if it were a copy. This photograph—the eight-by-ten—still retained much of its original color.

Original?

Ever so slowly, Jake reached for the photograph, all too aware that moving quickly would ignite a firestorm up his spine. He grabbed it, turned it over, and removed the stiff sheet of cardboard that kept the photograph from bending. Peeling the print from the glass, he studied the photograph and found the following words in small print around the white edging of the perimeter: *Anchorage Print. 1973. 18 of 24.*

He was holding a print made from the negative. Number eighteen of twenty-four.

Definitely an original.

Jake looked back to the image of Ana, wishing the woman could talk. She couldn't, of course. She could only stare back at Jake with that same startled expression, an expression that Jake was still pondering.

How in the hell had it arrived on her face?

She'd been painting fervently, that much was clear, but then what? The door had unexpectedly swung open? By someone with a key? It made sense. There'd been no knock. No warning. Just a door opening, and Ana Turov looking up, and a flash that captured that startled expression, and then...?

Someone offering a lame excuse, maybe even apologizing for the interruption.

Al?

The concierge had the original print. He'd also had access to Ana. Of course, he'd taken the photograph.

Uncomfortable, Jake shifted. Speaking of Al—where in the hell was that codeine?

He closed his eyes and did his best to take Claire's advice, to think about the ending. In his mind's eye, he saw Al returning with the codeine. He felt the pain dissipate from his lower vertebrae like steam. Then he imagined Al informing him that Nick Gold had won the painting—Nick Gold, a man whose client had more money than God. Jake's best guess was that Ana

Turov hadn't defected—she'd been murdered. Most likely by an American intelligence agency. And Nick's client wanted *Red Fury* for blackmail. After all, wasn't the painting proof she'd never left Blind River? If she had, wouldn't she have taken her masterpiece with her?

Thirty minutes passed, and then an hour.

Where in the hell were his drugs?

Maybe the first aide kit in the basement had been locked? Maybe Al had to track down a key? Or maybe Al had gone straight to Christopher Kidd? To warn him—Jake Boxer of *Bullseye* is *onto* you. If that was true, Jake didn't know *what* would happen.

Jake blinked. Swallowed hard.

He did his best to ignore the tick that had plagued him back in Moscow, but it was still there. All these years later—all that therapy—and he still couldn't shake it.

He had to get his mind into something else. He had to climb back into his fortress.

"Jake Boxer of *Bullseye* here," he mumbled to himself, smelling the pancake make-up beneath his nose again, feeling the hot lights on his face, "reporting to you live from Al Tulane, Jr.'s, room. Concierge of the Hotel Ascent. Armchair Cold War scholar, son of a murderer, and lover of Ana Turov's ghost."

Jake's gaze drifted to Al's small tube of hand lotion, a complimentary tube from the Hotel Ascent, of course. A box of Kleenex sat next to it, and on the floor, Jake spied a small black waste bin. He couldn't quite see inside of it, but he didn't need to.

He knew what sort of garbage was in there.

Ana's photograph...the lotion and tissue...it didn't take Freud to put it together. In a way it was kind of sweet—Al probably hadn't tugged it to another woman since meeting Ana half a century early. On the other hand, Ana was fifty years dead, which made it a little creepy, too. Not to mention the shot of Ana hadn't exactly caught her in the sexiest of moods. Too bad he didn't have other, more arousing photographs.

Jake looked at the edging of the photograph again: *18 of 24.*

He *did* have others.

Twenty-three others, to be exact.

Jake looked at the bedside table's drawer, a drawer that was easily within reach of whoever might be lying…or tugging it…in the bed. He got a hand on the drawer, pulled it open, and courtesy of that little crack in his L5, was blinded by a bolt of light. But the pain quickly abated, and he soon found himself staring at a naked woman. Jake reached into the drawer, snagged the stack of photos with his fingertips, and slowly drew them out.

The top photograph was of a nude woman, alright, but the head had been framed out, so all Jake could see was her body from the shoulders down. She was lying on a bed with a sheer sheet over her small breasts, leaving her lower half exposed.

She was twiggy thin, Jake noted, and underdeveloped. Just like Ana Turov.

The next photograph confirmed it. It had been taken of Ana from behind, her skinny pale butt in plain view, but in this one, she was looking back at the camera, a coy smile on her otherwise plain face. As Jake flipped through the nudes, the tortured artist in the startled photograph that had up until then defined Ana disappeared. In fact, in every photograph *except* the startled shot, she looked in complete control, as if she'd been the one telling the photographer how to frame the shot. Apparently, she was much more than a meek and timid artist, a realization that began to shift the shape of Claire's story. Perhaps Ana had not been the Soviet pawn he'd believed.

The identity of the photographer was put to rest with a shot of Ana in the bathroom. In it, Jake very clearly saw the photographer's hand in the bathroom mirror. A *black* hand. Jake also saw a piece of a sleeve. He'd been wearing a shirt, which meant Al had been clothed, a significant detail since Ana had been mostly *un*clothed.

Jake tried to imagine Al forcing the woman to take off her clothes and pose provocatively without alerting her Soviet guards…It was a hard scenario to swallow. Surely she would have tattled. No, the only way to get these pics were if she was *into* it.

If she'd *asked* Al to take them.

The nudes gave Jake a very different impression of the artist than that startled shot of her painting *Red Fury*. And the nudes weren't the only photographs in the stack. There were other pictures. Ana outside on the hotel's patio, taking in Blind River's mountain. Ana sheepishly posing with a newspaper and a headline that read: Soviet to Premiere Masterpiece for American Critics.

Then there was Ana seated amongst twenty or so very serious men. The group posed for the shot inside of the Glass Hall, the mountain looming over their shoulders through the impressive glass collage. They weren't her Soviet handlers. They wore expensive suits and ties, threads that might've been sold in New York or London. Not drab Soviet attire.

The critics, he realized.

The ones mentioned in the headline.

Ana looked nervous in this particular photograph, and for good reason. The men surrounding her would judge her painting, and that judgment would determine her artistic future.

Was the young woman a prodigy? Or just some stupid Soviet, talentless compared with her Western contemporaries?

What struck Jake most, however, was how old she looked here and how young she'd looked in the nudes. She'd been free in the nudes. But here, surrounded by the critics, she looked...*haunted* wasn't the right word for it. No, in this photograph, Ana looked scared. Scared of...the man sitting next to her.

Panic struck as Claire's words bounced around his skull.

Your therapist warned me not to mention him—she told me not to bring up Buck Masterson.

The sharp jab of a migraine joined the throb in his back. It was *him.* Jake was sure of it. The high cheekbones. The wavy chestnut hair. The sharp, all-seeing eyes. The man sitting next to Ana was decades younger than the death row inmate he'd interviewed in Huntsville, but Jake was all too sure of his identity.

Jake thought back to their first day in Blind River. Claire had been upset with one of Austin's texts, and as it turned out for good reason—every story had a source, and the state of Texas had just executed Claire's.

The man sitting next to Ana Turov was none other than Buck Masterson.

Jake didn't think twice about dialing 9-1-1—if only Claire had done the same thing. Only after several assurances that yes, he was *the* Jake Boxer, ex-host of *Bullseye*, and that yes, this was an enormous emergency—maybe the biggest to ever hit America—did the dispatch officer connect Jake to Sheriff Wilson Grout. It was three in the morning, and Wilson had been asleep, but he still answered after the third ring. Jake told him just enough to get him to the hotel, that the Kidd had sold Ana's painting mere hours earlier, and that it absolutely could not leave Blind River. It was a matter of national security.

The sheriff sounded skeptical but assured Jake he would be there just as soon as he found his boots and underwear. Jake hung up and considered Ana Turov's naked photographs. He thought back to what he'd told Al, that the Kidd had sold his lover's painting out from under him, and suddenly, Jake knew exactly why Al had yet to return.

Jake, he didn't leave to find out who won the painting. He left to try to take it back from Christopher Kidd!

Claire was right. And Al was in way over his head. If he *had* gone to take it back from the Kidd, well, odds were that he would only make things worse. And if Jake didn't get that painting before it left the hotel…

He didn't even want to think about it. Back in 1973, Buck Masterson had been in the employment of the CIA. God only knew what secrets lurked in Ana's masterpiece.

Jake dropped the nudie pics back into the drawer, slid it shut, then slowly scooted to the end of the bed. He put his shoes on the floor, slowly stood, and fell over immediately, knocking down half of the history books on the shelves along the way. Leaning against the rickety bookcase, he took a small yet excruciating step toward the door, then another. He crossed the room that way—using the bookshelf, then the kitchenette counter, and finally the wall—until he was opening the door and looking out into the hallway.

Empty.

Thank God.

To his left? The basement and the medical kit with the codeine. To his right? The lobby and the front desk and the wide revolving door, where he could meet Sheriff Wilson Grout.

Pulling Al's door shut behind him, he hobbled for the lobby. Though most of the guests were still asleep, the lobby was teeming with employees who were cleaning, packing up perishable food, and battening down the hatches for a three-month absence. The front desk came into view and Jake saw Summer, her back to him, working hard on her computer. He scanned the lobby for both Christopher Kidd and Al, but he didn't see either of them.

The Glass Hall, he thought. Maybe they're still there?

But then, as Jake stepped into the lobby, a small rubber ball whistled through the air, striking the hardwood floor just a few feet to his right before bouncing a good twenty feet back up.

He didn't hear a scream—it was much more like a full-throated shriek. At the same time, he registered the lights and sirens of a Blind River police truck through the revolving door, and he was actually foolish enough to believe that he'd called the sheriff in time to prevent anyone from getting hurt. Above him, several doors opened and a few groggy guests, woken by an argument, stumbled into the hallway just in time to see the wood banister on the fifth floor snap under a man's weight—a man who, moments later, followed that little red ball as he plunged all five stories, striking the floor with a sickening thud mere feet from where Jake was standing.

Jake stumbled backward, and by the time he regained his balance, he saw Christopher Kidd's body on the floor beside him, the man's neck broken, his purpling tongue wagging. Five floors above, where a piece of splintered banister waved over the lobby like the flag of a broken country, Al Tulane, Jr., was staring in horror at those big hands of his, still strong after all those years, undoubtedly thinking, *like father, like son.*

THIRTY-THREE

"YOU AND HANK getting along?"

At the sound of the sheriff's voice, Jake unpeeled his eyes long enough to take in "Hank," a massive, and mercifully stuffed, black wolf. The animal had been mounted on a pedestal adorned with granite boulders and fake snow—the centerpiece of a room still under construction.

"Took me a month to track him," Sheriff Wilson Grout said as he took a seat on a small step stool. "Got him in Roper's Valley, just on the other side of Highway 3. Took three shots to put him down, all of 'em square in the chest. The others only took one." The sheriff gestured beyond Hank. Ten more stuffed wolves were staged against the back wall, waiting to be posed with Hank, though only one was upright. The rest were lying on their sides, neglected and forgotten.

"So much for Blind River's winter belonging to the wolf," Jake muttered.

Wilson doffed his hat and drummed the brim with his fingers. "Oh, there's still at least one out there. Wolves run in packs—that means lots of girlfriends. Hank here had a favorite. Big bitch…nearly as big as him, but she ain't black. She's a mottled grey and brown. He was with her when I killed him. Gunshots spooked her good. I tried to track her, but the snow was deep and…well…The bitch got away, but not for long." Wilson's quick eyes looked Jake's battered body up and down. "How you feeling, Mr. Boxer?"

"Been better."

Jake was still lying in the same spot where the sheriff and his deputy had left him a few hours earlier—flat on his back on a leather couch. The room, like the rest of the north wing, was still under construction. Jake had heard Wilson call the room "The Hunt"—as cute a nickname as you get in Alaska—and it wasn't difficult to imagine the Kidd's affluent guests sipping cognac, smoking cigars, and making handshake business deals, all under the watchful eyes of the wolf pack that once haunted Blind River.

It was a dream that had never quite manifested, and now that Christopher Kidd was dead, never would.

In the chaos following the Kidd's death, Wilson had ordered his deputy to lock the hotel doors. No guests in, no guests out.

And certainly no paintings.

The sheriff and deputy had helped Jake to the couch, where Jake had quickly explained what had happened. He'd told Al that the Kidd sold his old lover's painting, and Al had most likely thrown the Kidd from the fifth floor in a fit of rage. It was *imperative* the sheriff found Ana's painting. If Al didn't have it, he told him to search four rooms—Nick Gold's, Mila Noël's, Mel Perkins's, and that of the Russians—that one of them had surely won it.

The sheriff had wanted to know why the painting was such a big deal. When Jake told him it had just sold for twenty-three million at the Kidd's annual auction, the lawman's blue eyes grew as wide as dinner plates. But now, sitting on the step stool in front of the black wolf, Jake saw something else in the sheriff's eyes—something that worried him gravely.

Doubt.

"I called Dr. Wallace," Wilson told him. "He's on his way with the van to transport you to Anchorage. In the meantime, I found you this, right where you said it would be."

The sheriff pulled a bottle of codeine from his jacket pocket.

Jake practically salivated. His skin crawled just looking at it.

Unscrewing the bottle, Wilson tipped the red liquid into a plastic measuring cup, then gave it to Jake, who swigged it down in a single, greedy gulp. It had been twenty-four hours since his last oxy. He would've swallowed wolf scat if someone had promised it would mitigate his pain, even a little.

"The painting…" Jake managed as the codeine lubricated his spine. "You find it?"

"Not yet."

"You *have* to find it…you have to find it *now.*"

"My deputies are interviewing guests and staff as we speak," Wilson said. "I already spoke to Al. He claims he killed Christopher Kidd in self-defense. That the Kidd had grown irate after Al confronted him about him bankrupting Blind River. A struggle ensued. Al shoved him away, but unfortunately, the banister split. He said it had nothing to do with some fifty-year-old love affair with Ana Turov, nor did it have anything to do with that painting."

Jake scoffed. "Did you look in his bedside table?"

Wilson nodded, then pulled a stack of photographs from his jacket pocket. Ana Turov's nudie pics. "They were right where you said they'd be."

Wilson slowly thumbed through the shots. His gaze lingered on one of Ana lying on the bed with her legs spread, the thin hand she'd used to paint *Red Fury* coyly covering her crotch.

"Skinny little thing, ain't she?" Wilson shook his head. "Look, I never took Al for a perv, but just because the old man jerked off to her every night doesn't mean he intentionally threw the Kidd off that balcony."

"You think it was an accident?"

"I've known Al for twenty years. The man doesn't have a bad bone in his body. I just sat with him for sixty minutes, and he was crying over the Kidd's death for fifty-nine of 'em. Know what he did with the spare minute?"

Jake shook his head.

"He cried over you and your broken back."

"Heart," Jake corrected, thinking about Claire.

Wilson nodded, then looked at Ana's photographs. "Gotta admit, this kinda blows my image of her. Always thought of her as a fragile, creative type. But I guess you gotta be something of an exhibitionist to paint—and God knows you gotta be bold to defect."

"She didn't defect. She was murdered."

"Now Mr. Boxer—"

"*Red Fury*," Jake interrupted. In his mind's eye, he saw the painting as clearly as he'd seen it at the auction. "It's a masterpiece. She wouldn't have left Blind River without it."

"She was defecting, Mr. Boxer. She was escaping the Soviet cudgel for the loving arms of America. Maybe she hid the painting. Maybe she thought she'd come back for it later but never did."

"Why not?"

"How should I know? People do stupid things. People turn their backs on their pasts. People have nervous breakdowns—some of them on live TV."

Jake blanched at the man's words. "I got a little too into my work, is all."

"You flipped out. And how do I know you're not *still* flipping out?"

A cold silence filled the room. Wilson held up the photograph of Ana Turov inside of the Glass Hall, the one in which she's flanked by the art critics.

What, exactly, had he told Wilson that morning? It was a blur. Jake's back had been pulsating with fire—the Kidd had been dead, just a few feet away—

You told him there were photographs in Al's bedside table. Photographs that would prove a dark and dangerous conspiracy. You told him to get those photographs, and the painting, and you'd tell him everything.

Right.

Jake's gaze drifted to the young Buck Masterson, seated next to Ana Turov.

"So explain it," Wilson said. "Explain to me why you're so convinced that Ana Turov was murdered in Blind River."

Tell him Jake. He's the only one who can get that painting before it leaves.

"Buck Masterson," Jake said finally. "Front row, the man immediately to Ana's right. A few years ago, he was convicted of a couple of cold cases—murders in Texas that took place back in the '70s. But Buck claimed that he'd only killed at the direction of the CIA. He was a boon for our show. We ran his interview during sweeps week and followed it up with investigations into each of his claims. One of them was rooted in a global conspiracy.

He talked about secret military machines being built under mountains. He claimed he'd intercepted ciphertext identifying a mole deep inside of the American government—"

"Wait a second. A mole?" Wilson said, interrupting. "Like a spy?"

"Yes. Like a double agent. But the Americans couldn't identify him— Buck had found the ciphertext, yes, but it was just a string of random letters. He didn't have the code to decrypt it."

"But if he did this…ciphertext…would identify the mole?"

"That's right. A mole who was sharing American intelligence with a network of foreign governments and international corporations, who was handpicking intelligence officers, generals, and CEOs to form a covert network that connected America, Europe, Africa, South America, Asia, and even the Soviet Union."

"And why would he do that?"

"To set a global agenda."

Wilson chuckled. "This show sounds familiar. Was it the one about the New World Order?"

"I prefer to call it an Old World Order—it's been around for forever."

A film of sweat broke across Jake's forehead. He blinked compulsively, then swallowed back the bile that had bubbled up his throat.

Had Wilson seen his tick?

Of course, he'd seen it. This man was the head of Blind River P.D. He saw everything. He thought Jake was nutso.

"Okay, so what does the painting have to do with Buck Masterson?" Wilson asked.

"Well, I'm just guessing here, but Buck did claim he had a Russian source who knew the cipher."

"And you think it was Ana?"

Jake shrugged. "Maybe she was his MPP?"

"MPP?"

"His perfect source. She was a prominent Soviet artist. She ran in privileged circles. She had access. She was privy to sensitive information, maybe to the information Buck wanted. And if she wanted to defect, she had a chip on her shoulder too. I can't think of any other reason why Buck would've been here at the same time as her. Yes, I think Ana was trying to pass Buck the mole's name."

"In her painting?"

Jake nodded, then swabbed his tongue about his mouth—it was suddenly dry.

"She knew the cipher."

"The code? The one the Soviets used?"

Jesus, was it just him? Or was the sheriff asking him the same thing over and over again?

"Yeah," Jake said, "just add it all up. There must be a reason Ana's painting sold for twenty-three million dollars." Jake looked back to the old photograph of Buck sitting next to Ana. "I can tell you this much, Buck Masterson wasn't here because he appreciated art."

Wilson chuckled, then leaned back and considered Jake's words, muttering, "Craziest goddamn story I've ever heard."

"Listen. Al doesn't know about the code, but the others, the bidders who came here to buy it, they *do*. That's why they're here. They don't care about the painting, they just want to identify the mole...I mean if all this is true...this guy...this spy...he changed the course of history...he could *still* be changing...changing it."

The pain had completely left Jake's body.

In fact, everything had left Jake's body.

Talk about good codeine.

The sheriff's stuff was the shit.

"And how exactly would she have coded this painting?" Wilson asked.

Half a century ago, spies were still using one-time pads to encode and decode secret messages. One-time pads contained a string of random numbers, which were also called the cipher. All one had to do was add each random number to each letter of the secret message (also called the plaintext) in order to create a *coded* secret message (also called the ciphertext). Of course, in order for both the sender and receiver to properly encode and decode the secret message, both parties had to use the same cipher—a cipher Ana would've tried to pass to Buck. A cipher Ana could've hidden anywhere. On the painting's frame, under the paint itself—hell, maybe she'd worked in some sort of ultraviolet material? Of course, even if the auction winner *did* find the hidden cipher in Ana's painting, it wouldn't do them a lick of good without the ciphertext. After all, they needed something to decode. And as far as Jake knew, only three people might have had the ciphertext—Ana, Buck,...and maybe Claire—and they were all dead.

But maybe they hadn't bought the painting to decipher a message. Maybe they'd bought the painting to destroy it—to make sure the mole's identity was lost forever.

"Jake? How would Ana have coded her painting?"

I already told you! Like a fucking one-time pad!

You're not speaking out loud, Jake.

I'm not?

"You feeling okay, Jake?"

"Bi'm beelin' bine," Jake spit out, his tongue suddenly quite uncooperative. Jake shook his head, tried it again. "Fine. I'm...I'm beelin' fine."

Wilson frowned, and his face smeared down the middle like melting wax. His next words echoed in Jake's ear, as if spoken within a deep cave. "Tell me about losing your shit on live TV. You thought Putin was following you in Moscow, right? That he was trying to kill you?"

"Bi'm better bow."

"So you're currently on your medication?"

Jake closed his eyes. No, I'm not on meds. Just therapy. And how in the hell did this guy know I *had* been? Claire weaned me off Risperdal years ago. Claire helped me beat my paranoia. Claire made life worth living. But now she's gone—oh, God she's—

"Jake."

Jake opened his eyes. They were filled with tears.

"Brussians," Jake muttered. "Bin bour botel."

"Brussians?"

"Bo! *Brussians*! BSB!"

"I'm having trouble understanding you, but if you're talking about the Russians, we're questioning them. We're also questioning the others—Mila Noël, Nick Gold, and Mel Perkins. We searched their rooms, but none of them had the painting. That leaves you, Jake."

"*Be?*"

"You."

"Be? Be. *BE?*"

Be feeling no pain.

Be floating away.

And *Bou* gave *Be* something other than codeine.

"I know you and your wife came here for a story, Jake. I know you're trying to reboot your show, *Bullseye*, and I *know* you have the painting," the sheriff went on.

"Bed Bury…"

"Yes, *Red Fury*. I like you, Mr. Boxer, and I'm sorry as hell about what happened to your wife. But I need you to talk to me. I need the truth. Then you can go to Anchorage to be with Claire."

He's lying.

Not now, Claire. Not when I'm feeling so…

Goooooooood.

Jake closed his eyes and sank into…no, sank *through*…the couch.

"Okay, Jake," he heard Wilson say, "if you're not gonna tell me about the painting, how about the diamond?"

Diamond?

Jake felt Wilson pry open the fingers of his right hand and press a small cool pendant into his palm.

"I recognized it from your wife's belongings," Wilson explained. "She was wearing it when she died, wasn't she?"

Jake didn't need to open his eyes to identify the stone. He knew it was Brody's necklace. Jake closed his fist and felt it prick his palm. It was the only thing he *could* feel. In that moment, Brody's puny diamond was so dense that it became the center of his universe, his infinity point. The only thing still pinning him to Earth.

Wilson's voice traveled down to him from outer space. "Funny how it got into Lancaster's pocket. Oh, a few of my men dragged his body from the river last night. Guess those horses of his finally got sick of him. Bucked him into the freezing water, then keeled over and died themselves. We also found a map in the sleigh, Jake. A photocopy of an old mineral survey from the nineteen fifties. You wouldn't know anything about that, would you?"

Ignoring him, Jake's glazed eyes drifted to the bottle of codeine. "What did 'cha…did 'cha *give* me?"

At least he wasn't speaking in *B*'s anymore.

"I'm asking the questions, Mr. Boxer, and I want to know why you were looking for the entrance to our mountain."

"Fuck your mountain," Jake heard himself mumble, his gaze returning to the taxidermied animal leering over Wilson's shoulder. "That *poor...* *poor...*"

He was going to say "wolf," but he never got it out.

Suddenly, he could only see the dead animal's eyes, its marble eyes, which were as lifeless as the sheriff's.

And as black as the sudden night.

PART FOUR

THE SPY

THIRTY-FOUR

I NEED TO TELL YOU SOMETHING, and it's going to make you mad.

At this point, does it really matter?

I'm not here for a travel article.

Of course, you're not. You're here for the painting.

Yes. But the painting isn't everything. The code in the painting—the secret—it's still relevant.

I know.

It's still dangerous.

I know.

And it killed the only man I ever loved.

I'm not dead yet, honey. In fact, I'm just getting started.

I'm not talking about you, Jake. I'm talking about—

Stop.

You have to hear it.

No, I don't.

Brody is the reason I dragged you to Blind River. We're here to get the story Brody died for, the one that also cost you Bullseye.

I already *have* the story. And when I get out of here, I'm going to re-launch *Bullseye*. I'm gonna blow the roof off this bastard.

No, Jake. You're not. You're going to die in Blind River, but you can still get the story out. And this is how you're going to do it.

Claire told him, and when Jake awoke in a cold sweat, her words were still rattling around his skull. The plan was simple, really, though it depend-ed on Claire's satellite phone, a phone, he noticed, now missing from his pocket. The sheriff must have taken it. But if he could find it...if it still had a charge...he could call Austin Foley, Claire's editor with the *American Post*, and give him the story.

Jake loathed the thought of Claire's boss running with the lead, but at least it wouldn't die with him in Blind River.

Okay, so he had to find it, and he *would*...just as soon as he sobered up from whatever Sheriff Grout had used to spike the codeine.

The tainted codeine...how long had he been unconscious?

And why couldn't he see?

His thoughts returned to the wolf, Hank. Sure, it was stuffed, but being locked in a room with an animal that size still made his hackles stand on end...only he wasn't *in* that room anymore, was he?

Yes, he was lying down, but he no longer felt the leather couch beneath him—he was on a mattress...a naked mattress.

A bed.

Okay, so they'd moved him into one of the Ascent's rooms, but where? He tried to concentrate—not easy with his headache. He remembered tak-ing the codeine, he remembered losing all feeling as the sheriff's slow af-fable voice—like melted chocolate—asked about the mineral survey he'd paid Lancaster to steal, and then the door had opened and another man had entered the room, and there were hands on him—comforting, strong hands of men who didn't have broken backs or broken hearts or dead wives. Those hands had moved him out of the room—and now there was this mattress and the moonlight—

Not completely dark, he realized as his head continued to clear.

Pale light was seeping through the drapes of a large picture window, illuminating a small kitchen table, a romantic fireplace, and the tip of a heart-shaped bed.

Jake was back in the Honeymoon Suite.

If the moon was up, that meant he'd slept through the entire day, a day unlike any other in Blind River, a day when the hotel closed its doors for the next three months. A day when the entire city shut down and locked its doors.

Jake did his best to quiet his thoughts. He told himself that it was okay, his captors wouldn't have left him to rot, not if they thought he might have Ana's painting.

Did they still think that? Or had they already determined he didn't? Had they simply left him to die?

Ever so slowly, he pushed himself up on his elbows. They'd taken his back brace, and his spine barked, but not too loudly. He was still able to game an angle on the bedside clock. A clock that was as dark as the room. He looked at the TV. There had been a gentle blue light marking the power button, but now that was gone too.

The power was out, and not just inside the hotel, Jake noticed. Main Street, normally glowing with street lamps, was dark as well.

He began to panic. They *had* left him to die. Everyone in Blind River— everyone in the hotel—*was gone!*

Well, almost everyone.

There was a dark silhouette at the kitchen table. The man was sitting perfectly still, his features indiscernible in the near absence of light. His hands were on some sort of machine, resting on the tabletop. Every so often, Jake saw a bit of movement and heard a click—a finger, perhaps, toggling a button on and off or twisting a knob. The man's ears were weird, covered in something blocky, like earmuffs—

No. Not earmuffs.

Ear*phones.*

"Brody…"

Jake's bogeyman didn't answer.

Yes, the things around his ears were almost certainly earphones, and his head was smooth, not because he was bald, but because there was no skin left, only bone. The man was recording a sound—

No. Not a sound.

A hum.

A hum that vibrated through the Honeymoon Suite at a low decibel, almost like an idling truck, but it was far richer, far more powerful. It was electric.

Just then a beam of light split Jake's skull and his stomach churned, and he suddenly recalled the symptoms afflicting the victims of another hum—the Dagestan Hum—that one had come with migraines, nausea, and insomnia, at least according to the locals.

Stop it, Jake. It's psychosomatic. Keep your shit together.

There's a hum, Claire. I can *hear* it.

The moon emerged from behind a cloud, and its pale light raked across Brody's bone-white skull, and then Jake saw a toothy grin as the dead man hissed, "*Picture us at the ending,*" before a bone-rattling ring from a telephone shattered Jake's nightmare.

Startled, he opened his eyes.

Yes, he was in the Honeymoon Suite, but no, Brody's corpse wasn't sitting at the kitchen table. But there was a *sound* in the air, and it was undoubtedly a hum—an electric, almost melodic hum.

The phone rang again.

The clock on the bedside table was dark, and so was the power button on the TV, but the phone was ringing. His sluggish brain tried to make sense of it.

A telephone ringing…without power…was that even possible?

He flashed upon a time in D.C., when a storm knocked the power out, and he was on the couch in his boxer shorts, waiting impatiently for Claire to come home, and just when he'd been sure she'd been washed away in a torrent of rain, the phone rang—the landline. It had been Claire, calling from the office. She'd been okay, but that wasn't the point. The point was that their landline had been low voltage and ran off a different power source than the main grid.

So maybe that was the case here at the Hotel Ascent?

The phone rang again, and Jake inched for it, got a hand on it, put the receiver to his ear, and said, "Yeah."

He could see his breath in the moonlight.

When there was no answer on the other end, Jake said, "Listen. I won't report this to anyone. I just want out. You can keep the painting."

Still nothing.

"Well, why'd you bother calling if you're not gonna say something?" he asked sharply.

Silence.

Fear gripped Jake's heart.

He was hearing things. There was no hum. The phone hadn't rung—he'd simply gone mad.

But then, finally, Jake heard a voice. "Do you really expect me to believe that Jake Boxer, host of *Bullseye*, isn't going to report this little fiasco if I let him go?"

Jake's mind turned. The voice…he recognized it. It was soft and cracked and he'd heard it before.

But where? Not in Blind River. Somewhere else…in Washington, D.C.? He didn't know—he couldn't think.

It was a voice that had aged, but not like a fine wine—no, it was far too strained for that. It sounded more like a man who'd lived for decades with a boulder on top of him—a survivor's voice.

"*Ex*-host," Jake reminded the mysterious caller. "I don't have a show anymore."

"What about NewsFlash? Are you still thinking about resurrecting *Bullseye* with Tabitha Fox?"

How in the hell did this guy know about Tabitha Fox?

"*Bullseye* on NewsFlash isn't going to happen," Jake said quietly. "Not after what happened to Claire."

"Yes, your wife. Regrettable, but what in life isn't? You should know that I just spoke to our mutual friend, Sheriff Wilson Grout. He's having a little trouble locating Ana's painting. The sooner he gets it, the sooner everyone goes home. So I offered to give you a ring, in hopes of jogging your memory. Is that okay?"

It was okay by Jake. The more this guy talked, the better chance he had to figure out just who, exactly, he was. And he had a feeling that this man was an integral part of Claire's story.

"Sounds good to me," Jake muttered. "I'd at least like to get out of here in time to vote."

The voice on the phone chuckled. He had a thin laugh, like someone who'd just barely survived a traumatic surgery. "Who cares about voting? There's no power in the presidency anymore."

"No?" Jake asked. "Then where is it?"

"Where it should be. In the hands of the people."

Somehow Jake doubted that.

"Republicans..." the man went on, "Democrats...they're all just riding the Carousel. Going around and around to nowhere.

The caller wasn't one of Claire's marks, and Jake doubted if he was in Blind River, but he needed to be sure.

"I want to speak to the sheriff," Jake said.

"You have a broken back. You can't move off your bed. You're in no position to be giving me orders."

"You're not with him, are you? That's why you can't put him on the phone. You aren't in Blind River."

"I'm exactly where I need to be, as are you. Now the mere fact that I'm making this call means the situation is dire. Fortunately, there's a way out of this for all of us—that includes you, son, so I want you to pay careful attention."

Jake heard a faint knocking coming from somewhere else in the hotel— and was that a scream? Or a howl? Or that weird hum? And was that a...

Yes. Yes it was.

It was a cough.

A *raspy* cough.

Mel Perkins.

Not on the phone—he'd heard him coughing down the hallway on the same floor—the *fifth* floor.

Jake's thoughts went to the list he'd given the sheriff.

Plastic Mel

The Russians.

Nick Gold.

Mila Noël.

One of them had won *Red Fury*.

Were they now all Wilson's prisoners?

His gaze drifted to the Honeymoon Suite's door. There had been two small LED lights on the lock, a red light for "locked," a green for "unlocked." Neither was illuminated, which meant the locking mechanism was stuck in whatever position it had been in when the power went out. And that position had been "locked," Jake was sure.

Whatever drug the sheriff had spiked the codeine with was beginning to wear off, and the terror of being trapped in that room for days—slowly starving—pushed a panicked grunt through Jake's lips.

"Who are you?" he blurted.

The man, who'd been rambling on about how Jake could save himself, if only he'd give up *Red Fury,* paused, then said, "I'm of little consequence, Mr. Boxer, a dinosaur who somehow survived the meteor."

"The meteor? Or the Cold War?"

"The *meteor,*" he snapped, then took a moment to calm down before saying, "Now, what *is* of consequence is the situation currently unfolding in Blind River. I'm afraid that you and your wife thrust yourselves into a very difficult situation."

"Thrust ourselves?"

"You're a journalist," he said. "You're always sticking your nose where it doesn't belong, one of the many reasons I *loathe* your kind, especially the entitled ones who mouth off on TV. But I have to admit, it was something else to watch you implode on the screen."

Jake interrupted him. "We've established that you know who I am. It's time you return the favor. And if you don't—"

"If I don't what?" He asked angrily. "You're going to hang up that phone? You're going to rot away in that Honeymoon Suite with nothing but the ghost of your dead wife to keep you company?"

"I have Ana Turov's ghost as well. And Brody's."

"You have *nothing.* And if you *don't* tell me where that painting is, I *will* let you die."

"Okay, okay, nobody wants that," Jake said, backpedaling. "I just…I just want to know who I'm dealing with. Can you at least tell me your name?"

Jake was running on instinct, and his gut told him to keep this man talking. To absorb every word he said. The phone was his lifeline, and the voice on the other end was the only one who could pull him back into the boat.

"My name?" the man said with a chuckle. "Well isn't that the twenty-three-million-dollar question? I'll tell you what, you give me the painting, I'll tell you who I am."

"I don't *have* painting."

"Yes, that's exactly what the others said."

The others.

So Jake *wasn't* the only prisoner.

"Well I *really* don't have it," Jake said forcefully, "and even if I did, it would be worthless to me."

"And why is that?"

"Because I don't know where Ana hid the code in her painting, and even if I did, I wouldn't be able to decipher it."

"But you could sell it to someone who could."

It was big information. Up until then, Jake had simply *assumed* there was a code. This man had just confirmed it.

"Buck Masterson was executed," Jake said coolly. "He's the only one who could've deciphered it."

"Yes. And Buck Masterson also had several interviews with your wife shortly before he was put to death."

"I'm not Claire."

"No. You're just her betrothed."

"We weren't working together," Jake said quickly. "Claire kept all of this to herself."

"And *why* would she do that?"

"Because...because she wanted me to go to law school," Jake mumbled. "Because this is all about catching the man who murdered her old flame."

"Sure it is." He sounded amused.

"Was it you?" Jake asked pointedly. "Did you torture and murder Brody White in Dagestan?"

"Mr. Boxer, I don't even know where Dagestan is."

"Then you must not have been watching my show very closely because I mentioned Dagestan every night."

"Believe it or not, I have more important things to keep in my head than your ramblings about a bullshit conspiracy theory for some 'Old' World Order."

He'd used Old World Order instead of New World Order.

No one but Jake used that terminology. This man *had* been watching *Bullseye*, quite closely. Probably *too* closely.

After all those years, was it possible that he actually had Brody's murderer on the line?

The other pressing question, of course, was the secret Ana had encoded in *Red Fury*. Jake was beginning to suspect that he was speaking to the man Ana Turov had identified in her painting. To the mole himself.

Jake had interviewed countless subjects—politicians, dictators, and yes, even spies—enough to know that he would never get this man to betray his identity, at least not without playing hardball, and that he might just have to sacrifice himself in the process.

But this was Claire's story—one worth dying for—though the thought was cold comfort for what he knew he had to do next.

Clearing his throat, Jake said, "I'm not saying another word until you identify yourself.

Irked, the man barked, "I told you, I'm inconsequential. What *is* of consequence—"

"You know the number," Jake said, interrupting, and then hung up.

Hardball.

Stupidball.

Same thing.

THIRTY-FIVE

As Jake waited on the heart-shaped bed for the spy to call back, he slowly became aware of two things: One, he didn't have to worry about starving. He would freeze long before that. And two, Claire's marks were definitely being held prisoner along with him on the fifth floor. Besides Plastic Mel's whooping cough, he heard the knocks and shouts and cries from the rest of them, especially from the attorney, Nick Gold, who was wailing far louder than the rest.

He also noticed things that could only be heard in an abandoned, powerless building. A lonesome creak as the building shifted. Rodents scurrying in the walls. The smattering of snow against the double-paned windows.

And the hum…distant and low and terrifying.

And then he heard another sound—one that was primal and raw. It was a lonesome howl, and it wove itself harmoniously around the hum. Had the animal been drawn to the sound? Was that why the winters in Blind River belonged to the wolves?

Jake saw Hank's black marble eyes, and then thought about the beast's bitch. The mottled wolf that'd gotten away.

"M-my name is Jake Boxer, your host at the new and improved *Bulls-eye*," he said to himself, "and that hum…that howl…they're real, *not* d-delusions." Jake paused, a thought striking him. "The hum…that's why…that's why they shut down the town—so that nobody will *hear* it. The hum…that's why Claire was trying to find the entrance into—*the mountain.*"

Yes, Claire. *That's* why you were on the ski lift with Sean Farris, head of the Blind River Tourism Bureau, when it fell. You were hoping he'd tell you the way in, because you knew that whatever Brody had discovered in Dagestan was also under Blind River.

Just for the hell of it, Jake picked up the phone and dialed 9-1-1. He heard a ring tone—there was power—but the call was almost immediately answered by an automated voice, saying, *We're sorry, but this line is not set up for outgoing calls. Please contact your local carrier for support.*

He hung up. Looked at the door. It was probably locked, but what if it wasn't? Didn't he at least have to *try* to open it? What kind of an idiot would he be if he died in a locked hotel room that wasn't really locked?

Of course, trying the door meant standing up.

Just the thought of moving made him want to puke. Still, he inched his way to the edge of the bed, then cautiously swung his left leg over and followed it with his right. Shifting his body, he positioned himself so that the edge of the mattress was nuzzled behind his knees. Next he had to stand, but he wasn't sure if his back could support him. Still, he put both hands on the bed and pushed himself up. He did it. He stood. He also wavered, half-expecting his legs to go out like they had in Al's room, but they held. Taking small steps, he made his way to the wall, which he used for support as he inched his way to the door.

Locked.

Fucking shit.

Somber, he rubbed his hands on his arms, desperate for warmth. He was still dressed in Alaskan formal—blue jeans and a well-starched button up—but he didn't have a jacket, and the heart-shaped bed's duvet had been stripped from the bed and stored for the winter.

His gaze settled on the drapes framing the picture window.

Creeping across the room, he reached the window, wrapped both hands around the drapes, and pulled, not so hard as to aggravate his back, but hard enough to pop the curtains from their plastic rings. Once free, he wrapped the drapes around his shoulders, and only then realized he was standing inches from the window. His breath fogged the glass. His eyes took in the old wooden railroad trestle that forded the river to Main Street and the town square's shuttered storefronts, just beyond.

All powerless. All dark.

And then he looked to the mountain. Its summit was pale in the thin moonlight, almost blue. His gaze locked onto the black granite spines, and Jake felt a biting wind in his face. He felt the ski lift jerk upward and then fall. He heard the screams…*Claire's* screams…as the black granite spines rushed to greet them.

Shivering, he closed his eyes and saw Brody packing his audio gear in their small Moscow hotel with the view of the infamous Lubyanka prison. Brody, who'd been tortured for his audiotapes, tapes the FSB had erased. Jake had always wondered what those tapes had sounded like, and now he had a pretty good idea. Though Blind River's hum wasn't fleeting, as the locals had described the Dagestan Hum.

It was constant.

It was working.

Something was happening inside of the mountain.

The telephone rang.

Startled, Jake spun for it and twisted his spine.

He screamed, fell to the cold hardwood floor, and lay there, gasping for air—*for mercy*—as the hot point on his spine blazed.

Answer the phone, Jake. You're playing hardball, remember? But you can't go to bat if you don't take that call.

You're right, Claire. You're always…*always*…right.

Half crawling, half slithering, Jake scooted across the frigid floor, cursing his throbbing spine. The phone was on the bed, but he didn't dare try to stand to answer. Instead, he grabbed the telephone cord and jerked. The receiver fell off the hook and skittered across the hardwood floor before Jake was able to get a hold of it. Breathing hard, he put it to his ear and then huffed the phoniest words that had ever come from his mouth in all of his thirty-eight years.

"I almost didn't answer," he said, "wasn't sure if you were…if you were really ready to talk."

The man…the mole…the *spy*…chuckled. "And you're panting, I'm sure, because you've got me *right* where you want me, don't you?"

"Damn straight, I do. Are you ready to tell me who you are?"

"No. But I am ready to tell you who I'm *not*, and that, Mr. Boxer, is someone who cares if you live or if you die. It's in my best interest to re-cover the painting, but if I don't, so be it. I'm not the one locked in a hotel room for what is sure to be a very long, and very cold, winter."

Jake considered the man's words, and then said, "Okay. Tell me about the hum. That's why you had Brody killed, isn't it?"

"Brody?"

"Brody White…he recorded the same hum in Russia—it's evidence of something you're trying to keep hidden—a *machine*." Yes, that made sense, Jake thought. It was almost certainly a machine. "This mountain was part of White Alice," Jake said, urgently now, "you were supposed to dismantle it when Ana Turov came to visit, but it's still operational."

"There's a word for people like you—paranoid."

"*That's* why you won't reopen the mountain for mining," Jake realized. "You're still *using* it."

"Enough with the bullshit. *Where* is the *painting?*"

Jake didn't have the painting, of course, but he needed this man to keep talking. No. Not just talk, he realized. He needed him to reveal what he'd built beneath that mountain.

Jake deliberated for just an instant before saying, "Call me back when you're ready to tell me what the hell is going on."

Jake hung up.

Hardball, baby.

Nausea, baby.

What had he *done?*

He'd just thrown away the story Claire had died for, the story that *he* was going to die for.

The phone rang.

He grabbed it.

"Talk or I'm hanging up again."

"Look out your window," the spy said wearily.

No easy feat.

Jake was still lying on the floor. He would have to *stand* to look out the window, something he probably couldn't do even if he wanted to.

"No."

"Why not?"

"Because I don't feel like it."

"You can't get up, can you?"

Jake didn't deign to answer.

"Okay," the voice said, "let me tell you what you would see."

"Don't need to. I know what I'd see. That mountain—"

"Yes, you'd see the mountain, and if you looked closely, you would also see the broken chair lift. Now somewhere beneath that wreckage is a snapped bolt covered with plastic explosive residue. When the snow melts, you might find it, but only then would you have concrete proof that your wife was murdered. Now what do you think the odds are that you'll find that itty-bitty piece of bolt?"

Jake didn't need to answer.

Pretty low.

"The Kidd didn't murder your wife, Jake. The sheriff did, and he tried to kill you too. His deputy gave you a quick ride up the mountain, hoping to get you on the ski lift with your wife. Hoping to kill you both in the 'accident.' But you had the gall to survive. And now you have something *I* want, and I have something *you* want. Give me the painting, and I'll tell you where to find the explosives he used to take down that lift. I'll give you the evidence you need to launch a *thorough* investigation, but it will be an investigation that ends with him, not me."

"You'd do that? Give up your men for the painting?"

"After I have the painting, I won't need my men."

Jake clammed up and considered the spy's offer.

The nameless mole kept talking. "It was Wilson's idea to murder your wife. I told him not to do it. That she was too high profile, and so were you. But he didn't listen. If it makes you feel any better, Mr. Boxer, I can assure you he will be dealt with in time. The organization I represent doesn't tolerate liabilities. Without us, our world ceases to exist."

"I'm sure."

"You don't believe me?" he asked, then fell silent a moment before asking, "What are we, Jake? Biologically speaking, I mean. We're apes. Smart apes, sure, but ultimately, we're little more than organs and muscle and bone and hair—and that's all we've been for millennia. But we also build things. We have technology. Technology that evolves in the blink of an eye. The wheel becomes the car. The concept of zero becomes computer code. Small inventions turn into systems incomprehensible to those who invented them. While we humans? We're still clipping our toenails, for Christ's sake."

"What's your point?"

"My point is that someday what we build will eclipse who we are, and though while I'm sure you *revile* my existence, on that day you would gladly sacrifice your wife to keep me in my position."

"I doubt it."

The spy sighed, then switched gears. "Why do you think America and the Soviet Union avoided war during the Cuban Missile Crisis?"

"JFK outmaneuvered them."

"No, because JFK talked to Khrushchev. Not directly but through back channels. At the time, there wasn't even a direct line between the White House and the Kremlin."

"But there was a phone line between America and the Soviet Union," Jake said, recalling Mel's words at the auction. "Between the Diomede Islands."

"That's right," the mole said. "A single phone line between two nations with enough nuclear technology to turn the world to ash. I hate to think what would've happened if we hadn't thought to provide humanity that simple service."

Jake looked at the mountain. "What does any of this have to do with what you assholes built beneath Blind River?"

"Don't bother yourself with such things."

"It's a machine, isn't it? What does it do?"

"Nothing. And it will keep on doing nothing long after you leave this place...*if* you cooperate."

"You're intelligence, aren't you."

"*Fuck* intelligence, Mr. Boxer. I'm a man of *vision*, and *because* of men like myself, in this country as well as others, we've thus far avoided world-ending conflicts. Without men like me, in both America *and* the Soviet Union, JFK and Khrushchev would've destroyed this planet. We're the ones with the vision to build upon the wheel and to ensure it doesn't run us over in the process, and I will not allow *you*, a washed up newsman, to jeopardize that. Now, I've told you what you want to know. If you hang up again, I won't be calling—"

Jake hung up.

Next, he grabbed the phone cord and yanked it hard. The plastic jack snapped as it popped out of the wall, making it impossible to reestablish contact.

Now, if the spy wanted to speak to him, there was only one way to do it—by unlocking that fucking door.

THIRTY-SIX

"GOOD EVENING, f-for those of you just tuning in, I'm y-your frozen host here at *B-Bullseye*, and do I have a whale of a tale for you."

Jake couldn't stop chattering. He was freezing, even with the drapes wrapped around his shoulders. He'd been on the floor for God only knew how long, but he hadn't moved since yanking the phone jack out of the wall.

"Okay, I g-g-guess it's a f-frozen episode of spies and murder and Old World Orders. W-wake up, Blind River. The name's Jake B-B-Boxer, and I've got you…I g-g-got you in m-my…m-m-my…"

He couldn't get out the word *crosshairs,* but he did manage to make little trembling guns with his fingers, and even fired them off, making the sound effect and everything.

Before this current bitter chill had fully soaked in, Jake had spent several hours with his ear against the wall, listening for the phone ringing in another room, figuring that, if they were holding the other guests prisoner, surely the mole was interrogating them as well, right?

Wrong.

The phone's mysterious silence tested his every nerve. He told himself that the sheriff must have been interrogating the other prisoners. That the spy had only called him because of his past. Because of Dagestan and his knowledge of the hum. That it took more sophisticated minds to interrogate him than Sheriff Wilson Grout or his deputy.

Maybe...

The only thing Jake knew for sure was that it would take the sheriff's eagerness to unlock his door—his only hope of escape—but that would never happen if the prisoner who won the painting had already given it up.

Jake looked at the ventilation system in the ceiling above him and longed for the hot air that once pumped in from the lobby's enormous fireplace. With the fire extinguished, nothing but cold air circulated through the ducts, dropping the temperature considerably. Jake pulled the drapes tighter around himself, his ear once again against the wall, straining to hear a phone ring, hoping...no *praying*...that Ana's masterpiece had yet to be found.

But all he heard was the hum.

The low drone shook the fine white sand from Claire's long toes and cracked the lovely ocean of glass into pieces—

Jake blinked, then rubbed his sticky eyes.

Christ, had he fallen asleep?

He'd only closed his eyes for a second, but between the cold and his exhaustion, he must have sacked out.

How much time had passed? Was it light outside?

Yes. Yes it was. Daylight was now seeping in through the picture window, and despite the cold, a new warm thought filled his head.

He'd survived his first night in prison.

One night of survival meant there could be a second, but he needed to move, or he'd freeze where he lay. It was time to stand, but his back had stiffened considerably, both from the cold and sleeping for God only knew how long in that awkward position on the hardwood floor. Still, he managed to straighten his legs, then get to his knees. From there, he was able to use the bed to help him stand upright.

It certainly hurt, but it also felt good to stretch.

It was also nice to see the dawn, even one as cold as this. It was the first bit of sunlight he'd seen since his imprisonment, which meant that it must have been around ten thirty on Tuesday morning. And then it struck him. It was also election day. November 8, 2016—a day when millions of Americans went to the polls to elect the next president of the United States. Not that it mattered. Democracy was dead. The system was rigged. The spy and his cronies had built a machine beneath Blind River's mountain…and beneath the one in Dagestan…that had somehow rendered the occupant of the big white house at 1600 Pennsylvania Avenue obsolete.

The voters weren't in control.

They just thought they were.

Jake's stomach knotted up suddenly, reminding him that a full day had passed since his imprisonment, and that he needed food. Badly.

There was nothing in the kitchenette's cabinets. The minifridge was un-plugged and empty.

There wasn't a crumb in the room, Jake realized glumly.

He had another fundamental problem as well—he was thirsty. He tried all of the faucets, even the shower, but there was no water. As a last resort, he lifted the toilet cover and heard Pete Lancaster's touristy voice in his head.

Eureka! Der's water in dat der swirly bowl!

Yes, there was standing water, already covered by a thin film of ice, and no, he didn't dare flush because he knew that the bowl wouldn't be filling back up again.

Housekeeping had left a few courtesy cups in the kitchenette, thank God, so Jake took one, dipped it into the toilet bowl, broke the ice, and scooped up water. He held it at eye level and was relieved to see that it was clear, not yellow.

Not that he cared. At the moment, he would've drunk anything.

Speaking of pee, he had to do it, and he eyeballed the drain in the shower. He had to shit too, but he couldn't go in the toilet—his only water source—nor could he bring himself to shit in that little shower drain, at least not yet. He was still holding out hope that at some point, the mole would have to send Wilson to open the door. At some point, he was going to escape.

No, he'd shit when he was damn well good and free, and far away from Blind River.

After peeing in the shower, he scooped out one more cup of water before returning to the main room, where the heart-shaped bed—the last place he'd ever held his wife—invited him to lie down and go to sleep and never stir again.

"Not yet," he muttered. "Not when I've still got toilet water."

He put the cup to his lips, swigged it down.

By then, the crack in his spine was imploring him to rest, but he knew that lying down would only invite the Big Sleep, and he wasn't ready for that. Not yet.

Fortunately, his wheelchair was still in the corner. He certainly would've been more comfortable lying down, but the pain of sitting would keep him conscious—pretty important if he was going to get the rest of Claire's story.

After slowly settling into the chair, he wrapped both hands around the cold push ring and wheeled himself over to the picture window. He sat there for hours, watching the sun pull its light across the horizon, until it was once again low in the sky. It was no longer snowing, but the unrelenting wind blew powder from the streets and rooftops alike. Jake thought the entire town looked blurry, as if smudged by an enormous thumb. Dusk settled. Jake's numb brain was focused on food, sleep, and the nameless new president when he first saw the wolf.

The animal crept out of the heavy pine just beyond the trestle bridge (had it been feasting on the Clydesdales? On Lancaster?), and then made its way onto Main Street. It was a large and husky animal, mottled with grey and brown.

"Hank's b-b...*b-b-b-bi*..."

He was trying to say "bitch" but couldn't get it out.

The beast slunk toward the trestle. She stopped where Main Street's frozen asphalt met the bridge's steel platform and plunked down on her haunches, tipped her nose to the darkening sky, and howled the loneliest cry he'd ever heard. Wolves were social animals, yet this one's pack had been murdered and stuffed and mounted in the inside of the hotel's unfinished north wing. The lone survivor was clearly the worse for wear. Even at a distance, Jake could see that the big animal was thin and that her hair was falling out in clumps, as if struck by mange or rabies or whatever the hell wolves picked up wandering about in the Alaskan wilderness. Yet she wasn't entirely alone. Her cry soon harmonized with the hum, and for a moment, both mountain and beast were one. The sound filled Jake with a mixture of fear and awe.

And then he heard the footsteps.

Someone was coming.

The sheriff? To open his door?

Jake rubbed his cold hands, next clenched and unclenched his fingers, hoping to warm them up, knowing that in just a few moments, his door would burst open, and he would have to fight one, or possibly two, cops. From his wheelchair.

Don't think about the odds, Jake. It's your only play.

Grabbing hold of the push ring, Jake shoved himself toward an old brass lamp on the small table to his right. He'd had his eye on it ever since formulating his plan: jerk out the phone line. Make them unlock the door. Lure them inside. Get them close by playing up the has-been reporter with the broken back angle, and then bash their brains in, just as Al's father had done to that "commie."

He jerked the lamp's plug out of the wall and unscrewed the nut at the top of light, then slid off the lampshade, making it a much more formidable weapon. He started to unscrew the light bulb but changed his mind. Maybe he'd luck out and hit the sheriff in his face with it? Maybe the bulb would shatter and the glass shards would blind him?

But what about the other guy? The sheriff wouldn't come alone; he'd have a deputy with him, most likely the same deputy who'd driven Jake from the café to the ski lift? How was he going to handle him?

He didn't know.

He'd play that by ear.

What he *did* know was that he was ready for it.

He'd do it.

Just as soon as Sheriff Grout opened his door.

Jake's breath made little clouds in front of his eyes. His poor fingers were so cold that they weren't even trembling anymore. They could barely grip that lamp. This had to happen. *Now.* While he still had the strength to fight.

The footsteps stopped.

He heard a door open…but it wasn't his.

They'd come for someone else, Jake realized, as he slowly lowered the lamp. Someone a couple of door's down from him.

And then he heard the sheriff's muffled voice shouting, "Get to the back of the room—right fuckin' now! Get to the back!" The barked orders were followed by two people cursing in Russian. Next, Ivana…or Helen Platt if one was to believe her…shouted, "Get your hands *off* me! We *don't* have the painting!" And finally, as the Russian man screamed, a door slammed shut, muffling his voice, and footsteps retreated down the hallway, leaving Jake alone with the howling wolf and the mountain's song. But now there was a *new* sound, a frantic pounding on the door the sheriff had just visited—surely from Ivan, the stony FSB man who'd been introduced to Jake as Tom Platt at the auction.

A few minutes later, a flicker of light drew Jake's eye back to the picture window. His first thought had been "drone," but the light had been far too low in the sky. It looked as though it had come from the circle driveway at the front of the hotel. He set down his brass lamp, grabbed the cold steel push ring, and rolled himself back to the window, which once again fogged over with his breath as he peered outside.

The light Jake had seen was from a flashlight, and it was beaming out of the lobby's revolving glass door, catching a nascent snowfall. A woman was shoved outside shrieking, and Jake heard the Russian man scream bloody murder and pound on his window, just a few rooms down. The son of a bitch on the other end of that phone had just dramatically raised the stakes, a turn that was acknowledged with a mad cackle from Nick Gold in a different room down the hall—his booming laugh echoing throughout the hotel.

All of the prisoners, apparently, were watching the show.

A second flashlight joined the first, both of them illuminating a terrified Ivana. The sheriff and his deputy were making damn sure that Ivan, and the rest of the guests imprisoned on the fifth floor, had a good view of the dark-haired woman—now barefoot and quivering in the snow, and clutching a bloody hand they'd slashed before tossing her to the wolf.

A little something to pique the animal's appetite.

One of the flashlights caught the cruel mottled face of the wolf in its beam. Jake had last seen the animal standing on the opposite side of the truss bridge. Now that she was closer, he was struck by the animal's size. Its head came up to at least the Russian woman's chest, and from above, the animal looked as wide as a horse.

Wolves don't attack people, Jake quickly reminded himself. That's what Pete Lancaster, that sleigh driver, had said, and Lancaster had been a local, so surely Lancaster would've known.

Right?

Jake looked back to the wolf.

The animal's ribs were pressing against its thin, and in some places hairless, hide. She was sick and long overdue for a meal. He was pretty sure Pete Lancaster wouldn't have said what he'd said if he'd seen this one.

Jake pounded on his window, desperate to distract the wolf, to buy the woman a little time, if only to finish whatever prayer to whatever God she must have been praying to, but it didn't work.

Jake closed his eyes, but he heard everything.

When Jake did finally open his eyes, the flashlights were gone and so were Ivana's cries and the wolf's God-awful yips. Even Ivan's desperate strained screams in the nearby room had turned into a whimper. The only other sound, save for that hum, were Jake's panicked breaths. He was sure that the show had been as much for *his* benefit as it had been for the poor dead woman's partner.

Talk or get fed to Hank's bitch.

It was persuasive as hell, and Jake found himself running down a long list of bullshit he could spew to avoid a similar fate. But in his heart, he knew it didn't matter what he told them. Until someone gave up the painting, it would end the same way for each of them.

He was freezing and terrified, and perhaps more than anything, he was hungry. No, not just hungry. He was *starving*. He had to get out of there. He'd made a living talking, convincing people to do what they didn't want to do.

He could work his way out of this.

All he had to do was get the spy back on the...phone.

Jesus Christ, why in the hell had he jerked that phone cord out of its jack?

Jake thought about the broken phone cord.

Maybe it would still work?

Maybe, if he plugged it in, he could at least negotiate a sandwich... maybe some chips...so at least he wouldn't be hungry when he was fed to that big ass wolf?

Desperate, he wheeled himself over to the phone cord and felt around in the darkness with numb fingers. He finally found the phone line—the end was broken all right, but he tried to plug it back in anyway. It took forever to find the jack in the darkness, and once he did find it, the plug wouldn't stay in the jack. It hurt like hell to bend down like that, and Claire was still dead, and that painting was still lost, and—

Footsteps.

Soft ones on the carpet outside of his door.

Jake gave up on the busted phone jack and eased his chair back around. He'd left the brass lamp near the door, or at least he thought he had. It was too dark to see, so he couldn't be sure. Slowly rolling forward, he strained as he leaned down, swiping his hand along the hardwood floor, feeling for the lamp—his weapon—and cursing himself for his stupidity.

Why in the hell had he dropped it? Why hadn't he just left it in his lap?

The footsteps stopped, but not outside of his door. Once again, they were outside of the Russians'. Jake heard his neighbor's door open, and then the sheriff shouted, "Give us the painting or you're next!" but there was no answer. Until Jake heard Ivan's pained growl, and Wilson's voice shouting, "Down! Down!" There were several gunshots. A window shattered. Men screamed. More gunfire bellowed. An eerie silence followed. Then Jake heard someone running down the hallway. Someone big. Someone running toward his room. Jake's door shuddered suddenly. It shuddered *violently*. Jake's fingers touched the brass lamp—thank God, he'd found it! The door shuttered again. Something splintered. Jake got the lamp in his hand. Held on tight with frozen fingers—*help* me, God. He felt his heart burst out of his chest and run away like a terrified rabbit from that big, terrifying wolf. Just before the door flew off its hinges, a thought bum-rushed Jake's brain: the cops had a key.

The sheriff wasn't knocking down his door.

It was someone else.

The door burst open.

A dark body hurtled toward him.

Jake swung his lamp.

It was a blind swing, but he knew he was facing the proper direction, and he stood when he swung. He had *momentum*. When he connected, he felt a bone-sickening thud, and the bulb burst into zillions of shards. He was falling forward, groping for the man he'd just struck, snagging him, and somehow dragging him down to the hardwood floor in a tangle of arms and legs. On impact, a starburst exploded behind Jake's eyes; the Devil twisted his spine, and he felt the sudden and queer urge to shit, cry, and die, all at the same time. But the attacker found his feet and a dark silhouette filled the picture window. Jake saw that it was the Russian. Ivan's chest was heaving, and he was bleeding profusely from the gut. Wilson had shot him, and Jake had done a real number on his skull with that lamp, but Ivan still had the haft of the fire axe he'd used to knock down the Honeymoon Suite's door in hand, a weapon he clearly intended to now use on poor Jake.

"Где картина?" he asked, his bushy mustache quivering.

"What?"

Jake, still on the floor, desperately reached behind him for his wheelchair.

The door was open, blasted from its hinges.

He could escape!

But he *had* to get into his fucking chair.

"Картина!" the Russian screamed, staggering forward. "Где она, блядь?!"

Jake found his wheelchair and pulled himself into it as the woozy Russian stumbled—having lost quite a bit of blood. He opened his mouth to say something else, but no words came—just a hiss, as if he were deflating. Jake grabbed the cold push ring, ready to roll out the door—to escape—but Ivan was stumbling toward him again, moving in slow motion while he bled out and navigated the sudden-funhouse of his broken skull. Ivan grabbed Jake. He tried to tip the wheelchair over but only managed to swing it around, so that Jake's back was now to the door. With little choice, Jake rolled himself backward, back to the open door. Back to the dark hotel. On the verge of death, Ivan teetered, then fell on him—*grabbed* him—one thick hand squeezed Jake's throat. The other tried to raise the axe—

But he couldn't swing it. Ivan was too weak.

They moved backward, closer to the open door. Ivan's legs were pumping, slowly but steadily, even while his grip tightened around Jake's throat. Together they rolled out of the Honeymoon Suite—*out of that miserable prison!*—and out into the fifth-floor hallway, toward the banister—the *broken* banister—where Al and Christopher Kidd had battled to the death. Crossing the hallway, Jake felt the chair hit the banister. Whatever was left of the wood cracked.

Buckled.

Split.

Jake grabbed the chair's push ring and held it. His lower lumbar roared. And the Russian, his clammy, pallid face just inches from Jake's own, groaned out his last and fell still. Jake shrugged the dead man from his lap. The body slipped to the side and plunged. Moments later there was a beefy thud, five stories below in the lobby, at nearly the exact same spot where Christopher Kidd had expired.

It was over.

Except, of course, that his wheelchair's thin rubber wheels were still teetering on the edge. Jake tried to roll the chair forward but couldn't muster the strength. The tires slipped. The chair tumbled backward. Jake flung himself forward, praying to kiss the fifth-floor hallway's thick carpet instead of the river-stone fireplace, far below.

THIRTY-SEVEN

It was dark and freezing and his wheelchair and a dead Russian were in the lobby five stories beneath him, but all Jake Boxer could think about was food.

Filet mignon.

Potatoes au gratin.

A salmon fillet…with just a *squeeze* of lemon.

Or a fucking box of Tic Tacs—*anything* he could *eat*.

Jake was lying on his empty stomach on the fifth floor's hallway carpet, his legs dangling on the other side of the broken banister. Yes, he'd just fought Ivan to the death, but somehow, he'd managed to keep those curtains over his shoulders. Grateful, he pulled them tight.

He was thankful to be alive. He was terrified to be alive.

What in the hell was he supposed to do next?

Then, down the hallway to his right, he noticed light spilling from one of the hotel rooms, its door slightly ajar. Electric light spilled in a supposedly powerless hotel.

Inching his way to the wall, he managed to hook his fingertips on the wainscoting, and then pull himself to his feet. Using the wall for support, he slowly worked his way down the hall, reached the room, and nudged the door the rest of the way open. A stray beam of light escaped, as if it had been held prisoner, too.

Flashlight.

He entered the room and saw two uniformed bodies, both sprawled at awkward angles on the floor. It was Sheriff Wilson Grout and his deputy, Travis Benson, the man who'd given Jake a ride from the café to the ski slopes minutes before the lift had fallen—a "favor" Jake now knew was part of their plot. They'd been hoping to kill both him and Claire in the lift accident.

Both of the lawmen had been shot to death. A gently falling snow was slowly covering them. It was almost a magical phenomenon, until Jake re-called hearing glass shattering along with the gunfire. Looking closer, he saw that the room's window had been shot out in the gunfight.

In a bid to intimidate the rest of them, the sheriff had made a fatal mis-take. He'd enraged a Russian FSB agent twice his size. The FSB agent must have wrested Wilson's weapon away from him.

There were two flashlights inside the room. The one shining out of the room's door was lying near the deputy's boot. The second flashlight, still in the sheriff's hand, shone straight up at the ceiling, creating an amber col-umn. This light was slowly pulsing—the flashlight batteries nearly depleted. Not that Jake cared. He'd spied a granola bar poking out of the sheriff's breast pocket.

With chocolate chips.

Jake let go of the wall and took a couple of wobbly steps. The next thing he knew, he was on his knees, cramming the granola bar into his mouth fast-er than he could possibly chew. It wasn't until he'd swallowed every last oat and licked the chocolate from the inside of the wrapper that he realized he'd consumed the entire bar mere inches from the sheriff's death mask.

The lawman's lips were frozen in an exaggerated grin, made all the more eerie by his bulging eyes, as if he were staring at some horror in the afterlife.

Jake looked away. His gut told him that this was the man who'd mur-dered his wife, and that he could finally leave Blind River with a clean con-science—he'd caught him. But Claire kept whispering in his ear.

My story…the reason I dragged you to Blind River…is still hidden somewhere inside the hotel.

The flashlights were bright enough to illuminate much of the room. Jake quickly spotted a revolver on the floor near the lawman's hand. He grabbed it and cracked open the cylinder. Empty. As was the deputy's gun. Both weapons had been depleted in their fight with Ivan. They'd be of little help without ammo, but Jake did find something that would almost certainly come in handy: the key ring on Wilson's utility belt.

A key ring that could most likely unlock every door in the hotel.

Jake unhooked the keys from the belt and pried the dimming flashlight from the sheriff's stiffening fingers. He would have preferred the deputy's flashlight—its batteries were stronger—but retrieving it would've meant either crawling over to where the deputy was sprawled out, or standing and then squatting again once he reached the flashlight. Neither option was palatable. Instead, Jake used the busted table to straighten up slowly, and then shuffle out of the room.

He stood in the hallway for a spell, catching his breath and listening. There'd been at least five officers working in Blind River, but that didn't mean they were all inside the hotel. The spy would want as few people in on Blind River's secret as possible. Besides, Jake had only seen a single vehicle through the Honeymoon Suite's picture window—the sheriff's F-150. Given all that, it was likely that only Sheriff Wilson Grout and Deputy Travis Benson had been involved, which meant, with the Russians dead, the only people left in the hotel were Mila Noël, Nick Gold, and Plastic Mel, all still prisoners somewhere on the fifth floor.

Speaking of Nick Gold…

Jake could hear the attorney carrying on a couple of doors to his left.

"I don't *have* your painting, but I *do* have money, *millions* of dollars, and it's yours. It's *all* yours. Just somebody open this fucking door!"

Jake thought about Nick Gold's hands all over Claire on the slopes of White Alice, and then he turned away.

He'd open that door last.

Slowly ambling across the dark hallway, with Nick Gold's cries at his back, Jake pounded on the next closest door with the butt of his flashlight.

"Hello?" he said. "Anyone there?"

No answer. He had to knock on two more doors before a woman's timid voice finally said, "I…I don't have it. I told you, I'm a curator for the Brussels Museum of Modern Art. We don't *have* twenty-three million dollars to spend on a painting—all of our art…it's all donated."

Mila.

Pulling the sheriff's keys from his pocket, Jake found the keyhole with the flashlight, then tried key after key until one of them finally caught. Just as soon as the deadbolt cocked back, the door swung at him. Jake stumbled back instinctively, and of course, his throbbing back seized up on him. Oh shit, he was going to fall, and it was going to hurt.

But Mila grabbed him, kept him upright, despite his bulky frame. He was about to say thanks when her nose flared and her wild, narrowly set eyes widened, and Jake felt something cold and sharp press against the soft flesh of his throat.

He froze.

"Jake Boxer," she muttered in her heavy accent. "The reporter with the dead wife. I knew you had something to do with this."

"Could you…could you *please* take that thing out of my neck."

She did just the opposite, pushing until his skin broke and he felt a trickle of warm blood. She glared at him, her black eyes twin dragons in their caves, ravished and menacing and ready to scorch the countryside.

"I'm on your team," Jake said quickly.

"If you're on my team, how did you get those keys?"

"That wolf," Jake said, "you saw it with that woman outside? That woman was a Russian FSB agent, and the sheriff…he killed her thinking it would make her partner talk. Instead her partner…well, it only enraged him. He killed them both—the sheriff *and* the deputy—and then he knocked down my door…so that he could kill me too."

"Why?"

Jake licked his chapped lips. "Probably because I'm the reason you've been locked in a hotel room for two days. I told the sheriff you might have won *Red Fury*. Or that the Russians might have. Sheriff Grout…he must have told them I blabbed, and so as soon as that big Russian got loose…" Jake closed his eyes and heard Ivana's screams as the wolf ripped her apart. "He just wanted vengeance. Look, I'm sorry you're here. It's my fault. I never would've said anything had I known the sheriff was working with him."

"Working with who?"

"You don't know?"

No. She didn't.

"Tell me everything," she said, and Jake felt the pressure ease off his throat. The pointy object she'd been threatening to slit his throat with was a curved glass shard; she must've smashed one of the complimentary glasses. Resourceful.

Jake, still clutching the sheriff's dimming flashlight, raised it a hair and the light spilled on Mila's face. He couldn't help but to gawk at her chapped and chewed-on lips. She was starving and thirsty and frozen, but despite all that, she still looked like Ana Turov.

"There's a code in your grandmother's painting," Jake told her, "a one-time code, the kind of code that was used during the Cold War. And that code identifies a mole deep inside one of our intelligence agencies. *He's* the one who took us prisoner. *He's* the reason we're here. The sheriff worked for him—he was trying to find and destroy the painting before anyone could use it to identify his boss."

"His boss...is a spy?"

"A double agent," Jake said. "And your grandmother was a double agent within the Soviet Union. She was an asset for the CIA."

Mila shook her head and seemed to deflate, her face suddenly old and withered. Jake wasn't surprised. It was a lot to swallow.

"Where did you get the key to open my door?" she finally asked.

"Sheriff's body. Four doors down."

"Any food?"

"There was," he said, "it was just a granola bar. I'm sure there's more around the hotel. There's another flashlight in the room. Why don't you get it, and we'll find a bite?" He held up the sheriff's dimming flashlight. "This one's about to die."

Mila looked to her right, to the amber light pouring out of Ivan and Ivana's old room, where the dead men were lying.

"Do you still think the painting's here?" she asked.

"We wouldn't be here if it wasn't." Jake said, his thoughts on the world-weary voice he'd heard on the telephone. "And that spy certainly wouldn't have risked calling us."

"There's no power," Mila said, over her shoulder, as she walked toward the Russians' room. "How could anyone have called?"

She left him to ponder the question.

They could've hooked up a small generator, Jake. Landlines...they don't need much. Remember?

Damn straight, Claire. That's right.

Jake blinked and swallowed back bile.

He was sure that he wasn't imagining the nausea, and that he hadn't imagined the hum. And if those were real, he was sure the voice on that phone had been real too.

Pretty sure...

He looked back to Mila, but she'd already disappeared into the room with the dead lawmen.

Alone again, Jake distracted himself from the monsters of his mind by considering the remaining rooms on the fifth floor. He could still hear Nick Gold carrying on behind him, but he hadn't heard so much as a peep out of Mel Perkins for quite some time—odd for a guy with such a brutal cough, unless...

Was the author of *Fifty Bricks* dead?

Maybe.

Who was he kidding?

Probably.

Hell, he'd nearly been dead *before* he'd been imprisoned.

Jake gave the thought a moment to stew, then lamented the loss of a potentially outstanding source...quite possibly his MPP.

But then...did he hear a rattling wheeze? From the room closest to the elevator? Taking great care, he slowly shuffled toward it, and as he got closer, he heard the quiet, ineffable susurrations of the near-dead. It *had* to be Mel. The old man was definitely saying something, but what?

By the time Jake reached the door, he realized there was a reason he couldn't understand the words, and it wasn't because the door had muted Mel's voice. It wasn't even because the man was so close to death.

It was because he was speaking in Russian.

To the spy on the telephone—to the man who built a global intelligence network.

*S*omeone *had* received a call from the spy besides him.

Jake practically rejoiced. He *wasn't* crazy!

Listening to the old man made Jake long for the acne-scarred translator he'd hired all those years ago back in Moscow, a translator who was surely dead by now, murdered for his involvement with *Bullseye*.

Jake was about to unlock Mel's door when a beam of light cut the darkness. He looked behind him, held a hand to his eyes, and saw Mila's approaching silhouette.

"What are you doing?" she demanded.

"Mel Perkins…" Jake said, his voice weaker than he had hoped. "He's in this room—we need to let him out."

"Why? We don't know who he is—*we don't know who he's working for.*"

The statement sent a shiver up Jake's injured spine.

Mila hadn't struck him as the sort of person who'd let an old man starve to death, but then he remembered that glass shard she'd held to his throat and reconsidered.

"Mila, he went to Moscow when your grandmother came to Blind River. They were part of the same 'Goodwill' exchange. After she disappeared, the Soviets imprisoned him in the Lubyanka. Maybe he knows something useful. And listen," he said. They both fell quiet and heard Mel Perkins speaking in Russian. "He's *talking* to the spy."

"On the phones that don't have power?"

Her voice was full of doubt.

"Yes," Jake said hotly. "He *knows* things. Maybe things about the painting. About the code. Don't you think we should let him out?"

Mila considered him silently, then shined her flashlight on Mel's door.

"You have the keys," she said finally. "Open it."

Jake quickly unlocked it. The door swung open, and they both shined their flashlights into the room.

Mel was, indeed, there. The old man lying on the floor, his mouth slowly moving as the Russian words left his lips. But he wasn't speaking Russian to the spy on the telephone. He was speaking Russian to the undisputed king of concierges. To Al Tulane, Jr.

"Всем сердцем," Mel was saying slowly, his head in Al's lap, his lungs full of phlegm. "Всем сердцем, всей жизнью своей клянусь служить родине, партии, и советскому народу."

"He's been saying the same thing over and over again," Al explained casually, as if he'd been expecting Jake to free them all along. "Yesterday, when he was still speaking English, he told me what it meant. You care to know, Mr. Boxer?"

"Do I have a choice?"

Al shook his head sadly, then said, *"With every heartbeat, with every day that passes, I swear to serve the Party, the homeland, and the Soviet people.* It was the oath administered to the KGB."

THIRTY-EIGHT

———————

"JAKE," MILA SAID, "I thought you said the Russian man was dead."

"He is."

"Then where is his body?"

Jake swallowed his oatmeal. He shifted uncomfortably in his wheelchair, which the group had rediscovered shortly after descending the hotel's *Gone with the Wind* staircase, leading down to the lobby. Despite its high-dive from the fifth floor, the chair was still in one piece, but its left wheel had bent on impact and several spokes had been snapped from the rim. Jake pulled his drapes, which were still over his shoulders, tightly around him as he scanned the lobby for the Russian. He was sure the FSB agent was dead—nobody could survive that fall—but Mila had a point.

Where the hell was his body?

"You don't have to worry," Jake said. "The sheriff shot him. I personally clubbed him over the head with a lamp and then he fell five stories. Believe me. He's dead."

"Sure, just like some fucking spy was calling you on a telephone without any power."

It was Nick Gold.

Of course.

They'd freed the dumpy lawyer shortly after discovering Al Tulane and Mel Perkins.

It was a decision Jake was already beginning to regret.

Nick was probably the healthiest of the bunch, but he wouldn't quit whining, and he was the only one who chuckled when they spoke somberly about what the mottled wolf had done to poor Ivana. He'd also scoffed when Jake asked if he'd received a call from the spy. As it turned out, *no one* in the group had heard a ringing phone, something Jake found difficult to believe. As a prisoner, Jake had heard every creaking bone inside the hotel.

Before leaving the fifth floor for the lobby, Nick Gold had insisted on plugging another phone into the jack inside of the Honeymoon Suite. Not only had there been no dial tone, there wasn't even an automated voice. But Jake knew what he'd heard. That spy's voice had not been a "confabulation," as his shrink had called some of his memories of Moscow.

You're not crazy, Jake. You know what you heard. The phone was probably hooked up to a small generator—it must have run out of gas.

Exactly. No one else can comprehend what these people are capable of. They didn't see what they did to Brody after he recorded the Dagestan Hum. But you and I, Claire...*we* know.

The sheriff apparently had used the lobby's sprawling front desk as a kitchen, which made sense. It was much closer to the fireplace than the real kitchen, and with the power out, a small wood fire (not big enough to heat the upper floors, that was for sure) had probably been their only source of heat. The sheriff and deputy had stored their food there too, and in addition to the oatmeal, the freed prisoners also discovered more granola, jerky, a bowl of fruit, and some hard cheese and bread.

But no dead Russian.

Jake, who was still holding Wilson's dying flashlight, turned it back on and shone it around the lobby, vainly searching for Ivan's remains.

While doing so, he noticed that the hotel had been trashed. Tables, chairs, and couches had been toppled like old Greek ruins. Strips of carpet had been ripped from the floor. Every cabinet and drawer had been emptied, and hotel supplies were strewn about like so much trash. The sheriff and his deputy had turned the place inside out in their search for Ana's painting—Jake could only pray that his search would go better.

Jake's flashlight fell on Mel Perkins, the best-selling author of *Fifty Bricks* and a Lubyanka survivor. At the moment, the author was perched on the edge of the fireplace—now alive with a modest but warm flame. It was a desperate bid to keep Death's chill from his bones. Al Tulane, Jr. held a spoon of oatmeal to the dying man's mouth. Every once in a while, Mel's tongue dabbed at the spoon, like a lizard. When he wasn't taste-testing his food, Mel was mumbling in Russian, though his words were now as thin as gas. No one in the group could understand him, but everyone kept a close eye on him, especially Al, who'd pretty much carried the dying man down all five flights of stairs himself.

As Jake considered Plastic Mel, the hum came back, though the rest of the group didn't seem to hear it, probably because they weren't listening for it. Jake, himself, could barely hear it, but it was there, and the harder he listened, the queasier he felt, like all of those Dagestan locals, complaining of nausea.

"You want to find your missing Russian?" Nick Gold said to Mila before jabbing a trembling finger at Mel. "He's sitting right there."

"He's *not* a Russian," Al said defensively, his rich baritone echoing throughout the lobby. "He's an American who spent *time* in Russia."

"What tourist picks up the KGB oath by 'spending time' in Russia?"

"*Lubyanka...*" Mel wheezed.

"Luby-what-the-fuck?"

"*Lubyanka,*" Jake corrected, his gaze on the dying man's tight, emotionless face. "That's where he learned Russian. It's the old KGB headquarters in the Red Square. There's a prison in the building's basement—part of the Russian Gulag—that's where he learned the KGB oath. His captors probably forced him to repeat it ad nauseam in an effort to brainwash him."

"And why were the two of you locked in a room together?"
Mila.

Her narrow eyes were set on Al. She had drifted to the far edge of the fire's glow, but she hadn't left it, Jake noted.

"Don't rightly know," Al replied, his gaze on his big hands. "I can only tell you what I told Sheriff Wilson, that I confronted Christopher Kidd after

Mr. Boxer here informed me of the boss's plan to bankrupt Blind River… and that he'd sold Ana's painting as a sort of financial getaway plan." Al's voice cracked with emotion. "I loved Ana…he *knew* how I felt about her… and I was mad that he hadn't told me he'd found her masterpiece…that he hadn't at least let these old eyes look upon it, much less *touch* it. He…he got in my face and I pushed him, but…he wasn't supposed to fall." His words fell away to a hoarse whisper, but when they came back, they were stronger than ever. "Sometime later, after most of the guests had already left, the sheriff and deputy escorted me to that room on the fifth floor—Mel was already there. We got to chatting, and by the time we realized the door was locked, that they weren't coming back, the last of the guests were already across the bridge and leaving the town square, way out of earshot."

"That true, Mel?" Jake asked.

If Mel heard him, the dying man made no indication.

Al, on the other hand, glared at Jake, his bushy eyebrows furrowed in the firelight. "Mr. Boxer. Of course, it's true. Why would I lie?"

Nick scoffed. "Oh, I don't know, maybe because *you murdered your boss.*"

"It was an *accident.*"

"And what? We're just supposed to take you at your word?"

"Blood," Mila interrupted, prompting every eye to turn.

She'd ventured deeper into the lobby, braving the darkness beyond the fire, and she'd trapped blood spatter on the lobby's stone floor in the beam of her flashlight.

Nick stood, incredulous. "But no body? The Russian falls five stories, *with* a gunshot wound, then crawls off somewhere to die?"

"No, he was dead," Mila said softly, her flashlight tracing not just blood spatter, but a blood smear. "Something dragged him away."

Mila turned her light to the front revolving door. It was cocked open, just wide enough for a wolf to slip through.

"Honey," Al said, breaking the uneasy silence. "Maybe you oughtta come back over here with us."

"I'm the curator for the Brussels's Museum of Modern Art." Mila said sharply, "*not* your *Honey.*"

Al just nodded, and Jake noted that Mila still made her way back toward the fire. Big shot or not, she'd apparently determined that anyone could be eaten by this particular wolf.

"My phone," Jake said, remembering the plan Claire had whispered into his ear. "*Claire's* phone. It's a satellite phone. We can use it to call for help."

"Great. Where is it?" Nick asked, sounding a little hopeful.

Jake shook his head. "I don't know. It was in my pocket before the sheriff drugged me. It's got to be here in the hotel."

"A lot of good *that* does us. Wait, I know. Maybe one of us can call it, you know—listen for its ring? Maybe with your magic landline that gets a dial tone without power?"

"If you're not going to be helpful, shut up," Mila said.

Jake studied the dark hotel. "The sheriff drugged me in a room in the north wing, second floor. The room with Hank the stuffed wolf. He called it the Hunt." Jake looked to Al. "Do you know it?"

"Of course."

"So maybe it's still in there." Jake looked to the stairwell, then considered his own wheelchair. "One of you should go look."

"Fuck that," Nick growled. "We stay together."

"He's right," Al said. "We stick together, at least until there's daylight. Even if your phone is up there, there's no guarantee it still has a charge."

"If we don't get that phone, we're never getting out of here. And that hum…It'll only get louder. The nausea, the headaches, they'll only get worse." Jake looked around at the group. Blank expressions all around. "What? You guys don't hear anything?"

"No," Nick said sharply.

"Yes," Mila said softly, contradicting Nick Gold. Her gaze going to the darkness outside. "I hear…*something.*"

Jake looked at Al, who pursed his lips before admitting, "I've been here sixty years, and this is the first time I've heard that noise."

Jake nodded. "There's a phenomenon called the Dagestan Hum that's very similar. It causes nausea, migraines, and insomnia. A close friend of mine tried to record it, and the Russians killed him for it."

"Bullshit," Nick said, sounding exasperated. "That sound's just the power grid cooling down. I lived next to one growing up and heard all sorts of weird electrical shit."

They're stalling, Jake. They don't want you to get my phone because they don't want you to be rescued. They want you to die here because we know too much.

"I'm not going to die here, Claire. I can promise you that."

"Who the hell are you talking to?"

It was Nick Gold. Staring at him as if he were crazy. He must have been talking to himself. And if he was talking to himself, maybe they were right. Maybe he *was* crazy.

Stop. You're not. They think you are, but you weren't in Dagestan, and you sure as hell aren't now. They're hiding something from us, Jake. They're trying to dismiss you.

It was true.

Nick Gold had ridiculed him over his claim that the spy called the Honeymoon Suite, and now Nick was dismissing the hum.

If they're good guys, they should all want to leave ASAP, right? And if they aren't, they'll do anything to stay. So put them to the test. See who wants to leave without that painting.

Good idea.

"I was talking to myself about the sheriff's truck," Jake said to Nick, following Claire's lead. "It's parked outside. I have the keys. We can use it to get out of here."

Not a soul stirred, not even Al, confirming Jake's suspicions.

They wanted the painting, and they weren't leaving without it.

No…*not* the painting. They wanted the code *inside* the painting. Surely the now-deceased FSB agents Ivan and Ivana had known about it, and Jake was willing to bet that the three individuals huddled around the dimming fire hadn't bid up to twenty-three million dollars to hang it over their mantel. But what about Al Bridge Tulane, Jr.?

Jake, don't be naive. Who's to say Al hadn't stayed on at the hotel because he'd been looking for the painting too?

"I guess we don't have to leave just yet," Jake said, breaking the awkward silence. "We may want to find the painting before we go. I mean, one of us was willing to pay twenty-three million for it. Seems to me that we should track it down."

"Twenty-three *million.*" Al whistled. His eyes were damp. "That would've made Ana's day."

"Not to burst your bubble," Jake interrupted, "but it wasn't for the painting. It was for a code."

"A code?" Nick said, sounding surprised. "In the painting?"

He's playing dumb.

I know, Claire.

"Well, yeah," Jake said. "That's why you're all here, right? For the story my wife died for? That Ana Turov was using her paintings to smuggle secrets out of the Soviet Union—"

Nick jumped back in. "First of all, let's get this straight. *I* didn't want that painting. And I bid with my *client's* money. Not my own."

"And what, exactly, does your client do?"

Mila.

Nick Gold leveled a cold stare at her, then said, "He works in telecommunications, and if he wants to way overpay for a stupid painting, I'm not gonna stop him."

Telecommunications.

The word harkened back to Jake's conversation with Mel Perkins during the auction. Hadn't the author had gone on a tear about the phone line between the Diomede Islands? About how, at the time, it had been the only direct line between America and the Soviet Union.

Jake looked at Mel, but the old man was out of it. His thin lips barely moving at all.

Looking back at Nick, Jake said, "Your client works in telecommunications?"

"Yeah, so what?"

"What's his name?"

"That's attorney-client privilege."

"We're stuck here together. We very well may die here together. I think we'd all like to know as much as possible—"

"Or what? You're gonna jump out of your wheelchair and strangle me? Kill the guy who won the painting, fair and square? The only one who might be able to find it? Oh, that'd be smart. *Real* smart."

"If I wanted to kill the person who won the painting, it wouldn't be you." Jake turned to Mila. "Would it?"

"Hey!" Nick said hotly. "*I'm* the one who bid twenty-three million dollars!"

"You're right," Jake said. "And if someone hadn't stolen your account information from your laptop that twenty-three million might've been in your bank when the Kidd tried to transfer the funds."

"You're telling me it wasn't?"

"That's exactly what I'm telling you. And that's why you never received instructions for how to pick up the painting. Instead, Christopher Kidd told the bidder who came in second. Didn't he, Mila?"

Mila licked her chapped lips and took a step away from the group, her flashlight still in hand.

"Before she died, my wife bugged Nick's room," Jake said. "I heard you using his laptop while he was passed out drunk. I can only assume you were stealing passwords for his account."

Nick Gold stood before Mila could answer, his hands balled into fists. "You bitch!"

"Easy," Jake said. "You hurt her and none of us get the painting, and I know all of you desperately want it."

Jake looked at Plastic Mel. "You, the American author who went to Moscow to write his novel while Ana was here, painting the mountain. When she disappeared from Blind River, the KGB suspected her of betraying the Motherland, of stealing secrets, and I assume they accused you of doing the same? But you didn't. And you had no idea what Ana had been up to. But you were guilty by association. A ten-year stint in the Lubyanka would strip anyone of their talents." Even so close to death, Mel winced at the observation. "Decoding that painting would be your revenge on a system that stole your career, wouldn't it?"

Mel didn't answer. He *couldn't* answer. He was too busy puckering for oxygen, like a fish out of water.

Jake moved his dimming flashlight to Al, who was still sitting next to Mel. "And you. You weren't in love with Ana, you were obsessed with her, which is why you keep those photographs of her in your bedside table drawer—and you're obsessed with her masterpiece. Yes, you may regret the Kidd's death, but it wasn't accidental. The only reason that bannister broke is because you *threw* him through it, didn't you?"

Al shook his head in weak protest, but that was all.

Jake moved on to Nick Gold. "Mr. Gold, you won't reveal the name of your client? Well you don't need to. Your client's the CEO of a successful telecommunications company, who also happens to be in business with the spy who called me in the Honeymoon Suite—*that's* why you're lying about not hearing that phone ring. You don't want us going down that road because your client is trying to *blackmail* the spy, and he can't blackmail him if the world already knows his name."

"Oh, for fuck's sake," Nick Gold groaned. "This bullshit is the reason your TV show was canceled."

Jake ignored him, looked at Mila. "And you, Ana Turov's granddaughter, you're fighting for her legacy, both artistically and politically. And you think that code can identify the man responsible for her death—"

"And what about you?" Mila asked, interrupting. "What about the guy who has 'America in his crosshairs?' Why do you want the code?"

"I don't. My wife did. I just want her story."

Jake looked back to the fireplace. Brody was now sitting next to Plastic Mel, those headphones clamped to his bone-white skull, the skin peeling from his face like cheese off an old pizza.

"I had a friend who died investigating that hum. The spy, the voice on the other end of the phone, is responsible for his death, and half a century ago, Ana Turov was trying to pass his name to the Americans. That's what's in the code—his identity—and that's why he's so desperate to keep that painting hidden."

"Jesus," Nick Gold said. "For the last time, an old spy *couldn't* have called you on the phone. *There's no fucking power.*"

"Oh, there's power here. More power than you could possibly believe. The current is rippling straight through this place."

Jake studied the dark mountain through a lobby window.

"The power's inside the mountain. There's something underneath it. Something that's only operational in the winter. The code in the painting names the man who built it."

The little group sat in silence for a moment, their heads cocked, their ears on that electric hum, on the noise the machine was making beneath the mountain.

"Okay," Mila said finally. "Let's say you're right. Even if we do find the painting, where's the code? I studied it at the auction. I didn't see one anywhere."

Jake was about to tell them they could worry about that *after* they found the painting when Mel Perkins suddenly wheezed, "The *shapes*...the *colors*."

He fell silent again, and for a moment, everyone thought he had died, but then he inhaled sharply, back from the dead.

"What's that supposed to mean?" Nick muttered. When Mel didn't answer, he stood, his big fat gut pushing out at the dying man. "*What's that supposed to mean?*"

The old man still didn't respond. Jake had an idea—he bet it had something to do with deciphering the painting, a clue possibly gleaned from Buck Masterson. Maybe Mel Perkins had met with the death row inmate? Maybe Mel told Buck he'd been invited to the auction to buy *Red Fury?* Maybe Buck, not trusting Mel, had then told Claire? Claire had last interviewed Buck, when? Two months ago? Buck could've told her about the auction then.

Jake thought about asking Mel if he'd spoken to Buck Masterson lately, but it was painfully obvious that Mel wouldn't be answering.

He was too busy dying.

"Okay," Jake said, his gaze going to Nick Gold, "we get the painting, and then we figure out what he's talking about."

Jake looked to the darkness beyond the pitch of the fire. His mind was racing.

Why had the spy called his room and no one else's? And what would the spy *do* once he learned that his minions, the sheriff and the deputy, were dead? Assuming Jake was right—that Ana had encoded the spy's identity—the spy would undoubtedly want the painting destroyed. But without the sheriff there to do his dirty work, wouldn't he have to resort to other, more drastic measures?

Blind River was a six-hour drive from Anchorage, *if* the roads were even passable. It would take the double agent too long to send reinforcements. Jake thought about the glint he'd seen in the sky the first day they'd been in Blind River. It felt like a lifetime ago, but he could still see it clearly in his mind's eye.

Not a weather balloon.

Not the sun bouncing around the falling snow.

A drone.

An MQ-9 Reaper drone hovering above them right then and there, hiding in the inclement weather, flown by CIA officers out of Langley who didn't answer to the president, but to a double agent who'd built something underneath this mountain, a mountain once utilized to eavesdrop on the Soviets. And now it was used for...what?

The same thing it was being used for in Dagestan. Something the spy had to keep hidden.

No matter the cost.

Jake could practically feel the pressure waves of a Hellfire missile rushing down at the hotel.

"We have to find the painting," Jake said quickly. "And if we're going to get out of this alive, we have to trust each other. So this is what's going to happen." Jake looked at Mila. "You're going to tell Nick where you moved his client's money." Then he looked at Nick, "And you're going to explain to your client that you were outbid. In return, Mila here will pay you the money she was going to pay Christopher Kidd, that's millions of dollars in your own pocket."

"And I get the painting?" Mila asked.

"Yes." Jake looked at Mel Perkins, "Whatsmore, Mel here gets his code. He gets his revenge. The shapes and the colors, right?"

Mel could do little more than flutter his eyelids—his way of saying yes.

"What about me, Mr. Boxer?" Al said softly. "What do I get?"

Jake, considering the concierge, said, "We won't report you for murdering Christopher Kidd. And yes, you'll also get to gaze on Ana's painting one last time. We'll even let you take a picture."

Al nodded. It was enough.

"And what about you?" Mila asked. "What do you get?"

"I get to publish the story."

The room fell quiet as they considered Jake's proposal. Then Nick Gold piped up, "Fine. But I want my money as soon as we get to Anchorage. She doesn't leave Alaska before it's in my account."

"Fine." Mila agreed. Looking at Jake, she said, "You're right. I did win the painting, but it never arrived. Christopher Kidd promised it would be in my room before checkout, but he never told me how it was coming." She looked at Al. "You killed him before it was delivered."

Al's face hardened, but he didn't say a word.

Jake thought about it, then vocalized a suspicion that had been simmering for the past hour. "Just because the Kidd died before you got the painting doesn't mean it wasn't on its way." Jake looked at Al. "Any idea where room service stores its dollies for the winter?"

THIRTY-NINE

THE ROOM SERVICE DOLLIES had been a common sight in the Hotel Ascent, especially in the mornings. So instead of scrambled eggs and a side of bacon, why not an original Ana Turov and a side of Cold War secrets? If Jake's hunch was right, they would find *Red Fury* hidden in one of the carts, still waiting to be delivered.

Al, the expert on the Hotel Ascent, told the group where the carts were stored—in the kitchen off the Glass Hall—and before they knew it, a reluctant Nick Gold was pushing Jake's wheelchair toward the ballroom. The chair limped along on its lame left wheel, jolting Jake's spine as it clomped across the floor, but it was still less painful than walking. Al and Mila, on either side of Mel Perkins, kept their arms wrapped around his thin waist, helping the ailing man navigate the couple hundred feet between the lobby's fireplace and the ballroom. They reached the entrance of the Glass Hall and Nick parked Jake to one side of the doors before opening them.

Mila shined her flashlight inside. Jake didn't. His had officially died moments earlier.

"Kitchen's over there," Al said, pointing across the empty ballroom to the set of easy swing aluminum doors.

They crossed the long, dark ballroom—their footsteps echoing far too loudly for anyone's comfort—and entered the kitchen. Once inside, Mila's flashlight illuminated baby blue tiled walls, stainless steel shelving, and three counters worth of gas stoves. Large strips of magnets ran the length of the wall where knives, spatulas, and pokers once hung, but the utensils were now boxed up and stored for the long winter. Too bad no one had boxed up the Russian's half-eaten body.

Mila averted her flashlight the moment the light touched the mangled corpse, but it lingered long enough to verify Ivan's fate. Yes, he'd fallen from the fifth floor to his death, and yes, his corpse had been dragged off into the depths of the hotel, most likely by the same mottled wolf that had consumed his partner.

No one in the group spoke. They knew instinctively not to talk but to *listen* for the soft pitter-patter of a four-legged animal. The wolf was somewhere inside the hotel.

"The service dollies are over here," Al whispered, eager to find the painting and get out.

"Over here" was in an endless hallway connecting the kitchen to what Jake assumed was the loading dock in back of the hotel. Before leaving, the hotel employees had parked the fifty or so service dollies along the length of the hallway, then covered them with blue plastic tarps. But they weren't covered anymore. Apparently, the sheriff and his deputy had already searched them. They'd stripped off the tarps and dumped each cart over. Some had been toppled on their sides, others were upside down, their silver serving platters and bulbous lids scattered about the hallway.

If the painting had been on a cart, the sheriff would've found it.

"Great," Nick groaned. "Now what do we do?"

Jake noticed something. Something the sheriff just may have missed. The top tray of each cart was thick, thick enough to store silverware.

Or a painting.

"Do the tops of the carts open?" Jake asked Al.

Al looked at the carts and shrugged. "Not sure, Mr. Boxer" he said. "Never worked in the kitchen."

Mila, handing her flashlight to Jake, righted one of the toppled carts and felt around the rim. She found a button, pushed it, and the top of the tray popped open. Jake shined his flashlight inside and discovered that the little storage space had an insulated interior. It wasn't meant to store utensils, but hot or cold packs, depending on the dish. The particular cart Mila had opened was empty, but the storage space appeared to be just big enough to hide *Red Fury*.

"Open them," Jake said, blinking hard, swallowing back bile. "Open them all."

Mila and Nick did the work while Jake held a flashlight. Al tended to Mel Perkins, now slumped against the wall, his bony buttocks on the cold tile, shivering. Nick dove into the work with zeal, righting a cart and searching for the button that unlocked the top. Jake held his breath. He didn't want Nick to find the painting; he wasn't sure they'd be able to pry it out of the lawyer's hands if he did.

Nick wrestled the lid off, revealing an empty storage space. Thank God. Irked, the attorney threw the cart to the side, grabbed another and searched for the button.

Meanwhile, Mila had just pried the top off her second cart.

Also empty.

"Al," Nick shouted. "Get your ass over here and help us before that wolf comes back."

Al bit his lip, then looked to Mel. "I'll be right back, okay?"

Mel nodded slightly, and Al lumbered over to help. As the three worked on the carts, Mel inched closer to Jake, and between coughs, whispered, "*The spy...he* called *you?*"

Not only was Mel speaking, but also it was the first time anyone had acknowledged that what Jake had claimed was true.

The spy *had* called him.

"Yes."

"What did he...what did he *sound* like?"

"Tired."

A strained smile stretched across Mel's face. "Motherfucker needs to *die...the shapes!* The colors—!"

Mel slumped into Jake, who did his best to get an arm around him—to give him a little support—without tweaking his own back too badly. The old man descended into another coughing fit, and Jake saw flecks of fresh blood on his lips.

"Al!" Jake shouted.

Al turned, saw Mel clinging to Jake's wheelchair, and rushed back over. Meanwhile, another dolly clanged.

Jake looked up. Nick Gold was about halfway down the hallway, his enormous stomach heaving as he worked, as he grumbled, "It's not here!"

"We haven't even gone through a third of them," Mila pointed out.

Nick Gold threw up his arms and turned to yet another cart. Pushed the button. Pulled off the top. Empty.

By then, Mel Perkins was once again in Al's arms. His breath had become as shallow and as precious as a hummingbird's.

The shapes and the colors.

Jake didn't know what it meant, but he was sure it had something to do with the code in the painting. If there were was any hope of deciphering that painting, Mel *had* to live.

The Devil tweaked his spine. Jake gripped his chair's armrests tightly, squinting. Breathing deeply. He'd moved too quickly, goddammit. He'd been too anxious. But how could he not be?

It didn't matter. They weren't going to make it. They weren't going to find that painting. Not before the wolf got them, or the drone circling over their heads—

Breathe, Jake. In and out. Picture us at the ending.

"I *can't* breathe, Claire—he's gonna *kill* us. He knows we're out of our rooms. He knows we're looking for the painting. He's gonna blow us up— *he's gonna use the drone.*"

"Drone?" Mila asked, prompting Jake to look at her.

You said that out loud, dummy.

Yeah. Yeah. Yeah.

"Drone," Jake said slowly, his gaze on Mila. "I saw one. He's been watching us. He's *still* watching us. The *spy*—"

"Hey! Get your flashlight over here," Nick shouted suddenly, "Now!"

Jake swung his light to Nick Gold. The lawyer was hunched over a cart toward the end of the hallway.

He had something in his hands.

Nick didn't need to state the obvious, but he did it anyway.

"Fuckin' *masterpiece*," he muttered, clutching what must have been Ana's painting, his knuckles as white as bone.

And then he turned and held it up.

"Masterpiece" was an understatement.

"Let me see it."

Jake extended a hand. He wanted to get the painting away from Nick Gold as quickly as possible.

But the attorney didn't hand it over. Instead, he glared at Jake's hand, as if the ex-newsman had just offered up the bubonic plague.

Mila, who'd taken her flashlight back from Jake, shined it in Nick Gold's face. "Give him the painting, motherfucker."

The lawyer swatted at her light, as if he could brush it away. "Get that light outta my eyes."

"Mila," Jake interrupted, "get the light off his face, and Nick, we had an agreement. You get the money. Mila gets the painting. Mel gets his secret. Al gets to go free. And I get the story. Now hand it over."

"Why do *you* get to hold onto it?" Nick asked, his face pulsing red in Mila's light. "So that you can pretend to find some code in there that doesn't exist?"

"No, because I'm in a wheelchair, a *broken* wheelchair," Jake stressed. "If I try to steal the painting, I think you'll be able to catch me."

The attorney, who was still a good thirty feet down the hall, pulled *Red Fury* close to his chest and glared at Mila, his breath visible in big bursts of steam. "I said get that fuckin' light outta my face!"

But Mila didn't get it out his face.

Jake thought about the first time he saw her—when she stormed away from her meeting with the Kidd at the Café Beaujolais. He thought about her holding that jagged shard of glass against his throat. He thought about where she'd gotten that jagged shard—that where there was one, there must be another—and he saw her reaching into her pocket with her free hand.

Jake, stuck in his wheelchair, turned to Plastic Mel, who was trembling and wheezing behind him, clutching his chest with a hand, drowning from the inside out, muttering, "*the shapes and the color*," over and over and over again.

Mel was of no help, and Al was too busy propping the thin old man up to take note of Nick Gold's drama. Suddenly, Jake saw a glint of glass as Mila's hand came out of her pocket. He was about to shout for her to stop when a howl did it for him. It was a lonesome and terrifying sound, and it rejoined the mountain's song—that queer electric hum—in a duet that made them sound like lost lovers.

It ended, and a long silence followed, until Mila finally broke it.

"That bitch is definitely inside the hotel."

The empty building was full of echoes, and it was difficult to pinpoint exactly where the howl had come from. Jake's best guess put it behind them, probably toward the loading dock. Mila must have thought so too, because she finally moved her light off Nick Gold's face and shined it back the way they'd come, beyond the Russian's gruesome remains, to the baby blue tiles on the kitchen walls and the aluminum doors that would lead them back into the Glass Hall.

"We should go that way."

Mel's watery eyes found the kitchen doors, now illuminated in the glowing circle of Mila's flashlight. The dying man's mouth was curling into itself—his carefully constructed face was finally collapsing—and his chest was rising and falling in slight, arrhythmic breaths. He was also doing something else, though. Something deliberate. He was nodding. Nodding as if to say, "Yes. The Glass Hall."

The shapes. The color. Jake...The glass collage!

That's it, Claire. That huge glass installation in the ballroom.

The wolf's howl billowed through the hallway again, and the group hurried for the kitchen's aluminum doors. Nick Gold even set the painting in Jake's lap before taking hold of the wheelchair's handles. Al and Mila once again wrapped their arms around Mel and dragged the wheezing man along for the ride, away from the wolf.

Once everyone was safely inside the Glass Hall, Al secured a little latch on the aluminum doors, and Nick Gold hurried across the ballroom's hardwood floor to the heavy double doors that led to the lobby.

"There's no lock!" Nick shouted as he closed the double doors.

Mila shined her light on a row of circular tables the hotel staff had left stacked against the wall. "There! Use those to barricade it!"

Nick turned to the stacked tables, grabbed one by the legs, and yanked it, toppling the rest of the tables to the floor with a humongous clatter.

If the wolf didn't know where they were before, she certainly did now.

Not that Jake gave a shit; he was holding *Red Fury*.

His hands tightened around the painting. A singular thought pulsed through his head: He'd done it. He finally had Claire's story...*and it was sitting on his lap!*

He ran his fingertips across the hard paint. He knew better than to touch it—it was fragile and irreplaceable—but at that moment, he *needed* the tactile sensation of Ana's desperate brush strokes. Touching it like that, he imagined the Soviet artist working slavishly on the painting. Her thin fingers gripping the brush like a weapon.

Jake looked at the ballroom's great window, at the massive glass collage. Before rushing to blockade the door with the circular tables, Nick Gold had left Jake's wheelchair in the center of the ballroom. The hum seemed to be louder there, and Jake was sure he could see the glass panes vibrating within their rebar web. Jake tried to discern the bulging mountain beyond, but the night and snowfall all but blotted *Ningakpok Iggik* from the horizon. It was a shadow—no, a shade of the mountain he'd seen in the day—the brooding soul of a killer that Ana Turov had somehow captured so perfectly on stretched canvas. The mountain's silhouette stared back at him apathetically, as if it couldn't care less about what happened in the next few precious minutes.

And why should it care?

The mountain had been there for thousands of years, and it would be there for thousands more.

Jake, and even *Red Fury*, were insignificant.

Al and Mila deposited Mel on a chair near the aluminum doors, which led back to the kitchen. Al remained by Mel's side, but Mila hurried across the ballroom to Jake.

"The cipher," she said quietly. "If it *is* in the painting, it won't be obvious. My grandmother wouldn't have wanted anyone else to see it, only the person who was *meant* to see it."

"Buck Masterson," Jake muttered.

She looked to him. "Who is that?"

Jake quickly explained *Bullseye*'s relationship with Buck Masterson, that even after they'd both quit the business, Claire had repeatedly interviewed the criminal, believing the death row inmate could lead her to Brody's killer. Apparently she'd been right. Buck Masterson had led them here, to Blind River.

By the time Jake wrapped up his story, he noticed that Al had been hanging on his every word, but Mila had only been half-listening.

She was hypnotized by her grandmother's painting, just as she'd been at the auction. Jake understood—the painting demanded attention. Ana had painted the rounded peak of the mountain dead center in the canvas, lending it a foreboding presence, as if the mountain had decided where it would sit for its portrait, not Ana—

Jake. The code.

Right.

Listening to Claire, Jake scrutinized the brush strokes and textures. *Red Fury* consisted mostly of tiny dabs of paint, some as small as pinpricks. The dabs on the granite mountain were of varying shades of red—from blood red to an almost white pink. The red dots smeared into one another, lending a *feeling* that the mountain had been captured with the use of hard lines, but in reality, it was much more akin to an expressionist's work.

She'd mimicked this same style along the river—a blue ribbon twisting through the bottom left quadrant of the canvas. From a distance, the river looked as if it had been painted with a single stroke, but in reality, it was made up of thousands of Ana's small precise dabs. She'd also used dabs of yellow and orange to highlight the river, to emphasis the waning glow of a dying sun.

The last hint of life before night overtook the landscape.

"So did you find the code?"

Jake looked beside him and saw Nick Gold, just a foot away. The lawyer was jittery and sweaty; his eyes kept jumping between Ana's painting and the doors that led to the lobby, the ones that wouldn't lock. "No," Nick said, "of course you didn't because this is all bullshit. Your wife bugged us for *no* reason—it's just a painting. A *lost* painting my idiot client wanted to spend *entirely* too much money on!"

"The Honeymoon Suite," Jake said, ignoring Nick's outburst and looking at Al. "Are you sure that's where she painted this?"

Al, still supporting a barely breathing Mel, nodded.

"Okay, then why didn't she paint the mountain from the Honeymoon Suite's perspective?" Jake pointed to Ana's rendering of the mountain's black spines. "Look. You can see four granite ridges in the painting, but from the Honeymoon Suite, you can only see three. Believe me, I spent enough time looking at it."

Jake turned his attention to the humming mountain through the glass collage, a black cutout against the black sky. The granite spines were only barely visible in the darkness, but he could still clearly count four. She'd painted the mountain from the Glass Hall's point of view, not the Honeymoon Suite's.

"The shapes and the colors," Jake muttered, looking back to Mel. "You sure it's the glass?"

But there was no answer. Mila shined her flashlight across Mel's frozen face. His lips were still curled in, but he was no longer gasping for air. In fact, he was no longer breathing at all.

Al hadn't even noticed.

"He's dead, Al," Jake said, maybe a little too loudly. Al blinked, saw that Mel was, indeed, gone, and somberly closed the author's eyes before making his way over to Jake and the others.

As the concierge crossed the ballroom, a thought struck Jake. For a man who'd been obsessed with Ana Turov for decades, Al had been remarkably indifferent to her masterpiece.

Why had he waited this long to venture over to see it?

Maybe because he'd been too concerned with Mel.

Maybe...

Jake turned his attention back to the painting. It was clearly meant for public consumption, to hang in a museum, but if Ana had simply hidden a bunch of letters in the painting, somebody somewhere would've spotted them. The Soviets would've known she'd been passing messages, even if they'd never deciphered the message. They would've executed her. No, Ana meant for the code to be read one time and one time only—here, in this room, where it was to debut for a host of art critics, including a man who really worked for the CIA—Buck Masterson."

Jake looked at Al.

"Did Ana know she was going to exhibit the painting in this room?"

"I imagine it was up to her."

"And that glass collage was here in 1973?"

"Yes, sir."

Jake turned and looked at the panes of glass: *at the shapes*. He looked to the painting: *at the colors*.

"The painting and the glass make the cipher…we use them together to decrypt the message."

The unmistakable click-clack of claws on tile reached them. The ornate double doors that led to the lobby were still closed, thank God. Two circular tables were still propped against them, one for each door, but an amber light flickered through the crack between the doors—light from the fireplace. As it was, Jake could only see the fire *above* the doorknob. A black shadow loomed beneath it. A *moving* black shadow. In a moment, with a gruff whine, it was gone, replaced by the fire's wavering light.

"What was that?" Nick asked. "What the fuck was that?"

Jake looked back at the painting.

"Buck Masterson," Jake mumbled, "he was a CIA agent, and he was here, in this room, posing as an art critic. Right, Al?"

Al shook his head. "It was a long time ago. There were a lot of critics here, I can't remember their names."

"This painting—Ana's code—it was for him. *He's* the one who told my wife about this place." Jake looked to Mila and Nick. "One of you must have gotten in touch with him. One of you must have called him and told him that Christopher Kidd was going to sell it. One of you wanted him to tell you how to decipher the code, but he didn't. He told my wife instead."

Nick Gold shook his head. "This is crazy! I've *never* heard of this Buck asshole!"

"He did not call me either," Mila said softly. "And I did not call him."

Jake looked back to Mel's body. It could've been the Lubyanka survivor, as he'd hypothesized earlier—maybe that's where Plastic Mel had learned about "the shapes and the colors?"

Or maybe the Russian FSB agents had called Buck?

Or Al.

Claire's words clanged around his skull like a hammer.

Jake studied the concierge. He was huffing hot air into his arthritic hands, once again indifferent to the unfolding events around him. Again, odd for a man who kept Ana's photograph on his bedside table, and a stack of her nudie pics in his drawer.

"You took Buck's photograph," Jake said, trying to sound casual. "He was here, in this room with the other critics, when you snapped it. Are you sure you didn't know him?"

"Mr. Boxer, at least twenty critics showed up. To a man, they left the day Ana and the painting disappeared—just hours before the unveiling. They were irate—they'd come a long ways. You have to remember, back then Blind River was even more difficult to visit than it is today. They all stormed off just as fast as they'd come."

If Al and Ana were lovers, wouldn't Al have searched desperately for her when she went missing, like you did for me? Wouldn't Al have spoken to the critics? To Buck Masterson? And if Al had met Buck Masterson—if Buck was here to get an important message from Ana—is it such a stretch to think that the two of them searched for her together? That they turned Blind River inside out looking for Ana and her painting? Is it such a stretch to think that Al had met Buck Masterson? And is it such a stretch to think that Al is lying to you now?

Claire's words drained through Jake's brain and settled in his heart.

"Let's say that you are right," Mila said, interrupting Claire's voice. "Let's say that Buck Masterson was here in 1973. This man was executed last week, was he not?"

"Yes. He was."

"Then how are we supposed to decipher a coded message if he's the only one who knew it? Don't we need a string of letters to start with?"

They expedited his death penalty appeals. Do you remember me telling you that? Do you remember how worried I was? Why was I worried, Jake? Think!

Because he hadn't told you the ciphertext. You knew you needed the painting to decode a string of letters, but he hadn't told you *what* letters you were supposed to decode. He wasn't going to tell you until you brought him the cipher.

But he did tell me, didn't he? In the end he found a way.

Jake remembered Claire's text.

Her last words to him.

Buck Masterson's last words, just before he was executed.

"*The Good Spy Dies Twice*," Jake mumbled, struck with the revelation. "Buck Masterson's last words before they executed him. Claire texted them to me before she died."

"So?" Mila asked.

"So, back in the day, spies passed along messages using ciphertext—seeming random letters that were strung together. But if you had the cipher—the numbers to decrypt each letter—you could read it." Jake looked at *Red Fury*. "The Good Spy Dies Twice. The initial letters—*T-G-S-D-T*—that's the ciphertext. And the painting and glass are the cipher to read it!"

His words soaked into the ballroom's walls.

Mila piped up. "Okay. So if this ciphertext is five letters long, the painting must be coded with five numbers, right? Then we just subtract Ana's numbers from Buck's letters and we have the message?"

Jake nodded, already one step ahead of her. He pointed to a single red dot on the painting, just beneath the black spine that was farthest to the right.

"A dark red dot. The darkest red on the painting. How many of those do you see?"

Mila quickly counted the blood red dots. "Fourteen?" she said. "No, fifteen."

"Right, and they're grouped. Look..." He pointed to the first lone dot, "Group one." Next he pointed to a group of two red dots, still on the mountain but toward the left edge of the canvas, "Group two." Then he pointed at a group of *three* red dots, practically dead center, "Group three."

He went on, pointing out each group: one through five. "Five groups of dots and five letters in Buck's ciphertext. The *dots* are the *code*."

"No. The *dots* are fucking dots!" Nick shouted, exasperated. "We *have* to get *out* of here!"

"He's right," Jake said. "They're just dots. Even the Soviet government couldn't toss her into the Gulag for something so innocuous. But Ana was smarter than her government. She left a code that could only be read in one place, at one time. Here, in this room, on November 6, 1973. The dots don't reference numbers to subtract from Buck's letters, they reference those windows."

The group followed Jake's gaze to the glass collage.

"The shapes and the colors," Jake said again. "The shapes refer to the windows; the colors to the dabs of dots on the painting."

Jake studied the single blood red dot marking the first number in the cipher. Ana had used it to mark the bottom portion of the granite spine that was farthest to the right, which also just so happened to be the same one that had killed Claire. He turned to the mountain. The sky was no longer black, but gray.

The sun was coming up.

Suddenly, Jake felt tungsten studio lights on his face, and he smelled pancake powder beneath his nose, and in his mind's eye, he found himself staring down the unflinching black eye of the camera, a camera that would beam his face into millions of households. He would warn his audience that Blind River's dark mountain, and the machine an American spy had built beneath it, was the gravest threat to freedom the world had ever known.

Jake's heart beat strongly for the first time in years.

Moving quickly, he held the painting up to the glass collage, relocated the blood red dab of oil paint, then found the exact same spot on the real mountain looming on the other side of the glass collage. He was looking at that particular spot through a skinny, oval-shaped pane of glass. Specifically, the *third* pane of glass from the *left* on the *second* row, or the seventeenth pane of glass—the number 17.

Time to compare it with the ciphertext: *The Good Spy Dies Twice*…or *T-G-S-D-T.*

Those letters translated into the following numbers: 20-7-19-04-20.

So subtracting 17 (the pane of glass indicated by the single red dot in Ana's painting) from 20 (the first letter in Buck's ciphertext—the letter *T*) revealed the number 3. Or the letter—

"*C.*"

Jake's breath caught in his throat.

He'd just decoded the first letter of Ana's message.

Four more letters and he'd have a name. He'd have the spy. He'd have Claire's story.

"That cannot be right."

Mila.

She was standing behind Jake, shining her flashlight at the painting.

"What? Why not?"

"Where you are standing in the room determines the pane of glass you're looking through." She hurried to the opposite side of the room, her footsteps echoing as she went. "From over here, if you looked at the same spot on the mountain, you'd be looking through the…" She quickly counted out the panes. "You'd be looking through the eleventh pane of glass. So subtract 11 from 20 and you get 9, or the letter—"

"*I*," Jake muttered.

Shit.

Of course. It was relative. The pane of glass would shift depending on where the viewer was standing in the room. That meant they could only decipher Buck's last words if they knew *exactly* where Ana had planned to exhibit the painting for the critics, and if they knew where Buck Masterson had been sitting fifty years ago. These were questions for Al.

Jake turned in his wheelchair, cringed as the Devil tweaked his spine, and saw that the concierge was now standing just behind him.

The rising sun's gray light was slowly filling the ballroom, exposing the ashen complexion of Al's face. The old man was covering his ears—trying to block out the hum, Jake was sure—as he stared out the window.

Surprisingly, he wasn't looking at the mountain. He was looking at the hotel's winter garden, which contained, of course, the witch hazel's twisting limbs and surprising yellow flowers, the plant Al had been so deliberately—and *lovingly*—pruning when Jake had lost Claire up on White Alice.

Al must have felt the heat of Jake's gaze because he looked back at him quickly, his breath short in his lungs, and gasped, "What?"

The click-clack of clawed footsteps in the lobby once again distracted him. The noise was followed by a loud clang that prompted Mila to whip her flashlight back toward the lobby doors. The light revealed Nick Gold, a folding chair in hand. He was slamming it against the doors that led to the lobby—where they could see the black shadow of the once-starving wolf pacing back and forth. She'd had plenty to eat but, apparently, she'd now developed a taste for human.

"Get outta here!" Nick was screaming, smashing the doors again and again with the chair. "Go away!"

"Nick!" Jake shouted. "Stop! You're just pissing it off!"

Spurred on by the noise, the animal began scratching at the doors, like a pet dog begging to get in. Nick stumbled away from the doors, turned his head, and puked suddenly. Groaning, he dropped the chair, clutched his head, and screamed, "Would somebody shut off that fucking hum!"

Jake saw Brody's pearl white teeth curve into a grin.

Yes.

It *was* the same hum he'd died for.

Panicked, Jake looked back to Al. "Where was Ana supposed to exhibit the painting?"

The concierge licked his dry lips and stepped toward Jake, and the ex-newsman noticed that the concierge's hands—the powerful hands he'd inherited from his murderous father—the same hands that had tossed Christopher Kidd off a fifth story balcony—were hooked like claws.

"*Al*," Jake pleaded, "where was Ana supposed to hang that painting?"

"I don't...I don't remember, Mr. Boxer."

Al stumbled back suddenly, as if waking from a nightmare, his hands went to his pockets, his big eyes opened wide.

What was wrong with him?

He remembers, Jake. He just doesn't want to tell you. But you don't have time to talk it out of him. Not with that hum. Not with that wolf. Talk to the museum curator—she'll know!

Desperate, Jake turned to Mila. "You're an art curator, right? How would you display the painting in this room?"

Sensing his panic, she answered quickly. "Artists love the north light." Her gaze darted around the room, studying how the rising sun was filling the corners. "Indirect sunlight," she said, looking to the southern wall. The wallpaper featured the same red-and-white chevrons that covered the carpets in the hotel hallways. "There. That wall would be best." She looked to Al. "What color was this place before the Kidd remodeled?"

Al squinted. "I can't...I can't rightly recall, Ms. Noël."

Mila clearly didn't believe him. She hurried across the room to the southern wall, then ran her hand along the seam between the wainscoting and the wallpaper until she found a loose corner. Using her fingernails, she picked out the corner and peeled the wallpaper back, revealing a layer of ivory paint.

"The paint before the Kidd remodeled," she announced. "It's ivory, a decent enough background for an exhibition."

Mila hurried back to Jake, who didn't hesitate. He gave her the painting.

As Mila's fingers wrapped around it, the color in her face darkened, and Jake knew that he'd just witnessed a sense of ownership taking root in her hollow face.

He found himself praying that she didn't run off with it.

Swallowing her greed, she rushed to the southern wall, the one with the best north light and with ivory paint beneath the obnoxious wallpaper. She looked up and saw a brass plate screwed into the ceiling. Turning toward Al, she asked, "There was a chandelier up there? Hanging from the ceiling?"

Al nodded and his mouth made a hard line, his hands digging deeper into his pockets.

Why, Al? What's *in* there?

Meanwhile, Mila had centered herself directly beneath the brass plate, turned back to the southern wall, and walked straight to it. Once she reached it, she turned back to Jake. "In that photograph of my grandmother, the one hanging in the Honeymoon Suite—how high did she have the painting on the easel?"

"The bottom was about even with her waist."

"Nick," Mila said. "Get over here and hold the painting against the wall."

Nick, who was lying on the floor in a puddle of his own puke, looked up and considered her through empty eyes.

"Do you want your client's money back or not?" Mila barked.

At the mention of money, the attorney somehow found his feet, then stumbled over, saying, "I just want that…want that *hum* to *stop*."

As Nick made his way to Mila, Jake looked back at Al. The concierge's hands were still deep in his pockets. He was no longer staring at the winter garden, but at the graying sky overhead.

"Hold it so that the bottom of the painting is even with my waist," Mila instructed Nick, oblivious to the danger above them. Nick, still slumping, did his best to hold the painting against the wall as Mila slowly walked backward, her eyes focused, looking for some magical viewing distance that only a curator, or an artist, would know. She stopped suddenly, saying, "Here. This is the spot where the paint strokes disappear. The spot where the painting presents itself." She looked up and saw that she was standing directly beneath the brass plate where the chandelier once hung. "A good place to seat your viewers—in the light."

Mila turned to her left and looked through the glass collage; she quickly gamed out the black granite spine matching the one Ana had marked with the single blood red dab in her painting. She was looking through the sixth glass pane on the bottom row, or the number thirty. By subtracting that from the letter *T,* the first letter in Buck's ciphertext, you get—

"You killed her."

Every eye turned on Jake, including Ana Turov's murderer.

Not that Jake noticed. He was squarely within the walls of his castle. Even his tick subsided. He finally knew the truth.

Yes, Jake. You do. You have my story—the whole story. Now use it.

"What's in your pocket?" Jake asked.

Al didn't move.

"It's a cell phone, isn't it? Claire's satellite phone."

"Why I don't know what you're talking about, Mr. Boxer."

"When are you supposed to call? When we've hit the point of no return? When the only way to stop us from uncovering his name is to use that?" Jake pointed to the overcast sky beyond the glass collage. Somewhere above the clouds was a Reaper drone. "Or maybe you don't need to call? Maybe he already has a lock on the signal transmitting from Claire's phone? All you have to do is stand next to the painting and that wall of glass that deciphers the coded text, and then...*boom.*"

Al smiled disarmingly—that great big I-love-everyone smile that had kept him employed as head concierge of the Hotel Ascent for decades.

"Sounds like you're writing me into that last *Bullseye* episode that got you canceled, Mr. Boxer."

"How old was he back then? The spy? In his late twenties? Even then, he had a vision for this place, didn't he? A remote surveillance mountain— already dug out and primed to build a machine deep inside, a machine that only operates when this place is closed for the winter. Even then, your boss was recruiting his global elite, a handpicked bunch he saw as a better fit to govern than those we elect." Jake took a breath, reconsidering. "Or did they recruit him? Regardless, he saw potential in you, a busboy with a daddy who *loathed* the 'commies,' who no one would ever suspect of having an affair with Ana Turov—a woman who'd somehow uncovered his true identity. She *confided* in you, and once she told you how she did it—that she passed her secrets through her paintings—you strangled her, you buried her in the garden, and you graced her final resting place with witch hazel, one of the only plants that blooms in the winter. How'd you sneak her body out of the hotel, Al? In a linen cart?"

Al didn't answer. His hands were back in his pockets.

Back on Claire's satellite phone.

Jake kept at it. "But you couldn't bring yourself to destroy the paint-ing—a masterpiece that was as much Ana Turov as her flesh and blood. So you hid it, but you *told* him you'd destroyed it. After all, how would he ever find out differently? Not when you'd hid it so well inside the hotel. Over the years, that spy built his machine, and you tended to it over the winters, didn't you? Everything was going just fine until Christopher Kidd found the painting while remodeling." Jake winced as he leaned toward Al, as fire shot up his bending spine. "You, the sheriff, the deputy. You all work for the spy, don't you? *You're all traitors.* You killed Claire because she was trying to get under the mountain, but you didn't know about the painting until I told you Christopher Kidd had auctioned it, did you? I'm curious, what did that asshole spy say when you called and told him? How pissed was he when he found out you never destroyed it? Pissed enough to convince you to do whatever it takes to destroy the painting now? To make sure his name remains hidden from the world, even if it means sacrificing yourself for the cause?"

"*P-I-M-W-Q,*" Mila said, interrupting, having deciphered the encrypted message. But then her face fell. "It doesn't mean anything. It's gibberish."

Jake, who still hadn't taken his gaze off the concierge, said, "That's be-cause Ana didn't speak English, did she Al? We shouldn't be decoding this into our alphabet, we should be decoding it into Russian. It's a good thing we have you here. That spy taught you how to speak Russian before she arrived, didn't he? At least enough for you to get by with. After all, you had to speak her language to seduce her, didn't you?"

Al, red in the face, was shaking his head repeatedly, saying, "You've got it all wrong, Mr. Boxer."

"No, Al. I've got it right. And now I want you to do something—I want you to listen to me. You think you're backed into a corner, but you're not. There's still a way out. The mouth of the mine is still open underneath this hotel, isn't it? You use it to tend to that machine throughout the year, don't you? You can take us to it—*you can get us undercover before that missile strikes*—"

"I...I really don't know what you're talking about."

"Picture us at the ending, Al. Picture us *alive!* This spy...he doesn't *care* about you. He's not *worth* it. We know his name; we can make him *pay* for what he made you do to Ana all those years ago, because you didn't want to kill her, did you? You honestly loved Ana Turov, just like I honestly loved my Claire. Don't you want to make amends for what you've done?"

Al stared at Jake for what might've been a lifetime.

"Да," he finally said. And then the weary old man looked behind him, back toward the aluminum doors that led to the dark kitchen, and the hotel's serpentine hallways beyond.

"The mine has stairs," Al muttered, his gaze returning to Jake's wheelchair. "Can you walk?"

"With help," Jake said, and then stood, reaching to steady himself on the old concierge's shoulder, desperate to escape the Glass Hall. Desperate to save Mila Noël, who was now scrambling toward him, struck with fear as a high-pitched whine descended upon them from the drone-filled skies above. Desperate to escape the horrors of the snarling mottled wolf that leapt upon Nick Gold as the attorney attempted to flee through the ballroom's doors to the lobby. Desperate for the truth encoded in Ana Turov's *Red Fury*—desperate for Claire's story—and, for the first time since Moscow...

Truly desperate to live.

Yes, Claire.

You're right. You're *always* right.

The missile struck moments later.

PART FIVE

Bullseye

FORTY

"It was a direct hit, sir. There's nothing left."

The old man let the drone pilot's words sit in his cell phone for a second, as if too timid to respond with a "Good job" or a "Way to go." As if frightened that the news was some big joke, that the reporter was still alive up there in Blind River, on the verge of uncovering his identity.

That the Carousel would finally claim his life for his failure.

The truth, however, was much simpler. He was eighty-two years old, and he'd spent sixty of those years living two lives, one as an intelligence operative for the CIA, the other as a global profiteer of state secrets. The stress had left him bent, weary, and in near-constant pain, both physically and emotionally. So when something undeniably pleasurable *did* happen—like the death of Jake fucking Boxer—he made sure to soak it up.

He only had so many good times left.

"Are you sure?" he asked finally.

"Our drone's been watching the site for twelve hours. There's been no movement."

No movement.

In twelve hours!

"Well," the old man said, his voice quivering with excitement, "it's all just another ride on the Carousel, isn't it?"

The old spy hung up. He was trembling, he noticed, and for once, it wasn't from neuropathy. It was because he'd done it. He'd destroyed the painting—the only thing left on earth that could've exposed his work as a double agent. He still couldn't believe how close that cable news show host had come to revealing his true identity.

Over the years, there'd been plenty of others who'd tried—starting with Ana Turov, who'd gleaned his name from the Soviets and tried to pass it to Buck Masterson—but no one had gotten as close as the *Bullseye* team. First, there'd been the show's soundman back in Dagestan; then Claire O'Donnell, the host's wife; and finally the host of the show himself, Jake Boxer. If it hadn't been for his eyes and ears on the ground—if it hadn't been for Albert Bridge Tulane, Jr.—the old housekeeper who'd watched over Blind River all those years—

Well.

He didn't want to think about what might have happened.

The whole trick of being a double agent was *not* getting caught, a miserable experience, he was sure. Just ask Robert Hansen, the FBI agent who'd been busted for selling secrets to the Russians and was now growing old in a supermax cell in Colorado. Though living the rest of his life in prison didn't worry him, something else kept him up at night. The thought of the Feds investigating his past, tracking down his old assets, and knocking on the Carousel's door made him shudder.

The world had no idea what they were capable of. The Carousel would light the world on fire to protect its secrets.

But now it wouldn't come to that, at least not yet.

Requesting the drone strike had been a calculated risk, one that would've undoubtedly been denied had that painting been anywhere other than in the middle of nowhere. Fortunately, the Carousel was already patrolling the skies over the small mountain town, keeping an eye on one of its many deep earth machines. Blind River was also closed for the winter—there wasn't another living soul closer than Anchorage. So no witnesses. And it would be March by the time the snow retreated and the roads were once again passable—a full four months away. Plenty of time for the Carousel to bulldoze the debris, fill in the crater, and clean up the explosive residue.

He could already see the headline in the Anchorage papers: Bankrupt Hotel Bulldozed After Owner's Death.

Would such an article even garner more attention? He doubted it. Certainly not as much as: Reporter Exposes Career CIA Mole, would have.

There was a knock at his door. The old spy practically leaped out of his skin.

"Mr. Anderson?" came a familiar voice. "Food's here."

He turned toward the woman's voice and pretended he had X-ray vision. He pretended he could see the social worker outside, holding her big bag of steamed broccoli, rice, and bread. A three-course meal that made hospital food taste gourmet, but what else should he expect from the city of Los Angeles? They came around once a day—an outreach program run by the city.

Whatever.

"Not hungry," the old spy shouted, though the Debbie-Do-Gooder didn't leave.

"Mr. Anderson," she said, "you need to eat wholesome, nutritious food. Not that junk from the convenience store."

He didn't eat "that junk" from the convenience store, of course. The Carousel paid him well. He wore fine suits and fancy jewelry, and he ate well, unlike the rest of the tenants at the Holly Hotel, a building that offered long-term single occupancy rooms and (maybe not so kindly) had been nicknamed the Chop. The tenants were almost all near-homeless, on the upper floors, at least, and most suffered from some sort of crippling psychosis—they *needed* the Debbie-Do-Gooder's broccoli and bread. The old spy, on the other hand, just needed the Chop for cover.

He'd arrived in Los Angeles a few years earlier, one of his many residences after retiring from the CIA (which believed he'd long ago retired to Key West). The government had no idea he'd assumed the role of Sheldon Anderson, retired machinist out of Tucson, Arizona, who'd moved to Los Angeles to be closer to his son. He wasn't hiding out from the CIA, of course. He'd assumed they'd mostly forgotten about their aging analyst. He was hiding out from the Carousel—the organization he'd sold secrets to for decades.

The organization that now knows where you live, he thought, staring at his cell phone. A phone he'd just used to call a Carousel drone pilot. But so what? There must have been hundreds of Carousel contacts in Los Angeles. He fit right in.

And Jake Boxer was dead.

The painting was destroyed.

He'd *won!*

Besides, he'd had little choice but to call them from his apartment. It had taken days for the sheriff to sweat out his suspects in that hotel—where was an old man like him supposed to hang out for that sort of time?

No, he told himself. You didn't have a choice. You had to call them from your apartment. And now you have to leave.

Again.

"Mr. Sheldon," came the voice, "I can hear you moving around in there. Are you gonna open this door? Or am I gonna open it for you?"

The old spy turned back to his front door.

Licked his lips.

Wondered if it was too late.

Wondered if the woman on the other side of the door was from the Carousel.

But why? He'd won!

But did it matter?

Of course, it mattered. He was a "Competent," the name they gave to untouchables. There was no central leadership in the Carousel, no bald evil genius stroking a white cat. They were a hive mind sharing a common goal—the positive evolution of the human race—and a Competent was allowed to move his or her own piece freely across the great chessboard. But if the Carousel removed you from the Competent column—if you were no longer to be trusted—they also removed your piece from the board, something that surely would've transpired had he allowed his identity to be revealed to the world.

But Christ, without him, without the secrets he'd given them, they'd be nothing! They'd *have* nothing! They certainly wouldn't have been able to build that machine underneath Blind River.

"Mr. *Anderson!*" the woman shouted. "You *need* a well-balanced meal."

He unlocked the door. Jerked it open to reveal a bulky black woman in tennis shoes and jeans and a light-blue windbreaker. He slipped one hand beneath his fine suit jacket for his holster and gripped his hidden .357. The cold steel was reassuring.

"I told you," he said, his thin lips curling, "I'm not hungry."

She didn't listen to him.

She reached into the large bag she was carrying.

He started to pull his gun from its holster. He pictured himself shoving it against her forehead. Pulling the trigger. Watching this Carousel killer's brains splatter all over the wall behind her—

"You have a microwave, Mr. Sheldon?"

Not a gun.

A to-go box.

And inside, through the clear plastic lid, he spied broccoli, several slices of whole wheat bread, and even some rice...*brown* rice.

The healthy kind.

"A *microwave?*" she asked again, annoyed.

He nodded, mumbling, "Sure."

"Well, enjoy. And, please, remember to remove the butter before you heat it up."

She ambled away, treading across the Chop's crunchy and stained carpet, then knocked on his neighbor's apartment door.

He turned back inside, closed his door, locked it, tossed the box of food onto the small kitchen table, and glared at it.

Who in the hell did she think he was?

He'd just ordered the first domestic drone strike in American history, and that woman thought he was going to microwave a packet of butter wrapped in foil?

Of course, he'd take out the butter.

Forget about her, he told himself. Eat the food. It's time to leave, and if you eat first, you won't have to stop until you're out of Los Angeles.

Shuffling over to the counter, he placed the box in the microwave, set the timer to thirty seconds, and hit Start. Having to move was annoying, but he wouldn't exactly miss the place. Sure, Los Angeles had been convenient.

Every Competent was paid a quarterly stipend, and there were plenty of drops and pickups in downtown, but his apartment was no bigger than a crappy motel room. Management had been renovating the apartments on the lower floors, but the city had zoned the upper floors as single occupancies—they couldn't kick out the tenants, but they didn't bother updating the amenities either. The paint was peeling, the plumbing was clogged, and the wiring blew a fuse seemingly at random. The view was okay. He was five stories up and overlooked the corner of Spring and 5th Streets, where a uniquely Angelino mix of cappuccino-sipping hipsters and drug-addled near-homeless staggered in and out of the Chop. Where the stench of exhaust and stale piss often wafted through his window. Downtown Los Angeles, and the Chop in particular, had been a miserable place to retire, sure, but the tradeoff had been anonymity. Until now.

The microwave crackled.

Confused, he turned and saw that the box of food was sparking inside the microwave. The plastic lid was melting. He opened the microwave quickly, releasing a tuft of pungent smoke, and glared at his scorched and ruined food.

He'd forgotten to take out the butter packet.

What else had he forgotten?

What else had he overlooked?

He trembled for several minutes before reassuring himself that it was okay. Jake Boxer was dead. The painting was destroyed.

And he didn't like broccoli anyway.

Grand Central Market sat on the corner of Broadway and 3rd Street, just two city blocks from the Chop. Once a sad collection of second-class eateries, it was now the culinary heart of downtown, a thriving indoor market that featured scores of restaurants serving up the best food in Los Angeles. It was always jam-packed, and ordinarily, the old spy would've steered clear, but he was getting on a train that afternoon—he was leaving Los Angeles for good—and Stacy Nowak from two doors down had told him the buckwheat pancakes at the market's famous Belle's Counter were to die for. After the broccoli catastrophe, he felt as though he deserved them.

Whatever the hell a buckwheat was.

Leaning heavily on his cane, and wearing one of his fine suits, he shuffled through the crowded indoor market. It was dinnertime, and the Angelinos were all rushing for grub, foolishly believing that their time mattered. The old spy knew better.

They were all sheep.

He was their shepherd.

A long time ago, he'd been a sheep too. Back in the '60s he'd actually signed up to fight in Vietnam, and it was there that he learned the dangers of blind allegiance, mostly as a result of the My Lai Massacre—a brutal episode that saw American soldiers slaughtering women and children—a massacre his superiors had forced him to take part in. It had been sheep slaughtering sheep, he'd realized several sleepless nights later, and he swore that from that day forward, he'd never be a sheep again.

Fearing he'd talk, his superiors reassigned him to Blind River, Alaska. His orders were to defend a radar installation, but no one, including the Soviets, gave two shits about it. In fact, the atmosphere around the installation was so blasé that the military engineers simply left the radar system's top secret schematics lying around out in the open for any cynical foot soldier to see.

Or copy.

It wasn't until years later, while working as an analyst for the CIA, that he'd learned of the abandoned experiment in Blind River. He hadn't stolen schematics for a radar array. He'd stolen schematics for some sort of deep earth machine that had been designed to operate remotely, and completely unmanned. Aside from an irritating and only sometimes-noticeable hum, the high-tech machines were invisible to the outside world. He didn't know exactly what they were supposed to do, but over the years, he surmised that it was some sort of top-secret subatomic particle detector, though what the Carousel would want with something like that was beyond him. He could only assume it was an extension of nuclear physics—the military had learned how to split the atom, perhaps they were trying to weaponize subatomic particles as well?

Regardless, the project under Blind River had been quickly shuttered, in large part due to its hefty price tag, but by then he'd already sold the schematics to the Soviets. Later, of course, he would learn the true identity of his buyer—a Soviet, yes, but not a Soviet who was loyal to the Motherland.

A Soviet who was loyal to a *global* agenda—a sophisticated and powerful man who was friends with generals and billionaires not just in the USSR, but also around the world. A man who possessed a vocabulary larger than "country" and "duty." A man who'd quietly begun sharing his vision with the elite few. That must have been how they'd gotten to the shuttered machine under Blind River—there had been a number of powerful Americans riding the Carousel over the years—Christopher Kidd's father had been one of them.

"What can I get you, sir?"

The old spy blinked out of his thoughts and looked up, almost surprised to find himself at Belle's Counter, next in line to order. "I hear the blueberry buckwheat pancakes are to die for."

"Coming right up. Need help finding a seat?"

"No," he said sharply, and the kid behind the cash register—a doughy teenage boy—shrugged and smiled awkwardly, as if saying, "Just trying to help!"

But he didn't need help. His secrets had destroyed empires and democracies alike. He could find his own goddam seat…that was, if any had been available. The place was packed, and his joints were killing him, and—

"Right over there, sir!" It was the pudgy kid again, jabbing a fat index finger at an empty seat at the long counter, one he'd apparently missed. "Help you with your chair?"

"No!" the old spy hollered, moving slowly for the empty seat.

Now that he'd set his mind on moving, he couldn't wait to get out of this town.

The old spy took his seat at the counter, wedging himself in between a young man and woman both wearing standard Los Angeles affair—so casual they were fancy—and sporting three-hundred-dollar haircuts. A TV was playing in the corner and everyone was glued to the news reports covering whatever the hell was going on in the aftermath of the election.

It didn't take long for his food to arrive. The pancakes were warm, the blueberries gooey. They looked a hell of a lot tastier than broccoli. He drenched them in maple syrup, stabbed a hunk with his fork, and was about to take a bite when he hesitated. He could see the blueberries, but where in the hell was the buckwheat? And what if he didn't like it? What if those buckwheats ruined what would otherwise be a lovely—and exceedingly rare—pancake experience?

Wouldn't that be a miserable thing.

Well, he thought. If it did...if that fucking buckwheat got the better of him...he would hunt down the person who'd sown it and stop them from ever growing a buckwheat again. It would be easy enough. All he needed was a name—just one name. The name of the fat teenager who'd taken his money would do. If he had the kid's name, he could grab someone the kid loved. He could then blackmail the kid to get to the cook, and if he got to the cook, he could find the bag the buckwheats had come in. Once he had that bag, he could find the packaging plant that had bagged the buckwheat, which would lead him to the buckwheat farm itself. Once he was at the field, he could tie up the farmers and force them to hand over the old schedules. From there, he could find the hired hands who actually planted the buckwheat seeds that had ruined his pancake and kill every last man, woman, and child. All of that, and all he needed to know was *one name* to get him started, to get him on the right trail.

He shook these thoughts away.

The painting was destroyed.

Jake Boxer never *revealed* his name.

The Feds couldn't use it to beat a line to the Carousel's door, and so long as *they* were safe, *he* was safe. It was the best an old spy could do.

As it turned out, the buckwheat, whatever it was, was delicious—though he had a hard time discerning it from the blueberries and the syrup. In fact, he was so taken by the deliciousness of the blueberries and the buckwheat and the maple syrup that he didn't even realize Jake Boxer's bloody and bruised face was looking down on him until the television's video feed cut back to the NewsFlash anchor.

The old spy nearly choked on his pancake.

Jake...Boxer?

No. It couldn't have been him.

Jake Boxer was dead.

He focused on the television, just to be sure. Jake wasn't there. Rather Tabitha Fox—America's foremost purveyor of smut and gossip—was staring at the camera. Tabitha, a "journalist" who'd made a name for herself that election season by criticizing Hillary Clinton's fashion sense, was an explosion of a woman—curves everywhere, makeup caked on like cement, and a sky-high mop of curly blonde hair. She was apparently reporting from a studio in D.C., because he could see the Capitol through a window in the background.

"We interrupt our normal programming to bring you this special report: Jake Boxer, a friend and colleague of NewsFlash, has just survived what he's calling the first military strike on American soil." She turned her attention to a small monitor with a fuzzy image of an indiscernible man. "Can you tell us what's happening, Jake?"

Silence.

"Can you *hear* me?" she asked, flustered. "Are you *there?*"

It was then that the old spy heard it. A voice he'd last heard a day earlier, when he'd called Jake Boxer's room in the Hotel Ascent. When he'd tried to convince the ex-journalist to reveal the location of Ana Turov's *Red Fury*. When Jake Boxer had ripped the phone cord out on him.

"Hold on," the man who might have been Jake Boxer grunted, "should work in a second…on a…satellite phone—"

The words cut away, and Tabitha's expression grew grave.

"Jake…*Jake?*"

The old spy exhaled, relieved.

Maybe Jake Boxer *had* survived the Hellfire missile, but only for a moment. Maybe he'd succumbed to his wounds. Maybe he was dead.

"Tabitha," Jake said suddenly, and strongly, and the cameras cut to a live stream from his satellite phone, a live stream that was jerky and froze too often, but worked. "Tabitha, can you hear me?"

"Yes. I can hear you, Jake—and I can see you. Where are you?"

"Near the…near the mouth of an old mineral mine," Jake said, wincing and in pain, but alive. "Beneath a hotel in Blind River, Alaska."

No you're not. You were in the ballroom when the missile hit. You were there with Ana Turov's masterpiece. You didn't know where the entrance to the mine was, no one did except—

"Al," Jake barked on the television screen, "come hold the phone."

Jake handed the phone to someone off-camera, and as the phone's camera turned, the old spy caught a glimpse of the broad, affable face of a man he'd paid to murder Ana Turov decades ago. Of a man who'd supposedly been loyal to his cause.

Albert Bridge Tulane, Jr.

In a daze, the old spy set his fork down on his plate and looked around. A thick silence had filled the packed market. Every eye was glued to the TV.

"Turn it off," he heard himself say. "Someone...someone turn this shit off!"

But no one listened to the crazy old man in the nice suit who hadn't been able to find his own seat at the market.

No one cared.

On the television, Al finally got the camera right, framing Jake Boxer in a wider angle, and revealing Ana Turov's granddaughter at his side, holding a painting.

No.

Holding a masterpiece.

"What's going on up there?" Tabitha asked. "Have you been hurt?"

Jake, who was leaning against the mouth of the mine, the hotel's rubble all around, nodded. "A drone, Tabitha...a drone fired a missile at us."

"I'm sorry. Did you say a drone?"

"Yes...a drone. They were trying to destroy this painting. They were trying to destroy the Glass Hall—*the code's cipher.*"

"Slow down, Jake. You're not making sense—"

"Хольц," Mila said, interrupting.

"I'm sorry, can you repeat that?" Tabitha asked.

"It's Russian," Jake said, "for Holtz."

The old spy had heard enough. He stood, put his cane down, and on three legs, hobbled for the double doors leading out of the market. Every eye was still glued to the TV, but he knew all too well that there were always eyes he couldn't see.

"Holtz?" Tabitha asked. "Okay, so what about it?"

Jake didn't answer.

Standing at the market's exit, the old spy turned back to the television. Ana Turov's granddaughter was now looking at Jake Boxer, and Jake Boxer was staring glumly at his feet.

"Jake," Tabitha said. "Jake, can you hear me?"

Yes, Jake could hear her, but no, Jake didn't answer.

A smile crept across the old spy's face.

He couldn't do it.

After all those years, after his very public meltdown on live TV, after losing his show, after losing his wife in Blind River, Jake Boxer could no longer look the camera in the eye.

But then the old spy's grin fell as Jake muttered, "Holtz. That's the name Ana put in her painting. It's the last name of a man who worked for the CIA back in the early seventies. Ana Turov was trying to tell us that he was a double agent. That he *is* a double agent."

Tabitha shook her head. "I'm sorry, a double agent? Is this some sort of a joke?"

"No," Jake said, and for the first time in years, looked the camera right in the eye. *"This* is *Bullseye."*

AUTHOR'S NOTE

I am indebted to many people for the production of this book, though none more so than my wife, so I'll thank her first. Marcelle—my bounce-board, first reader and first editor—you are amazing and loved!

My editor, Daniel Spinella, for his keen eye that really whipped this book into shape. My agent, Paul Fedorko, for his continuous support and invaluable feedback. Cover designer Yen Tan, who created a tremendous cover for this book and series. Sergei Skarupo, who translated my English into Russian with an assist from Kusia Hreshchyshyn. Dr. Stephen Liu, for his medical expertise and help putting Jake Boxer in a wheelchair. My brother, Ray Hosack, for providing the gritty nuts and bolts of policing over the years. My sister, Kara Fowler, for her psychological expertise that helped with my portrayal of Jake Boxer. The early readers of my work—Shari Shattuck, Sharon Doyle, Sherri James, Chris Summitt, Bree Ramage (Drew Rice!)—without your invaluable feedback I would still be stuck on Chapter 1.

John and Diane Rice, for their on-going help with our household while I fiddle with these books.

And, of course, my parents, Harold and Sharon Hosack, for helping me better understand the Cold War, and their support in just about every aspect of my life.

NEXT ON BULLSEYE...

THE CHAOS AGENT

Book 2 of the Bullseye Series

COMING

2017

MARK HOSACK is the author of *The Good Spy Dies Twice* and *Identity*. He also writes screenplays. Mark lives in Los Angeles with his wife and kids.

SIGN UP FOR MARK'S NEWSLETTER AT
markhosack.com/newsletter

OR FOLLOW HIM ON SOCIAL MEDIA AT
facebook.com/markhosack
@markhosack

www.markhosack.com

CPSIA information can be obtained at www.ICGtesting.com
Printed in the USA
LVOW07s1820191016

509435LV00004B/984/P